Critical acclaim for The Virtual Trilogy

...a tautly plotted thriller . . .
Virtually Maria will not fail you . . .
(Irish News-Belfast)

. . . a very slick fish in the growing pool of
cyberthrillers . . .
. . . irrepressible and surprisingly irresistible.
(RTE Guide)

. . . a ground-breaking love story . . .
(The Examiner)

. . . brilliantly conceived, exquisitely executed
and eminently readable . . .
(Commuting Times)

. . . published to great critical acclaim . . .
(Ireland on Sunday)

Virtually Maria – A gripping, action-packed, tautly
plotted thriller . . .
(Publishing News)

Virtually Maria - EASONS Book of the Month

MASTERPIECE

——

A NOVEL

Also by John Joyce

The Virtual Trilogy

Virtually Maria
A Matter of Time
Yesterday, Today & Tomorrow

Fire & Ice

Captain Cockle

Captain Cockle and the Cormorant
Captain Cockle and the Loch Ness Monster
Captain Cockle and the Pond

Black John - The Bogus Pirate

Black John - The Bogus Pirate's
Cartoon Workbook of Marine Beasts

MASTERPIECE

JOHN
JOYCE

This edition published by Spindrift Press 2014

 **SPINDRIFT PRESS**

www.spindriftpress.com

ISBN 978-0-9574439-0-7

The moral right of the author has been asserted

ACKNOWLEDGEMENTS

uld like to acknowledge the help I was given by all those I met
my research on *Masterpiece* at the various locations mentioned
novel.

ould also like to acknowledge the professional editorial
nce I received, both from Rebecca Laty in the UK and from
Blum Guest in Paris.

ddition, my very good friends Dick Bates and Geoffrey
van provided me with many valuable insights, for which I am
ely grateful.

lly, as always, I would like to thank my wife Jane for her
t and, in particular, for accompanying me on my researches
such exciting and glamorous locations as London, Dublin,
d Madrid including the Louvre museum, Atocha Station and
the far less salubrious surroundings of the sewers of Paris.

book, like those before, is lovingly dedicated to you.

nk you.

ABOUT THE AUTHO

Award-winning science writer Dr John Jo'
the *Virtual Trilogy* of technothrillei
Theo Gilkrensky – *Virtually Maria, A M*
Yesterday, Today and Tomorrow – as well
ESP thriller *Fire & Ice, the Black John the Bo*
Workbook of Marine Beasts and the *Captai*
underwater adventure books for

He was presented with the Glaxo EU Fell
Writers by the Prime Minister of Irelanc
contributed a great many articles to scier
publications. His first published novel *V*
selected as Book of the Month by the Eas(

John Joyce is currently working on the
adventure *Mastermind*.

For information and updates on all Jo
log on to:

www.spindriftpress.c

This is a work of fiction. All character
institutions and organisations in this nov
of the author's imagination or, if real, a
without any intent to describe their a

I w
durin§
in this

I v
assista
Laurie

In
O'Sull
extren

Fin.
suppo:
arounc
Paris a
even t(

Thi:

Tha

FOR JANE

MASTERPIECE

THEN

PARIS

Planning the crime had taken a year of Sabaut's life. There had been the special equipment to prepare, surveys to carry out, endless research into computer security systems and, of course, the tunnel. During all that time, he'd marvelled at the ultimate simplicity of what he was about to do. It had the same perfect form a masterpiece of art presents to the untrained observer, the same fusion of inspiration, sweat and pain into a seemingly effortless beauty.

Now he crouched in the darkness of the tiny cave it had taken him six weeks to dig. Light from the small torch strapped to his head glistened on the clay walls, on the two steel cases and the waterproof canvas bag he'd hauled in on his hands and knees. Only a steel plate, held in place by four metal catches, separated him from the storeroom.

He held his hands up to the light and watched them shake from the exertion of climbing the last few metres from the sewers below. The sickly sweet stench of those endless caverns still filled his nostrils. Sabaut was not a young man. His arms and legs ached from weeks of work on the tunnel. His vision swam. The walls of the cave pressed in. Points of red light danced in front of him and a cold sweat broke out on his face. The strain of the past year seemed to rise up and crash down on him like a wave. He closed his eyes and tried to steady himself. The red lights faded and his breathing returned to normal.

Nicole! I'm doing this for you.

Sabaut opened his eyes again. His hands no longer shook.

He leant forward and reached for the panel's four metal catches.

"I'm at point one," he said into his throat microphone.

"Proceed," said a familiar voice in his earpiece.

Sabaut opened each of the catches in turn, switched off his head torch and lifted the panel aside. He was peering into a dark silent space, filled with shapeless forms. He waited for a moment and then, satisfied that nobody was in the room, he reached up and turned on his light. A face stared at him out of the blackness. Its sightless eyes did not blink in the torch beam. Nor did its expression change.

"*Bon soir,*" Sabaut said softly. "*Ça va?*"

The statue did not reply.

Sabaut played the torch around the vast low-ceilinged chamber, taking in the rows of exquisitely carved faces, curving bodies and prancing animals, all frozen in stone. The building had started life as a fortress almost a thousand years before and this room, deep below ground, was now used as a storehouse. Sabaut knew there were no alarms here, and no cameras. These would begin at the next level.

He reached back through the panel and pulled the two cases and the bag through. Slipping the straps of his torch over the head of the statue, Sabaut peeled off the mud-stained boiler suit he'd worn in the tunnel and changed into an old shirt, faded jeans and scuffed brown shoes. Then he pulled on a light blue work coat, checked the security badge was prominently displayed on the breast pocket and turned to the first case. With practised ease he assembled the collection of stainless steel plates, rods and rubber wheels inside. Finally, he turned to the second case, opening the clasps and gently lifting the lid to reveal two exquisite oil paintings.

In another two minutes, he stood before a thick wooden door at the end of a narrow stone corridor, illuminated by strips of fluorescent light. He knew he was still more than ten metres below street level, in one of the fifteen kilometres of underground passageways and service tunnels that honeycombed the earth beneath the great buildings above. Beyond the door the security cameras would start.

"I'm at point two," he said.

"Shutting cameras down now!" came the reply. "You have fifteen minutes before the alarms reset."

Sabaut opened the door and stepped into a brightly lit passageway with white walls and a smooth concrete floor. The Cyclops eye of a security camera peered down at him from the ceiling.

Was it still live?

An orange light flashed on the walls around him. The hiss of tyres and the whirr of an electric motor sounded as a yellow cart pulling a trailer loaded with wooden crates and cardboard boxes rolled past. The driver raised his hand in salute as he passed and drove on.

Sabaut walked for over fifty metres to a service lift, stepped inside and pressed the button marked 'Entresol'. As the polished door slid shut he saw the reflection of a tall, grey haired porter with a stainless steel trolley looking back at him. The heavy moustache he'd grown especially for the job and the thick-framed spectacles, repaired with electrical tape, gave just the right impression of an honest hard-working man.

Sabaut smiled as the lift doors slid open. He turned to his left and, pushing the trolley in front of him, made his way down a darkened mall of exclusive retail outlets, information points and souvenir shops to the vast space beyond.

He hardly looked up as he passed beneath the soaring lattice of metal and glass that formed the giant pyramid above his head, or took in the escalators, ticket kiosks, coffee docks and balconies that welcomed over six million visitors a year. For six days out of seven, this atrium would be swarming with visitors from all over the world, pilgrims who had come to pay homage to one of the greatest art collections in existence. But now, early on the morning of the one day in each week when the museum was closed to the public for maintenance, the only sounds to be heard in the Musée du Louvre were the distant drone of floor polishing machines, the squeaking wheels of Sabaut's trolley and the hollow clap of his shoes on the marble floor.

He crossed the great atrium into a corridor closed to tourists and art lovers. A pair of grey-painted double doors stood shut across his path, protected by a security camera, a card reader and an electronic keypad.

Sabaut glanced up at the camera, drew out a swipe card and ran it through the slot. A green light blinked on the keypad. Sabaut entered four numbers, pulled open the door and wheeled the trolley into a long, brightly lit corridor that smelled of floor polish. He glanced at the names on the office doors as he passed.

At the far end of the corridor was the room that really interested him, marked by the pair of armed security men standing guard outside. Their faces looked familiar but, with a staff of over two thousand men and women at the Louvre, it was unlikely that either of them would recognise him from his fleeting visits to the restoration area in the years Nicole had worked there.

However, it was not impossible.

"Good morning," he said, wheeling the trolley in front of him. "What are you guys doing here? Is it that time of year again?"

The guard on the left glanced at Sabaut's identification badge.

"She's down for analysis and restoration before she goes back up to that new exhibition area in the Salle des États tomorrow." he said.

"The one the Japanese TV company sponsored?"

"Bullet-proof glass, hermetically sealed, new alarm systems, the works! It cost almost five million euro."

Sabaut shrugged. "Perhaps it's worth it," he said. "After all, she is valued at over eight hundred million. Can I leave this inside for the restorers?"

"What is it?" asked the other guard, leaning forward.

Sabaut carefully lifted the dust sheet covering the trolley.

"A Monet from the Grand Gallery, down for its annual check-up. They forgot to bring it across last night and the curators want it back on display by the end of the week. I wish the management took as good care of its staff as it does with its precious paintings."

Both guards nodded in agreement. The one on Sabaut's left pulled the dust sheet back into place.

"Not one of my favourites," he said. "Hurry up then. They're paranoid about security when she's down." The door opened with a hiss.

"I'll just be a moment," Sabaut said and pushed the trolley forward. The restoration room smelt of surgical spirit. Its white walls, complex X-ray machinery and tables of tools and long-stemmed lamps gave the impression of a vast hospital laboratory or a workshop for luxury cars. There were no windows and no other exit. The room was sealed, airtight and hermetically-controlled, with security cameras panning down from every angle. Sabaut took a deep breath and stared along the endless rows of tables bearing covered paintings. Were those cameras still live? Or were they watching nothing more than the image of the empty room that had been frozen into their feedback circuits before he'd entered?

"I'm at point three," he said softly.

"You have ten minutes and twenty seconds," said the voice.

Sabaut pushed the trolley down the main aisle between the covered paintings, to the far end of the room. There, on a table set apart from all the rest, was a single small painting covered by a Plexiglas dust shield.

He slipped on a pair of fine cotton gloves, checked the dust shield for hidden alarms and lifted it off, laying it gently down beside the table. For a moment, he allowed himself the bittersweet luxury of gazing down at the enigmatic smile of a young woman sitting on a balcony with her hands crossed on the arm of her seat.

Colours came to him . . . the blues and greens of Nicole's palette as she worked during the evenings in their apartment near the Pompidou Centre . . . the spun silver and gold of her hair . . . and finally, the dark red swirls of blood on white porcelain. . . .

Jean-Jacques Sabaut pushed that memory aside and lifted the Monet onto the table. Then he leant down and began to work on the bottom shelf of the trolley.

This is for you, Nicci. This is my masterpiece. Just as the paintings you left behind will be recognised some day for the works of genius they are, so this act in your memory will also find a place in history.

The lower shelf of the trolley was made of stainless steel with a lip eight centimetres deep. Reaching underneath, Sabaut found the hidden catch that released a padded tray. He bent down, gently removed the contents and laid it on the workbench.

It was an expertly aged and treated piece of poplar wood, seventy-seven centimetres tall by fifty-three centimetres wide, with four wooden battens running across its back to prevent it from warping. On its upturned face a portrait had been painted, identical in every respect to the original that lay beside it on the restorer's table.

How many years had Nicole worked here in the Louvre, studying the art and form of this painting's legendary creator; copying his pictures, matching his brush strokes, studying his pigments, so that she could do his genius justice in her restorations?

She'd started the project as a joke—just to see if it could be done. But, as the reviews of her own original paintings had grown more and more hostile and Nicole's artistic spirit had begun to buckle, it had become a serious obsession. If the critics would not accept Nicole Sabaut as an artist of the present, then she'd expose their hypocritical worship of the artists of the past. Nicole had unlimited access to the restoration room. She had the talent, the expertise and the materials to create the ultimate forgery. All she had to do was to substitute it for the real thing, then take her vengeance upon the jackals of the art community when she unmasked them as the mindless hypocrites they were.

Sabaut lifted Da Vinci's masterpiece from the restoration table and turned it lovingly in his hands, examining the front and back of the poplar wood sheet. Nicole had been right. The wood was warping ever so slightly. The museum had been justified in building the new display to protect it from further damage. Sabaut smiled. If he succeeded tonight, and Nicole's forgery was encased inside that bullet-proof display before it was hermetically sealed, then it could remain that way forever.

His fingers touched what appeared to be a blob of wax on the bottom edge of the poplar panel. Looking at it closely, it seemed as if the wax had been there for centuries, but Sabaut knew better. Taking a pocket knife and unfolding the blade, he gently prized what was actually a red plastic plug away from the wood. A cylindrical electronic security tag fell into his palm. He smiled again, remembering Nicole's precise instructions, and transferred the device and its 'wax' cover to a corresponding hole in her perfect forgery.

Then he laid the two paintings side by side on the table and looked down at them. Apart from the presence of the tag, they were identical in every respect except one—the knowledge that Leonardo's masterpiece carried the very soul of its creator in the delicate brushstrokes and that it was a priceless national treasure of France, the essence of which could never be replaced.

Taking this painting from the Louvre was an awesome responsibility. What if something were to happen to it in the tunnel? Was it fundamentally right, in spite of his solemn vow to Nicole, to proceed?

"You have six minutes," said the voice in his ear.

A cold sweat broke out on Jean-Jacques Sabaut's face as he gazed down at the two masterpieces in front of him—one genuine, one not.

"Five minutes."

"I hear you!"

To hesitate any further risked discovery and capture.

The two portraits smiled back at him like rival lovers, challenging him to choose between them.

Sabaut took a deep breath, covered one of the paintings with the Plexiglas lid, gently placed the other into the secret compartment beneath the trolley and shut the metal flap.

To anyone looking at the trolley from above, the bottom shelf was empty.

He took the fake Monet Nicole had made and hid it behind a stack of other paintings in the corner of the restoration room. Nicole had often told him that, for all its security arrangements and cataloguing, the Louvre had still not managed to make a complete inventory of its three hundred thousand pieces of art.

He turned, looked back at the painting beneath the Plexiglas cover one last time, and pushed the seemingly empty trolley back to the doors of the restoration room. The two guards hardly glanced at it as he pushed it past them and along the brightly lit corridor to the atrium, the elevator and down into the bowels of the great museum to the storeroom where he'd entered.

He turned on the light, shut the door behind him and started to dismantle the trolley.

"You can release the cameras now," he said into his throat microphone. "I'm back."

"Understood."

Sabaut pulled his boiler suit back on, carefully removed the painting from the stainless steel tray and placed it lovingly in the reinforced carrying case. The stench of the sewer flared his nostrils as he reopened the panel in the wall. Then he took his headlight back from the statue, bid it farewell and, with a last deep breath of sweet air, he was gone.

Forty minutes later, he stood by a rusted metal ladder leading upwards to a steel plate set into the pavement at the south-east corner of the Place de la Concorde on the north bank of the Seine. From above came the muted roar of traffic bursting from the underpass beneath the Pont de la Concorde. Below him was the babble of gently flowing sewage. He'd already dumped the trolley and the bag containing the clothes and security tag into it. Now all he had was the precious case.

"I'm at the manhole," he said.

"I'm in place. Hurry!"

Sabaut took the case in his left hand, gripped the wet metal rungs with his right and ascended the ladder. Once at the top, he braced his shoulder against the manhole cover and pushed, sliding it sideways onto the pavement. The sound of distant sirens, the roar of traffic and the muffled hum of a city at night time washed over him. Cold, clean air rushed through the manhole and into his lungs as he climbed out.

After the silence and the stinking blackness below him, he paused for a moment to take in the lights, the sounds and the wide open space of the Place de la Concorde as the great sweeping searchlight from the Eiffel Tower swung across the stars. Then he pushed the cover back into place and looked across the Quai de Tuileries to the Seine. The black van was there, on the other side of the road.

Sabaut got to his feet, took the case and ran towards the vehicle, glancing to his right at the underpass as he went. He'd reached the middle of the road when a silver BMW, travelling at speed, burst out of the tunnel. Sabaut darted forward and twisted his body to one side, just in time for the offside wing of the speeding car to slice past him harmlessly.

There. The devil looks after his own—

With a roar and the briefest flash of blue light, the police motorcycle that had been chasing the BMW, exploded out of the underpass, swerved out of control as it tried to avoid him and smashed into his legs.

Sabaut felt nothing but the unimaginable impact of the machine, as it caught him below the knees, spun him upwards into the whirling lights of the city and slammed him down onto the unforgiving surface of the roadway. His head cracked against the edge of the pavement. A deafening hiss roared in his ears. As it cleared, he heard the sound of running feet and the wail of sirens. Cars skidded to a halt close by. Men shouted and twisted metal scraped against stone. Voices crackled over radios.

A man's voice asked if he could hear him. Sabaut tried to move his legs, but his body was numb.

A familiar engine pulled away and faded into the distance. The van had gone.

All that planning . . . all that risk . . . his revenge against the art world for Nicole's death . . . all gone in a second!

The painting! What about the painting?

"I had a case," he said. "Where is it?"

The voice told him to lie still. Then, somewhere off to his right, he heard the unmistakeable sound of the case scraping on the roadway. Someone was lifting it.

"Don't open . . ." Sabaut said. But then came the snap of the catches being flicked back. For a moment, it seemed to Sabaut that the world had fallen silent. Someone's voice, raised in excitement, was calling to his colleagues to come and look. There was a clatter of footsteps.

Sabaut turned his head. He blinked his eyes. He had to see.

But there was nothing . . . nothing but the dark.

NOW

DUBLIN

"Any questions?" said Flynn, looking up the rows of tiered seats in the half-empty lecture theatre towards the young woman at the very back.

He'd been watching her ever since he'd arrived and found her sitting there on her own with a trim manila folder in front of her.

Was she a spy from the Dean's office?

Attendance at his lectures had been declining steadily. People no longer found his theories on the origins of terrorism as topical as they'd been after 9/11, when his name had been on everyone's lips as 'the man who saw it coming'.

Back then, his opinion had been sought on every terrorist incident across the globe and the college had fêted him as a prize addition to its academic staff. His book had climbed to the rarefied heights of the bestseller lists and his public lectures had packed the biggest theatres on campus.

But now his contract was due to be terminated and even this small theatre, one of the older Victorian rooms at the back of the college, was hardly more than half-full.

If the woman in the back row wasn't from the Dean's office, then who was she? She'd taken no notes during his lecture, which meant she wasn't a mature student or a journalist. Flynn was sick of journalists. They'd been bad news throughout his academic career and even more so since his open letters to the American embassy criticising their strategies in Afghanistan and Iraq. A junior reporter Flynn recognised was loitering in the front row right now, just waiting for a sound bite he could use to splash across tomorrow's paper. The microphone of his digital recorder was aimed at Flynn like the barrel of a gun.

Flynn glanced again at the woman in the back row. She looked petite and precise. Her dark shoulder length hair was beautifully cut and she was elegantly dressed, in a navy blue business suit and white shirt. Flynn would have put her in her early to mid thirties and would have guessed that, for the want of hearing her speak, she wasn't Irish. Mature Irish students, in Flynn's experience, didn't take that much care of their appearance when they attended evening lectures in Dublin colleges, while full-time undergraduates tended towards false tan, fake nails and sports/casual outfits with expensive jeans from Abercrombie and Fitch.

So, if she wasn't a student or journalist, then perhaps she was the woman from that European security committee with the ridiculous acronym who'd been sending him all those emails and phone messages. That would explain the disapproving way she kept staring at him with those bright brown eyes of hers, as if he was something she'd found stuck to the bottom of her shoe.

He looked around the theatre, searching for raised hands between the empty spaces. Nobody moved.

"Anybody?"

The woman raised her left hand.

"You said that all terrorism is the product of oppression," she said. "Isn't that a gross oversimplification?"

Flynn recognised her accent and precise diction immediately from the messages on his voice mail. It was her! Why the hell had she come all this way just to ambush him in public?

"Hold on. Aren't you the—?"

Then he caught sight of the reporter in the front row, recorder at the ready, waiting for his response to her question. He combed his fingers through his hair while he thought of an answer and looked back up the theatre at the woman.

"It's no oversimplification," he said slowly and clearly, so that the journalist would have no problem quoting him accurately. "It's a basic fact. Oppression creates anger. Anger creates a climate in which extremism can flourish—simply because extremist actions become acceptable to an oppressed population with no other way of protecting itself—particularly if those actions become excusable as 'acts of rebellion' against those in power over them. That's why the German people tolerated Hitler's extremist actions, because they saw themselves as downtrodden, bankrupted and humiliated by the Allies after World War One and would support anyone who could salvage their national pride. If Germany hadn't been so oppressed, it's unlikely that Hitler's actions would've been tolerated and millions of lives would've been saved from the conflict that followed."

The journalist in the front row lost interest and tapped his teeth with his pen.

"It's the same today all over the world," continued Flynn. "If you disenfranchise the Palestinians by giving their land to the Jews, you get anger. If the United States supports this oppression by aligning itself with Israel against a Muslim country you get anger, extremism and the sort of terrorist attacks we saw on 9/11, in the London Subway bombs and in Madrid."

"And here in Ireland?" asked the woman. "How would you apply your theories to what happened in the North?"

So she knew all about him. Were those his personal details in the file in front of her?

All at once he was back, fishing for mackerel with his brother Sean on the shore in County Cork.

"These strategies of yours, Daimo," Sean had said. "These ideas about how oppressed people can make those in power sit up and take notice. There's a few of my friends up North would like to speak to you about them."

"Doctor Flynn?" the woman asked again.

The reporter stopped tapping his teeth with his pen and held it poised over his notepad, waiting for Flynn's reply.

"The same basic principals have applied here in Ireland over the last hundred years as they have all over the world," he said, snapping back to the present. "If you oppress the Catholics in Northern Ireland, you create anger, which in turn supports the Irish Republican Army. This produces a backlash from Unionist paramilitaries such as the UVF, which creates more anger, which breeds more violence, which leads to more deaths. The only way to resolve a situation like that was to break the vicious cycle by promoting dialogue and eventually removing the oppression. If you create dialogue — however impossible and distasteful it may seem in the short term — you promote long-term understanding. If you create understanding, you eliminate extremism and eventually achieve peace, which is what happened in the North."

"And in worldwide terms?"

"The same principals apply," Flynn said, holding up his left hand and counting off the points on his fingers. "You promote dialogue, create understanding, eliminate extremism and achieve peace."

"I understand your theories, Doctor Flynn. But what do you say to the people on either side whose loved ones have been murdered? How do you stop them hating the people who did that?"

The journalist turned in his seat to look back at her and then stared at Flynn.

Flynn ran his fingers through his hair again as he thought of a sound bite that he could dare see in print.

"Theirs is the hardest task of all," he said at last. "For it's only by breaking the cycle of hatred, so that death does not always bring revenge, that violence can be stopped."

"That's not an easy thing to ask."

Their eyes met. For an instant, Flynn saw a deep sadness there. He thought of the way Sean had been shot down, and what their mother had said to him afterwards, when she came to visit him in prison that last time, just before she died.

"No," he said. "It's not."

After the few remaining members of the audience had filed out of the lecture theatre, Flynn walked up through the rows of seats.

Seeing him approach, the woman snapped her file shut, slipped it into the leather case on her lap and stood up. She was taller than Flynn had imagined and looked like someone who worked out regularly. It was obvious to him who she was now. The chic business suit, the French accent and the manila file said it all.

"Would you by any chance be Madame Gabrielle Arnault?" he asked, holding out his hand. "I'm Damien Flynn. I'm sorry you felt you had to come all this way."

She took out a business card and handed it to him. Flynn saw the Europol logo, her full name, rank and contact details.

"You wouldn't return my calls or my emails, Doctor Flynn. So you forced me to come in person."

"I'm sorry to have wasted your time, *mon Capitaine*," he said, and handed the card back to her. She folded her arms on her chest and fixed him with her dark brown eyes.

"We're offering you a lucrative contract position, Doctor Flynn. You've done consultancy work before."

"I told your office weeks ago I wasn't interested in working with government enforcement agencies. They should have told you that."

"They did, Doctor Flynn. And I must say, it doesn't surprise me, considering some of the more questionable organisations you've worked for in the past. But this work is vital to European security and I've an urgent requirement for someone with your qualifications, experience and contacts in Europe. Besides, your book was recommended to me by someone whose judgement I respect."

"And who might that be?"

For the second time, her mask slipped. Flynn glimpsed the sadness behind her eyes again. "Someone who was impressed by your ideas," she said. "Is there somewhere we can talk in private?"

Flynn decided to stand his ground.

"There's no point in talking to me about a job. I'm sorry you felt you had to come all this way, but I still won't work for you."

The woman glanced over his shoulder to make sure there was

nobody within earshot. Then she turned to him and spoke in a slow and deliberate whisper.

"Doctor Flynn, I wouldn't have wasted my time coming all the way from The Hague to meet you if this wasn't of the highest priority. You were trained by Russian instructors in Libya during your time as a member of the Irish Republican Army. Following this training you spent time in Moscow and you've continued to attend classes in the Russian language here at the university."

"That's common knowledge, Capitaine Arnault. What's your point?"

"As part of the research for your book, you conducted a detailed analysis on the danger of nuclear weapons smuggling from unsecured arms depots in the former Soviet Union. You proposed a number of potential scenarios involving such weapons falling into the hands of terrorists and how those scenarios might be dealt with."

"I did. What of it?"

She fixed him directly with her bright brown eyes.

"One of those scenarios is about to be played out. There are currently two nuclear weapons on the black market and heading for unknown targets in Europe."

"I have a room here on campus," Flynn said. "We can talk there."

Gabrielle Arnault followed Flynn out of the lecture theatre, down a dilapidated corridor with cracked tiles and peeling paint, and into a cobbled courtyard. The fading hum of Dublin's commuter traffic reached her from beyond the campus walls. The orange glow of neon lights filtered upwards to the stars. Since Madrid she had found that smoking calmed her nerves. So she stopped for a moment, took a packet of cigarettes and a gold Colibri lighter from her bag and lit up, drawing the smoke into her lungs and releasing it with a hard sigh into the cold night air. She had been meaning to quit smoking for some time, but had not yet managed it. Perhaps it was the idea of being without that lighter . . ?

"Over here," Flynn said, and set off briskly across the cobbles without a backward glance.

Gabrielle had decided that she would not like Flynn long before she'd boarded the plane to Dublin. Now the rightness of that decision had been confirmed. The man was uncouth, unkempt and arrogant. His long dark hair looked as if it hadn't been washed in weeks and his beard, flecked with ginger and grey, hadn't seen a pair of scissors in months. His cotton shirt, which at some stage in its career must have been white, was so badly worn at the collar points that part of the plastic reinforcing showed through, while his heavy tweed jacket only looked respectable because the many stains it bore blended in so well with the tweed pattern.

And, of course, the man was a former terrorist. It was only at Felipe's recommendation and the insistence of her direct superior in Europol that she was here at all. This mission was too important to let her personal feelings get in the way. She'd been ordered to recruit Flynn. That didn't mean she had to like him.

She opened her bag and replaced the lighter. It had been a present from Felipe, in lieu of being able to select the perfect engagement ring. Sometimes she felt—

"Come on," yelled Flynn across the courtyard. "It's this way."

She followed him to a long, three storey red-brick building that spanned the entire width of the quadrangle. Flynn patted his pockets, produced an old brass key and opened door number three. Then he led her into a dark hallway that smelt of mould, past a pair of rusted bicycles and up a flight of wooden stairs to the fourth floor. Another door, another key and they were standing in a large, high-ceilinged room lined with empty bookcases. Cardboard boxes full of books stood stacked in the centre of a faded patchwork rug. The room smelt of dirty laundry, floor polish and curry.

Flynn slumped into a worn leather chair next to a dark oak desk. The only things on the desk were an open laptop and two photographs – one of a team of young men in karate outfits holding a sporting trophy and another, more faded picture of a young woman holding a child.

"So," Flynn said, without any offer of a seat or something to drink. "Somebody's finally done it?"

Gabrielle lifted a pile of newspapers from one end of a moth-eaten sofa, brushed the stained material with her hand and perched gingerly on the very edge. Then she opened her document case, pulled out a printed form and a pen, and handed them to Flynn. Flynn reached into the inside pocket of his tweed jacket, took out a pair of wire-rimmed reading glasses and unfolded them.

"If you mean that somebody's devised a plan to smuggle two operational nuclear weapons out of Russia and onto European soil, then yes, somebody has," she said. "Could you sign that please, it's a confidentiality agreement. Everything I discuss with you from this moment on is of the utmost sensitivity."

Flynn scanned the document, signed it, and handed it back. "You're not going to stop terrorism with bits of paper," he said. Then he sat back and ran his fingers through his hair. Gabrielle noticed that he closed his eyes when he was thinking.

"You're presuming these devices originated in Russia?" Flynn said.

"We have some information, but it's very fragmented. Russia is the most obvious source of such weapons after all. Following the collapse of the Soviet Union, the second largest stockpile of nuclear weapons in the world —"

"You could drive a truck in and pick up a hydrogen bomb for the price of a square meal. The Russian authorities couldn't even afford to feed their men, let alone guard their facilities. Twenty seven thousand weapons of mass destruction, along with enough weapons-grade plutonium and uranium to make three times more, left unguarded or unaccounted for. It's a miracle nothing's happened up until now. Any idea who's behind it?"

"No. All we have is information of an incident involving two tactical nuclear devices—artillery shells with atomic warheads— that may be on their way to Europe from Kazakhstan. Nuclear smuggling is a concern to Europol. You speak fluent Russian.

You're an acknowledged expert on terrorism. You still have contacts in terrorist networks that might be useful to us. I'm mandated by Europol's Committee on Electronic and Techno-Terrorism to offer you a consultancy contract to assist us in finding this weapon."

"Couldn't the Americans do that for you? They've spent more than ten billion dollars since the collapse of Communism trying to keep a lid on this thing. They must know where those warheads are."

"That's true," Gabrielle said. "The Americans and the International Atomic Agency have been very efficient in the past. But even they have reported nearly two hundred nuclear smuggling incidents over the last fifteen years and less than half of Russia's nuclear storage sites are up to American security standards. If a terrorist organisation has enough money and the right contacts, they can buy a fully assembled bomb or the material and know-how to make one. You're a former terrorist yourself. You were trained by the Russians. We need you to advise us on these contacts, Doctor Flynn. Captain Felipe Rodriguez, the man who founded COMMETT, read your book and recommended that you be asked to join us."

Flynn opened his eyes.

"Then why has he taken so long to contact me?"

"Because he's dead, Doctor Flynn," said Gabrielle, holding his gaze.

"I'm sorry. I really am."

"I've been assigned to carry on his work and to run the COMMETT programme," Gabrielle said. "I intend to succeed in this for his sake and I will. You wouldn't have been my first choice as an advisor but—"

"And why not?"

Gabrielle hesitated while she considered her answer.

"Because of your history as a terrorist for the Irish Republic Army. You'd still be in jail had it not been for the Good Friday agreement."

Flynn scowled at her.

"And all this is in that file you had in front of you during my lecture?"

"It is."

"Can I see it?"

Gabrielle reached down, unzipped her document case and passed him the file. She watched while he read, licking his finger and thumb to turn the pages as he did so.

She'd completely understated her feelings when she said he hadn't been her first choice. She could hardly bear being in the same room as a man who was capable of inflicting the kind of pain she'd endured in Madrid. She was only here on sufferance to the memory of Felipe and under the orders of Europol. If Flynn turned her down now, she'd happily walk away with a clear conscience that she had at least done her duty to COMMETT.

"It says here that I was only captured because I mistimed the explosion and allowed myself to get caught in the blast," Flynn said, closing the file and handing it back to her. "That's British propaganda."

"Then perhaps you'd like me to update the file with the facts?"

"Some other time. Right now, I'd like to know why you've gone to all this trouble to recruit me if you obviously hate my guts."

"Europol is empowered to recruit civilian advisors from any speciality in order to ensure that we obtain the most accurate advice. As I've already told you, Captain Rodriguez admired your work. My superiors decided that the best advice they could get on nuclear terrorism would be from a former terrorist. That's why I'm here."

Flynn raised his eyebrows and looked at her over the top of his reading glasses.

"No matter what you think of me personally?"

Gabrielle slid Flynn's folder back into her case and zipped it shut.

"If you agree to work with me, I'll show you the respect you deserve and I shall expect the same in return, whatever our personal feelings are for each other. After all, what do my feelings matter when two nuclear devices could be exploded in any European city at any time?"

Flynn took off his glasses and frowned at her.

"And what if I still don't want to work with you?"

Gabrielle didn't flinch. She reached into her case, took out another business card and laid it on the arm of his chair. Then she got to her feet.

"That's your choice, Doctor Flynn. But from my own research into your present circumstances, Europol is the only potential source of employment you have. This college receives large donations from sources in the United States. Your book condemning the American security forces for failing to fully appreciate the terrorist threat and your letters to the US authorities about Iraq and Afghanistan have raised embarrassing questions which put that funding at risk. I know your contract here has been revoked and that you've been asked to leave by the end of the month. Even though you and your wife are separated, you still have to provide maintenance for her and your daughter. If you want to accept our offer, please call me on that mobile number. If not, then thank you for your time."

Flynn looked away. She saw his eyes lingering over the empty bookshelves and the cardboard boxes that filled the centre of the room.

"I don't work just for the money," he said, staring back at her again. "A person who's made the sacrifices I've made for a cause I believed in doesn't do it just for the money."

Gabrielle picked up her case and got to her feet. She glanced at the photos on Flynn's desk.

"Then do this for a cause. You claim to be a world expert on terrorism and you talk of understanding the terrorist mind. Work with us to prove your theories are correct. Work with us to pay for all the suffering you caused with that bomb in England. Do it to protect your wife and daughter. After all, those nuclear weapons could be exploded as easily here in Dublin as in Paris or Rome. Ireland has offended many extremists by allowing America to use Shannon airport as a stopover for its military aircraft during the war in Iraq. This country is as valid a target as anywhere else."

Flynn got up from his chair and walked to the window. Looking past him, Gabrielle saw the lights of Dublin twinkling against the night sky.

"If I was to take this contract, to whom would I be reporting?" Flynn said, with his back to her.

"To me directly, as head of section. I insist on that."

"And what if I don't like taking orders from a young woman?"

"You'll be taking orders from a Captain of the French Police and a senior advisor to Europol," said Gabrielle. "And neither of those two organisations condone sexism."

"*Touché, mon Capitaine.* And this work you want me to carry out— is it purely in an advisory capacity or would you expect me to get my hands dirty?"

"If you mean 'will you be expected to operate in the field', then the answer is no. Europol's mandate is purely to advise any two or more Member State police forces that request our special assistance. We're not mandated to carry firearms or to make arrests. You will not be expected to place yourself in danger in any way."

Flynn turned away from the window and smiled.

"Pity," he said. "I was looking forward to some excitement."

3

"Bottom line," said the man sitting across the table from Gorshkov. "Two nuclear warheads, delivered to the destination of our choice. How much?"

The dark eyes fixed on his from across the table. Up until this point, the negotiations had been easy, or as easy as any bargaining for such high stakes can be. The man and his assistant, a slim brunette in a beautifully cut business suit, had agreed to all of Gorshkov's demands regarding security. They'd waited in their hotel suite for three days, making no phone calls and receiving no visitors while Gorshkov had checked out their story. They'd agreed to be searched, blindfolded, transported in a closed van to their present location and confined in this room with Gorshkov and his two bodyguards, all of whom were armed.

But then again, thought Gorshkov, when a man exposes himself to as many risks in acquiring illegal nuclear weapons as he had, he cannot afford to be too careful in screening new buyers, particularly if his employers were powerful and vengeful men. Indeed, Gorshkov would not have risked their wrath at all by entering into an independent deal of his own had the potential reward not been so great—enough money to retire on and disappear to somewhere warm.

The man across the table stared at him while he waited for an answer. Gorshkov had tried to push up the price by exaggerating the difficulties he'd encountered in acquiring the bombs, the expenses incurred and the dangers he'd faced. The man had listened carefully to each new twist in Gorshkov's story. He was not dressed like a terrorist but then again, terrorists came in all shapes and sizes these days. He wore a dark suit over a blue silk shirt, open at the neck, with no jewellery or watch, since Gorshkov had insisted that all such items be left at the hotel in case they harboured bugging devices.

Looking carefully at his face, Gorshkov thought the man might have been Spanish, or even an Arab judging from the short black hair, the neatly trimmed beard and the dark brooding face. He spoke fluent Russian with a slight accent, and he'd been recommended to Gorshkov by one of his contacts in Kazakhstan. Nevertheless, he'd still pushed all his old information sources to make sure the man's story checked out. With his life on the line, Gorshkov couldn't afford to make a mistake.

The woman sitting slightly behind the man had the same dark looks and the same intelligent eyes, but there the similarity ended. While the man was broad-shouldered, like a hunting dog or a trained soldier, she had the graceful strength of a Siamese cat or a prima ballerina. Gorshkov had been a connoisseur of ballerinas in his halcyon days as a high-ranking officer in the KGB. He'd loved their effortless beauty and perfect performance, their unquestioning acceptance of his offers to spend the weekend at his *dacha* outside Moscow and their hard, boyish bodies in his bed.

But that had been a long time ago, before his proud jaw had vanished beneath his jowls and his hair had receded to the point where his head had come to resemble a glistening pink sphere. In those days, however Machiavellian the politicking and the internecine wars had been under Communism, he'd always been sure of coming home to his state sponsored apartment, his generous food allowance and his monthly salary. Nowadays, he found himself taking even greater risks for far higher stakes, with no such job security whatsoever behind him. In modern Russia, murder and extortion were now in the hands of private enterprise, and subject to the same ruthless laws of supply and demand.

Gorshkov glanced at his own hands, puffy and soft on the table in front of him, and felt his paunch press against his belt. He was getting old and fat. It was time to take his money and run. With enough cash he could still buy the kind of women he'd once been able to acquire as a perk of his job, in a climate that suited his bones—Thailand perhaps? He'd always had a taste for younger girls.

He glanced again at the dark-haired woman and imagined how it would feel to have someone like her. Did she and the man have something more than a professional relationship? Gorshkov didn't think so. He'd listened to recordings of their conversations in the hotel room and heard nothing but constant bickering. They weren't even friends. This was a pity, since any intimate connection between them might be exploited later on, if the deal went sour and pressure had to be applied.

"Well?" repeated the man. "Two atomic weapons—how much?"

"I have a problem," Gorshkov said, raising his eyebrows. "One of the items you were interested in has already been sold. I'm afraid it was previously committed to another customer. They took it ashore in another boat while we were off Marseilles."

The man's eyes bored into his.

"Is this another trick to push up the price?"

Gorshkov gestured his exasperation with his hands, glancing over the man's shoulder to where two of his own bodyguards stood with their AK-47 assault rifles at the ready.

"If only it were," he said. "Then we could negotiate and reach an agreement. Perhaps if you'd come to me sooner?"

"So there's only one warhead for sale? My employers won't be pleased."

"And who are those employers?" asked Gorshkov pleasantly.

"You know I can't say."

Gorshkov shrugged. "I do apologise. But you must realise I have to be sure of any new customers and background security checks take time. How else could I be sure you're not government agents, sent to trap me?"

"I thought you were sure," the man said. "You took enough time checking us out. Come to that, how can we be sure you yourself aren't part of some elaborate scheme to trap our employers into showing their hand? In fact, how can we be sure you even have one nuclear weapon for sale?"

Gorshkov smiled. "You can be certain of that," he said. "Come next door with me and see it for yourself."

The woman glanced at her partner and spoke for the first time.

"You mean you have the bomb right here?" she said in English. "I thought you had it hidden somewhere safe and were taking us to inspect it."

"This will save time, Madame," said Gorshkov. "That's why you were put through so much inconvenience over the last three days regarding security. We had to be sure you weren't going to call the police down on our heads."

The man with the beard still glared at Gorshkov across the table.

"And the price?" he asked.

"Ten million Euros," Gorshkov said.

"That's far too much. For ten million Euros I could take a lorry up to any of your abandoned military bases in Siberia and buy a dozen warheads myself."

"You could. But it would take you at least six months to make the contacts you need to get the weapons back past the International Atomic Agency inspectors without being detected. I can sell you a fully functional nuclear weapon here and now. And, from what I can already guess of your plans, you need that device immediately for your operation to succeed."

For the first time, the man was defensive.

"What do you know of our plans?" he said.

Gorshkov sat back in his seat. "You're working to a tight deadline," he said slowly. "You need a bomb by the end of this month to simulate an atomic test in Iran. That will destabilise the region and precipitate a world fuel shortage. Then your investors in Texas will make billions on the oil reserves they already have stored in floating tankers or left untapped in wells all over the world."

"You're very well informed," the man said. "I'm impressed."

"It's my training, my contacts and my own suspicious mind at work," Gorshkov explained with a smile. "In these circumstances, given the enormous fortune your American backers have to gain, you must agree that ten million Euros for immediate access to a working bomb is a very reasonable price."

The man thought for a moment.

"And that ten million Euros would also pay for your silence?"

Had it not been for the two armed guards in the room and the loaded pistol in his pocket, Gorshkov might have felt threatened.

"Of course," he said, "just as I'd expect my delivery of this nuclear warhead to include yours."

The man nodded. "Right then. At least we understand each other. Perhaps it's time we inspected the merchandise."

Gorshkov heaved himself to his feet and led them to a steel door, held closed by metal toggles. He motioned to one of his men, who pulled open the toggles and wrenched the door back. The clang it made as it struck the wall rang round the room like a bell.

"Mind yourself, Madame," Gorshkov said pointing downwards. "You have to step over that metal lip," and watched the woman's tight backside move beneath her business suit as she negotiated the sill. The bearded man and Gorshkov's guards followed them into the hold of the ship.

The dark cavernous space throbbed with the soft pulse of a distant generator. Light from armoured glass fixtures high above their heads shone weakly down on the stark metal walls that glistened with condensation. The hold was empty, except for a steel stairway leading to a door high up on the far wall and a large wooden packing crate the size of a coffin in the centre of the floor. Gorshkov bent down, grabbed a steel crowbar from the floor and prised off the lid.

Inside the crate, held down with canvas slings and swathed in polystyrene packing, was an obscene metal slug, painted bright purple and tapering to a point. The emblem of the hammer and sickle and a confusion of Cyrillic script were emblazoned on its casing.

"There," he said, "one nuclear-tipped artillery shell—eighty kilotons atomic yield."

The woman stepped forward and examined it.

"Red Army 365 Lightning Bolt type. It looks genuine enough, but I'll have to check."

She took a small black box, the only item she had been allowed to bring on board—and then only after it had been opened and minutely inspected—attached a probe on a cable and passed it over the contents of the case. A low clicking sound echoed around the room, rising and falling as the woman moved it around the bomb.

"At least it's radioactive," she said. "So it's probably genuine."

Gorshkov tried to look hurt.

"Madame! You insult me."

The man peered down at the shell, raised his head to Gorshkov and nodded.

"You'll receive twenty-five percent of the agreed price as soon as we can arrange it, twenty-five percent on delivery and the remaining fifty percent following a successful detonation," he said. "I can have the money wired to any bank account in the world."

"I prefer cash," Gorshkov said.

"Two and a half million is a lot of cash to arrange if you don't want it to be traced," the man said. "And bearer bonds are traceable, no matter what they tell you."

"And the intelligence services of the world have ways of tracing electronic transactions. No matter what you say," Gorshkov said, drawing on his own experience of doing exactly that for the KGB. "I'll take my money in diamonds then. They must be uncut. Nothing less than fifty carat."

"That might take time, and we're up against a tight deadline."

"Those are my terms. Do you want the bomb or not?"

The man thought for a moment. "Okay, I accept. Contact me at the hotel within twenty-four hours."

The woman glanced at the man. Her eyes were very beautiful and full of promise, with long full lashes. Gorshkov had an idea.

"That's all very well," he said. "But I'll need some security against payment. Until you can raise my diamonds, the woman stays with me, just in case you decide to walk away from the deal."

The man didn't hesitate. "Of course. I understand."

Gorshkov glanced at the woman, just in time to catch the blaze of anger directed at her partner before it faded.

"Good," he told the man. "I'll have my men blindfold you and escort you back to your hotel. Madame, I'm sure I can make you comfortable here with me until tomorrow."

He motioned to the two guards. One laid his Kalashnikov back against the wall, safely out of reach, and moved forward, pulling a wide strip of black cloth and a pair of handcuffs from his jacket pocket. The other man held his gun steady, keeping watch on the man, who put his hands behind his back, ready to accept the cuffs.

Gorshkov turned to gaze upon the woman, standing calm and erect. His mind slipped back to the joys of his dacha and the young ballerinas cavorting in his bed . . .

The clatter of feet on metal shattered Gorshkov's fantasies. The door at the top of the stairway burst open and a man shouted down at him.

"We've picked up a radio signal . . . a high-speed squirt transmission . . . very loud . . . it could only have come from here on the ship."

Gorshkov leapt forward, tore the Geiger counter from the woman's hand and smashed it down on the metal deck. It shattered into a dozen pieces. Gorshkov knelt and sifted through them with his fingers. Then, finding nothing, he stood up and rammed his heel down on the radiation probe. Bending down again, he pulled the small silver disc of a miniature radio transmitter from its shattered head and held it up to the light. Then he swore violently and grabbed the woman by the arm.

"Yura!" he shouted to the man at the top of the staircase. "Get some men down here and take the bomb to the helicopter. Borya, Seriozha, wait until we've left, then kill this man."

4

Flynn felt the adrenaline surge through his body as Gorshkov's man shouted his warning from the top of the stairwell.

They were blown—unarmed and trapped—with three gunmen in a steel room that offered no cover. Their only hope of survival was the AK-47 Gorshkov's guard had propped against the wall.

Flynn shifted his weight to his left foot and kicked back with his right, catching the man behind him full in the stomach. The man retched, doubled over and the handcuffs went clattering to the floor. The guard behind Gabrielle turned, snapping back the bolt of his gun to load the first round into the breech, ready to fire.

Flynn dived for the unattended weapon. His shoulder hit the metal floor and he slid towards the wall, reaching for the gun, bracing himself for the roar of automatic fire that could shatter his body at any moment. His outstretched fingers closed on the strap of the weapon and he jerked it towards him, clawing at the bolt and flicking off the safety catch.

The guard crashed on top of Flynn like a falling tree, crushing the breath from his lungs, breaking though his defences and closing on his neck. Flynn heard Gorshkov yelling orders and the sound of running feet. The man bore down on him, his thumbs crushing Flynn's windpipe and his sour breath hot on Flynn's face.

Flynn brought his right knee up into the guard's crotch. The man jerked backwards, just at the roar of the other guard's gun exploded. Bullets screamed off metal. The man on top of Flynn jerked forward in a cloud of blood and slammed into the wall, sliding down on top of Flynn in an untidy heap of arms and legs. Flynn wriggled out from under him and hauled up the AK-47, swinging its barrel to cover the room. The other guard raised his gun to fire again.

Flynn had no time to aim. He simply squeezed the trigger and hosed the centre of the room,   the rifle juddering in his hands. The man's chest shattered and he slumped against the stairway.

Gorshkov and Gabrielle were gone. Two Russians were dead.

Now the mission was blown and the only way they could recover the second bomb was to take Gorshkov alive. Flynn ripped the magazine out of the fallen guard's gun, stuffed it into his pocket and ran up the stairs.

Gorshkov knew his only hope of escape was getting airborne before the police closed in. Once the woman had sent that radio signal it could only be a few minutes before whoever was looking out for her came to the rescue. And with a nuclear weapon involved, there was bound to be an overwhelming and immediate response.

Gorshkov had been in too many tight situations during his long and bloody career to leave his escape route to chance. Two bursts of machine gun fire sounded from the stairwell behind him as he pushed the woman through the door into the corridor beyond. Good. That was the dark-haired man out of the way. Now there was just this woman, and she made the perfect hostage.

Drawing his pistol and ramming it into her spine, he shoved her in front of him, down the corridor and through another steel door onto the deck of the ship. To his right, glittering in the sunshine, lay the inner harbour of Barcelona with its great steel tower, its cable cars and its gleaming cruise liners. To his left was the dockyard, the breakwater and the vast expanse of the Mediterranean.

But Gorshkov's eyes were fixed on the bright yellow helicopter on the aft deck, its rotors already whirring into a blur. The four men who'd brought up the bomb closed the rear door of the machine and raced down the gangplank to the waiting cars on the dock below. His bomb was safe aboard the helicopter. It was time to make his escape.

"Move!" he roared, grinding the gun into the woman's back and slamming her shoulder with his left hand. She lost her balance and fell forward onto her knees. Gorshkov kicked her backside to get her onto her feet. Then he cocked his pistol and aimed it at her head.

"Move!"

With a crack like gunfire, a signal flare burst above their heads and an amplified voice boomed out across the harbour.

"*Vnimaniye*! Attention cargo vessel Cape Sarych. This is the Spanish Police. Put down your weapons and surrender!"

Then, as if on cue, the crews of nearby yachts, holidaymakers promenading on the pier and dockers working on the wharf suddenly sprouted automatic weapons and trained them at the ship.

"Attention!" shouted the voice again. "Shut down that aircraft and throw your guns into the sea or we open fire!"

"Run!" shouted Gorshkov. "Run to the helicopter!"

Before he could kick her again, she was up and sprinting towards the machine with a speed that surprised him. In an instant she'd reached it, ducked below the thrashing blades and was pulling open the pilot's door.

She's panicking, thought Gorshkov. She's confused.

"No! Get in the back!"

The downdraft from the rotors tore at his clothes as he ran after her. He reached out to grab her shoulder but she spun round as gracefully as any ballerina and slammed her right heel into his groin.

A sudden numbness, followed by a tidal wave of pain, rolled over Gorshkov. His eyes bulged in their sockets and he toppled forward. His gun clattered to the deck plates. The last thing he remembered was being bundled into the back of the helicopter next to the bomb. Then the woman snatched up his gun and slammed it down on his skull . . . .

Gabrielle levelled Gorshkov's pistol at the pilot's head.

"Get out! Get out or I'll shoot!"

The pilot stared at her is disbelief.

Even against the roar of the engine and the scream of the rotor blades, the boom of the pistol inside the cockpit was deafening. The pilot's jaw dropped and his wide eyes swivelled to the neat hole in the Plexiglas of the far side door.

Gabrielle heard gunshots behind her. A bullet whizzed overhead. Gorshkov's men had seen her overpower their leader and were taking action to protect him.

"Get out!" she screamed at the pilot.

She was angrier than she'd ever been in her life.

"Out!"

The pistol exploded again. A second hole appeared in the Plexiglas. The pilot scrabbled at his safety harness, wrenched open his door and leapt onto the ship's helipad.

Gabrielle pulled herself into the cockpit and slammed the door, sliding across to the pilot's seat and strapping herself in. Her feet found the rudder pedals. Her hands settled on the joystick and collective pitch lever as Gorshkov's men hurtled down the deck towards her. With a quick glance at the gauges, she opened up the engine, tilted the blades so that they bit into the air and pulled the helicopter up off the ship.

Three days of being cooped up in a hotel room with Flynn, unable to speak anything more than small talk for fear of hidden microphones, was bad enough. But his eagerness to leave her alone with that pervert Gorshkov was the final straw.

The deck of the ship fell beneath her as the helicopter swooped out over Barcelona harbour towards the open sea. She moved her feet on the pedals to turn the machine and looked back at the ship.

Gunfire had broken out between the police on the dock and the Russians. As she watched, a tall familiar figure ran along the side of the ship towards the stern, waving at her to come back.

Flynn burst out of the corridor from the hold just in time to see
Gabrielle taking control of the helicopter. A gaggle of Gorshkov's
men had also spotted her and were running towards the helipad,
brandishing weapons. Could she take off in time to avoid being
hit? She was a perfect target through the clear bubble of the cockpit
window.

"Here!" Flynn screamed at the Russians, letting off a short burst
from his rifle into the air. "Over here!"

The men turned and raised their weapons towards him. Flynn
leapt behind a bulkhead as a swarm of bullets zipped past his head.

He snatched a glance back at the aft deck, just in time to see the
helicopter pull clear . . . and head straight out to sea. She was bound
to be pissed off with his agreeing to leave her with Gorshkov. But
was she really abandoning him?

He dodged around a ventilator and down a flight of stairs to the
lower deck. In the harbour below, a pair of police launches zoomed
in from the seaward side, their loudhailers calling out in Russian
for everyone to throw their weapons into the water and surrender.
From the landward side, the shriek of police sirens and the squeal
of tyres sounded from the quay.

Flynn glanced back at the police launches. They were bristling
with guns and firing wildly. If he kept his own weapon, he could as
easily be shot by an excited Spanish policeman as by the Russians.
He looked back up the stairway, saw that nobody was following
him and threw the Kalashnikov over the side, raising his arms in
surrender.

It was a mistake. No sooner had the automatic rifle hit the water
than the gang of gunmen from the rear deck burst into view at the
top of the stairwell, bellowing and firing down at the police. The
launches fired back. The Russians looked down the stairwell, saw
him and turned their weapons in his direction.

"Shite!"

Flynn spun round, ran to another set of stairs and launched
himself downwards as the Russians opened fire. Bullets hissed

over his head and ricocheted off the metal deck below. He missed his footing, slid down the last six steps, and found himself lying at the rounded stern of the ship. Above him, and getting closer by the second, were a dozen angry Russians with guns.

In front of him was the sea.

He ran to the rail and glanced upwards.

The bright yellow helicopter was hovering well out of range over the harbour He could just make out the white oval of Arnault's face, staring out at him through the canopy.

He waved to her, beckoning her back to pick him up. But she just pointed downwards at the water.

She was telling him to jump.

"Bloody women!" hissed Flynn. Then he leapt over the side into the harbour.

5

Gabrielle sipped her coffee from a standard blue and white European Commission cup and glanced out at the panoramic view offered by the conference room reception area of The Hague. The headquarters of Europol at number 47 Raamweg looks like any other office building, with all the red brick, chromed steel and glass expected of any department of the European Commission in Brussels or Strasbourg. Security is the same, with its passport checks, photo identification and self-adhesive visitor badges bearing the blue circle and yellow stars of the European Union flag. There are the same grey offices, with the same regulation grey-painted furniture and the strictly regulated access to window space, allocated by rank—one window for a junior officer, two for a senior executive and three or more for top management staff.

"They'll be ready for you in a moment," chirped the secretary at the desk. "Your item is at the top of the agenda."

Gabrielle nodded and placed her cup back on its saucer, trying to keep her nerves under control. She was dying for a cigarette and toyed with Felipe's lighter in her pocket. Smoking was prohibited inside the building. This was her first ever briefing to the full Europol Management Board and today, of all days, she needed to be in control. The Barcelona operation was up for discussion and the fate of the whole nuclear smuggling investigation, as well as Felipe's vision for COMMETT, hung in the balance.

Gabrielle felt her heart jump as the internal phone on the secretary's desk purred. The woman picked it up, listened and nodded to her.

"You may go in now," she said. "They're ready for you."

Gabrielle took a deep breath and ran her hands down the skirt of her French National Police uniform to flatten the creases.

Then, taking the folder she'd brought up from her office, she stepped forward and pulled open the heavy wooden doors to conference room number one.

She found herself standing at the head of the meeting, looking down the horseshoe of polished wooden tables and chairs common to most EU conference rooms. In each place sat a representative of the various European Member States, with their paperwork and a microphone in front of them. At the base of the horseshoe, near the door where she'd entered, sat the meeting's rapporteurs, a secretary from admin, Europol's Director and two Deputy Directors. Gabrielle noticed the folders were marked with a red label and the words 'Strictly Confidential'.

One of the Deputy Directors rose to greet her. He was a tall man in his late forties, with thinning black hair, bright blue eyes and a bulbous nose. He looked like a farmer, a builder, a man who worked with his hands. But Gabrielle knew him as the Deputy Director covering the EU terrorism threat and, as such, her direct superior. His name was Commander Gerald Parkinson and, before taking this four-year European appointment, he'd been the deputy head of one of the elite anti-terrorism squads at the London Metropolitan Police.

"Bonjour, Capitaine Arnault," he said, in very passable French. "I won't waste time on introductions. You probably know most of the members, at least by reputation."

He smiled and motioned her to sit at the top table to his right, nodded to the Director and pressed the red button on his microphone, going live to the translation booths along the left-hand wall of the meeting room and, through headphones, to each member of the Management Board.

"Ladies and gentlemen," he continued in English. "With the Director's permission, I'd like to introduce an important member of my team, Capitaine Gabrielle Arnault, temporarily on secondment from the RAID unit of the French National Police and currently heading up COMMETT, our Committee on Electronic and Techno-Terrorism. Capitaine Arnault, we're all anxious to hear your report on the recent incident in Barcelona. In particular, we'd like to hear your thoughts on the whereabouts of the remaining nuclear device."

He nodded to Gabrielle, who put on her headphones and opened her notes. Her hands shook as she reached for a glass of water, took a sip and leant forward to the microphone to speak.

"Monsieur le Directeur, ladies and gentlemen—"

Parkinson interrupted her, reached over and turned her microphone on. Gabrielle nodded her thanks as the red light came to life and tried to recover her composure. After another sip of water she continued.

"As you're all aware, ladies and gentlemen, the mandate of Europol includes the provision of assistance and advice to EU Member States on the threat of nuclear terrorism. Six weeks ago, intelligence reached us that two tactical atomic artillery shells from a former Soviet Union stockpile in Kazakhstan, each with an explosive power equivalent to eighty thousand tons of TNT, had resurfaced on the black market. When it appeared that these shells had been transported to Europe, and the threat presented by these devices covered more than one Member State as per the Europol mandate, COMMETT was ordered to devise a plan that might lead to their recovery with the minimum of risk."

She glanced up from her notes. The red light above a microphone at the far left-hand side of the meeting room had winked on. The tall, elaborately coiffured woman seated behind it spoke in very rapid Spanish. Gabrielle had to wait a couple of seconds for the translation to come through in French on her headset.

"Surely Capitaine," the translation began, "nobody who is fully informed about the Barcelona recovery operation could ever describe it as proceeding 'with the minimum of risk'. Two men died in a full-scale gun battle in a public place in the very heart of the city and a nuclear device was allowed to come under gunfire as it was flown from the scene in a helicopter! And please tell me, how did your unit became so deeply involved in this action when the Europol mandate specifically limits your activities to the provision of advice and intelligence? Surely the policing of the action should have been in the hands of the Spanish authorities?"

"With respect, Señora Hernandez," Gabrielle replied. "Europol was working very closely with, and at the specific request of, the Spanish police. The two fatalities took place only after the Russian gang selling the weapons was forewarned to our operation by their interception of a radio transmission calling for the Spanish authorities to move in and recover the bomb. The gang went for their guns and two Russians were killed. They were the only deaths that resulted and there were no other casualties."

The red light in front of Señora Hernandez flashed on again.

"Nevertheless," she said, "those deaths occurred as a direct result of Europol action at the scene. So I ask again, Capitaine Arnault: how was it that members of your group, this . . . COMMETT committee of yours, were meeting with the smugglers when your mandate should have been to provide no more than technical advice and intelligence to the Spanish authorities?"

"Again with respect, Señora Hernandez, for COMMETT to seek out, locate and infiltrate a group of technically sophisticated nuclear smugglers meant creating credibility within the networks in which they operate, so as to win the confidence of the smugglers themselves. In this case, I was advised by a specialist consultant that the best way to do this was to pose as prospective buyers of such weapons, a tactic that has served the American FBI well in the past. This consultant had expert knowledge of nuclear smuggling networks in Russia and is a fluent Russian speaker but, once contact was made with the smugglers, a meeting arranged and trust established, it became impossible to replace him without raising suspicion."

Señora Hernandez was still not satisfied.

"And in this case, the Europol personnel involved were yourself and this civilian consultant . . . this Doctor Flynn, whose actions precipitated the two deaths? Is it not foolish to place such a dangerous policing operation in the hands of a civilian consultant, particularly one who is himself a former terrorist?"

Heads turned around the table. Gabrielle felt completely out of her depth. She glanced at Parkinson, who leant forward and pressed the light on his own microphone to speak.

"If I can be allowed to explain, Señora, it was I, as Deputy Director in charge of the anti-terrorism brief, and not Capitaine Arnault who insisted that the consultant in question be allowed to maintain his position as the key negotiator with the Russians until the exact location of the weapons was identified. Once this was achieved, it was the intention that the bombs be safely recovered by the relevant European police force. The deaths in Barcelona were precipitated by the fact that one of the bombs was actually aboard the vessel where negotiations were taking place and had to be safely recovered by whatever means necessary to avoid catastrophic loss of life and property. It was not a failure of procedure on behalf of Capitaine Arnault or the members of her team. I'd also like to remind the Board that all Europol operatives are prohibited from carrying firearms. The only guns aboard that ship belonged to the smugglers themselves. According to Doctor Flynn's statement, which has been corroborated by both Capitaine Arnault and a detailed examination of the scene by your own forensic experts, one smuggler was hit by fire from his own side. The other death occurred in an act of self-defence."

Señora Hernandez shook her head. "Nevertheless," she said. "Your COMMETT group went far beyond the standard operational procedures laid down by—"

"I think your point is well taken, Señora," said the Director of Europol, "but there are far more serious matters facing the Board here today. Commander Parkinson, Capitaine Arnault, the second weapon is unaccounted for and may still be at large in Europe. There are a number of European summit meetings taking place over the next month that could be prime targets for such a device, including an important international energy summit which is due to be attended by a number of heads of state, including the American president. Do you have any idea where the weapon could be? Can the suspects arrested in Barcelona give us any information?"

"The head of the Russian smuggling gang, Alexandr Gorshkov, has been questioned by the Spanish authorities for the last thirty-six hours in Barcelona," Parkinson said, "but he denies everything that was said on the ship and will not give us the names of his contacts in Russia. I think he's more afraid of them than he is of us."

"Which means we could be facing the most serious terrorist threat in European history," said the Director. "If a group such as Al Qaeda has that device then we could be facing an infinitely more catastrophic disaster than the London or Madrid bombings or even the terrible events of 9/11. I've set up links with our colleagues in the various international security services, called for the reintroduction of border checks for any vehicle large enough to carry the device and rerouted surveillance satellites to monitor trace emissions of radioactivity across the European continent. Europol has also made contact with the Russian security services in the hope of finding clues in Moscow. But even with all this activity, we still have no idea what the target might be or when this bomb might be detonated. Therefore, I suggest we recess for a short break before reconvening to discuss what emergency measures we might take without panicking the entire population of Europe. In the meantime, I would insist that you all strictly observe the 'Top Secret' nature of this matter. It is not to be discussed outside this room."

He switched off his microphone and stood. Around the horseshoe table, Europol board members shuffled their papers as the meeting adjourned to consider the crisis.

"Capitaine Arnault," said Parkinson. "We need to talk."

He led her out of the conference room, across the reception area into a spacious office with four windows looking out over the city.

"You did well in there," he said. "You stood your ground. What's more, your initial analysis of the case and your actions once that analysis had been made allowed COMMETT to succeed where other agencies have failed. I think Señora Hernandez was jealous that you had a success on Spanish soil, when it should have been the Spanish intelligence agencies that got there first."

"Thank you, Commander."

"Nevertheless, there is a line that should not be crossed. Señora Hernandez was right regarding the mandate of Europol. We should have identified Gorshkov, relayed the information to Spanish intelligence and proceeded in a purely advisory capacity. Not carried on as part of the operation itself."

"I agree, Commander," Gabrielle said, "but, Doctor Flynn and I were trapped in an impossible situation. We had to improvise."

Parkinson took a thick folder from his desk and opened it. "Was the idea to pose as potential buyers really Doctor Flynn's or was it yours?"

"As I told the Board, he advised me as an expert consultant and I, as section leader, accepted his advice. Locating the bombs and recovering them safely was our primary objective and I felt the risk involved was acceptable."

"I understand you almost came to blows with Flynn on the quayside in Barcelona after he was pulled out of the harbour," said Parkinson.

"We had a difference of professional opinion."

"Over what, might I ask?"

"Gorshkov had insisted I remain on the ship as his hostage while Doctor Flynn raised the money to pay for the bomb," said Gabrielle trying not to sound like the plaintiff in an application for divorce. "I felt that Flynn was too willing to leave me behind. He felt I could have come back with the helicopter and picked him up from the ship to save him from jumping into the sea. I had to remain well out of range of gunfire from the ship, because I was carrying not only the nuclear weapon itself but also Gorshkov, our only information source to the second bomb. Both arguments were valid. We've settled our differences and the matter is now closed."

Parkinson peered at her over the top of the file.

"And how do you feel about his performance as a member of COMMETT?"

"He's the best in his field. He has precisely the right set of skills we need for the mission."

"But he's something of an individualist, by all accounts?"

"Experts of his calibre often are, Mister Chairman."

"I understand you share the concern raised just now by Señora Hernandez, regarding the fact that Damien Flynn is himself a former terrorist—a senior member of the Irish Republican Army."

"Yes Commander. I'm also concerned that he worked as what can only be described as a mercenary after his release from prison in 1999, before settling down at one of the universities in Dublin. That's why he would not have been my first choice for COMMETT. But that's only my personal opinion."

"And yet the contacts he made during that time were what enabled you to penetrate Gorshkov's operation," said Parkinson.

"Like I said, Commander, it's only my personal opinion. The success of this mission comes first. I'm fully committed to that."

"Look Gabrielle," said Parkinson, in a tone of voice that reminded her of her father, "I know you don't like Flynn and, given your experience as a direct victim of terrorism in Madrid, I can sympathise with you, but we're dealing with a massive terrorist threat here and we need to use any and every resource at our disposal. Your fiancé Felipe Rodriguez knew it—he recommended Flynn—and I know it too. I spent years fighting people like him during their bombing campaigns in London. They're committed, they're clever and they're totally, utterly ruthless. While I don't condone what the IRA did, while their actions caused the deaths of a lot of innocent people, I still respect their cleverness and cunning in carrying them out."

He laid the file flat on the desk in front of him and looked directly into her eyes.

"That's why I insisted that you recruit Flynn in the first place, even though the hiring of former terrorists with murky pasts is a new and potentially dangerous idea to the more conservative minds around the Board table in there. With the stakes as high as they are, given that nuclear weapons are involved, it's better to have people like Flynn inside the tent pissing out than outside the tent pissing in. The question is, can you, as leader of COMMETT, continue to work with him?"

Gabrielle stood stiffly to attention. "Yes Commander. I can."

Parkinson continued to examine her for a moment. Then his gaze softened.

"All right then. We've had a spectacular success through unconventional means, but we need to be careful. I wouldn't like to see COMMETT overreach and burn out before it has a chance to establish itself. So take whatever advice Flynn gives you, use your best judgement as Section Leader and, if you have any problems, come straight to me. Is that clear? You have my mobile number?"

"Yes Commander. Will that be all?"

"Yes, Capitaine. Thank you."

Gabrielle picked up her file of papers, walked back through reception to the lift and returned to her office two floors below. She swiped her security card in the lock, opened the door and threw the file onto the desk.

Then she stopped. Something important was missing . . .

"You owe me a new suit."

"And you were supposed to wait outside in the lobby until I got back!"

Damian Flynn lay sprawled across the couch Gabrielle sometimes used as a bed when she had to work late. His arms were behind his head, his eyes closed and his long legs crossed at the ankles. On his chest lay the framed picture of Felipe and herself in the restaurant overlooking the Square of Columbus in Madrid. On the low table next to him lay a Europol file, face down. She crossed the room, took the picture and replaced it gently on her desk.

"You shouldn't have been so quick to leave me as a hostage to that pig Gorshkov!" she said.

"Perhaps," replied Flynn. "But if you had remained as his hostage, I can't imagine anyone seducing a dirty old devil like Gorshkov into giving us the secret of the second bomb's whereabouts faster than you. Besides, taking off in the chopper and abandoning me on that ship to be shot at by a gang of gun-crazed Russians was hardly quid pro quo. How were you so sure I could swim?"

"I read your Europol file. How were you so sure I could fly?"

"Touché, mon Capitaine. But I've been reading Europol files of my own."

He lifted the file from the table next to the couch and turned it so that she could read the title. It was her personnel file, which me must have taken from her desk along with the picture.

"That's confidential."

"Very interesting though," said Flynn, flicking through the pages. "Father was a policeman from a long line of policemen in Brittany . . . nice part of the world by the way, very much like parts of Ireland . . . grandfather was a hero in the Resistance during the war . . . now that is interesting. Looks like you went into the family business, mon Capitaine. You certainly went up the ranks fast enough. Two medals for bravery in the Gendarmerie . . . leading role in a critical hostage situation against terrorists from Action Directe which brought you to the attention of *Recherché, Assistance, Intervention, Dissuasion*. . . which we terrorists all know as RAID . . . assigned to work on detailed strategies to combat plane hijackings, protect the Channel Tunnel, trains and commercial aircraft and . . . wait for it . . . a secret action to successfully defuse the bombing of a French nuclear power station. Now I never heard about that one! Which in turn brought you to Europol where you met one Felipe Hernandez seconded there a year before from an elite Spanish anti-terrorism unit. Together you dreamt up the idea for COMMETT and here we are . . . "

"That's enough!" snapped Gabrielle and grabbed the file back from him.

Flynn let it go.

"You hate me for being what you see as a terrorist," he said. "But that label can be applied to members of your family too. It's there in black and white."

"I don't see how!" spat Gabrielle.

"This grandfather of yours, the gallant hero who won so many medals in the French resistance during the war, did he by any chance plant bombs in cafés, blow up cars or shoot German soldiers in ambush?"

"Of course he did. He was a freedom fighter. France had been invaded by the Nazis. It was the only way to strike back."

"And couldn't you say the same thing about the British occupation of Ireland, or the use of Russian or American troops in Afghanistan? One man's freedom fighter is another man's terrorist. It just depends which side you're on."

Gabrielle stared at him with icy hatred.

"If you've read that file, Doctor Flynn, you'll know that I was almost killed by a terrorist bomb in Madrid. So I don't need to play academic mind games with you about the definition of terrorism. I've lived through it as a victim."

"And what makes you think that I haven't . . ." began Flynn.

Then he saw the look in her eyes and held up his hands in mock surrender.

"Okay. Okay," he said. "Let's call a truce for now and stick to the job in hand. Has Gorshkov told the Spanish police anything yet?"

Gabrielle took a deep breath to steady herself.

"No. And I don't think he's going to. I doubt if he even knows where the second bomb is or who took it away on that other ship off Marseilles."

"I think you're right," Flynn said. "But if I'd had a bomb as powerful as that back in my days as a terrorist I'd have done one of two things—explode it without warning where it would do the most harm, or use it as a weapon of blackmail to get what I wanted. The questions are: which of those options are they going to pursue and can we find the bomb before they explode it?"

Gabrielle thought of the energy summit the Director had mentioned.

"I'm sure we'll have the answer to your first question soon enough," she said. "All we have to do is wait."

"Okay then," said Flynn. "Let's call it a truce for now. I'm heading back to Dublin for the weekend. I'll see you on Monday."

"Bon voyage," Gabrielle said and carefully locked her personnel file in her desk drawer.

Then she picked up the photograph of herself and Felipe, touched the glass gently with her finger and started to cry . . .

6

It should have been one of the happiest days of Gabrielle's life. Here she was, in the beautiful city of Madrid with the man she was going to marry and her wedding only a week away. In a few minutes, her mother and father would arrive by train, bringing Gabrielle's wedding dress with them for its final fitting. At the weekend they'd all fly back to Brittany for the ceremony and the celebrations. Then she and Felipe would honeymoon in Tunisia for three weeks before returning to work in The Hague.

She should have been so happy.

A heavy shower burst as they emerged from the Metro, forcing them to shelter under the awning of a nearby news stand. Across the wide plaza, past the central fountain and the glistening roofs of bustling cars, the great semicircle of Atocha Station concourse bulged into the sky. Early morning commuters jostled them. Umbrellas bobbed and weaved on the pavements. Gabrielle squinted at her watch and brushed raindrops from its face.

It was 7:15. She had fifteen minutes before her parents' train arrived.

"Felipe. I—"

"The rain's stopped," he said, taking her hand. "Come on." It was the first thing he'd said to her since they'd left the hotel.

He led her across the pedestrian crossing, through the crowd of commuters and down the ramp to the left of the station concourse, almost dragging her behind him. A solid line of red striped taxies proceeded past the entrance, picking up fares and shouldering their way back into the traffic.

"Felipe!" But he didn't seem to hear her.

They joined the stream of commuters filing their way through the lobby with its Labarila Grill, its aroma of freshly ground coffee, its car hire booths and souvenir stands and into the towering concourse. Grey steel girders rose against the brickwork walls and soared out to meet each other under a great glass canopy. Tropical ferns, irrigated by a mist of spray, stretched up to the softened light from banks of electric lamps.

Felipe still led her by the hand. She pulled away from him.

"What?" he snapped.

"We have to talk."

"We talked about this last night," he said. "It's nerves, Gabrielle. That's all it is."

"But it's—"

"I'm going to check which platform they're arriving at," he said. "You wait here."

Then he was gone, striding through the milling crowds towards the information board, leaving Gabrielle hurt and angry in the centre of the concourse by the palms. She watched him go, head and shoulders above the crowd. She thought back to when she'd first met him and how she'd tried to please him—just as she'd spent her life trying to please the men she loved.

Felipe Rodriguez was a handsome man, with bright brown eyes and a smile that could have won him any woman in the Europol office. He had a way of seeing beyond the nuts and bolts of things to the larger principles. Gabrielle, ever the pragmatist, envied him this gift and wanted to learn how to acquire it. So, when he leant across the planning table at the end of a particularly long and involved meeting and said, "You know there's a better way to do this, don't you?" she'd agreed to join him for coffee in his office to discuss it.

"The secret of understanding terrorism," said Felipe, addressing her in word perfect French, "is to understand the terrorist mind. Did you know, several experts accurately predicted the attacks of 9/11 in advance?"

Felipe took a book from the shelf behind him. "This was written by a reformed Irish terrorist turned academic and published twelve months before the attacks on the World Trade Centre," he said, turning to a bookmarked page and opening it in front of her. "I think it's time we took such experts seriously and brought them in to advise Europol directly."

"Don't we have enough experts of our own?"

"On conventional policing—yes. But crime is evolving into new areas and new technologies faster than we can cope. The internet, mobile communications, biological warfare and even the threat of stolen nuclear weapons are all relevant issues today, so we need a specialist technical unit to bring in outside experts and advise on new strategies and tactics. You've experience of strategic planning from your work in RAID. Will you help me create it?"

Felipe weaved through the crowd, towards her. She had to tell him that they were taking things too fast. That perhaps the whirlwind romance they'd enjoyed in the wake of their successful project together was over and they should stop and think. She'd felt it from the moment he'd proposed to her and been too caught up in the moment to say 'no'. She'd sensed it last night in the restaurant overlooking the Square of Columbus as Felipe argued with the waiter over her order. And she'd known it for certain after he'd made love to her at their cheap hotel off the Cala Manuella Mallestrano, where she'd wrestled with the truth in the darkness, listening to his breathing as he slept.

She had to tell him now, before her parents arrived, before it went any further.

"It's over here," he said, reaching for her hand. "Come on."

"I'm serious," Gabrielle said, standing her ground. "I can't go through with this now. I tried to tell you this morning at the hotel, but you wouldn't listen."

Felipe glanced from side to side. To Gabrielle, it seemed he was more afraid of causing a scene in public than the truth of what she had to say.

"It's just nerves," he said again. "You'll get over it."

"I won't. I've thought about this, Felipe. We're making a mistake. We're rushing into this too fast."

He moved closer to her, taking hold of her arm.

"So what do we do? Your parents will be arriving at this station any minute now. We're to be married next week! Do we just tell everyone the whole thing's off ?"

Gabrielle reached up, took his hand and disengaged it.

"It's the rest of our lives," she said. "The rest of our lives!"

The anger and confusion blazed in his eyes.

"I don't understand you," he snapped. Then he turned sharply and pushed his way through the crowd, heading for the platforms.

Gabrielle stood staring after him. It would be so easy to say nothing more and let the tide of wedding arrangements wash over her. Perhaps Felipe was right. Her parents were arriving. What could he say to them before she got there? What would they think?

Gabrielle pushed her way through the sea of moving people towards the information board. Looking up, she saw their train had already arrived. She noted the platform and went past the barrier, into the throng of people disembarking. She burst through just as her mother and father appeared in the doorway of the carriage in front of him.

"Felipe!"

He turned to her.

Her mother called her name from the carriage door. She had a large box in her hand. Her father was behind her, smiling.

"Felipe!"

For an instant, she thought someone had taken a flash photograph right next to her. There was a brilliant burst of light, a deafening roar and a searing blast of hot air that gripped her in its fist and slammed her against the train on the far side of the platform. She lay buried in bodies as her ears hissed and a terrible numbness filled her. She couldn't see the light, even though her eyes were open. She couldn't breathe. She tried to call out, but her voice sounded too small to be heard. Through the hissing roar she heard the faint sound of screaming, men shouting and the distant wail of sirens—far, far away.

Then she felt movement.

Someone was searching through the pile of bodies. Light flooded in. She clamped her eyes shut against the pain. A policeman bent over her. His mouth moved, but she couldn't hear his words. Behind him, ambulance men trying to cope with the carnage were ripping bandages from a sheet of white silk.

It was only later, when she was recovering in hospital, that she realised it had been material from her wedding dress.

7

Paris sleeps, if any city can ever be said to sleep, between 02:00 and 04:00 in the morning. The stream of headlights on the Avenue des Champs-Élysées and around the Arc de Triomphe slows to a trickle, the Metro echoes with the hollow slap of footsteps instead of the roar of trains, and the lights of bars and night clubs flicker and die. Apart from the low snore of sound that is the background noise to any sleeping city, all is quiet.

Against this stillness, the diesel engine of the little street-sweeping vehicle seemed unusually loud as it bustled like a giant beetle off the Place du Carrousel and into the great enclosed space of the Cour Napoléon of the Musée du Louvre. Its flashing orange light blinked against the stern faces of statues lining the walls of the great courtyard and glittered on the soaring glass pyramid covering the main entrance to the museum. Security staff, watching from cameras mounted high on the building, noted its presence but paid it no heed. It was 02:05 on a Tuesday morning, and every Tuesday the museum is closed to the public for maintenance.

The giant green beetle fussed around the courtyard, stopping at each of the cylindrical metal litter bins and lifting them one by one to collect their contents in its hopper. Only in the farthest corner, to the north-east of the Cour Napoléon, where the security cameras have a blind spot, did the vehicle and its handlers pause for an extra moment. Then it crawled out into the courtyard and, with a whirr of brushes and a hiss of water jets, proceeded to clean the area around the pyramid, the enclosed ponds and concrete benches, before shuffling back onto the Place du Carrousel and vanished into the night.

No alarm was raised; the water dried on the paving. The black metal cylinder in the north-east corner of that great courtyard remained what it appeared to be, a place for depositing litter.

Security in France is maintained through an uneasy alliance between two powerful organisations: the Police Nationale, a civilian force responsible for urban areas and run by the Ministry of the Interior, and the Gendarmerie Nationale, a military force primarily responsible for rural areas and military installations, run by the Ministry of Defence.

Responsibility for security in France's capital city, however, is uniquely centralised under a single individual known as the Préfet de Police, appointed by the President of the Council of Ministers and whose jurisdiction extends to the departments of the inner ring of Greater Paris and their thirty thousand staff. It's a highly responsible position, covering all manner of security in Paris as well as day-to-day matters such as identification cards, motor vehicle registration, protection of the environment and the management of police and fire fighters. Such a responsible position demands a man with a clear head and a good night's sleep behind him. So it was with no little surprise and a great deal of annoyance when Jacques Retour, incumbent Préfet de Police, answered the personal telephone that rang by his bedside at 02:15 on that morning of Tuesday 12 October. At first he thought it might be his youngest daughter Marie-Claire, wanting a lift back from yet another party. In many ways Jacques Retour wished he'd been blessed with sons.

"Allo?"

A man's voice, unknown to the Préfet, spoke.

"Am I speaking to Monsieur Jacques Retour?"

"Who is this?" The Préfet flicked on the bedside light. At this time of the morning, it could only be an emergency. His wife stirred in the bed beside him.

"Never mind who I am," said the voice. "The important thing is who I represent. You have a very important email, Monsieur le Préfet, probably the most important communication you will ever receive. It has been sent to your personal email account which you can access from the computer downstairs in your study. I suggest you go down and read it now. Then you should make a phone call, either to Europol or to the head of police in Barcelona, to confirm we have the capability to do what we say."

"Who is this?" Retour said again, but the line was dead. How on earth did the man get the number? It was known only to the officer of the watch at the Préfecture on Place Louis Lépane, who was under the strictest orders to pass it on to nobody.

"What is it, Jacques?" his wife murmured.

"It's business. Go back to sleep."

Retour got out of bed, pulled on his silk dressing gown and flicked off the bedside light. Then he felt his way to the door, onto the landing and down to the book-lined study and the big oak desk where he worked while at home. He opened his laptop, put on his gold-framed reading glasses, logged onto his email account—again supposedly private and confidential—and peered at the computer screen. At the top of the list of received items on his Inbox, above the inevitable spam mail that had come in during the night, sat a mail marked 'urgent' and 'action required'. It had originated, apparently, from the Department of Justice and was entitled 'Justice for Africa'.

"Monsieur Le Préfet. You will be aware, as all of Europe is aware, that a colossal debt is owed by the countries of the European Union to their ravaged and abandoned colonies on the continent of Africa. For centuries, the countries of Europe have pillaged and looted the natural resources of that great continent for their own selfish ends. Now, in the twenty-first century, the European Union has turned its back on Africa, leaving millions to die of starvation, disease and the effects of drought due to climate change.

There is no excuse for ignorance. Satellite television beams the images of starving African people and their dying children into your homes every day, just as images of consumerism, pollution and squandered resources are beamed from Europe to Africa. The great charitable organisations do what they can, but it is not enough. The governments of the EU do too little, too late. The time has come for radical change. Broken promises must be repaired by drastic action.

It has been calculated that the resources pillaged by the great powers of Europe from Africa over the last hundred years alone are worth over €100 billion. That debt must be repaid if the lives of millions are to be saved. Talk has proven useless. Appeals have been ineffective. Force is the only language Europe has ever understood.

Therefore, if that debt of €100 billion is not repaid by midnight tonight, using the means our organisation will describe, property to the equivalent value of that debt will be destroyed at and around the Musée du Louvre by an atomic explosion of eighty kilotons.

Monsieur Le Préfet, you are hereby ordered to immediately evacuate the city of Paris to a safe distance of no less than 100 kilometres radius from the Louvre to avoid needless injury and loss of life, should we be forced to explode the device. Do not approach the Louvre or attempt to remove any of the artworks therein. The security system there is now under our control and a catastrophic loss of life will occur if you force our hands ahead of the deadline.

You will be contacted again today by email at 06:00 hours with instructions as to how the payment must be made.

Once again, we urge you to contact either Europol or the Head of Police in Barcelona to confirm that we can carry out this threat.

Justice for Africa"

Retour read the message again. It had to be a hoax. Some young hacker perhaps, who had wormed his way past the firewalls into the Department of Justice computer system, pulled his personal phone number and email address off the database and gone to work. What they were asking was impossible. Leaving the Louvre unprotected would be unthinkable. Yes, there was an evacuation plan prepared for Paris in the event of an emergency and had been for some time. Retour himself had overseen the updating of it in the wake of the

9/11, Madrid and London subway attacks, but to put it into effect in less than twenty-four hours might lead to total panic. And anyway, how could he be sure this was not a hoax?

He opened his contacts database and scrolled down to the list of contacts under 'L'. As Préfet de Police, his responsibilities included security and protection of all public buildings. He could settle this matter here and now and perhaps recover a few hours' sleep.

The found the number and dialled.

"Hello, is that the security office of the Louvre?"

The voice on the other end of the line sounded distracted.

"Yes, who is this please?"

"This is Jacques Retour, Préfet de Police. What is your situation there?"

"Ah . . . Monsieur Le Préfet, we were about to ring your office. What's going on? Is this some kind of exercise? We had no notice. "

Retour felt an icy hand grip his heart.

"What's happening down there?"

"You don't know?"

"Just tell me."

"The computerised security system, Monsieur Le Préfet. It's gone mad. We're locked out of all the cameras and alarms. None of our authentic usernames or passwords work. The automatic doors have closed and the escalators are shut down. It's as if someone else is controlling it all from outside."

Retour closed his eyes and tried to think.

"Listen to me," he said. "I want you to get all your people out of the building and over to the fire assembly points outside. Tell them nothing except that this is an emergency drill and ensure that no one speaks to the press. Act normally, but act quickly. I'll make sure the police throw a cordon around the Museum immediately to maintain security. Contact your Director and have him meet me at my office at Place Louis Lépane at once. You can call me through the switchboard if there are any developments. Is that clear?"

"Yes, Monsieur Le Préfet."

"Thank you. Please go ahead."

So the threat was real. Someone had actually taken over control of the Louvre security system. Was the threat of the bomb also real? He thought of the beautiful buildings and museums around the centre of Paris he saw every day on his way to work and the priceless art treasures they contained. They could never be replaced. The evacuation plan, although carefully calculated, had never been tried in earnest. He thought of the enormous effort it would take to move the entire population of Paris to safety by the deadline. All at once, the simple life he'd enjoyed so long ago as a young and ambitious lawyer in Toulon seemed a lifetime away.

He lifted the phone again and dialled his own office. The duty officer answered.

"Marcel, this is the Préfet. Call the heads of the Police, the Gendarmerie and anyone connected with the Special Evacuation Plan to my office for a meeting in one hour. Then I want you to get whoever is in the office right now to run a web search for an organisation called Justice for Africa. . . Yes, that's right. And send a car and escort around to my house immediately."

"Is this an exercise, Monsieur Le Préfet?"

"I hope so, but treat it as if it were the real thing. We'll know for sure within an hour."

He ran back upstairs, woke his wife and told her to contact all three of their children, wherever they were, and take them to her parents' house at Saint Malo immediately. She protested, until she saw the look in his eyes. Then she picked up her mobile phone and started to dial.

Retour dressed, ran back down to check his computer again and forwarded the Justice for Africa message to his official email address at his office. Then he picked up the phone and dialled the Elysée Palace.

The President of France came on the line just as the blue flashing lights of Retour's police car and motor cycle escort pulled up in the driveway outside.

8

In the main incident room of the Préfeture de Police on Place Louis Lépane, in the shadow of the great cathedral of Notre Dame, Jacques Retour laid a telephone back in its cradle and looked up at the assembled senior representatives of the police, military and civil authorities he'd summoned from their beds. They looked back at him with dazed and bleary eyes from around the great conference table over steaming cups of black coffee and burning cigarettes. To Retour, the whole scene felt surreal, like the set of one of those dreadful American action movies, but perhaps that was just the pressure of circumstance he found himself in, and the time of night.

"I've just received confirmation from Europol that an atomic device, a Russian nuclear artillery shell matching the kiloton yield given in the email from this so-called Justice for Africa, may indeed have been successfully smuggled into Europe" he said. "We are therefore facing a very real crisis, perhaps the greatest Paris has ever faced: the destruction of the city itself."

"You can rely on the offices of the Mayor, Monsieur Le Préfet," announced a tall official with silver hair who, even at this hour, was immaculately dressed.

"And on the security services of the Police . . . . "

"And the Gendarmerie," said the two representatives of those organisations, cutting across each other.

"We already have a major incident plan drawn up for the evacuation of the city in such circumstances," Retour said. "I've ordered the organisations involved to stand by and, now I have definite confirmation that the threat is real, we'll put it into immediate effect. There are clearly defined roles for each of your Departments regarding the phased evacuation of the city. This will proceed section by section, starting with the inner areas closest to the Louvre and working outwards to the evacuation centres in the safe zone, a hundred kilometres out. Private cars are to be kept off the streets and public transport and metro facilities will run at maximum capacity. Army transport units will assemble on the outskirts and move into the centre along the designated routes as soon as we give the word. Traffic control is a matter for the Police. They know the city and its bottlenecks far better than anyone and will do the most efficient job in the time available. They will direct the Army staff. Is that clear? Colonel Renard, do you have anything to add?"

The Army expert in nuclear ordinance at the far end of the table spoke.

"Going on the Europol report on the illegal weapon seized in Barcelona, we're dealing with a Russian nuclear artillery shell with an explosive yield of around eighty kilotons of TNT. Anything within two kilometres of the point of detonation will be completely destroyed and the blast wave will demolish buildings up to six kilometres in all directions. Beyond that, there'll be moderate damage to buildings up to seventeen kilometres out, along with first degree burns. In all, I'd agree with the estimate given by these terrorists that we need to evacuate out to at least a hundred kilometres to ensure any degree of safety for the population of Paris."

"And the damage at the point of detonation?" the Director of the Louvre asked.

"It will be absolute, Monsieur," replied Renard. "The temperature at the fireball of a nuclear explosion is over a million degrees. Everything within a hundred metres will be vaporised and everything within two kilometres totally destroyed."

"But the greatest art treasures in the world are in the Louvre and in a dozen other museums that surround it. The Musée d'Orsay, the Musée Rodin, and the Musée d'Art Moderne at the Palais de Tokyo all contain collections that are priceless and irreplaceable. The loss to humanity would be too great to bear. Is there no way we can evacuate them to a safe place?"

"We may be able to remove some of the artworks from the other museums, as long as we can do it unobserved, but we cannot even entertain the possibility of salvaging anything from the Louvre while the terrorists have control of the security system," said Retour. "I appreciate your concern, Monsieur le Directeur, and I agree that the loss of the Louvre and the other museums would be a tragedy, but my responsibility is to the people of the city. It's too great a risk."

"And if the bomb doesn't go off?" The question came from Commissaire Claude Pichet, the senior officer of RAID, a thickset police officer with close-cropped hair and the battered face of a Hollywood gangster. Retour knew him as a very tough and focussed officer, a man who'd led a successful intervention against a mad bomber who'd taken twenty-one children and their minders hostage in a siege at a school in Neuilly some years before. The bomber had been shot dead at the scene, but all the children had survived. Retour took some comfort in Pichet's proven ability to resolve major acts of mayhem with such surgical precision.

"I've been in contact with the President directly," he replied. "He in turn has convened an emergency meeting of the European Security Council. They're discussing options to meet the demands made by this Justice for Africa group and the payment of their ransom with both the Banque de France and the Central European Bank, should the situation get that far."

"Indeed," Pichet said. "But there are more proactive steps to investigate. We could for example, find the device and disarm it ourselves, or we could track down the organisation that planted it and force them to disarm it for us."

"We could indeed, but we have only twenty-one hours to do it."

Pichet continued. "With respect, Monsieur Le Préfet, twenty-one hours is plenty of time if we know exactly where to look for the bomb, and we already know it's either inside, or in the immediate vicinity of, the Louvre. As to this Justice for Africa group, you told us earlier that nobody can identify it as an existing organisation, either on the web or through the services of our intelligence agencies?"

"No. We can't. It appears to be a new outfit on its first mission. None of the other African NGOs or lobby groups have heard of it. My enquiries to intelligence organisations in America and the United Kingdom have also drawn a blank. The source of their email cannot be traced. It could have come from anywhere in the world, as could the phone call I received at my home earlier this morning."

"And yet an operation as complex as this calls for a significant degree of organisation," suggested Pichet. "The ability to acquire, place and detonate a nuclear weapon, the technology to hack into and gain control of the security system at the Louvre, all speaks of considerable organisation and technical ability, does it not?"

"It does. What's your point?" asked Retour.

"You told us earlier that a similar device had been smuggled into Europe and that the Spanish police recovered it on the advice of a new specialist group within Europol. I understand the officer in charge of this group is a former member of my own RAID unit. Can I suggest I call her and formally request that her Europol group be called in to advise us on our situation?"

"You can indeed, Commandant Pichet. Please make that call."

9

The thing Flynn missed most after the breakup of his marriage to Siobhan was simply being touched. What he yearned for, even more than sex, was the feel of her fingers on his skin, her lips on his and the comforting luxury of lying next to her in bed. The incident in Barcelona, and the violent deaths of the two Russians on the ship, had brought back old nightmares. He remembered the stink of cordite in the ship's hold and, above all, the feeling of a dead man's blood on his face. He didn't want to die without making one last attempt at peace with Siobhan and their daughter Aoife. So, as soon as the inevitable paperwork and analyses on Barcelona had been completed in The Hague, he'd flown to Dublin for the weekend to try and patch things up one last time.

But it hadn't worked out. Things had gone well enough for most of Saturday morning, while they were still trying hard to be civil to one another. They'd taken Aoife to the shopping centre in Dundrum on the LUAS tram system and had chocolate cake in the Dome Restaurant overlooking Stephen's Green. But by Saturday afternoon, the effort of trying to play 'happy families' had been too much and their masks had started to slip. A stupid argument flared up, superficially over who'd do the washing-up, but in reality about far bigger issues than either of them could deal with. They spent Saturday night in separate rooms and by Sunday lunchtime, Aoife had gone out with her friends and Siobhan was asking him the time of his return flight to Brussels. He walked out on Sunday afternoon, spent the night at the airport hotel and got the Aer Lingus 06:50 'red eye' to Brussels the next morning.

So, when an attractive woman with blonde hair had brushed against him accidentally during the coffee break at a meeting on security in the Le Bourchet Centre in Brussels for the forthcoming international energy summit, he'd struck up a conversation with her. This had led to a shared lunch in the big communal dining area on the top floor of the conference centre, followed by dinner in one of the better seafood restaurants off the Grand Place, a few too many glasses of wine and a nightcap at his rented flat facing the cathedral near the Place Sainte-Catherine. Her name was Juliette, she was part of the EU Commission Directorate on Foreign Policy and, like Flynn, she was currently unattached.

"You still haven't told me what your do for a living," she said as they lay side by side in Flynn's bed with the lights of the city filtering in through the open curtains.

"I'm a consultant to Europol on security issues. That's why I was at the meeting today."

The distant wail of police sirens and the hiss of rain sounded on the closed windows.

"It all sounds very mysterious," Juliette said, running her long fingernails through the hairs on his naked chest, "a lot more exciting than my job in foreign policy."

"Foreign policy can be exciting—studying new cultures, learning new ideas, meeting new people—"

"People like you?" Juliette said.

"People like me. You said it yourself. It's exciting."

"Do I excite you," she said playfully, running her hand down his chest and onto his stomach.

She'd captivated Flynn from the moment she'd brushed past him. It had been almost electric, to have someone new touch him like that, even in passing. No wonder he missed it.

He leant over and kissed her, gently at first and then deeper, as her tongue played with his.

A low buzz sounded from his pile of clothes on the floor.

"I must excite you a lot," Juliette said, running the inside of her thigh along the top of his leg. "That mobile phone of yours has been buzzing for the last hour and you haven't answered it."

"I don't know how to turn it off. Just ignore it. It's usually some trivial thing at the office or a wrong number."

She rolled over onto him. Her hair fell like a curtain around their faces as she kissed him. Flynn closed his eyes and lost himself in the warmth of her, just as the sound of police sirens rose several decibels and the flash of blue lights lit the ceiling.

The doorbell rang. Flynn heard a brief exchange of angry voices, the crash of doors, and the sound of pounding feet on the wooden stairs outside the flat.

"Holy Shite!"

Someone hammered on the door. Juliette rolled off the bed, taking the covers with her. The hammering started again.

"All right, all right for fuck's sake! I'm coming!"

Flynn threw a shirt over his back, grabbed his trousers and stuffed his legs into them. Then he hurried to the door, pulled back the security chain and opened it.

Gabrielle Arnault stood there in full uniform, glaring at him.

"You should have answered your mobile !" she snapped. "Then I wouldn't have had to waste precious time trying to find you."

"Jesus! Can you keep it down a bit? I have neighbours, you know!"

Flynn was about to bar her way, when he saw the two large Belgian policemen behind her.

She marched past him.

"Then you should answer your mobile. Please get dressed, Doctor Flynn, we have a flight to . . . Oh! Good evening, mademoiselle. My name is Gabrielle Arnault. I work with Doctor Flynn. Please excuse us."

Juliette rose from the other side of the bed, holding the sheet to her chest.

"Sorry, Juliette," Flynn muttered. "Like you said earlier, it's an interesting job."

Gabrielle slammed the door of the police car with more force than necessary and ordered the driver to take them to the airport as quickly as possible. She was tired and upset, having been woken from a troubled sleep in her room at the Brussels Europa Hotel less than an hour beforehand. The fact that Flynn had not answered his mobile, in complete disregard for his duty to COMMETT, made her angry. Bursting in on him, while he'd been in bed with a woman, had left her embarrassed. There had been nobody in her life since Felipe, nothing that she cared about except making COMMETT a reality, and the whole incident had touched a sensitive nerve with her. She pulled out her lighter and a packet of cigarettes, and lit up.

"Are you drunk?" she snapped at him as the police car pulled out of the Place Catherine behind its motorcycle escort.

"I had a few glasses of wine, for fuck's sake! I'll get some coffee on the plane. What the hell's this all about anyway? What can be so important that it gives you the licence to haul me out of bed in the middle of the night?"

He started to roll down the car window and flap at her cigarette smoke with his hand.

"They found the second nuclear weapon," Gabrielle said. "It's in Paris and there's a blackmail threat, just like you predicted, by an organisation calling itself Justice for Africa. If the European Union doesn't come up with a hundred billion euro by midnight tonight, they explode the bomb."

"Jesus!" breathed Flynn, and stopped rolling down the window.

"So you need to be sober when we reach Paris. It's going to be a long day!"

The car reached the ring road and accelerated past the imposing façade of the Gare Centrale with its motorcycle outriders clearing the way.

"You're really pissed off at me, aren't you?" Flynn said.

"Yes."

"Why? What I do in my spare time and who I do it with is my business. You had no right to come barging into my flat like that.

What is with you? Are you jealous?"

The question caught Gabrielle by surprise. She didn't think of herself as a prude. She and Felipe had enjoyed each others' bodies. But she hadn't been with anyone since he died. Somehow it didn't seem right. All there was for her was COMMETT and the burning desire to make Felipe's dream a reality. Was it guilt? Or a substitute for something she couldn't even define?

"Don't be ridiculous," she snapped back at Flynn.

"So who requested our assistance?" he asked after a few moments.

"RAID and the Préfet de Police in Paris. They made the connection between our bomb in Barcelona and their bomb in Paris. I served with RAID before I was seconded to Europol. My old commanding officer asked for my help. They employ civilian consultants just as COMMETT does. They understand the value of expert advice in specialised situations. Your services were also requested."

"What kind of advice can we give that they haven't already got?"

"The bomb's been planted somewhere in the Musée du Louvre. Whoever put it there's hacked into the Louvre's computers and hijacked the museum's entire security system for themselves. This means they can use the cameras and alarms to make sure that the bomb isn't touched and the artworks remain in place to be destroyed if their ransom isn't paid. To break into a system as advanced as that from the outside requires very specialist knowledge. COMMETT has another external consultant like you, who has previous experience of doing this. With luck, they should be able to tell us how to override the Louvre security systems so we can reach the bomb and disarm it undetected."

"You mean someone's hacked into it before?"

"The case was never proven against her," Gabrielle said. "In any event, she's a reformed character and working for us now. Like you, she's a legitimate and highly respected security consultant, one who specialises on the threat of cyberterrorism. The French authorities specifically asked for her by name."

"And what about the bomb? Who will you get to advise you on that?"

"RAID has experts on defusing nuclear weapons. I was trained myself when I was in service with them. But the atomic shell we're dealing with is an obsolete type which may employ fail-safes and booby traps we have little knowledge of. Therefore I've called in a former Soviet expert. She'll be joining us in Paris."

"Another woman! Am I going to be the only man on this gig?"

Gabrielle held her anger in check. "No, there's one other man. He's already been brought in to advise on this case by the management of the Louvre and the Préfet de Police and is waiting for us in Paris. It was this man who asked for you, by the way. He's a former art dealer who knows you from your previous experience of selling stolen paintings to finance your activities in the IRA."

"You're never going to forgive me for being a terrorist, are you?"

"My feelings don't matter, Doctor Flynn. All you have to do is your job."

Flynn grunted. "And who is this art dealer anyway?"

"I haven't been told. But I understand his experience is vital to RAID's strategy for getting into the Louvre."

"Look," Flynn said as they approached the airport terminal building. "I'm sorry about what just happened and . . ."

"I care about my work, Doctor Flynn," she said stiffly. "The success of COMMETT means a great deal more to me than you realise. So please act professionally throughout this operation and, in future, answer your mobile when it rings."

The car pulled past the main departure area, turned through a guarded gate onto the main apron and came to a stop.

"Look," shouted Flynn against the roar of jet engines as they climbed out into the rain. "If you find it so fucking difficult to work with me, why include me in the team?"

"Because my Deputy Director has faith in your abilities and because the art dealer in Paris asked for you personally."

Flynn thought about this for a moment.

"I'm sorry I slowed us up," he said. "Is there anything I could be doing on the flight to save us time when we get to Paris?"

Wind and rain swept the apron as they reached the steps of a white Aerospatiale executive jet bearing the EU logo. Gabrielle ducked through the door and strapped herself into one of the dark blue seats at the rear of the cabin. They were the only passengers on board. She pulled a folder from her briefcase and gave it to Flynn. Inside was a large-scale map of the centre of Paris and a set of architectural blueprints. "There," she said. "Memorise these if you can. You'll need to be completely familiar with this information if we get the green light to go in."

She had no sense of homecoming as the Europol jet circled Le Bourget airport to the north-west of Paris, settled on its glide path and touched down in a cloud of spray. A grey dawn was breaking as a police car whisked them across the tarmac to the other side of the field where an Alouette jet helicopter was already warming up.

"Are we flying out of Paris again?" she asked the pilot as she strapped herself in.

"No, Capitaine. You're flying in. You'll see why we have to use the helicopter in a moment."

With a roar of turbines and the heavy chop of its rotor blades, the machine lifted off from the tarmac, turned and headed south-east into the rising sun and the centre of the city.

"Jesus!" said Flynn. "Talk about rush hour!"

Looking down to her left and right, Gabrielle saw that every road out of the city was choked in both lanes by a steady stream of civilian buses, coaches and army transport vehicles crawling towards the suburbs. Military helicopters circled the horizon like flies. She saw roadblocks on the feeder routes flash below them, whole fields of abandoned cars and dense crowds of people around bus depots and Metro stations.

"It's actually happening," she said, as the sheer scale of the threat hit her. "They're clearing the city."

In less than five minutes the towers of Notre Dame loomed between the buildings and the Alouette settled unsteadily into a clear space surrounded by police cars, vans and motorcycles. They were in the vast courtyard of the Préfecture de Police on the Ile de la Cité in the middle of the Seine, only a few hundred metres away from the Louvre on the north bank of the river.

A uniformed policeman dodged in under the rotor blades, opened the helicopter door and led them up a wide wooden staircase to the main operations room. Gabrielle noted the tension in the air—as thick as the cigarette smoke—the litter of papers and phones on the main conference table and the digitised map of the city filling the vast plasma screen along one wall of the room.

A small, dapper man in a dark blue business suit, with thinning black hair and a neatly trimmed moustache, put out his hand.

"Capitaine Arnault, Monsieur Flynn? I'm Jacques Retour, Préfet de Police. I'm very glad you could come."

"Have there been any further developments since we were last briefed?" Gabrielle asked.

"The evacuation of the city is going according to plan. We've placed a no-fly zone for all aircraft over the city, except for police and military helicopters of course. The media don't like it, but I'd rather have bad press than one of their helicopters colliding with ours above our heads."

"And on the ground?"

"There's a complete army roadblock around Paris at a hundred kilometres out, on both the auto routes and all the smaller roads. Civilians are being evacuated street by street and hospitals cleared, right out to the roadblock. Only personnel essential to the evacuation remain in Paris, and even they will be moved out as we near the deadline at midnight tonight."

"What have the public been told?" Flynn asked.

"That we're facing a terrorist threat," Retour replied. "They're being told that a number of conventional high explosive bombs are hidden in unidentified locations around the city. We've held the nuclear story back to avoid panic and loss of life. There's a tight lid on all media coverage, with strictly controlled briefings to the main print and broadcast outlets on the hour. We're appealing for calm and co-operation. It would not be safe to tell the public the truth."

"Have you heard from the terrorists?" Gabrielle asked.

"We've received an email detailing how the ransom is to be paid," said Retour. "It's to be transferred electronically from the European Central Bank to a number of accounts in Switzerland, the Cayman Islands and elsewhere. I imagine the money will be transferred again immediately from those accounts to others we know nothing about and the original accounts closed after the transactions have taken place."

"But do you really think the European Union will pay?" asked Flynn.

Retour shook his head.

"A hundred billion is a lot of money," he said, "even for the Central Bank of Europe."

"I know," Flynn said. "And less than twenty-four hours is an extremely unrealistic deadline in which to expect a multinational bureaucracy like the European Union to respond. Are you sure this threat is really what it seems?"

A heavyset man in dark combat fatigues looked up from a map table and came over to them. He saluted Gabrielle stiffly. Then his leathery face split in a wide smile.

"Ça va, Gabrielle? It's a pity we have to meet again under these difficult circumstances. How's life with you since you took that soft job in Brussels?"

"Ça va bien, patron. Allow me to introduce my colleague from the Committee on European Techno-Terrorism, Doctor Damien Flynn. Doctor Flynn, this is my former commanding officer, Commissaire Pichet of RAID."

"Ah," Pichet said, "the tame terrorist who tracked down the bomb in Barcelona. I look forward to your analysis of the situation as someone from the other side of the law, so to speak."

Flynn stepped forward, but Pichet declined to shake his hand.

Gabrielle saw Flynn stiffen.

"Are you really sure you'd like to hear it?" he asked.

"Of course. Good anti-terrorist action can only benefit from good intelligence, no matter where it comes from. Please give me your thoughts."

"There are a number of points that confuse me," Flynn said. "Firstly, the people who are putting this city at ransom claim to be promoting a humanitarian cause, and yet they're threatening to destroy billions of euro's worth of property and the most valuable collection of art in the world. Doesn't that seem like a contradiction in terms to you?"

"Their email to me earlier this morning said they'd tried every other avenue to get Europe's attention and had failed," explained Retour.

"But if they've tried all other avenues before, how is it nobody's ever heard of them?"

"I don't know. They said they were desperate to right what they see as an enormous injustice by the only means left to them."

"And yet," Flynn continued, "for a desperate organisation, representing a starving continent, they're extremely well resourced. They have the money and the means to purchase nuclear devices on the black market and set up secret bank accounts in faraway places. That doesn't sound like a desperate humanitarian organisation to me, Monsieur Le Préfet. That sounds like a very well organised criminal gang. If I was you I'd—"

"Enough of this theorising," said Pichet, beckoning them to the digitised map of the city and stabbing its screen with his stout fingers. "We have a very practical task to take care of here, to defuse a nuclear weapon against a very tight deadline. Here is the Musée du Louvre, where we believe the bomb is placed. And here is the Musée d'Orsay, the Musée Rodin, the Musée d'Art Moderne and a dozen other museums and art galleries, all well within the bomb's radius of total destruction. The Director of the Louvre is anxious that as much of this artwork is moved to safety as possible. That doesn't present a problem with the other museums but, since the security system of the Louvre itself is now under the control of the terrorists, removing art treasures from there presents a risk that may be too great to take."

"Commissaire Pichet and I have debated this at length," said Jacques Retour. "And, in light of certain expertise being available that could give us the opportunity to examine and disarm the bomb, I've agreed to a plan which would benefit greatly from your assistance."

"Does this have anything to do with your request for a certain computer expert on the COMMETT payroll?" Gabrielle asked.

"It does, but first I'd like you to meet someone we've brought here specially to advise us on practical details. He's waiting in the next room."

There were, in fact, two men waiting for Gabrielle and Flynn in the smaller meeting room just off the operations centre. One was a well-dressed figure with thinning grey hair, wearing a business suit and a worried expression. The other man, sitting at the far end of a conference table, was wearing a sweater, a light blue shirt and a pair of faded jeans under a dark blue overcoat. He had a mane of long white hair, brushed back behind his ears and a thin, sad face which still retained a twinkle of amusement around the eyes. He didn't get up when Gabrielle entered. Retour carefully closed the door behind him once Gabrielle, Flynn and Pichet were inside.

"Capitaine Arnault, Doctor Flynn," he said. "Please let me introduce Monsieur Jean-Claude Trichet, the Director of the Musée du Louvre." The well-dressed man stepped forward and shook hands with Gabrielle.

"It's a pleasure to meet you," he said. "I hope you can do France a great service today. Commissionaire Pichet recommends you highly. I'll put every facility of the Museum at your disposal."

"To do what, exactly?" asked Flynn.

"Our primary mission is to locate and disarm the bomb in the Musée du Louvre," Pichet explained. "To do that, we need to enter the Museum undetected. And to accomplish that, we need not only to enter the Museum without being seen from the outside, but also without tripping the alarm system inside the building, which is fully controlled by the terrorists. Is that clear?"

He paused for a moment. There were no questions.

"Since we plan to send a team in to defuse the bomb anyway," Pichet continued, "I don't see why we can't remove a few of the most valuable masterworks from the Louvre, as we're doing with the other museums in Paris, in case things don't go as planned. To get into the Louvre undetected, under the very eyes of the Museum's own security system, we need not only your expert services but also the assistance of this gentleman here."

"Hello, Jean-Jacques," said Flynn, smiling at the seated man. "Fancy seeing you here."

"You know him?" asked Gabrielle.

The man got painfully to his feet, held a thin white stick out in front of him and hobbled forward to meet them.

"It's a pleasure to meet you, Madame," he said, holding out a bony hand for her to shake. "My name is Jean-Jacques Sabaut, and I'm the second man ever to steal the *Mona Lisa*."

10

Gabrielle knew she had a problem as soon as Sabaut was introduced. But before she could talk to him about it, he'd reached past her and was extending his hand again, this time in the direction of Flynn's voice.

"And Damien, mon cher ami. It's good to hear you again after all this time. You're no longer selling stolen paintings to raise money for the cause, eh?"

"No, Jean-Jacques. I'm on the side of the angels now."

"But how do you both know each other?" repeated Gabrielle.

"It was a long time ago," said Sabaut, "during my days as an art dealer in Paris. Damien used to come to me with items he and his comrades-in-arms had acquired to raise money for their cause. That's why I've followed his career all these years and that's why, when they told me that Europol was involved, I asked if Damien could be my eyes on this little adventure. I need someone I can trust, someone who knows Paris and the world of art."

"To be your eyes?" asked Gabrielle.

"Yes, my dear, quite literally. After I'd successfully removed the *Mona Lisa* from the Louvre some years ago, I was immediately involved in a tragic accident that left me blinded and unable to walk. It was ironic in many ways. Imagine a man whose whole life is dedicated to the visual arts suddenly being robbed of the gift of sight. That's why they released me from prison after a very short time. They felt I'd suffered enough and, after all, what harm can a blind art thief do?"

"I'm sorry," Gabrielle said, and helped him to a chair.

"Don't be sorry, Madame. I still have all my other senses, and a very good brain besides. Today I have the chance to use my knowledge to assist in saving the greatest art treasures in the world from destruction. What greater purpose can a connoisseur of the arts have than that? And Damien will help me achieve it."

"Are you sure now, Jean-Jacques?" asked Flynn. "With all due respect, the security systems we're dealing with today are way more advanced than they were in your time."

Sabaut shrugged. "Ah! Young people today think they're the only ones who can understand modern technology. But I'm an avid student of all things technological, particularly where they relate to my passions, and I still keep up to date. So I don't think there'll be a problem, apart from my obvious handicaps. And I plan to use Damian's eyes and the application of technology to overcome them."

Gabrielle felt awkward in Sabaut's presence. She couldn't relate his obvious good humour and the wry smile he carried with the suffering he'd endured. How could a lover of art and visual beauty, albeit one who dealt in black market paintings, ever accept the loss of his sight?

"I thought there was only ever one successful theft of the *Mona Lisa*, Monsieur Sabaut," she said. "Back in 1911."

"Ah, that was a very amateurish affair," Sabaut said, dismissing it with a wave of his hand. "Vincenzo Peruggia, a worker at the Louvre, simply took the painting down off the wall in the Salle Carré and walked out of the museum with it under his coat. It's not a large painting you see, and so it's easily concealed. The museum staff thought it had simply been moved somewhere else to be photographed and nobody realised it was stolen until twenty-four hours after it was gone. My theft of *La Giaconda* was an infinitely more professional enterprise and I'm here to tell you and your colleagues how I got in and out of the Louvre without being challenged. That's what you really want to know, isn't it?"

"Indeed it is, Monsieur. How did you do it?"

"Have you ever read *Les Miserables* by Victor Hugo?" Sabaut asked, smiling mischievously. "I got into the Louvre by the same means that Hugo's hero Jean Valjean escaped the soldiers of the revolution. What is that line again? Ah yes. 'Paris has another Paris under herself; a Paris of sewers; which has its streets, its crossings, its squares, its blind alleys, its arteries, and its circulation, which is slime . . .' The ground beneath our feet here, and all over this city, is honeycombed with enough tunnels to reach from Paris to Istanbul, nearly two thousand kilometres of them. Some of those tunnels pass directly under the Louvre. There were indeed problems when the Museum was extended underground into that fine atrium with the impressive glass pyramid you see today, when those tunnels were accidentally breached. I simply found out where the repairs had been made and created my own extension into a storeroom on the lowest level."

"I can see how you got in and out," Flynn said. "But when you were inside, how did you get past the cameras?"

Sabaut smiled again and tapped the side of his nose with his finger. "Ah Damien, this is where this technology of yours comes in. I had an accomplice, a very dear friend of my late wife's, who was an expert in computer systems. Everything these days is controlled by computers, isn't it, Madame? I don't need to tell you that. Together we devised a way of hacking into the main security computer from the outside and fooling the camera systems into believing they were looking at empty space as I passed by. With that protection, I was able to walk into the restoration area on the night before the *Mona Lisa* was to be installed in the sealed display case where it now resides and replace it with a perfect replica. Had I not been knocked down by a police motorcycle as I left the scene of the crime, that replica might still be hanging there today undetected."

"And your accomplice" asked Gabrielle carefully, "this friend of your wife's? How would you feel about working with her again?"

"She left me for dead as I lay injured in the middle of the road that night and I haven't spoken to her since," said Sabaut. "Perhaps she was ashamed. Perhaps she was scared. But she never contacted me, or visited me in hospital or in prison. I kept her name from the police and I've erased it from my memory. I don't know where she is today."

"You know we can't get inside the Louvre without her?" said Gabrielle gently. "She's as much a key to this mission as you are."

"I doubt it," snapped Sabaut. "I'm sure a resourceful young woman like you, in a position of power in Europol must have many other experts you can call on, including the people who designed the alarm system in the first place."

"I'm afraid not, Monsieur Sabaut," Gabrielle said. "Doctor Flynn, the other consultants I asked for must have arrived by now. Would you mind asking them to join us?"

Flynn leant close to her and whispered, "If one of those other consultants is who I think she is, then there's going to be fireworks."

"I had no idea the French authorities were going to bring Sabaut in on this case," hissed Gabrielle. "If it's a problem we'll just have to deal with it."

"Then let battle commence," replied Flynn and opened the door to the main situation room.

The two women he led back into the meeting were complete opposites. The first was a blonde in her early fifties, tall and painfully thin, with bright intelligent eyes and the slim, strong hands of a concert pianist. The second woman was in her mid forties, short and heavy, with close-cropped gingery hair, thick fingers and a wide smile that lit up the room.

"Gabrielle!" she cried. "So good of you to invite me to your party. *Ça va?*"

"*Ça va bien*, Constance. How have you been keeping? Well out of trouble I hope."

Constance LeClerc, computer expert, hacker extraordinaire and consultant on cyberterrorism to COMMETT, strode into the room and embraced Gabrielle with a bear hug.

Sabaut sat wide-eyed and transfixed, staring sightlessly in the direction of Constance's voice. His mouth hung open for a moment, then he hauled himself to his feet and waved his stick in her direction.

"Constance?" he shouted across the room. "How could you have abandoned me that night?"

Constance put her hands to her mouth and stared at him.

"Jean-Jacques? Is it really you?" She took a step forward and touched his arm. Sabaut recoiled as if she'd been a venomous snake and would have fallen if Gabrielle had not grabbed him and eased his shaking body back into his chair. Constance put out her hand to support herself against the meeting room table. Her eyes darted from Pichet to Retour and finally rested on Gabrielle. For a moment they rested there, full of pain and accusation. Then she turned to Sabaut.

"There were police everywhere that night, Jean-Jacques. I was terrified of them finding the equipment in the van. They would have arrested me and thrown me in jail. There was nothing I could do for you and I panicked. I drove away. I was so sure you'd tell them I'd helped you that I left the country. Did you tell them?"

Sabaut still shook. His face hardened. "No, Constance. I didn't. You were Nicole's friend, and mine. However angry I was with you, I was the one who persuaded you to assist me. I couldn't betray you. Nicole would never have forgiven me."

"Do you mean to say this woman is the one who assisted Sabaut in the first robbery?" said Retour. "She should have been arrested and charged, just as he was."

"With respect, Monsieur Le Préfet," said Gabrielle. "All that is in the past and far less important than having Madame Le Clerc help us now. If she still agrees to assist us, as she's already promised Europol, then I'd like to request that we drop the matter of her previous involvement altogether."

For a moment, Retour looked as if he was going to protest. Then he nodded his agreement.

"Monsieur Sabaut. For this mission to succeed, it is absolutely vital that you and Madame Le Clerc work together," said Gabrielle. "Can you do that?"

Sabaut turned his head towards her and then towards Constance. He ran his open palms down over his eyes and then brought them together in front of his face, as if in prayer.

"Constance," he said softly. "I will work with you for one reason, and for one reason only – for Nicole's memory. It would have broken her heart to see even so much as one painting in the Louvre destroyed. Can you do the same?" and he put out his hands. Constance took them and looked down at him.

"Pour Nicole," she said softly. "Merci Jean-Jacques. Merci bien."

Then she turned to Gabrielle.

"Is the person who designed the Louvre security system and the upgrades that were made after our robbery here in the building?" she asked.

"Yes," said Jean-Claude Trichet. "His name is André Bloc and I've asked him to join us. He's waiting outside."

"Then, if somebody could show me where I can connect my laptop, I'll let you know if I can still penetrate the Louvre security system without detection."

Gabrielle turned to the blonde woman who'd entered the room with Constance. Her name was Lyudmila Petrachkova and, before the collapse of the Soviet Union, she'd been a senior technician with MinAtom, the Ministry for Atomic Power in the USSR.

"Did you have a chance to familiarise yourself with the photographs we recovered in Barcelona?"

"I did," Lyudmila said. "The Barcelona device was a basic artillery shell, but there will be additional refinements on the version we encounter here today to protect it from tampering and to allow it to be detonated remotely at any time, if that is what the terrorists decide. Do we know exactly where the bomb is located within the building?"

"No," said Pichet. "Not yet."

"All nuclear weapons rely on radioactive material to create an atomic explosion," Lyudmila explained. "If the bomb in the Louvre is hidden above ground, in a car or a truck, it might be possible to detect that radiation remotely from a helicopter or even a satellite."

"We've tried that," said Pichet. "But whoever put the bomb in place was very clever. Somehow, they managed to contaminate the entire courtyard of the Louvre and the area outside it with low levels of radiation, not enough to cause a health hazard, but certainly enough to mask any competently shielded device placed in the vicinity."

"How could anyone do that and not be noticed?" asked Constance.

"By spreading radioactive powder or liquid," suggested Lyudmila, brushing back a strand of blonde hair from her face. "A liquid would be more effective, as it wouldn't blow away. But to apply a liquid you'd need a spray of some kind and it would be impossible to spray an area as big as the Louvre courtyard without being seen."

Gabrielle thought for a moment.

"A street-cleaning truck!" she said. "There must be hundreds of them, all over the city. Even if it was seen by the Louvre security cameras, nobody would pay any attention to it."

"And what if that the truck is still close by?" asked Lyudmila. "The device we're looking for would easily fit into the cabin of a small vehicle."

"There are no vehicles around the Museum," Pichet said. "They've all been removed. There may be others in the underground garages and delivery bays, but we'll only be able to search them once we have control of the security cameras and can get inside undetected. I'd be honoured, Capitaine Arnault, if you and your expert would accompany me as part of a team to find the bomb and disarm it."

"I'll go with you," Flynn said.

Pichet lowered his voice. "You'll do no such thing," he hissed. "I already have one convicted criminal forced upon me by the authorities to assist with this operation in the form of Monsieur Sabaut. You'll be part of the team only because he has insisted on it and my superiors somehow believe his judgement. Your role, given your previous experience in removing art from museums without the owners' permissions, will be to help my men remove as many of the most valuable paintings as you can carry. But if I even smell a problem with you, I'll have you tied up on the spot and picked up on the way back."

The meeting began to break up as people moved into their teams ready for the mission. But there was one thing Gabrielle was still anxious to ask Sabaut.

"So tell me, Jean-Jacques. Why did you steal the *Mona Lisa* in the first place? You must have known you could never sell it. Who would want a stolen piece of art that is so instantly recognisable?"

Sabaut smiled. "There you are wrong. I could name half a dozen extremely rich men and women who'd pay a king's ransom to possess that painting, people who already have secret collections of the world's greatest stolen art treasures they display only to themselves."

"You did it for money then?"

"No," he said. "I did it for my wife, Nicole."

"Why? Did she want it as a gift? Were you trying to prove something to her?"

"Nicole was dead," said Sabaut.

"I'm sorry."

"The establishment killed her. She was a brilliant and gifted artist, one of the most talented of her generation. Nicole Legrand, you might have heard of her. She experimented with forms of perspective and portraiture that were completely revolutionary. But, her first love, her greatest love of all perhaps, was the work of Leonardo. She took a job as a restorer in the Louvre, simply to be near his work and feel his genius. He too was a pioneer, just like her, an artist ahead of his time. But unlike Leonardo, her work was scorned by the critics and left to hang on the walls of our apartment in obscurity until she died. Do you know what it's like for an artist to go unrecognised, Capitaine Arnault?"

"I can imagine."

"Can you really? It's soul destroying. It's like a mother who constantly gives birth to dead children. There is the inspiration of conception, the long, hard labour in the creation of the piece itself and then, when it should be born into the world and acclaimed as a true work of art, there is nothing . . . nothing but the scorn of ignorant critics and rejection of the galleries. At least a mother whose baby dies at childbirth is the subject of sympathy and understanding. My Nicci was crucified year after year, picture after picture by small minds that could not see the genius right in front of their eyes."

"But she kept painting?"

"A creative artist can do nothing but create," said Sabaut. "It's a force as strong and unstoppable as the birth of a child. What happened was that her work became darker and more introspective, until one day, after her last exhibition had been savaged by the critics yet again, I came home and found her lying dead in the bath with her wrists slit open. She couldn't take it any more. She was a sensitive artist, a person ruled by her passions, and the heartache was too great for her to bear."

Gabrielle could find no words to say. She touched Sabaut's arm.

"What they did to Nicci was a crime," Sabaut said. "They took her spirit and they crushed it, as an ignorant child crushes a butterfly. They slated her paintings time and time again. They denied her exhibitions. They called her talentless and trite . . . until her soul could take no more of it. Then, like so many great artists before her, she sought the only relief that remained, and left me to carry out her revenge. That's why I stole the *Mona Lisa*. To prove to the critics of this world that her art was at least the equal of the man they have so slavishly worshipped for so long."

"But how would stealing the *Mona Lisa* do that?"

"As I told you, Nicci was a passionate student of the works of Leonardo and she worked in the restoration section of the Louvre. Other students make sketches of Leonardo's work. They study his techniques and form. They read books and attend lectures. Nicci was different. She became Leonardo, in his methods, his materials and his very inspiration. And over the years of study and practice she was able to duplicate his very essence and, ultimately, accurately duplicate his greatest work, *La Giaconda*, the *Mona Lisa*."

"You mean she was able to forge his paintings?"

"Not forge. Duplicate! There is a world of difference. A forger slavishly copies the work of a great master feature by feature with one end in mind, to deceive the art world into thinking it's real. But Nicci was able to take a slab of aged poplar wood and the materials Leonardo would have used, and duplicate the very essence of his *Mona Lisa*. I had that painting in my apartment after she died and I thought, what a sweet revenge it would be for me to substitute it for the real thing and have the so-called 'experts' of the art world continue to drool over it. Then, after a few months, I could announce that these hypocrites who had driven my Nicole to her death with their criticisms, had been completely fooled by her genius."

"It's an interesting idea," said Gabrielle.

Sabaut continued. "But then of course, as is the cruel tradition of art, her work was suddenly 'rediscovered' by the intelligentsia and hailed as the key to a whole new way of seeing the world. All this happened after my accident, while I was lying in a hospital bed in prison. I've been blind for five years now, Madame Arnault and, even though I'll never be able to gaze upon their beauty again, I find myself back here today because of Nicole and that painting."

"Do you still have your wife's duplicate of the *Mona Lisa*?"

"Indeed I do," Sabaut snorted. "The authorities made a cruel show of giving it back to me when I was released from jail, simply because I could no longer appreciate its beauty. It's hidden in our old apartment, along with her other paintings. Now that I'm blind, I'll probably have to sell most of them in order to survive. But Nicole's *Mona Lisa* is going with me to my grave."

Gabrielle squeezed Sabaut's arm and stood up.

"Then let's make sure that doesn't happen today," she said, and went to join the others.

11

Flynn watched the police helicopters swarming above the city as the army coach edged its way westwards along the southern bank of the Seine, surrounded by the sea of traffic evacuating the population of Paris. He was hung-over and sleep-deprived. He was also pissed off at Pichet for calling him a 'tame terrorist' and for relegating him to carrying paintings for the museum technicians when he should have been assigned to the bomb detail with Arnault.

The last time he'd been in the French capital was when he'd been trying to sell a collection of Renaissance paintings stolen from a country house in Wicklow. Back then, the Quai Anatole had been lined with stalls selling cheap paintings, books, magazines and souvenirs, while the river had been alive with sightseeing *Batobuses* and snakelike cargo barges. He'd enjoyed a good time then, touring the less reputable galleries and black market dealers, looking for a good price by day, drinking red wine and chasing the dancers in the strip clubs by night.

But today the green-painted shutters were up on the souvenir stalls and the river was empty of all traffic except for a lonely police launch. It was incredible to think that the heart of Paris and all the security forces left behind to save it could vanish in an instant if the bomb they were searching for exploded. All this creative genius, all this history, and all these lives could go up in a puff of smoke. Helping his brother Sean to pack a van with Semtex to take out a busload of British soldiers was bad enough, but the destruction of a whole city was obscene.

"Look Daimo, it's like this. To get noticed you have to cause them pain. That's what it's all about, causing them pain. And when that pain gets too great, when too many of their soldiers are going home in body bags and they're afraid to go shopping for fear of getting blown to buggery, then perhaps they'll sit down at a table and talk to us about peace."

Today, somebody had found a way of causing enough pain to make the entire European Union sit up and take notice.

The bus shouldered its way out of the main traffic flow, turned right across the graceful curves of the Pont de la Concorde Bridge and came to a stop in a tree-lined square near the Musée de l'Orangerie, well out of sight of the Louvre. The door of the bus hissed open, letting in a blast of cold autumn air.

"Even if the terrorists have observers around the museum, the trees will block their view of us here," Arnault said, fastening the zip on her black jumpsuit. Her armband and ID tag read 'Police', as did those of everyone on the bus. To Flynn, she looked completely in her element and excited at the prospect of action. He, on the other hand, felt uncomfortable to have that word on his arm. But, with so many security officers already on the streets in similar gear, at least none of their group would look out of place. He followed her out of the bus and into the sunshine, where the rest of the group had already gathered around a screen protecting a manhole in the pavement and were checking their equipment.

"Are you sure these radios can't be overheard?" he asked.

"The headsets are completely secure," Pichet said. "We use them for all our anti-terrorist missions and the waveband is scrambled. But don't put your helmet and headlight on until you're in the tunnel. I don't want anyone guessing what we're about."

Flynn nodded grudgingly and turned his radio headset on. "Jean-Jacques? Can you hear me?"

Sabaut's voice came through loud and clear. "I hear you, Damien. Where are you?"

"At the manhole near the Musée de l'Orangerie. They're opening the cover now."

"Then welcome to the Paris beneath Paris. I hope you don't have a sensitive nose."

"Very well," Pichet said. "The team dealing with the bomb will go into the tunnel first. That's myself, Madame Petrachkova and Capitaine Arnault. Then you, Monsieur Flynn will follow the second team of nine men, under the direction of the Museum's director of security. It's your responsibility to remove the paintings he indicates to safety. Is that understood?

Flynn nodded, first to Pichet, and then to the nine technicians from the Louvre standing around him with flat metal cases.

"Check your throat microphones and headsets!" said Pichet. "Everyone, sound off. Capitaine Arnault?"

Gabrielle stepped to the edge of the manhole and looked down. This was the moment she'd been dreading, the one terrible thing she'd been trying to put out of her mind. Ever since she'd found herself buried under a pile a bodies on the platform of Atocha station, she'd panicked at the thought of confined spaces. In her apartment at the Hague, she slept with her bedroom door open and a nightlight by her bed. Time and again, she'd wake up with the covers over her face and claw them off in blind terror before she realised where she was. The post-trauma stress counselling had helped, but she had not wanted to make too much of her claustrophobia for fear of being declared unfit for duty. Now that lie was about to catch up with her. She felt sick. Her chest tightened. She was going to faint.

"Capitaine Arnault? Is your radio working?"

Gabrielle brought her breath under control and closed her eyes for a moment.

"Oui, Patron. My radio's fine. I'll follow you down."

Pichet descended into the tunnel, followed by Lyudmila.

Part of Gabrielle's brain, the part that was a professional police officer, carefully watched where the other members of her team put their hands and feet. The other part, the terrified woman who had lain under a pile of dead and dying bodies, screamed silently. Death was down there in dark places, death for her and those she loved. She tried to move her legs, but she was paralysed.

"Come on, Gabrielle," said Flynn behind her. "You don't want to keep me and the lads from our shopping trip, now do you."

She looked back at him.

"Stay close behind me," she said and sat with her legs hanging into the blackness. Then she reached forward and lowered herself down the ladder until she was standing on firm ground in the dark. Her breath came very fast. Pinpoints of light swam in front of her eyes. She had to see where she was. She had to know she was here in Paris, and not back at Atocha station.

"Flynn?"

"Get away from the ladder, Gabrielle, or I'll step on your head!"

She reached sideways, found the damp wall and steadied herself. Then she rammed the helmet onto her head and snapped on the light. She was standing on a narrow stone shelf beside a greenish-grey river. The smell was unique and indescribable. It was not the rich aroma of farm manure, or even the pungent stench of human faeces. It was alien and almost sweet, an evil organic odour that felt as if it was seeping into every orifice and pore in her body. She knew that, years from now, she would still carry that smell with her wherever she went, however many times she washed her body. Nothing she could ever do would get rid of it.

She waited until Flynn was right behind her and then moved forward after the lights of Pichet and Lyudmila, following them into the darkness, heading east towards the Louvre.

"Keep up please, Capitaine Arnault," Pichet said. "The tunnel is straight for about a hundred metres and then curves inwards towards the Louvre."

The walls of the sewer pressed down on her, crushing her chest. She had to hear another voice.

"Constance?" she whispered into her radio. "How are you doing with the security system?"

Back at the Préfecture de Police, Constance LeClerc sat in front of her laptop at a large desk surrounded by three other computer screens and a bank of monitors which had been hastily assembled by the technical staff. Behind her, and to her left, sat Jean-Jacques Sabaut. To her right, sat the systems designer André Bloc and the Préfet de Police. With her short squat body, her crop of gingery hair and her large round spectacles, Constance looked like a grounded owl. Her stubby fingers fluttered over the keyboard in front of her like feathers.

"I'm being careful, Gabrielle," she said into her headset. "I'm examining the external feeds to the Louvre computer system to see if there's a way through the protective firewall the hackers have sealed to make all the authentic passwords useless. Right now Monsieur Bloc and I are trying a different way into the system, through the Louvre's public web page. If we can pretend to log on as one of the staff who designed it, we might be able to get past the firewall the hackers have corrupted onto the server that supports it. If we can do that, then we might be able to access the security cameras and insert a computer virus to constantly repeat their digital feed into a continuous loop of empty space."

"Isn't that what you did for Jean-Jacques when he broke into the Louvre before?"

"It was, but there are two additional factors at play now; the improvements made to the system since our break-in by Monsieur Bloc and his team, and whatever booby-traps the terrorists might have programmed into it. I don't want to upset either of them. The building I'm in now is less than a two hundred metres from the Louvre, so we'll be the first to be vaporised if the bomb goes off."

She turned to the young man sitting next to her. "Monsieur Bloc, I'm familiar with your security system as it was when Jean-Jacques and I last broke in. So perhaps it would save us time if you tell me only about any new modifications you've made since then."

André Bloc spread out a sheet of schematics on the table.

"We added more motion sensors in the service areas of the museum at the lower levels, and more cameras in corridor intersections and stairwells," he said. "There are also pressure sensors in the floors around key artworks, to detect the weight of a human body, and a significant upgrade of the security software that supports the system itself to prevent an intruder hacking in. It includes new firewalls and anti-intrusion programmes."

"How often does the system check itself?" asked Constance. "The old system monitored its own settings automatically every fifteen minutes, in case someone had hacked in and reset the cameras or the anti-intrusion devices. How long is the time interval now?"

"We thought, in view of the improved capability of hackers nowadays and the increased possibility of intrusion into the system, that we would increase our computer security and install a wider range of sensors. Another measure we took was to cut down the reset time to sixty seconds."

Constance raised her eyebrows.

"A minute is a very short time, Monsieur. If I can hack into the system, could I change the reset time to allow our people longer inside the museum before the system checks itself?"

"If you can hack in," said Bloc with a trace of pride in his voice . "I'd be very surprised if you could even infiltrate the main servers in the first place."

Constance linked her fingers above the keyboard in front of her and clicked her joints, as if she was about to perform a piano concert.

"Young man, just watch me," she said.

The homepage of the Louvre website opened, with its information pages, contact details and virtual tours. Constance turned to the systems designer.

"What safeguards do you have to prevent external computers logging on as editors to the website?"

"There are simple password protections," said Bloc. "I can give you those."

"Okay." She typed in a series of instructions on her keyboard.

A new screen opened. It asked her to identify herself as an editor, with full name and password. Constance did so. A list of commands scrolled across the screen.

"Are there security firewalls on any of these?" she asked.

"Not until the next level," said Bloc. "How did you get past the password protection the first time."

"Your predecessor was a very close friend of mine," said Constance. "She allowed me full access."

"Do you mean Madame Damereaux?"

"Exactly," Constance said, smiling wistfully at the screen. "As I said, we were very close. Now, this is new. Where do I go from here?"

"It's an added security precaution," said Bloc. "The system has identified your laptop as an external unit not cleared on the main network. It won't let you any further until you've proven you're not a threat."

"And if I register the laptop as a recognised terminal within the system and link it to my own user name and password? Will that throw up a warning to whoever has control of the system now?"

"It shouldn't."

"Can't you be sure? I really don't want to be vaporised just yet!"

"Wouldn't it be safer just to cut the electrical power to the whole museum?" asked the Préfet de Police. "That way, all the cameras would go down, the lights would go out and our teams could do what they wanted. We're wasting time here!"

"The Louvre has its own emergency generators, Monsieur Retour," said Bloc. "They cut in immediately after the power goes off and can't be overridden from the outside. Any power cut will also be registered by the computer and show up as a warning to the terrorists."

"I agree with Monsieur Bloc," said Constance. "The terrorists know what they're doing. They took control of the system without your staff at the Louvre even knowing they were there. We can't afford to make a mistake now."

It was the longest walk of Gabrielle's life. Every second of silence was a fight against the nightmare crowding in on her from the walls. The narrow footpath above the grey sewage and the sharp inward curve of the stone walls were difficult to navigate. The flicker of torch beams made it hard to keep her balance and the sickly sweet stench was becoming unbearable. Her last meal, a snatched croissant with jam on the plane from Brussels with Flynn, repeated itself in her mouth. Her stomach heaved and she fought it back. Now was no time to show weakness. If only someone would speak!

"We turn left at the next junction," said Pichet's voice in her headset. "Is everyone okay?"

"If we wanted a toilet stop, we couldn't have picked a better place," said Flynn. "I suppose nobody wants to break for lunch."

"Let's keep going," Pichet said. "Only thirty minutes more until the turn-off for the Louvre."

"Beats the Metro hands down," Flynn said. Gabrielle found herself humming a tune to break the silence. It was a lullaby her mother had sung to her back in Roscoff.

"*Et bien!*" Constance said. "Are you sure that's all we need to do to get past the firewall and insert the virus?"

"Yes," said Bloc. "Anyone with my clearance would have full access."

Constance pressed the return key. For a moment nothing happened. Then the computer gave a grunt and a small square appeared in the centre of the screen.

"User already logged on," it said. "Access denied."

"Oops!" Constance said. "We have a problem."

12

"What kind of problem?" asked Gabrielle into her microphone.

Constance's voice sounded loud and clear in her earpiece.

"I can't get past the firewall. How far are you from the Museum?"

"We should be there in fifteen minutes or less," Pichet said, consulting a map of the tunnels.

"Don't make it less. I may not have the cameras fixed by then."

"Let's keep moving," said Pichet. "She may be able to solve the problem, or she may not but, if we wait here, we'll only lose time."

"Constance?" said Gabrielle. "Do you think the terrorists know we're trying to hack into the system?"

"They may have a booby trap programme installed to alert them if anybody tries to log on, but I think we'd have had some kind of warning of that by now. What I'm seeing on screen is the standard notice from the main computer about another user being logged on and blocking access. Our problem is—how do we get around it without alerting the terrorists?"

Gabrielle heard Constance consulting someone else back at the Préfecture. "How long did you say it takes the standby generators to kick in after a power cut?"

"A few seconds," said the Préfet's voice in the background. "But when we discussed it earlier you didn't think it was an option."

"If the power goes out in the Museum," said Constance. "What happens to the security system? Do the computers go down too?"

"Yes. Anyone using them would have to reboot and log on again," Bloc said.

"And the alarms?" asked Constance.

"Everything goes down, but only for a few seconds."

"That would be all we'd need," Constance said. "If we had the code for the virus written and ready, we could log on using the security director's password as soon as the system reboots. That would allow us to insert the virus through the firewall and log off again before the terrorists think it's anything more than a random interruption to the power supply."

"We'll be at the Museum in ten minutes," Pichet said. "How long to write this computer virus?"

"Half an hour," said Constance, "perhaps longer."

"We'll go as far as we can now," Pichet said. "There's no point in holding back until we get to the Louvre."

They trudged on into the darkness, their feet echoing along the brickwork. The heat rose, making the stench seem even more oppressive. Gabrielle wondered if she could hold herself together until they emerged in the Louvre. She remembered Sabaut's description of the vastness and complexity of the sewer system and how people had got lost in its twists and blind alleys. If she got lost now and found herself alone in the dark, she'd go mad.

"Monsieur Sabaut?" she said. "Are we anywhere near the turn-off for the Louvre?"

Sabaut's voice sounded in her headset. "Look for a bend in the canal and the numbers '5663' on the wall to the left."

"I see it," Pichet said, pointing his torch forward.

"Follow that fork for another two hundred metres and you'll see a branch to the right, barred with a chain and marked 'Danger of Collapse - Maintenance Access Only'. That's the beginning of the tunnel that was breached when the glass pyramid was added to the Museum. Ten metres along you'll see a vertical smear of yellow paint. Ten bricks further on you'll find that the brickwork becomes loose. That's where I made my entrance to the storeroom in the basement."

"How's Constance coming with the cameras?" asked Gabrielle.

"She's shooed us all out of the room so that she and the system designer can concentrate on creating this computer virus of theirs," Sabaut said. "I'll tell you when the power's due to be cut."

"How far can we go before we have to stop and wait?" asked Pichet.

"Up into my tunnel as far as the panel. It's a very tight space up there, but it'll bring you out inside the storeroom."

Ten minutes later, the two teams stopped by the strip of yellow paint Sabaut had identified. Gabrielle watched Pichet pull a stout knife from his belt and count a number of bricks to the left, before easing the blade into the wall and pulling the first brick free. Then everyone leant a hand to prise the loose bricks out and stack them on the walkway beyond the growing gap in the sewer wall. Gabrielle peered inside. A tunnel about a metre wide stretched into the blackness beyond the beams of her headlight. Cold sweat broke out on her face.

"I'll go first," Pichet said and lifted himself into the opening, followed by Lyudmila and Flynn. Gabrielle took a deep breath and pulled herself up into the tunnel. It was carved directly from the clay, slippery and damp, with rotting wooden boards providing a makeshift floor. She eased herself upwards on her elbows with her torch pointed forward, humming the lullaby her mother had taught her, as she tried to put the nightmares out of her mind.

The damp clay felt soft and yielding, just like the bodies at Atocha. She was trapped in a narrow tunnel with people above and below her. The screams of dying people grew in her ears. The cold sweat on her face turned to blood. From up ahead, she heard someone knocking on a hollow metal panel and Pichet's voice say "We're there! What about that security system, Madame LeClerc?"

Gabrielle folded her arms over her head and hoped nobody would see her falling apart.

Constance looked up at the big electric clock above the computer terminal. On her laptop screen was the page she'd navigated to from the Louvre website, fully completed with the security director's username and password. Beside her, André Bloc sat at a similar machine showing the home page of the Louvre website.

"On this data stick," said Constance, holding up a USB no longer than a pen top, "is the computer virus containing a complete set of instructions to the digital surveillance cameras all over the Louvre. It tells them to record thirty seconds of footage at each of their locations, and then play it back in a continuous loop until commanded to stop. The instructions also tell the motion sensors, pressure switches and infrared detectors to increase the settings on their alarm thresholds to a hundred times beyond that needed to trigger a warning."

"And how does that help us, exactly?" asked Retour.

"Normally a pressure sensor, such as those installed under the carpets near the entrances and exits, would send a signal to the security board if even a small weight, like a dog or a child, was placed on them. Now, you'd need to drive a lorry over the sensors to set off an alarm. Likewise the amount of body heat needed to trigger the infrared sensors has been increased to that of a forest fire and the motion sensors, which rely on air movement, will only trigger if wind speeds equal to those of a tornado were to rip through the museum."

Retour was not convinced.

"Isn't that a big gamble?" he said. "Is there any way to test it before our teams go in?"

"You can see the Louvre from that window there, yes?" said Constance. "The floodlights facing this building are also controlled by the security computer in the museum. They'll flash three times and then stay on once the virus is installed. To anyone watching the building, it will look like a simple fault, but we'll know the virus is working. Now Monsieur Retour, I need you to cut the power."

She slid the data stick holding the virus into a port on the main computer.

Retour picked up a phone and gave his instructions. "You'll have it in two minutes," he said. "At eleven fifty eight precisely."

Everyone in the room looked up at the clock. A minute passed. The second hand moved on around the bottom of its second arc and began to crawl closer to vertical.

"Here it comes," Constance said.

All computer screens connected to the mains power supply abruptly went blank and then flicked back into life.

"The Louvre web page is down," said Bloc. "It should be up again in a few seconds. Here it comes, now."

Constance hit the return key on her machine. A blue square popped up in front of her eyes, accompanied by a clear ping from the computer speaker.

"Welcome to the Louvre Security System" said a message on the screen. "You have logged on successfully."

Her fingers fluttered over the keyboard. Her little finger snapped down on the return key again.

"It's done," she said. "I'm logging off. Look out of the window."

On the far side of the Seine, the eastern façade of the Louvre flashed three times and then stood brightly lit against the late afternoon sky.

"No explosion so far," said Constance. "Capitaine Pichet, Gabrielle and Damien. Welcome to the Musée du Louvre!"

Flynn heard someone humming a lullaby, followed by the sound of sobbing. He flicked his radio off and shone his torch back down the tunnel.

Gabrielle lay curled up like a baby, gently rocking to and fro with her hands over her head.

"Gabrielle!" he hissed. "Turn your radio off!"

She looked up at him. Her eyes were streaming with tears and her face was a white mask.

"Turn your radio off!"

Her hand went down to her headset.

He heard a faint click in his ear and reached down to her. Her skin was cold. She gripped his hand.

"Talk to me, Gabrielle!" hissed Flynn. "It's okay. Nobody can hear you now. Just talk to me!"

"I was in Madrid . . . at Atocha station! I was there with my family when it happened. I was *there*!"

"It's okay," said Flynn. "I'm with you. You're not alone. We'll be out of here in a moment. Sure we will. Just keep talking to me. . ."

Flynn heard Pichet release the metal clips holding the panel in place. Then came the distant click of a switch and light flooded down into the tunnel.

"So far, so good," whispered Pichet. "I'm through into the storeroom and no alarms yet. Follow me up, all of you."

Flynn looked down at Gabrielle and smiled.

"There," he said. "What did I tell you?"

He let go of her hand and waited as each member of the team ahead of him squirmed out of the tunnel into a storeroom and reached back to help Gabrielle through. She wiped her face with the back of her sleeve and pulled herself upright."

"Thank you, Doctor Flynn," she said. "It's just that . . ."

"It's great to know you're human after all, mon Capitaine," said Flynn. "Besides, the smell makes your eyes water very badly, doesn't it? Pichet and Lyudmila went this way. I think we'd better follow them."

He led her across the storeroom, between the rows of statues and into a dark stone passage. From there, they followed Pichet and Lyudmila down a brightly lit corridor, up a flight of stairs and into a vast open space. To their right was a deserted shopping mall, in front of them three motionless escalators and a set of ticket desks. A pyramid of glass and steel soared above their heads, glistening in the late afternoon sun.

"We did it," said Flynn. "We're in!"

13

No alarms sounded. No lights flashed. The only sound Flynn heard was the squeaking of feet on the polished floor.

"Very well," Pichet said. "We'll divide into two teams as agreed. Capitaine Arnault, you and your Russian colleague follow me with the Geiger counter and search for the bomb. I suggest we start at ground level up on the Cour Napoléon and descend into the garages and storage areas. It would be wise to go up through one of the galleries and not the main entrance at the Pyramid, just in case the terrorists have someone watching outside. Monsieur le Directeur, you take your men and retrieve the paintings you want to save. Take Monsieur Flynn with you."

The Security Director nodded. Flynn watched Gabrielle run to an escalator and disappear up into one of the galleries with Lyudmila and Pichet.

"Follow me," said the Security Director. "We'll start in the Denon Wing on the first floor, Room Five."

They turned left up a flight of stairs and into a high-ceilinged gallery that seemed to stretch on forever. There were paintings as far as Flynn could see; paintings dating back for hundreds of years. Face after face looked down at him from the portraits lining the walls. He thought of all the time and effort of so many gifted artists that had produced them over the centuries. The enormity of the loss that would be sustained if the Louvre was destroyed suddenly struck him. It was truly irreplaceable.

"Monsieur Retour?" he asked. "Has there been any word from the terrorists or the EU Parliament about the ransom?"

"Ah! It's come home to you at last, hasn't it?" said Sabaut over Flynn's headset. "You're in the Denon Wing, standing in the presence of genius. You're looking at the very best that human imagination and artistic craft has to offer, the pure distillation of that side of the human soul that makes us yearn to be more than we are. Do you still think it would be a crime to pay the ransom, knowing that it would go to as worthy a cause as the relief of suffering in Africa?"

"There's been no word from the terrorists and the Parliament is still in deadlock," cut in the Préfet de Police, "and Monsieur Sabaut, if you could confine your comments to the provision of technical advice, it would be greatly appreciated."

"I rest my case," Sabaut said. "Just do your best, Damien, and bring back those paintings before they're blown to atoms."

Flynn saw the Security Director turn right, off the main gallery and down a sloping corridor into a large room, hung with very few paintings, and followed him inside. In the centre, on a red wall behind a glass panel that stretched from floor to ceiling, and protected by a wooden rail, was a very familiar face. She seemed to smile at him, as if she'd been expecting him.

"We're here," said Flynn. "We're at the *Mona Lisa*."

"How does she look?" Sabaut asked.

"Like she was waiting for us."

The nine technicians from the Louvre fanned out across the room with their steel carrying cases, moving from painting to painting - *The Virgin in the Rocks* , *The Virgin, The Infant Jesus and St Anne, Head of a Woman, Portrait of a Young Lady* - disengaging the taut wires suspending them from their picture rails and lowering them to the floor. They went to work on the frames, carefully prising back the pins that held the canvases in place, removing the paintings and placing them inside the padded steel cases.

Then three of them surrounded the *Mona Lisa* and started unscrewing the hidden bolts holding the glass panels in place.

"How long will it take to remove the painting?" asked Flynn.

"If I may be allowed to advise," Sabaut said. "There are two sheets of bulletproof glass and a hermetically sealed case to get through before you can reach *La Giaconda*. It will take time. You can see why I chose to liberate her while she was down for her annual inspection, before the display cabinet was completed."

"It's fortunate that Leonardo preferred wooden panels to large canvasses," said the Security Director as he watched his men working. "Get those packed into the cases and back to the tunnel as soon as you can."

Flynn saw the technicians around the *Mona Lisa* struggling with the first panel of bulletproof glass. He helped them lift it down and prop it up against the wall. It seemed incredibly heavy as they laid its base down on the floor. Flynn thought of the pressure sensors under the carpet.

"Are you sure the alarms are off, Constance?"

"They aren't switched off. I told you that. It's just that their sensitivity settings are turned way down. You'd have to make a very loud bang in there to set them off."

Gabrielle followed Pichet through a hall packed with sculptures. All at once she was back with Felipe at the Prado museum in Madrid, looking up at the great statue of Valazquez at the main entrance. Felipe had been a fan of all the great Spanish masters; Valazquez, Goya, Dali and Picasso, and had extolled their genius over all other artists in the world, including those of Italy and her native France. They'd stopped for a long time in the great long gallery where Picasso's *Guernica* had been displayed. The painting was enormous—the size of three garage doors—and full of pain and suffering, with wide eyes and arms and legs at strange angles in shades of black, grey and white. Gabrielle had not understood that painting until the next morning when, no more than a hundred metres from where *Guernica* stood, the terrorist bombs had gone off at Atocha station.

Commissaire Pichet stopped at the end of the ground floor gallery, punched in the security code to isolate a door to the North East courtyard and turned a key in the lock. Looking nervously at the door surround, he pulled on the release bar. The door swung inwards with a clack. No alarms sounded.

"We have the door open," he said. "The courtyard's clear. There are no vehicles. No kiosks or stands. Nowhere to hide the bomb. I suggest we go down to the garages and start looking there."

"Just a moment," Gabrielle said, scanning the courtyard. "What else do cleaning carts do beside spraying the streets?"

Retour's voice came back to her over her headset.

"They brush the gutters and empty and rubbish bins."

"I see the bins. The bomb would easily fit inside one of those, wouldn't it?"

"It's possible," Lyudmila said. "If the mechanism was inserted vertically."

She heard Retour reply over her headset. "Then search them. You have your Geiger counter?"

"Yes," Lyudmila said. "But it's already showing background radiation from the paving stones."

"Try turning the sensitivity down and test each bin in turn," suggested Pichet. "Capitaine Arnault. If you could use the radio wave detector to scan for any remote trigger, that would help us, but make sure you watch out for tripwires."

"It'll take some time," said Gabrielle, looking around the courtyard. The afternoon sun, now low in the sky to the west, cast deep shadows in the Cour Napoléon, throwing the sightless statues into stark relief. From where she stood, she counted at least a dozen bins on this side of the great space and even more beyond the pyramid to the west.

"It has to be done," Pichet said. "Take your time and do it right. There are no second chances with this."

Flynn watched as the museum technicians moved from painting to painting. They were on their third Da Vinci, his *Portrait of a Lady of the Court of Milan* when one of the technicians at the *Mona Lisa* said, "We have a problem. The second panel of glass is jammed in its runner."

He looked across to the two men standing between the wooden railing in front of the *Mona Lisa* and the painting itself. One of them had a battery operated screwdriver poised at the point where the glass met the wall. The other watched him with his hands outstretched across the panel, ready to support it.

Flynn moved towards them. There was a loud crack, a shout, and the glass covering the painting toppled onto the railing. The technician was taken by surprise, fell backwards and lost his grip on the glass. The huge panel, now unsupported, hit the wood, tipped over it and plunged towards the floor.

Flynn shouted a warning to the man next to him and dived forward. He rolled across the carpet, landing on his back with his arms and legs outstretched beneath the falling panel as the other man followed suit. The glass slammed into them, their arms and legs shuddered and, for a second or two, they lay there with the panel poised above them.

But then, before the other technicians could reach them, the great pane of glass slid sideways at an angle, tilted awkwardly and its top right corner jabbed into the floor.

"Shite!" hissed Flynn. "We've done it now!"

Voices sounded in his earpiece at once—Retour's, Pichet's and Constance's.

"What's happened?"

"We dropped one of the glass panels in front of the *Mona Lisa*. One of its corners dug right through the carpet. It's bound to have set off the pressure alarms."

"There's nothing on my screens," Constance said. "The sensors are spaced out individually over the floor. They don't cover the entire area. You must have been lucky and missed them."

The technicians lifted the glass and carefully placed it on the floor.

"Thank you," said the Security Director looking down at Flynn. "That could have been a disaster."

Flynn staggered to his feet, still shaking.

"I'm surprised it wasn't," he said. "How much longer will all this take?"

"Another ten minutes or so to get the hermetically sealed cabinet around the *Mona Lisa* open and that's it. The technicians on the other floors have the paintings they came to retrieve. The statues and the larger paintings will have to remain. There's no way we can take them out."

"How many artworks are there in all?"

"Almost four hundred thousand objects in the Louvre alone," said the Security Director, "and hundreds of thousands more in the other museums in central Paris. If that bomb goes off they'll all be lost."

"Then let's hope we don't drop any more panels," muttered Flynn. "Gabrielle? Any progress with the bomb?"

Gabrielle looked up from the third bin they'd examined in the Cour Napoléon. It had taken them ten minutes to get this far, and the bin was empty. At this rate it would be another hour if they had to examine each bin in the courtyard, and that was before they even tried to disarm the device.

"You take the paintings and get out," she said. "This is going to take us longer than we thought."

Lyudmila pointed to the next bin, hidden in shadow at the south-eastern corner of the courtyard.

"The Geiger counter shows an elevated reading over background radiation," she said. "We'd better investigate."

"How do we do that?" asked Gabrielle.

"We check for booby trap devices. We monitor the frequency of the radio transmission to and from the bomb. Whoever planted it here has to have a mechanism for either detonating it or, if it's already on a timer, for shutting that timer off, should we agree to their demands. If we can tap into the bomb's radio command system, we may be able to override it and shut down the weapon without taking it apart."

"And if we can't?" asked Pichet.

"Then we have to open the casing and get at the bomb inside. It'll have a triggering mechanism to detonate the conventional explosives around the plutonium core. If we can prevent that trigger mechanism from functioning, then we can stop that core being compressed into critical mass and block the nuclear explosion. It's as simple as that."

"Simple," said Gabrielle. "Where do we start?"

"With the radio signal," Lyudmila said. "Commissaire? What do you see?"

Pichet looked at the digital read-out on his radio detector. "There's a faint carrier wave coming from the bomb."

"That could be a tamper alarm, designed to warn whoever controls the bomb if it's interfered with," Lyudmila said. "It could be linked to a trembler device, such as a simple mercury switch—which we could freeze with liquid nitrogen—or to a latch on the door of the bin. Either way, if we can set up a more powerful signal on the same frequency and transmit the message that all is well, then we build ourselves a safety net if we make a mistake."

She reached into her backpack, pulled out what looked like an old-fashioned transistor radio and extended its aerial. Then she set the digital display to exactly the same wavelength as the one on the detector.

"Do you concur?" she asked Pichet.

"How powerful is your transmitter? Are you sure it's capable of overriding any signal put out by the bomb?"

"It's linked to a military communications satellite overhead," said Lyudmila. "That will boost its signal a thousand times."

"Then go ahead."

Gabrielle held her breath. Lyudmila pressed a button on the transmitter. A green light blinked on.

"So far, so good," Lyudmila said. She lay the transmitter down on the paving, crouched down and peered around the base of the bin. "I don't see any booby trap wires or switches to detect if the bin is moved."

"Do you need to move it at all?" asked Gabrielle. "If all you need to do is disable the trigger. Couldn't you do that where it stands?"

"We'll see."

Lyudmila reached back into her kitbag, pulled out an old-fashioned leather roll of tools and spread it on the ground. Then, taking a small round mirror on a telescopic rod and a thin flashlight, she reached over the bin and peered inside.

"It's solid below this ashtray," she said. "There's definitely some large object there."

"Can we reach it?" asked Gabrielle.

"There's a panel on the front of the bin, just like all the others. We could start by opening that."

"What about booby traps? Can you see between the bin casing and what's inside from the top?" asked Pichet.

"There seems to be just the inside hinges of the panel and the locking mechanism," said Lyudmila.

"Can you see the bomb itself?" asked Gabrielle.

"There's a large cylinder. It's painted purple."

"Just like the bomb in Barcelona.

"We've found it," said Pichet into his throat microphone. "Monsieur le Directeur, take the paintings and get out, now!"

"We should also evacuate all the security forces remaining in the city," said the Préfet de Police. "The team with the paintings needs only to exit the museum through the sewers and be transported to a safe distance. The bomb disposal team are expert enough to work on their own. We only need a skeleton crew here at the Préfecture to assist in case of a further emergency. I'll remain here in command. All personnel not directly supporting the team in the Louvre should leave now."

"I'll stay by the radio," Sabaut said. "There may be some problems with the escape route and they could need my advice.

"You could just as easily stay in touch with them by radio from a safe distance," said Retour. "Why stay?"

"Honour among thieves, Monsieur. I'd rather not let those in the Louvre see me leave them behind."

"And I'll stay with Jean-Jacques," Constance said. "If I was to change location now it would interrupt our monitoring of the security systems."

"Very well," Retour said. "I'll call the President and the EU Parliament and tell them we've located the bomb."

"We have the paintings and we're back near the atrium," said Flynn as his team assembled beneath the great glass pyramid. The ten most valuable paintings in the Louvre, those that would fit through Sabaut's tunnel, were with them.

"Flynn, you help take the paintings back through the sewer to the Place de la Concorde," said Pichet. "The coach is waiting there with a police escort. It will take you and the paintings to a safe distance. The roads out of the city are clear now."

"With respect, Monsieur le Commissaire. Capitaine Arnault is up there with you," Flynn said. "As a Europol consultant I report directly to her. The paintings can go. I'll stay here at the Louvre and help in any way I can."

"Doctor Flynn," Gabrielle said. "Your job is only to advise me. You have advised me enough and there is nothing more you can do. Now go! That's an order!"

Flynn hesitated, remembering her face in the tunnel. She was right. He would only get in the way if he went upstairs and peered over her shoulder while she and the others tried to defuse the bomb. The paintings had to be taken to safety. But it still felt wrong to leave her there.

"All right," he said. "Just make sure I see you again."

"Are you absolutely certain there aren't any booby trap wires around the door of the bin?"

"Gabrielle. I'm as sure as I can be," said Lyudmila. "Would you like to take a look yourself?"

"Sorry. Go ahead and do what you think best. I'll call Flynn and see how far he's got with the paintings."

She stood away from the bomb and spoke into her radio.

"Flynn? Where are you?"

"We're about halfway back to the Place de la Concorde. You might want to turn your headset off while you're trying to disconnect the bomb. Your running commentary is making us all very nervous down here."

"Sorry. I'll only call you if there are any developments."

"Thanks. But I'm sure we'll be amongst the first to know if anything goes wrong."

"Okay. Out!"

She turned back to Lyudmila and Pichet.

"The first thing is to get access to the bomb," Lyudmila said. "To do that, we either have to get this door open, cut open the casing or approach it from the top through the ashtray. Any suggestions?"

"The access door's too obvious," said Pichet. "It could be a trap."

"Do you have an optic fibre camera?"

"I do."

"Let's use it to examine the underside of the ashtray and see if that's booby-trapped."

Lyudmila slipped a swan-necked device from her toolkit and inserted the end carefully into the gap between the ashtray and the inner bin. For a moment she gently manoeuvred the tip of the device while watching the little monitor.

"There's a mercury tilt switch taped right under the ashtray pan. If we move the bin or take the tray out, the fluid mercury inside will move, connect the two leads inside to make a circuit and trigger the bomb. But we can disarm it by freezing the mercury with liquid nitrogen, taking off the pan and cutting the circuit permanently."

She pulled a small steel cylinder like a tiny fire extinguisher from her pack, peered in through the opening, pointed the nozzle and pulled the trigger.

Gabrielle jumped at the sudden whoosh of gas that followed. A cloud of white vapour poured out of the bin and settled on the paving, frosting the slabs around the base of the bin. There was another whoosh, another cloud, and Lyudmila put on a pair of gloves, before leaning forward with a screwdriver.

In a moment the ashtray of the bin was off and a small frozen device lay exposed on top of the purple cylinder below. Pichet bent over it with a pair of wire clippers and carefully cut it out of the circuit.

"One down," he said. "Now we can try reaching the bomb."

Gabrielle switched on her radio.

"Flynn? Where are you?"

Flynn emerged into sweet-smelling air at the Place de la Concorde and looked back towards the Louvre, but it was just out of sight. The setting sun had turned the westward sky to an ominous fiery red, transforming the Eiffel Tower into a black steel skeleton.

"I'm out of the sewer. The coach and escort are here. We're loading the paintings now. The city's deserted. There isn't a helicopter in the sky or a car on the streets. How are you doing?"

"We have access to the bomb. We've jammed any radio trigger and defused a booby trap on the outer casing. We'll be going for the main trigger in a few minutes. Just get as far away as you can."

He turned to the coach. The museum technicians and the RAID team had finished loading the paintings into the luggage compartment and were inside and waving at him to follow. Flynn looked back again, towards the Louvre

"Understood," he said. "Good luck."

Gabrielle turned back to Lyudmila and the RAID man. They were both bending over the bin, looking down on the purple cylinder inside.

"It must be nose-down inside the bin," said Lyudmila. "Either that or they've removed the workings of the bomb and placed it inside this new casing. Otherwise we'd be looking down on the pointed tip of the shell."

"Perhaps it was too heavy to transport in its original casing," said

Pichet. "In any event, having it in this thinner barrel will make it easier to cut into if we have to. Do you want to try from the top here or open the door and go in from the side?"

"Are you sure there are no booby traps on the door?"

"None that I can see," Lyudmila said. "We'll go in from the door. I can see an inspection plate opposite it on the inner casing. We should get direct access to the mechanism that way."

"The door opens with a simple Allen key," said Pichet. "Will you do it, or shall I?"

"Go ahead," said Lyudmila. "I'll watch for wires." And she picked up the torch and mirror to peer into the bin from the top while Pichet applied the Allen key to the lock on the door.

Gabrielle heard a click as the catch opened.

"Okay?" asked Pichet.

"Go ahead," Lyudmila said. "Gently. No, stop!"

She was too late. A high-pitched beeping split the still air of the courtyard. Pichet swung the door open. Gabrielle looked past him, to where a flat screen in the side of the purple casing was showing a digital display counting down from 20 . . . 19 . . . 18 . . . 17

She switched on her radio headset.

"Flynn!" she screamed. "Get as far away as you can. It's going to blow!"

14

"Oh my God!"

Flynn glanced back up the Seine and then screamed at the bus driver.

"Go! Go! Go! The bomb's going to explode!"

For a second the driver didn't believe him. Then he turned, saw Flynn's radio headset and the look on his face. The bus accelerated frantically between the pair of motorcycles waiting to escort it, knocking Flynn off his feet as it raced across the Pont de la Concorde and skidded onto the deserted Quai d'Orsay, heading west towards the Eiffel Tower.

They were well within the danger zone of the nuclear explosion. Their only hope was to get the coach far enough around the curve of the river to shield themselves from the x-rays, heat radiation and blast wave that would come swooping down on them at any moment.

Flynn pulled himself upright as the bus shot forward along the river bank. He knew the initial flash of the bomb could blind him. But, as the great lattice needle of the Tour Eiffel soared above them on the left, he couldn't resist a glance towards the Louvre.

"Gabrielle!" he said out loud. "I'm sorry!"

For Gabrielle, time stood still. Her vision narrowed into a tunnel like the barrel of a gun. Pichet and Lyudmila still stood next to the bomb—Pichet staring at the open flap and Lyudmila scrabbling in her toolkit.

For a split second she thought of running to the shelter of the archway to the inner courtyard.

Then the impossibility of escape hit her.

In a few seconds she'd be part of a nuclear fireball as hot as the core of the sun. The beautiful statues that stared down at her from the walls of the courtyard, the hundreds of thousands of priceless artworks all around her and the magnificent buildings of the city, for kilometres around, would be vaporised, demolished, devastated.

She heard Flynn's voice in her headset.

Then, as the seconds ticked away to nothing, Gabrielle closed her eyes. She thought of Felipe and her parents.

She heard her own voice call out to him —

A loud crack echoed around the Cour Napoléon, followed by darkness.

Flynn held his balance as the coach careered towards the bend in the Seine. He heard Gabrielle call out to Lyudmila and Pichet over his radio — followed by what sounded like a gunshot.

"Gabrielle!"

He looked back. Above the trees and rooftops of the city, where the Louvre must have been, a strange purple cloud rose to meet the light of the setting sun.

Gabrielle opened her eyes. She was alive. The darkness all around her dissolved into a strange purple mist that turned to dust as she watched. Her whole body was plastered with it. As the cloud thinned she saw the outline of the courtyard and the great glass pyramid softened by an even coating of purple.

"Lyudmila? Commissaire Pichet?"

A pair of shapeless purple forms on the ground next to the open bin moved and became two living people. Lyudmila and Pichet got to their feet and tried to rub the purple dust from their eyes. Gabrielle ran to them. Apart from a few cuts and scratches, they seemed intact.

"What happened?" grunted Pichet like a man waking from a dream. "We should all be dead."

Gabrielle turned to the bin. The nose of the purple canister had blown clean off. Inside, it was empty. Above them, in the light afternoon wind, a cloud of powdered dye drifted slowly westwards to the Seine.

"Is the dust radioactive?"

Lyudmila reached down for her Geiger counter, wiped the dust off the display and turned the device on.

"It's clean," she said, shaking her head in bewilderment. "It has to be some kind of joke."

A terrible thought dawned on Gabrielle.

"Flynn!" she screamed into her headset. "The bomb's a decoy! Get back here with the paintings as fast as you can!"

"What?"

The bus and its escort had just made the turn by the Musée Chirac onto the Quai Branly out of direct line of sight of the bomb. The driver shouted a warning and pointed across the river. Flynn squinted against the setting sun and shielded his eyes with his hand.

Shooting towards them at right angles across the approaching Pont d'Iéna bridge from the north bank of the Seine was a pair of drab-painted Range Rovers and a large black van. The thought flashed through Flynn's mind that they must be part of the French military.

Then the first Range Rover veered right, ploughed through the two motorcycles in their escort and sent them spinning into the air. The second veered behind them out of sight, just as the black van smashed into the coach, slamming it across the central divide of the road, onto the opposite pavement and through a hedge into the main turnstile to the Eiffel Tower.

Flynn was thrown forward against the bar in front of his seat. The breath whooshed from his lungs and the world spun as he toppled over the bar and into the coach stairwell. He heard the crash of glass, the shouts of the other men in the bus and the boom of a shot being fired at close range. His mouth, eyes and nose were assaulted by the searing fire of tear gas, blinding him instantly and closing his throat. Fighting back the pain, he staggered to his feet, punched the emergency release for the door and fell headlong onto the pavement, gasping for air.

Through the tears streaming from his eyes he saw the second Range Rover pull to a stop and spew heavily armed men in gas masks and combat suits. Bolt cutters were being used on the luggage compartment of the coach. The security cases containing the paintings they'd just rescued from the Louvre were being yanked out.

A man yelled and a shot zipped above Flynn's head. He flattened himself against the tarmac, playing dead. But even as the shock of what was happening washed over him some small, still part of his mind wondered how on earth whoever was robbing them ever planned to get the paintings out of Paris with so many police and army personnel in a cordon around the city.

Then the thundering whine of a powerful helicopter pounded overhead. Sliding past the Eiffel Tower for a perfect landing in the Parc du Champ de Mars was the bulbous insect shape of a giant MiG-31 jet helicopter, its enormous rotors thrashing the air and the setting sun glistening on its plexiglass canopy. The armed men surrounding the bus looked up, fired warning shots above the heads of those on the ground and ran between the four great legs of the Tower towards the waiting machine, taking the paintings with them.

Flynn heard the distant wail of sirens coming from the other side of the Seine.

Then the low roar of the Russian helicopter rose to a shrill scream as it lifted off, tilted forward and shot straight down the Parc du Champ, skimming the tightly mown lawns and neat flower beds and sliding over the École Militaire. In a few seconds it had vanished into the growing darkness to the east and the only sounds Flynn could hear were the coughing of tortured lungs from the men in the coach and the rising shriek of approaching sirens.

The *Mona Lisa* and nine of the most valuable paintings in the world had just been stolen.

15

"This has to be the greatest confidence trick in history," snapped Jacques Retour, addressing the assembled RAID, Police and Europol personnel in the main operations room of the Préfecture de Police, "and we have been the world's greatest fools."

Gabrielle was in hell. The accusing eyes of the Préfet fixed on her and at once she was a little girl again, standing in the stone-flagged kitchen in Roscoff while her father scolded her for some childish crime. She'd betrayed Felipe's dream and lost the greatest art treasures in France. COMMETT was doomed. Her career was ended. When this meeting was over she'd find a quiet corner somewhere and kill herself.

Flynn stood next to her. His eyes were red-rimmed from the tear gas and a plaster covered a cut on his forehead. Beside him were Lyudmila and Commissaire Pichet, both looking self-conscious. Like Gabrielle, purple dye stained their hair and faces. Outside the window, the chop of helicopters, the constant wail of sirens and the honk of horns filled the night air as the city crawled its way back to normality.

"There will be hell to pay for this," continued Retour, stepping forward to stand in front of Gabrielle. "The President himself has summoned me to explain this outrage, the Ministry of Justice wants my head and every news outlet in the world is demanding to know what happened here today. In the meantime we've put out the story that the missing paintings were removed to be repaired following the release of dye in the museum forecourt by an unnamed protest group claiming reparations for Africa, but it's only a matter of time before the real story comes out. When that happens I shall resign. I blame myself for listening to the advice I was fed by the Police, the Gendarmerie and, most of all, by our so-called advisors from Europol. Capitaine Arnault, I have already drafted a formal complaint to your superiors in The Hague. You and your team will be lucky to have jobs by the time you return."

"With due respect, Monsieur le Préfet," said Commissaire Pichet. "I was the one who formally requested Europol to assist us. I would also like to point out that Doctor Flynn did warn us that this situation was not what it seemed, and I ignored his advice and proceeded as if it was a real threat, along with your full support, Monsieur le Préfet. Capitaine Arnault conducted herself with extreme bravery when she stayed behind with her colleague to dismantle what we all believed was a fully armed nuclear device. The blame for this incident does not rest with her alone, or with Europol, but also with ourselves here in Paris."

"Very gallant, Commissaire," snapped Retour, glaring at him. "But I'm sure that, in the long and exhaustive enquiries that will inevitably follow this whole debacle, many questions will be asked as to why convicted criminals such as Jean-Jacques Sabaut and other so-called 'civilian advisers' from Europol were allowed to influence the police and security forces of France in an operation that led to the theft of the greatest art treasures in the world from right under their noses."

"But Monsieur le Préfet. . ."

"Enough!" shouted Retour. "I am summoned by the President. Commissaire Pichet, you may stand your men down, but make sure our Europol advisors remain in the building. I'll need to speak to them again when I return."

He stormed out of the room. Gabrielle heard the door slam.

"I'm sorry," Pichet said, turning to her as the meeting broke up and the various representatives filed out of the room to make their own reports to their various department heads. "Monsieur Retour is in an impossible position. He alone is responsible for security matters in Paris and it is he who has to answer for all this to the President and the people of France. To save his job he must find someone else to blame. You and your team are the most convenient scapegoats. I'm sorry about this, and I'll support you in whatever way I can. Good luck."

He saluted Gabrielle and led his men out of the room, leaving her with Constance, Lyudmila and Flynn. Gabrielle slumped down at the conference table, torn between immediately resigning her post and trying to think of a way to salvage COMMETT from this terrible disaster. The purple dye would take weeks to work itself out of her hair. For a while nobody spoke.

"Where is Jean-Jacques anyway?" asked Flynn.

"I don't know," Constance said. "I haven't seen him since the fake bomb exploded and everything went crazy."

There was another long silence, broken again by Flynn.

"You have to take your hat off to them though, don't you?"

"I don't understand," Gabrielle said. "Who are you talking about?"

"I mean—whoever pulled off this scam. Just think about it for a moment. They create a non-existent terrorist organisation that represents a cause any of us would support—the relief of poverty and oppression in Africa. Then they persuade the combined forces of the French Police and Gendarmerie, along with Europol and the Musée du Louvre to help them remove the ten most priceless paintings in the world from a high security facility and deliver them on a plate. And, as if that wasn't enough, they then convince the French authorities to remove all police cars from the streets and all helicopters from the skies so the paintings can be stolen without anyone giving chase. Whoever put that plan together is brilliant, imaginative and incredibly well resourced."

"You actually admire them?"

"Don't you?"

"No! I certainly do not!" Gabrielle snapped. "They've deprived the entire world of ten priceless works of art, including the consummate piece of artistic genius on this planet. They've disrupted the city of Paris, and they've cost me my job as well as the future of COMMETT, which includes you and everyone else in this room. So if you appreciate strategies, Doctor Flynn, give me a plan to get those paintings back!"

"That was going to be my next move," Flynn said, easing himself into a chair opposite her at the conference table, leaning back and closing his eyes. "The obvious key to retrieving those artworks is to find out who's responsible—"

"Obviously!"

"This Justice for Africa organisation is a front. Nobody's ever heard of it and nobody else has claimed responsibility for what happened here today. If Justice for Africa were a bona fide African interest group they'd be shouting about the success they've just had all over the media. Let's face it, it's the biggest publicity stunt in support of their cause they could ever dream of!"

Constance poured a cup of coffee from a flask, set it on the table in front of Gabrielle and sat down beside her.

"So who do you think we're dealing with?" she asked.

"Only three kinds of organisation look for access to nuclear weapons," explained Flynn. "The first would be a national government. I think we can rule them out, since the theft of the Mona Lisa certainly isn't good diplomacy. The second would be a terrorist organisation. But you'll remember, right from the start, I said that was unlikely. Terrorists explode their bombs without warning for revenge, to provoke their victims into political action of some kind, or to demonstrate their power and attract new followers. That wasn't the case here."

"So who else is left?" asked Constance.

"Obviously a criminal gang," Flynn said. "We already know a criminal conspiracy to smuggle nuclear weapons into Europe exists. That was proved to us in Barcelona—"

"Some gang!" cut in Constance. "They have trained men with guns, a jet helicopter and even a nuclear weapon. What kind of criminal organisation has access to resources like that?"

"The Russian mafia," Flynn said, "which worries me a great deal. If we're about to go up against an organisation as powerful as that, I think we should fly back to Barcelona and ask our friend Gorshkov a few more questions first."

16

To Gabrielle, as she woke in the same seat of the same aircraft she'd arrived in from Brussels with Flynn the previous night, the last thirty-six hours had been a bad dream.

After a series of heated conference calls with Commander Parkinson and various members of the Management Board of Europol, followed by the drafting of a long and detailed report on everything that had happened, she felt exhausted, humiliated and demoralised. All she wanted to do was sleep. But they'd be landing back in Barcelona in a few moments and she needed to be sharp. She put the file on Gorshkov she'd been reading down on the seat next to her and hoped the Spanish police would be more co-operative than the authorities she'd left behind in France.

Flynn sat across the aisle from her with a laptop on his knee, tapping keys and sucking on the legs of his reading glasses.

"Like I said in Paris, we're up against some fierce opposition," he muttered, almost to himself.

"What do you mean?"

"I mean the Russian mafia. Did you know they control forty percent of private business and sixty percent of state-owned companies in Russia, along with eighty percent of all Russian banks. They don't hesitate to use extreme violence and they take on unemployed assassins from the armed forces and security services to do it. There are ten thousand fatal shootings every year in Russia. This case is starting to worry me."

"It was the fall of Communism," Gabrielle said. "Organised crime moved in and filled the void left by the system. The security forces were underpaid and demoralised. They couldn't cope."

"That's who Gorshkov works for," Flynn said.

"No wonder the Spanish police haven't been able to get any information out of him. Why would he be afraid of them when he has the protection of an organisation as powerful as that?"

"On the contrary, I'd say that right now Gorshkov is very much afraid—not of the Spanish police, but of what his masters in the Russian mafia will do to him for allowing himself to be caught with that second nuclear device. Right now, I'd say the last thing Gorshkov wants is his freedom."

"So what do you suggest we do?" asked Gabrielle. "Request the Spanish authorities to turn him free?"

"Not exactly, but conspiracy and suspicion are in the blood of men like Gorshkov. They look for them everywhere. You know those Russian dolls, the ones that fit inside each other? The Russian mind is like that. They expect nothing to be what it seems."

"How will that help us?"

"When we get to Barcelona, I'll show you," said Flynn.

The headquarters of Barcelona Municipal Police is a large modern office building, completely out of place amongst the traditional Spanish architecture around it to the west of La Rambla, the main thoroughfare of the city. The front lobby, which features an enquiry desk, a waiting room and, frequently, a long queue of petty crime victims, leads into a large open-plan area and side offices where detectives and police officers work. Beside the building, looking north, is a large car park and at the back are the interrogation rooms and holding cells.

It was in one of these rooms that Alexandr Anatolevich Gorshkov sat at the bare metal table, waiting for his visitors from Europol . The interrogation room, although Spartan and functional, was like a five-star hotel compared to most of the torture chambers he'd worked in during his time with the KGB and, later, its successor the FSB. His Spanish interrogators, while probably considered *hombres duros* or 'hard men' by their peers, were limited by their own laws from using the kind of methods Gorshkov had practiced during his career. The food was edible and the bed in his cell was tolerable. In fact, Gorshkov felt far more comfortable here than he would have done outside on the street.

At least he was protected.

Gorshkov's lawyer, the young and ambitious man from Moscow sitting to his left, was good. In preparation for the Europol meeting, he'd pointed out that no sound or video recordings had been made during the entrapment on the ship, therefore no permanent record of what had been actually said existed. While Gorshkov didn't imagine that fact would prove much of a defence in court, particularly given the evidence of the bomb itself in his possession, it would at least slow the prosecution down. Gorshkov didn't want the Spanish authorities to act quickly, nor did he expect them to. He'd been part of a bureaucracy most of his life and knew how such organisations worked. What he wanted most of all, was to remain within the protective walls of the Spanish police headquarters for as long as he could, to give his masters in Moscow time to cool down.

To slow the process of justice as much as possible, Gorshkov had insisted his lawyer be present at all of the interrogations and that, feigning ignorance of any other language, he would speak through him in Russian. That, of course, had frustrated the Spanish authorities even further, and delayed his interrogations even more. The door of the interrogation room opened. A police stenographer entered, followed by the Europol representatives he'd been told to expect.

They were the man and a woman they'd sent to trap him on the ship.

The dark-haired man with the beard spoke fluent Russian. That would make things more difficult. Gorshkov watched him as he pulled two chairs forward and sat down at the table with the woman, facing him. The man's eyes were red-rimmed and sunken and there was a cut above his eye. He looked exhausted.

Gorshkov, who himself was an expert at interrogation technique, felt he could use that to his advantage.

The young woman, the one with the tight body of a ballerina, had traces of purple around her hairline. Gorshkov smiled when he noticed it.

"A pity your lady friend doesn't speak our language," he said to the man in Russian. "I see she's had what you call 'a bad hair day'. Is that how you say it?"

"You know what happened in Paris then, Alexandr Anatolevich?" replied the man, again in Russian.

"I watch the news. They allow me that."

"You're very confident. I understand you have a good lawyer and that he's claiming entrapment and wrongful arrest."

"Your Russian's very good, my friend. And yes, that's exactly what he's claiming."

"The reason I speak Russian, Alexandr Anatolevich, is because I learned it from Russian instructors in Libya and, later on, in Moscow. I'm also a student of Russian history, particularly the period of the middle and late twentieth century. You know what a *suka* is?"

Gorshkov smiled and shook his head. "Do you mean literally or figuratively?"

"Please don't toy with me, Alexandr Anatolevich. You know very well what I mean."

"Meant literally, *suka* is the Russian word for 'bitch'," explained Gorshkov amiably. "But you and I both know that the term is also used to describe a criminal who's decided to cooperate with the police. I'm no *suka*. I've done nothing wrong. I've committed no crime, so I've nobody to betray anything to."

Gorshkov's lawyer leant forward from his notes. "Can I ask what the point of all this questioning is?" he said.

"Let him continue," said Gorshkov, who was in no hurry. "This history lesson is fascinating."

"During the Second World War," said the man, "Josef Stalin made an offer to imprisoned criminals. In exchange for their service on the western front against the Nazis, he said he'd give them a full pardon at the end of the war. But, when hostilities ceased, he broke his promise and sent those prisoners who'd fought for Russia back to prison. These men were immediately branded as collaborators by their fellow prisoners, even though they'd betrayed nobody. Many of them were set upon and killed. Those were the 'Bitch Wars', Alexandr Anatolevich. Do you see any parallels here to your own case? What are those who hired you to provide the bomb promising? And will they keep their promise once they think you've collaborated with us to identify them?"

A shiver of unease passed through Gorshkov's body.

"I must protest," said his lawyer. "Are you insinuating that my client is part of a criminal conspiracy?"

The man laid a cardboard file on the table. It carried a dark blue circle with yellow stars and the word Europol.

"This file details your client's long association with the Solntsevskaya mafia group in Moscow," he said. "And his remarks about my colleague's hair just now indicate that he knows exactly what went on at the Louvre yesterday and who was behind it, even though precise details of what happened were not released to the press. I also know—because I was present on his ship at the time with my colleague here—that your client offered to sell us a Russian atomic artillery shell of an identical type to the casing found at the Louvre yesterday as part of that same elaborate hoax to steal paintings valued at over three billion dollars."

"You cannot prove what my client told you aboard his ship," said Gorshkov's lawyer. "It's hearsay. As for that file, I demand to know the source of your information."

The man smiled pleasantly. His eyes bored straight into Gorshkov's.

"I don't need to prove anything," he said. "All I need to do is suggest a possible scenario."

"Let's hear it," said Gorshkov, staring defiantly back at the man. "Although I know it's going to be rubbish."

"Let's say a man who'd committed a crime for a powerful criminal organisation got caught and fell into the hands of the police," said the man. "Whose interests would be best served by having him dead — the police, who want him alive to get information on his employers, or the criminals themselves, who want to keep their secrets safe and remain anonymous? It's only a hypothetical situation, you understand, Alexandr Anatolevich. I'm sure your employers have your welfare at heart at all times."

It was exactly the scenario that Gorshkov himself most feared. Bad enough that he'd made a serious error of judgement in his desire to boost his retirement fund at their expense, but if the men in Moscow thought he was about to betray them, even the walls of the Barcelona police headquarters would be no protection. He felt himself sweating, even though the air conditioning was whirring above his head at full blast.

"I don't see how the situation you describe pertains to my client," said Gorshkov's lawyer. "He's done nothing wrong."

"To practical considerations then," replied the man. "Do you know if the windows on this cell are made of bulletproof glass to protect your client from snipers? Does anyone test your client's drinking water to make sure it isn't poisoned or check his food before he eats it? Is he guarded day and night against assassination? And were you, his legal representative, appointed by the court or by someone else — someone with interests in Moscow perhaps?"

"What are you implying?" snapped Gorshkov's lawyer.

"Nothing. I'm simply asking practical questions. If your client was, hypothetically speaking, working for a powerful criminal organisation, they'd know he was being held here in this facility. If you were in their place, would you keep whatever promises you'd made regarding his safety, or would you take the cheaper and far safer option of silencing him forever? It's just a hypothetical question, you understand, but I'd like your client to think about it carefully, while he's here in Barcelona with time on his hands."

Gorshkov was very worried now. He'd heard stories of what happened to people who displeased the big men in Moscow, stories that made him shudder.

"You may leave us for a while," he said to his lawyer. "And I want that woman with the purple hair out of here too, along with the police stenographer."

The lawyer protested, but finally got to his feet and followed the two women out of the room.

When he was alone with the dark-haired man, Gorshkov said,

"I have a serious problem."

"Tell me about it, Alexandr Anatolevich. Perhaps I can help."

"I'll explain it to you this way. Let's pretend I work for a chemical company that needs fresh orange peel as the raw ingredient for some new drug they've created and a rival chemical company wants the oranges too. There are only so many oranges and I need them all to meet my employers' needs. What should I do?"

"You tell me."

"I talk to my rivals," said Gorshkov, "and I learn that while my company needs the peel, the other only needs the juice inside, so we strike a deal and everybody's happy."

"How is that relevant?"

"A while ago I was approached by a cruel and powerful man, representing the sort of people in Moscow you describe, to obtain and deliver a small atomic bomb. Then, shortly afterwards, another rich customer I'd worked with in the past came to me looking for a second device. No sooner had I acquired those two weapons from Kazakhstan than I received your order for two more. That left me in the awkward position of having orders for four bombs, but only possessing two. So I talked to my original customers and found that, while my Moscow buyer was anxious to purchase the inner workings of a warhead, the other only needed the outer casing to give the impression that the real bomb was inside. So I held back one complete weapon to satisfy you, sold the core of the second bomb to my Moscow client and the outer casing to the other. My problem is that I told neither of them that the other existed. My Moscow client is a vengeful man. If he thinks that what my second client did in Paris with the casing he bought from me will in any way jeopardise his own plans, he'll kill that man and me along with him. That's why I'm going to take you up on your offer of protection."

The man shook his head sadly.

"Alexandr Anatolevich. You have two problems, not one. Tell me now, who was the client you sold the casing to and what's happened to the bomb mechanism you removed and sold?"

But Gorshkov was still enough of a businessman to know when to drive a hard bargain.

"If I tell you their names now," he said. "What's to stop you just walking away? No. You get me out of here to somewhere the men in Moscow won't be able to reach me and then I'll talk."

"We may have a deal," said the man. "My colleague has a private jet at the airport. If you agree to come with us we can be safely inside Europol's headquarters in The Hague in two hours and you can talk to our superiors there."

Gabrielle stood up from her seat in the open-plan area as Flynn came out of the interrogation room.

"There were two other buyers," he said, "one for the inner workings of the second bomb and one for the outer casing. If we can track down the first buyer we take the bomb out of circulation and, if we track down the second, we get the paintings back."

There was still hope! Gabrielle felt a wave of relief break over her. If they could recover both the paintings and the bomb, Europol would have to keep COMMETT alive.

"But we need to get Gorshkov to a safer location right now," continued Flynn. "I wasn't kidding him when I said he's in great danger. Either of those buyers, particularly the one with the real bomb, needs him dead as soon as possible."

"I'll call the jet and get a take-off slot," she said. "You talk to the Spanish police about an armed escort to get us to the airport."

She pulled out her mobile phone and dialled. Behind her, she heard Flynn talking to a senior officer. The man shouted an order and immediately, two armed police officers appeared outside the interrogation room door. Gorshkov's lawyer was protesting, but getting nowhere. He stormed off into the lobby and disappeared. She reached the jet, got a take-off slot for within the hour and called Europol. Flynn returned at the head of an armed escort—six uniformed men and women in bulletproof vests and riot helmets.

"They have an armoured van coming round to the car park," he said. "We'll ride with them to the airport."

Two men brought Gorshkov out of the interrogation room.

"We meet again, Madame." said Gorshkov in perfect French. "Good to see you again."

"Indeed," said Gabrielle, trying to hide the excitement in her voice, and followed him and his escort to the side entrance of the station. Outside in the car park, a rain shower was pattering off the roofs of the parked cars and turning the tarmac a glossy black.

The police van was too high to reverse right up to the door and stood parked about three metres away with its back doors open. Gabrielle saw two officers waiting inside the van. The others had donned waterproof jackets and formed a narrow gauntlet leading up to it. Flynn was beside Gorshkov, on his right, leading him. Gabrielle was just behind and to his left. They stepped out into the open.

"In spite of what I said earlier, the purple colour in your hair is really quite attractive," said Gorshkov, turning to her. "It sets off your—"

Gorshkov's great bald head exploded with a sound like a baseball bat hitting a ripe melon, ripping off the back of his skull and splattering his brains over Gabrielle's face in a spray of blood.

"Sniper!" screamed Flynn. "Get down!"

Gabrielle froze, as Gorshkov's lifeless body crashed backwards onto the wet concrete. Flynn reached out and grabbed her, pulling her down. Her hands went to her mouth, frantically scrubbing her lips to keep out the blood and brains. Finally, she fell forward onto her knees and vomited behind the van, her stomach churning and heaving as the nightmare scene replayed itself over and over in her mind.

Chernenko, the assassin, quickly dismantled the specially adapted SV-98 sniper's rifle and arranged the components into their allotted trays in the customised violin case on the bed of the hotel room. Chernenko had used an earlier model of the same silenced gun to kill Taliban leaders in Afghanistan during the Russian occupation and knew it was accurate to a thousand metres. The shot that had just killed Gorshkov, taken quickly over only a hundred metres across the dual carriageway leading into the city, was a challenging but by no means impossible assignment for someone who had once been a member of the Russian Olympic rifle team and had killed so many people so efficiently in the course of their career.

The first death had been Chernenko's father back in Leningrad, when Chernenko had been no more than twelve years old. The man had been a drunk and a sadist, who abused his children and beat their mother systematically over the years until she finally escaped him by dying of a brain haemorrhage in her sleep. His favourite method of torture had been to take the hands of any child who'd offended him and hold them as close as he could to the open fire. Chernenko could still smell the raw alcohol on his breath as he crept about their bedroom after dark; feel the course stubble of his chin and the heat of the flames, getting closer and closer.

One night, after a particularly sadistic torture session, Chernenko waited for him in the darkness at the top of the rickety flight of stairs leading up to their apartment. In the morning, the local police ruled that his death had been a simple accident and no questions were asked. That was when Chernenko realised how easy it was to kill.

To escape the grey misery of the state orphanage that followed, Chernenko had enlisted in the Russian army as one of its youngest recruits and excelled in every area of combat, particularly those that involved killing. Graduation to sniper school followed, which in turn led to four tours of duty in Afghanistan with the elite Spetsnaz commandos and a string of surgically performed executions.

But even now, after all the years, the one thing Chernenko could not abide was the stench of alcohol.

And the one thing Chernenko feared was fire.

Chernenko had no reason to doubt that Gorshkov was dead. The mercury-tipped 308 bullet had been designed to strike at the speed of sound and open out like the petals of a flower inside the target as it suddenly decelerated, expending all its energy outwards.

Its impact would have utterly destroyed Gorshkov.

Retrieving the single cartridge case the rifle had automatically ejected onto the carpet, Chernenko took the violin case, went to the hotel room door and attached the pre-printed 'This room is ready for service' label to the outside of the knob, before leaving.

Nobody paid any attention to the well-dressed musician with the wide-brimmed hat and violin case who strode through the hotel lobby a few moments later, raised a large black umbrella against the rain and the gaze of the security cameras, and hailed a taxi.

17

Gabrielle sat huddled on the bed of her hotel room as the sun rose over Barcelona, clasping her hands across her chest and shivering. She felt she was made of porcelain. Her heart was an inflating balloon in the centre of her chest. In a moment, unless she stopped holding herself together, the balloon would swell until it shattered her body into a million pieces just like . . . just like Gorshkov's head.

That obscene moment played over and over in her mind like a repeating video clip . . . Gorshkov turning and smiling . . . his bald head coming round and back . . . and the awful sound of bursting . . . . over and over and over . . .

She'd showered again and again at the police station. She'd scrubbed her face until it stung. She'd given all her clothes to be burned and taken a set of police overalls instead.

But nothing could remove the awful metallic taste in her mouth or the grotesque images that had been seared into her memory . . . round and back and burst . . .

The rest of the day, like the one before in Paris, had been a round of witness statements, reports and recriminations. What did Gorshkov really know? Who was his lawyer talking to on his cell phone outside the interrogation room? Where was that lawyer now?

The Spanish police had no idea who had killed Gorshkov. The only evidence they had was his mutilated body, a collection of misshapen bullet fragments and minute traces of gunshot residues from a hotel room overlooking the rear entrance of the police station. Hair and fibre analysis of the room had shown nothing, since it had taken over an hour to identify the source of the shot and nobody had thought to tell the hotel cleaning staff not to do their job in the meantime.

Flynn told Gabrielle she was in shock. He said there was no point making the trip back to Paris that night.

"Get some rest and we'll fly back in the morning when you feel better," he'd said.

But Gabrielle couldn't sleep. She felt no more rested now than when she'd gone to bed.

She'd just finished dressing when her cell phone rang. The number was familiar.

"Gabrielle. This is Parkinson speaking from Europol. Are you alone?"

"Yes sir. I am."

"I need you to return to The Hague and report to me in person as soon as possible."

"But I emailed my report on yesterday's incident here in Barcelona to you last night, Commander. I've also been debriefed by the Spanish authorities. They've agreed to forward details of that session to you."

"I need to talk to you in person, Gabrielle. There are things we need to discuss about the future of COMMETT."

She sat back down on the bed.

"What things, sir?"

"I'm sure you can guess. The incident at the Louvre has attracted a great deal of attention, and all of it negative. We've had protests from the highest levels and the very existence of Europol itself has been called into question. I'll not permit this organisation to be completely undermined because of one stupid failure, no matter how much criticism it gets."

"I understand, sir."

"Do you really? Then you can imagine what we must discuss when we meet."

"You want to disband COMMETT."

Parkinson paused for a moment.

"Yes. I'm afraid so. I also understand you've been under a great deal of strain this last forty-eight hours, and that you witnessed a particularly vicious murder at very close range yesterday. Is that true?"

The image of Gorshkov's death flashed in front of her eyes . . . round and back and burst . . .

"Yes, sir."

Parkinson's voice softened.

"You underwent trauma therapy after that terrible incident in Madrid, didn't you?"

"Yes, Commander."

"Have you been attending counselling since?"

"Not for some time, sir."

"I think it's time you took sick leave, Gabrielle. Report to me tomorrow in The Hague, and then you're relieved of duty for a month. We'll discuss your reassignment back to RAID when you're fit to take up your position again."

"But Commander—"

"Thank you, Capitaine Arnault. Please bring your identification and security passes with you when you come."

The line went dead.

Gabrielle replaced the receiver and held herself tight across the shoulders. The balloon in her chest was at bursting point. In a moment, she'd shatter into a million pieces.

She heard a knock at the door, and Flynn's voice.

"Gabrielle? Come on. The plane's waiting."

"It's open," she said in a voice that sounded as if it was coming from far away. "Come in."

"What's wrong?" said Flynn when he saw her face.

"We've been disbanded. That was Parkinson on the phone."

Flynn put down the overnight bag he was carrying.

"Shite," he said. "I'm sorry. How long have we got?"

"I don't know. I have to report back to The Hague today and then I'm on sick leave for a month. I'm to be reassigned back to RAID. Europol will probably pay you the balance of your contract and then terminate your services. You won't be out of pocket."

Flynn ran his fingers through his hair and took a deep breath, as if he was looking for the right words.

"Look, Gabrielle," he said. "I really am sorry. You tried so hard to make this work."

She felt her body tear open under the pressure of the balloon in her chest. The pain burst out in great whooping sobs that she couldn't control. She had failed . . . failed . . . failed. In her mind she saw Felipe and her parents that one last time at Atocha station and heard the awful sound of Gorshkov's head bursting under the impact of the bullet.

Flynn gently shut the hotel room door, sat down awkwardly on the bed beside her and put his arm around her shoulder.

"Look," he said clumsily. "COMMETT was ahead of its time. Bureaucracies like Europol aren't ready for radical thinking like that. You're a good police officer. You'll bounce back."

"But I *had* to make it work. I *had* to make it succeed."

"I know. Perhaps a few weeks off isn't a bad idea. You're a professional. You've been under a lot of stress, seen a lot of trauma. Take some rest. Lie in the sun. COMMETT was a great idea. You'll have others."

"You don't understand," she sobbed. "It wasn't my idea. It was his."

"Who?"

"Felipe Rodriguez, my fiancé. COMMETT was his idea, his brainchild. Not mine. He said there had to be a better way . . . a way to understand why these things happened. Bringing in experts like you was his idea, not mine."

"Was he the young man in the photo in your office?"

"We worked on the project together," Gabrielle said, wiping her eyes. "We did the research, we looked at costs and feasibility . . . and we got carried away in the excitement of it all. Getting married seemed the most natural thing in the world to do. But it wasn't right. I knew that on the morning he died."

"I'm sorry —"

"You have to help me get those paintings back!" she said, turning suddenly to face him. "It's the only way we can save COMMETT and keep Felipe's idea alive."

Flynn pulled back from her and raised his hands.

"Whoa, Gabrielle. You're upset. You're probably still in shock. Let's not make any hasty decisions right now. Getting those paintings back from the Russian mafia would be very, very dangerous, even with the full support of Europol, which we don't have any more, so let's just wait a while and leave things sit. Okay?"

"But you have contacts. Jean-Jacques Sabaut said you knew people in the art world, people with connections, people who might be able to help us track down the paintings."

Flynn got to his feet. "This is way too dangerous for us to get mixed up in on our own. I know how you feel, but let's just get back to the airport and we can talk some more about it on the plane."

He picked up his bag, then lifted hers from the bed. To Gabrielle, seeing him lift her case on the presumption that she had to follow it was just too much.

"And to think Felipe wanted to hire *you*!" she shouted at him, "the great Doctor Damien Flynn who knew so much about terrorism! The world expert! The author! The man with all the answers! Pichet was right, you're nothing but a 'tame terrorist'. You don't care about anything but your own skin —"

"Don't ever tell me that I don't care," Flynn snapped. "I fucking care and I've got the fucking scars to prove it. I just don't want to get myself killed that's all—or you!"

Flynn picked up his bag. His hands shook.

"Come on," he said. "The plane's waiting on us."

Gabrielle's phone rang.

"Gabrielle?" said Pichet. "We have a problem in Paris."

"What is it?"

"Jean-Jacques Sabaut's gone missing. At first we thought he'd just run off somewhere, but we sent a man round to his old apartment and found what appears to be a suicide note."

18

The taxi dropped Gabrielle and Flynn next to a Starbucks in a pedestrian area off the Boulevard de Sébastopol. Street theatre was in progress on the wide steps outside the Pompidou Centre. Black wooden silhouettes of human beings were being laid flat on the ground every second to symbolise a death in Africa.

"That's as far as I can take you," said the driver. "The damned *flics* have closed the rest of the road."

Gabrielle looked past the lines of postcard racks and souvenir stalls to where a pair of police cars blocked a side street. The entrance was cordoned off with incident tape. A crowd of sightseers had gathered. A TV crew lurked, watching and waiting for anything worth filming.

"Thank you," she said, and handed over the fare. "Just back up a bit before you drop us off. I don't want to get out too close to the cameras."

"Were you part of that thing the other day?" asked the driver nodding to the black silhouettes outside the Pompidou centre. "That hoax at the Louvre? Those guys really stuck it to the *flics*, didn't they? Forced them to clear the whole city and then let off a fake bomb. Clever bastards. I hope they get away with it."

Gabrielle got out of the cab and walked with Flynn to the police line. "I'm with Europol," she said to the nearest policeman and showed him her identification. "This man's with me."

The gendarme looked at the photo on the pass and at Gabrielle and Flynn. Then he waved them through.

"Commissaire Pichet asked us to expect you," he said. "It's the last house on the right. You see the guards on the door? Just tell them who you are."

She ducked under the tape and down a narrow street. Book shops, restaurants and beauty salons shouldered each other. The aroma of Indian, Chinese and Mexican cooking mingled with the scent of hairspray and overflowing rubbish bins. At the end of the street, just before it joined the Rue Étienne Marcel, was an old house, divided into apartments. A gendarme who looked young enough to have just left school stood next to the open door.

"The forensic people have been here already, Capitaine," he explained, after she'd identified herself. "But I'm on strict orders not to let anyone in unaccompanied."

"That's quite all right," Gabrielle said. "You can show us around."

He led them down a long, dark corridor that reeked of cat, to a flight of stone steps and an ancient elevator with a worn brass cage over the door. They climbed the stairs and entered an inner courtyard overlooked by the windows of the apartments above. Most of the windows were open.

Faces peered down and then withdrew out of sight.

"Hardly the Paris Hilton, is it?" said Flynn.

Jean-Jacques Sabaut's apartment was all on one level. A small kitchen and dining area gave way to a spacious studio under a large roof window framing the sky. Furniture was sparse: a futon, a desk with a laptop and an inkjet printer with plenty of paper. The futon had been stripped of all its bedclothes. There were dark stains on the thin mattress and an abandoned white cane. Traces of black fingerprint dust still lingered on the paintwork, like soot.

"Just wear these if you want to touch anything," said the young gendarme, and handed her a pair of surgical gloves.

"Looks like signs of foul play," asked Gabrielle, "any other evidence of a struggle?"

"Nothing beyond the blood stains on the bed," the gendarme said, "but no body. The sheets have been taken to forensics. We also found an empty bottle of painkillers, but I heard he suffered from back pain ever since the accident that blinded him, so that was nothing unusual. The reason the investigators suspect suicide, is because he left a note. It was typed on the computer and printed out."

"Do we know what it said?" asked Flynn.

The gendarme held out a white envelope.

"Are you Damien Flynn?" he asked.

"That's right."

"Then this is for you. It isn't the original. The police have that. Commissaire Pichet asked us to print out a copy for you before the original went to the lab for tests."

"Why hold a copy of the note for me?" asked Flynn.

"Because it was addressed to you specifically, Monsieur."

Gabrielle watched Flynn take the envelope, open the letter and read it.

"Fuck!" he said. His hand shook as he passed the single sheet to her.

"My dear Damien, I couldn't leave without apologising to you personally for the embarrassment and inconvenience you must be experiencing in the wake of my actions over the last two days. Years ago, as I told your colleague Gabrielle, I broke into the Louvre to steal *La Giaconda* and replace it with the perfect replica my dear wife Nicole had created. I did this as a gesture of defiance to the art establishment and to demonstrate my wife's genius to the critics who drove her to her death.

Since then, confined by my blindness and my bitterness, I've had time to think. I dreamed of an even greater scheme to demonstrate the futility of the art world and the vanity it generates.

The scheme you and your colleagues so valiantly tried to thwart here in Paris this week was my own personal creation, a masterpiece of criminal art worthy of the pieces it removed from the Louvre.

My deepest regret is that you will be cruelly rewarded for your faith in me with disgrace and ridicule. I cannot live with that guilt.

As a last special favour to me, I would like you to make sure that the self-portrait of Nicole is delivered as a token of my sincere apology to Constance, who still has eyes to gaze upon my wife's beauty. She loved Nicole, and I know she misses her, as I do. Try to forgive me if you can.

Your friend.

Jean-Jacques Sabaut."

Gabrielle reread the letter, feeling the ground shifting beneath her feet, trying to make sense of it all as the new reality set in.

"He played us all for fools," Flynn said, slumping down into the chair next to the desk. "And I fell for it. Fuck!"

Gabrielle read the note again and laid it gently on the desk. Then she moved to the wall next to the kitchenette and looked up at the framed portrait of a beautiful woman with gold and silver hair.

"She looks very sad," she said, reaching up and touching the frame. "But I wonder if Jean-Jacques really was the kind of man to take his own life?"

Gabrielle turned and looked around the room, trying to remember the conversation she'd had with Sabaut just before the mission and how he'd spoken of his wife's death, weighing different arguments in her own mind.

"Sabaut was blind and in constant pain," said Flynn. "He'd lost the woman he loved. He . . ."

"But he'd lived with that loss for years. He'd been blind for years. According to this note, he'd plotted and planned for years to carry out the most ambitious art theft in history and he'd actually made it work. Why kill himself now, on the completion of this 'masterpiece' of his? Nobody would have suspected him if it wasn't for this confession. Besides, if it was a suicide, where's his body?"

"But there's nothing beyond a few blood spots on the bed to make it look like foul play," Flynn said, "It has to be suicide. Perhaps he took a taxi to the Seine and drowned himself?"

Gabrielle read the letter again. "If you take out just one line, you'd have a confession and not a suicide note at all," she said. "See? There at the end. If you delete 'and I cannot live with that guilt' he could be just typing you a confession before going into hiding."

She turned to the desk where Sabaut's computer stood. The 'ready' light was still on.

Flynn got to his feet and stared at the portrait of Sabaut's wife.

"She was very beautiful, wasn't she?" He ran his fingers over the heavy frame of the picture, lost in thought.

"This computer," said Gabrielle to the young gendarme. "Have the police touched it?"

"They dusted it for prints. They'll take it down to their lab when you're finished and analyse what's on it."

Gabrielle moved the mouse. The machine flashed into life and a synthetic voice said "Computer ready."

"It's a screen reader," said Flynn. "A programme that allows blind people to hear what's on the screen. You can turn it off here," and he pressed three keys on the keyboard. The computer screen cleared to show lines of text.

"Look," Gabrielle said. "The note's still up. Come over here. I want you both to witness this."

She placed the printed copy of the note Sabaut had left Flynn on the desk and compared it to the live version on screen. They were identical. Then she moved the cursor to the curved backward arrow at the top of the screen to undo the last edits made to the document.

The sentence 'And I cannot live with that guilt' vanished.

"There," she said. "I was right. Either Sabaut inserted that sentence into the note himself at the last minute or someone else arrived and did it for him. Let's look at the document history."

She brought up File, Properties and General on the screen. A list of times scrolled in front of her; when the document was created, when it was modified and when it was last accessed.

"You see," she said. "He created that file at 8:35 pm just after the robbery, but it was modified an hour later at 9:40 pm. Do the police know when Jean-Jacques went missing?"

"Nobody noticed him leaving the apartment that night," said the gendarme. "And even if they did, they're not saying."

"Then perhaps we should be looking for other clues. Did he send any emails?"

She opened the email facility. There had been no sent messages for twenty-four hours and only spam messages coming in.

"Jean-Jacques was with us at the Préfecture all day on Wednesday during the robbery," she said. "He was missing by the time we came back to be debriefed. He would not have . . ."

"Click on that," said Flynn, pointing to the inbox.

It was an e-ticket confirmation for an airline flight departing from Paris, Charles de Gaulle for Turkey at 09:00 on the day after the robbery.

"Did the police find his passport here in the apartment?" asked Gabrielle.

"No," said the young gendarme.

"Had he packed any bags?"

"Let's see," said Flynn. He looked around the apartment, opening cupboards and wardrobes. Above them, high on the wall, was a small trapdoor that led into the roof space. Grabbing a chair, Flynn stood on it, clicked the catch open and peered inside. He reached in, pulled out a small backpack and lowered it down to Gabrielle. She undid the flap and peered inside. There were neatly folded clothes and a washbag.

"Check the front pocket," Flynn said.

Gabrielle did so and pulled out a passport and printed boarding pass, both in the name of Jean-Jacques Sabaut.

"There's no way a blind man who could hardly walk could have hidden this bag up here," Flynn said. "Besides, why would anyone with an airline reservation and packed bags leave a suicide note? Jean-Jacques was abducted. We'd better go and tell Constance."

19

To Gabrielle, the wrought iron railings, the tall windows and the polished bellpush of the exclusive apartment building off the Boulevard Haussmann spoke of history, traditional values and a great deal of money.

Flynn laid the carefully wrapped painting on the scrubbed limestone doorstep while she pressed the buzzer for apartment number six. A voice answered.

"Constance?" she said. "It's Gabrielle Arnault and Damien Flynn. We need to talk to you."

She heard a distant buzz and the heavy wooden door clicked open. A modern elevator, equipped with a security camera and an emergency telephone, transported them to a narrow corridor at the very top of the building, lined with ferns and framed Victorian prints of Parisian life.

The apartment door was already ajar. It led to a tastefully decorated hallway hung with Salvador Dali reproductions. Gabrielle paused for a moment in front of the portrait *Gala Nude Seen From Behind*. For a moment she was struck by how similar it was to the painting of Sabaut's wife, Nicole.

"Isn't it wonderful how Dali managed to capture the flow of her hair?" said Constance from the doorway. "Come on in, both of you. Has there been any word of Jean-Jacques?"

They walked through into the lounge. Gabrielle took in the high ceiling, the huge glass doors to the balcony overlooking the city and, incongruous in that tasteful apartment, a bank of industrial metal shelving that heaved under the weight of flatscreen monitors, hard drives, tower units, printers and scanners. A thick rope of coiled electric leads snaked to a bank of sockets mounted low on the wall. A large-screen laptop sat in pride of place in the centre of a work table, in front of a modern orthopaedic swivel chair.

"There's been nothing," Flynn said. "We were wondering if you might know anything."

"I haven't seen him since that evening in the Préfecture," said Constance. "I tried phoning the authorities to see if they knew where he was and I phoned his apartment, in case he was there. I even called round. But there was nothing from anyone. That was when I called Commissaire Pichet and asked for the gendarmes to look inside. I've heard nothing since."

Flynn set the painting down next to the computer desk and took Sabaut's note from his pocket. He unfolded it and handed it to Constance.

"It looks like bad news, I'm afraid. He left this."

Constance Le Clerc read the note. Her hand went to her mouth.

"This has to be some kind of joke," she said, moving unsteadily to the swivel chair and sitting down. "Was Jean-Jacques really behind all this?"

"He was part of it, if you believe that letter," Flynn said. "He says he did it for the same reason he stole the *Mona Lisa* the first time, to avenge his wife's death."

Constance stared at the note again, shaking her head.

"So he fooled us all," she said, almost to herself, "even me!"

"He fooled everyone," Flynn said.

"But then why would Jean-Jacques take his own life?" said Constance. "He'd beaten everyone. He'd had his revenge. He must have been paid a king's ransom to get those paintings. Why kill himself now, when he'd won?"

"We don't think he did," said Gabrielle. "There was no body and his passport and travel documents were still at his apartment. Even his white cane was left behind. Flynn thinks he was abducted and perhaps murdered. There were also blood spots on the bed."

"But who would take him?"

"Probably the same people who financed the raid on the Louvre," said Flynn. "Another witness, a man who arranged to supply the bomb casing booby trap Gabrielle encountered, was assassinated in police custody in Barcelona yesterday. Perhaps whoever was backing Jean-Jacques was just tidying up loose ends."

Constance's hands went to her mouth.

"So Jean-Jacques's dead?"

"It's possible," Gabrielle said. "I'm sorry, Constance."

"Oh no . . ."

Constance turned to the wall and started to cry. Gabrielle put her arms around her and held her. Flynn got up and paced to and fro across the apartment.

Finally Constance raised her head, dried her eyes on a handkerchief and pointed to the package Flynn had brought.

"And that's the self-portrait of Nicole, the one he refers to in his note?"

"It is," Flynn said, lifting the painting from beside the computer desk and handing it to her. "He wanted you to have it."

Constance took the portrait over to the dining table in the centre of the room, undid the packing and stared down at the sad and beautiful face looking up at her from the canvas.

"Oh Nicole," she said, softly stroking her thick forefinger over the painted face, "We were students when we met, young and passionate. For a long time I was jealous of Jean-Jacques when he won her away from me. Is there anything we can do to find out what really happened to him?"

"Not in any official capacity," Gabrielle said, "COMMETT is being disbanded and I have to report in person to The Hague. Then I'm on enforced sick leave for a month, pending a re-assignment to RAID."

"Then how about unofficially?" asked Flynn, nodding his head to the bank of computer equipment behind Constance. "You haven't left Europol yet, have you? Chances are you still have access to their databases, right?"

Gabrielle was tired. The last few days had been the worst since she'd lost her family in Madrid.

"I don't know."

"Why don't we try it and see?" Flynn said. "Constance? Is that all right with you?"

Constance nodded and powered up the machines. Then she rose from her chair, so that Gabrielle could take her place at the keyboard.

"What do you want me to do?" Gabrielle said, looking up at Flynn.

"I want you to forget the rules and regulations for a few minutes, mon Capitaine," said Flynn. "And get us some information."

"I'll not do anything illegal," Gabrielle said.

"You don't have to," said Flynn. "You'd be doing a little extracurricular research on a particular facet of organised crime. You're allowed to do that at Europol, aren't you?"

She held her breath while the computer searched for a connection to the Europol website, typed in her virtual network username and password and the screen cleared.

"I'm online to Europol," she said.

"Ask yourself," Flynn said, pulling up a chair beside her, "what hard facts do we have about this case?"

"We know the Russian mafia's involved," Gabrielle said.

"And we can assume that whoever backed Jean-Jacques in stealing the pictures has an interest in art," Constance said, "either as a collector, or as a supplier to collectors."

"Then we need to identify collectors who specialise in valuable and illegally obtained works of art," Gabrielle said. "And there can't be many of those, certainly not many who would have the money, men and machines behind the raid on the Louvre and still be able to buy the complete secrecy they'd need to stay out of jail."

"How do we do that?" asked Flynn.

"Simple," said Gabrielle. "We pull up the Forbes list of the wealthiest men in Russia. Then we identify those interested in art and cross-reference them with the Europol and Interpol databases. There may be crosschecks available from the Russian security service records, but I doubt it. They aren't as open with information as they should be simply because they don't want anyone else to know how far behind they've fallen in the fight against organised crime."

She typed furiously for a few minutes and then turned the screen so that both Flynn and Constance could see it. "That's the top one hundred richest people in Russia. See anyone you recognise?"

"I don't," Flynn said, "but I do remember that list caused quite a stir in the Russian business community when it came out. A lot of rich people got very frightened because they thought the Russian mafia would start taking an interest in them . . ."

"Or perhaps they were worried that the authorities might start asking questions as to how they came to be on the Forbes list in the first place?" said Constance.

"Indeed," Flynn said. "Now save that list and see if you can bring up the Europol or Interpol lists of known Russian mafia contacts."

"That might take a bit longer," Gabrielle said.

"No problem," said Flynn. "After all, it's not like we have jobs to rush off to now, is it?"

In an hour's time they were staring at a list of fifty names.

"I had no idea so many business leaders in Russia had criminal connections," Constance said.

Gabrielle nodded. "If they were all arrested at once, the economy of Russia would be knocked back to the Stone Age. But fifty names are still a lot to investigate in detail."

Constance said, "Then how about trying to find a connection with the Louvre robbery? We could Google a list of the top art collectors in Russia and Europol's list of known dealers in stolen art."

"There are a dozen matches," Gabrielle reported after a few moments searching.

"But what if the final customer for the *Mona Lisa* and the other pieces from the Louvre is a person with no obvious connections to the

Russian mafia?" said Flynn. "That would really upset our analysis."

"What else do we know?" asked Gabrielle. "Let's searh Gorshkov's file. He's the only Russian mafia connection we're sure of."

She pulled up the information. Gorshkov's photo on his Europol file brought back the nightmare of his head snapping back under the impact of that bullet the day before.

Gabrielle took a deep breath to steady herself. " 'Alexandr Anatolevich Gorshkov, former Colonel in the Second Directorate of the KGB . . . responsible for domestic counterintelligence and internal security, including the hunting of foreign spies and domestic traitors in the USSR.' The Second Directorate was also responsible for countering organized crime. That must have been where Gorshkov made his contacts in the first place."

"He had an import-export company as a legitimate front for his smuggling activities," Flynn said. "Is there anything on that?"

"Yes," said Gabrielle, pointing at the screen. "A great deal of information. Gorshkov's company operated in both the Caspian and the Black Sea. Most of its business was tied up with the oil industry in the Caspian. There are offices in Atyrau, that service the Kashagan offshore oilfields, and also in Baku in Azerbaijan, supplying the refineries and offshore installations."

"Do any of the names on our list of potential suspects have contacts with the Caspian oil industry?" asked Flynn.

"Eleven," Gabrielle said. "Spread between Baku and Atyrau."

"Interesting. If Jean-Jacques had been meaning to meet Gorshkov before he disappeared, could he have flown to either of those places from Turkey?"

Gabrielle did a search. "There are direct flights to Baku with Aeroflot and Turkish Airlines. A flight to Atyrau in Kazakhstan would have involved changes, but it's still possible."

"I suppose there's no way to access Gorshkov's company files from here?" asked Constance.

"I doubt it. The police in Barcelona were trying to obtain them. Europol was also after them through the Russian police, but neither succeeded."

"I may have a contact who could help us," Flynn said. "Since none of us have much to do at the moment, perhaps we should give him a call."

He went to the window at the far end of the room, took out his cellphone, checked the address book and dialled.

Gabrielle heard a muffled conversation taking place. Then Flynn came back, grinning broadly.

"Good news," he said. "He's willing to meet us in person and, in view of where he is and what he's doing, I think we should take him up on his offer."

"We still have to get back to The Hague," Gabrielle said. "I have to report."

"You're still thinking like a policewoman," said Flynn. "You'll be a lot better prepared to face Europol if you start thinking like a criminal for a change. Believe me."

20

The interior of Finnegan's Irish Pub would have looked perfectly at home in Dublin, Cork or Belfast. The walls above the dark wood panelling under the high ceiling were hung with Irish flags, hurling jerseys and battered wooden *sliothars*, while the muddied faces of Gaelic football squads beamed victoriously from framed photographs. A huge sign displaying the familiar long-billed toucan bird and the words 'St. James's Gate – Home of Guinness' dominated the bar. The same clientele Flynn would have expected to find in any Irish city pub—young office workers and pressurised executives with open ties—fought to catch the eyes of staff to get a bite of lunch and a drink before heading back to the office.

But to Flynn, the marvellous thing about Finnegan's Irish Pub was that it had been built, not in Ireland, but on the eastern shore of the Caspian Sea in the oil city of Baku, capital of Azerbaijan.

The ginger-haired man, sitting alone with a notebook and a voice recorder at a corner table had always meant trouble for Flynn. Gerry Murphy was the kind of journalist who always posed the awkward question, always knew the right 'anonymous source' to ask when nobody else would tell him the truth, and who could never be bought off. In short, he was extremely good at his job.

"Damien," he said, wiping the head of a freshly pulled pint of stout from his lips and beckoning to Flynn and Gabrielle to join him. "What'll you have? The Guinness here is the best outside Dublin. I swear to God!"

"A pint then," said Flynn. "Gerry, this is a friend of mine, Gabrielle Arnault. She's a freelancer doing a story for *Paris Match* on the oil industry and pollution in the Caspian Sea."

Murphy winked at Flynn and held out his hand to Gabrielle.

"*Enchanté*, Madame. I should be so lucky to have friends as beautiful as you. And there's plenty of oil industry and pollution around here for you to write about. What can I get you to drink?"

"Pernod with ice, if they have it, thank you," Gabrielle said and they sat down.

"Since when did you make friends with journalists?" asked Murphy as he put the drinks in front of them. Flynn raised his pint, took a sip and smiled.

"Since I became an academic and learned the value of proper research. Miss Arnault's a friend of a friend. She was looking for an overview on what life's like out here for a colour piece in *Paris Match*. I was in town on another matter, knew you were working here and promised to set up a meeting. It's as simple as that."

"And what 'other matter' might that be?" asked Murphy, eyeing Flynn suspiciously.

Flynn took another sip of his beer. "You're right. The Guinness here's very good."

"And that's all?" Murphy asked.

"That's it."

"Like that friend of yours you and your brother asked me to help out in Belfast years ago? That ended up with me being questioned by the British Army for two days. I nearly lost my press card over that one."

"You'd have lost more than your press card if it hadn't been for me. Remember that time when a few of the lads wanted to kneecap you, or the time I had to vouch for you when they thought you were a spy and had that gun to your head?"

"I remember," Murphy said. "And I'm grateful. But will you promise me that, if I help you now, I'm not going to end up in jail?"

"I promise, on my mother's grave."

Murphy considered this for a moment.

"In that case, I also want you to promise me that when the shit hits the fan on whatever it is you're really up to out here, I get an exclusive on the story. Is that a deal?"

"It's a deal," Flynn said.

Murphy put down his pint and turned to Gabrielle.

"Right then, Madame. Where do you want me to start?"

Gabrielle reached into her bag, took out her own digital recorder and put it on the table next to Gerry's.

"Just background," she said. "It's an article on how western consumerism and industrial growth are causing environmental problems in other developing countries. Stories about chopping down the rain forests in South America to make mahogany drinks cabinets, destroying mangrove swamps in Asia with prawn farms to make scampi, polluting the Caspian so that rich people can fill their SUVs. That sort of thing."

"I'm impressed. I didn't know *Paris Match* took such things so seriously."

"Our readers do, Mr Murphy. Being 'green' is very chic, which makes our editors take notice. Is it okay if I use a recorder? My shorthand is not as fast as it could be."

"No problem."

"Okay, just for background. Tell me your thoughts on the impact of the oil industry here in Azerbaijan."

"Caspian Sea oil is to the western world what the riches of India were to nineteenth century Europe," said Gerry, with a journalist's gift of story, "So everyone in the civilized world wants a piece of the action. Total oil reserves here are second only to Saudi Arabia. They can pump out a million barrels a day right now and triple that over the next three years. The industry's had a big influence on things around the Caspian, particularly here in Azerbaijan, and across the water in Kazakhstan, where eighty percent of the oil reserves are located. That's where all the money from outside investors is going and why you can look around this bar and see so many foreigners in suits and ties."

"And who's putting all that money in?" asked Flynn.

Murphy looked at him, and then at Gabrielle.

"I thought she was supposed to be the journalist," he said.

"The companies, Mr Murphy?" Gabrielle said.

"All the big US names. Chevron's in Kazakhstan, and the Azerbaijani giant Socar's here, along with Azeroil and the Gazprom, which are both Russian. The Americans want the oil as cheaply and reliably as possible. The Russians want to make sure it all gets piped across their soil on the way out, so that they can charge huge taxes on it."

"But what argument can the Russians make for that?" asked Gabrielle.

"Let me show you," said Murphy. He cleared their glasses to the edge of the table, dipped his finger in his pint and drew a crude map on the glass top.

"The Caspian's as landlocked as a garden pond," he said. "Tanker ships can't get in or out. So every drop of oil that comes out of the Caspian fields has to be piped to an open body of water with a connection to the sea that tankers can reach."

"Like the Mediterranean?"

"Exactly, or the Black Sea to the west or even across Iran, Afghanistan or Pakistan to the Persian Gulf in the south. But, since those last three countries aren't on speaking terms with the west most of the time, the smart money's on a western pipeline through Russia to the Black Sea. There's even talk of a pipeline under the Caspian to link the Kazakh oil fields with those here off Azerbaijan and then run the whole lot from Baku straight through Russia to the Black Sea. The Russian oil company Azeroil's behind that one."

"That sounds like a huge project," said Gabrielle.

"Huge and astronomically expensive," said Gerry, taking a sip of his pint. "Rumour has it that the cost of an undersea pipeline's so high the price of oil would need to double to make it pay."

Gabrielle thought about this for a moment.

"But if the price of oil did go up and the project went ahead," she said, "then the Russians, and this company Azeroil in particular, would be sitting on an absolute goldmine with all the pipeline taxes to themselves, plus a secure export route from the Caspian free from all the political instability in Iran or Afghanistan."

"So the big money's to be made not in drilling the oil, but in getting it out?" Flynn said.

"Which paper did you say you worked for, Mr Flynn?" asked Murphy.

Flynn ignored the question. "I'm sure Madame Arnault is more interested in the personalities involved than the politics. That piece you did last year, Gerry, the one on the Russian oil billionaires, the oligarchs and their connections to the Russian mafia. That caused quite a stir. Did you ever get any backlash on that?"

"I'm glad to see you've been doing your homework," Murphy said. "But what's that got to do with Caspian oil and environmental pollution?"

"You always check your facts before you publish, Gerry. When you were researching that article, did you come across a guy called Gorshkov?"

Gerry put his pint down and stared at Flynn.

"Hey now, do you mean that smuggler who got shot in the head in Barcelona? You're not thinking of getting mixed up with that kind of shite, are you?"

"Gorshkov had an import-export company here in Baku?"

Gerry Murphy looked nervous. He glanced around the bar, like a wild animal checking its watering hole for predators.

"There," he said, leaning forward and switching off Gabrielle's recorder. "I knew all that *Paris Match* bullshit was just a front. You're not pushing some illegal scam to raise money for your friends in Belfast now, are you Damien? Because if that's your plan, this conversation ends here and now."

Flynn nodded to Gabrielle, who reached into her pocket, took out her Europol identification and discreetly showed it to Gerry.

"I'm sorry, Gerry" Flynn said. "But I didn't think you'd speak to us at all if you knew who we're working for."

"Damn right, I wouldn't. I may not speak to you even now."

"This is very important, Mr Murphy," Gabrielle said, slipping her Europol card back in her pocket. "People have died and a great many more people may be killed unless we have information. You won't be quoted as a source, or involved in any way, beyond simply giving us background information to help our investigation."

"And no comebacks?" said Murphy.

"None," Gabrielle said. "I promise."

Murphy glanced at Flynn. Then he leant forward again. "All right then," he whispered. "Word on the street here in Baku is that Gorshkov had contacts all over the place. Some say he was former KGB. Some say he had connections to the Russian mafia. If you wanted something done in a hurry, or you needed bits of equipment nobody else could get, then Gorshkov was your man, just as long as you had the money to pay for it. All the big oil companies used him, for all sorts of things. He could fix anything."

"And if I was to tell you that he also dealt in smuggled weapons, would that surprise you?" Flynn said.

Murphy shook his head. "Nothing would surprise me about Gorshkov. Arms smuggling wouldn't have been a problem to him at all."

Flynn glanced around the bar and leant forward.

"And if Miss Arnault here wanted to interview some of his office staff about the economic impact of the oil boom here in Azerbaijan, could you tell me where Gorshkov's offices might be?"

"Out at the Serebrovsky oil installation on Artyom Island," Gerry said. "It's east of the city on the peninsula. But you'll need to make an appointment and you'll need a really watertight cover story. Russian bureaucrats take their bureaucracies very seriously. I'll write down directions for you."

He scribbled a few lines on a page of his notebook, tore it off and handed it to Flynn.

"I'll make a call," Flynn said and, pulling out his mobile phone, went to the bar to borrow a local directory.

"Two things," said Gerry to Gabrielle as he watched Flynn.

"If you're going by taxi, make sure you give the driver these directions before you start off and make sure they follow them, otherwise they'll take you out into the middle of nowhere and threaten to leave you there unless you hand over your wallet."

"We're driving a hire car," Gabrielle said. "What's the other thing?"

"When you get to Gorshkov's office," Murphy said, looking up from the paper, "for Christ's sake, don't tell them I sent you."

Gabrielle followed Flynn out of Finnegan's into the sunshine and down Alizadeh Street to the tree-lined corniche with its wide promenade where they'd parked their hired car. To her right, the shining white palace of the Socar oil company stood, stark in the early afternoon sun. The three giant shards of glass making up the Baku Flame hotel towered above the mosques of the old city, which fought a losing battle against the rising crop of ultramodern buildings all around them. In front of her, the turquoise waters of the Caspian glittered across the trees of Primorsky Park and, from the centre of the bay, a fountain soared into the sky. The city was alive with energy, sunshine and the raw power of oil.

Oil was everywhere in Baku, in the shining new corporate headquarters of the oil companies and the fantastic architecture of the smart new hotels, in the business suits of the executives in Finnegan's and even in the air itself, where the faint scent of oil wafted in from the sea.

"I'll drive," said Flynn. "You navigate."

She wondered briefly what the drink-driving laws were in Azerbaijan, got into the car and belted herself in. There was no sense in courting disaster. Flynn turned the battered Volga and headed north around the walled citadel of the old city, past the airport and eastwards into the country.

Oil was here too. It dominated the landscape with the brown rusting skeletons of abandoned derricks towering into the sky and the nodding heads of pumps sucking the oil out of the land like giant metal mosquitoes. Then, as the road dipped down to a narrow bridge leading to Artyom Island, she saw that the oil industry had made its way out into the ocean. Stretching out to sea around the low-lying island was a fantastic man-made complex of raised roadways and oil derricks above the glitter of the waves.

The Atyrau offices of Gorshkov's company were housed in a grey concrete building just to the right of the main gates. On either side, a chain metal fence encircled a huge compound containing pipes, drilling bits and machinery of all kinds. Behind the building stood a modern warehouse the size of an aircraft hangar. It looked like a recent addition. Flynn parked the car. Gabrielle watched him press the ceramic bellpush and waited. Harsh Russian consonants barked through the wall-mounted intercom Flynn muttered a greeting, a magnetic lock buzzed and Gabrielle pushed the door open.

They were inside a drab reception area facing a desk. A young blonde woman wearing a telephone headset looked up from her computer. Flynn glanced down at the trade magazines littering a coffee table, picked one up and spoke to the receptionist. She nodded and reached for a telephone.

Flynn turned and smiled.

"I dropped the environmental angle," he whispered to Gabrielle. "When I called ahead from the bar I told her we're in the area to do a piece on the Trans-Caspian pipeline for a trade magazine and pretended our appointment had already been agreed with head office but mislaid on their system. You're the journalist and I'm selling advertising space. Is that okay with you?"

Before she could decide, the door behind the reception area opened. A small man with thick glasses and a thin moustache emerged. He seemed annoyed. Flynn spoke to him. Then the man turned to her and spoke in perfect French.

"*Desolé*, Madame. I had no idea an appointment had been fixed for today. You're from *Oil and Gas International*?"

Gabrielle patted her pockets, as if looking for a business card. "Indeed, Monsieur, my name is Marie-Therese Foucard, this is Patrick

Finnegan from our London office and we're doing an advertisement feature on the proposed Trans-Caspian pipeline. We understand your company is a major supplier of equipment and technology to some of the main contractors and we'd like to do a commercial profile. Perhaps we can also interest you in taking advertising space with us."

The man nodded. "I'm Mikhail Olegovich Komarov and I'm the general manager here. I have another meeting in fifteen minutes. Do you perhaps have identification from your paper? No? Well I'm sure I can give you enough general information to at least begin your article. Then, if there's anything else you need after that, you can always reach me here," and he passed Gabrielle a business card. "Please step into my office."

Komarov was as guarded in his answers to Gabrielle's questions as he could be, and confined any information he gave to general issues on the oil industry in Baku. Regarding his own operation in particular, he simply provided leaflets containing technical and general material, having first apologised for it being in Russian and not French. Flynn said they could translate.

"And is this the only operation your company has here on Artyom Island?" asked Gabrielle.

"All our operations on this side of the Caspian Sea are based here in these buildings," said Komarov guardedly. "The only other facility we have is a small warehouse out on the Serebrovsky complex. It's situated on a disused part of the walkways just offshore and kept for storing the explosive charges we use for seismic surveying. Our operations on the other side of the Caspian are based at another facility in Atyrau, from which we supply the Kazakh oilfields."

"Can I ask which of the main contractors your company supplies?"

"You mean their individual names?"

"That would be useful, yes."

Komarov turned to a brown cardboard folder and opened it. Gabrielle glimpsed a list of companies in Cyrillic script.

"Can I ask," he said, "why you need this information?"

"To give a better profile of your company," said Gabrielle.

Komarov looked at the folder again, ran his finger down the list of names and then closed it.

"I do apologise," he said. "But it's not our policy to give out printed lists. There's nothing personal about this. It's just that, in the past, publications such as yours have used our list to call our suppliers and pester them to buy advertising space. It gives us a bad name and the oil business is very competitive. I'm sure you understand."

"Indeed," Gabrielle said. "Those are all the questions I have Monsieur Komarov, but Monsieur Finnegan would like to talk to you about advertising."

Flynn then started to speak enthusiastically in Russian. Komarov responded monosyllabically. As Gabrielle watched, Flynn became more and more animated. He took the copy of *Oil and Gas International* he'd picked up in the reception area and moved a pile of papers on Komarov's desk so that he could place the magazine there to demonstrate the quality and depth of its coverage. An open file of documents fell to the floor. Gabrielle bent to help Komarov retrieve them. Flynn and Komarov talked for another minute or so. Then Flynn held up his hands as if in surrender to Komarov's defences, picked up the magazine and stood up.

"Thank you, Madame," said Komarov shaking Gabrielle's hand. "I'm sorry we can't take advertising space in this issue. Perhaps some other time."

"Thank you for your time this afternoon, Monsieur," Gabrielle said. "I hope we haven't delayed you from your meeting."

It was only when they'd driven two or three miles back towards Baku that Flynn reached into the glove compartment for the magazine and handed it to her.

"Page forty-two," he said. "Special industry feature."

She opened the magazine. Slipped inside between pages forty-two and forty-three was the typed list of companies that Gorshkov's company supplied that Flynn had stolen from Komarov's desk.

"I can translate that," Flynn said. "It would be worth cross-referencing the names of those companies with the lists of mafia interests, art lovers and oligarchs we drew up in Paris."

"And that other facility Gorshkov's company has, out on the edge of the complex," said Gabrielle, "the one where Komarov said they keep their explosives. It might be worth getting the authorities to investigate it for the second bomb."

"I've got a better idea that might save us some time," Flynn said.

21

In the darkness, the Serebrovsky oil complex looked almost beautiful. Moonlight softened the stark lines of the elevated roadways and the rusted lattices of oil gantries into a single black spider's web suspended over a silvery sea. Orange plumes of burning gas above the drilling platforms burst upwards towards the stars and glittered on the oily water below.

"Over there," Flynn said. "That hut on the outer perimeter."

Gabrielle pushed the handle on the old Johnson outboard to her right, swinging the bow of the inflatable dingy to the left, heading straight for the moon. She had serious doubts about doing things Flynn's way and had told him so from the start. Firstly, her training as a police officer told her this was an illegal search, an act of trespass in a foreign country and, as such, a criminal action for which they could both be arrested. Secondly, if that hut contained explosives, as Komarov had claimed, then it would more than likely be guarded and they could be caught. Thirdly, if it was guarded, the guards would have guns. She also wondered why Komarov had been so forthcoming with details about this facility when he'd been so guarded about everything else. She sensed a trap.

"We should go back to Baku and report this," she'd said.

But Flynn had no faith in the local authorities and had insisted that they needed to check things out themselves, which was why he'd gone to the trouble to hire this inflatable dinghy from a local fisherman for cash.

"We're the ones who are here *now*! Reporting back to Europol would take too long and the bomb could be moved," he said.

"And what if we're caught?"

"We won't be, not out here. They have strict security at the main gates, but nothing out to sea. Fishing boats weave in and out of those pilings all the time and nobody stops them. They probably don't want to upset the locals. Even if we do get into trouble, we can stick to our original story about being investigative journalists doing an environmental piece or, even better, we're a honeymoon couple who got lost. What could be more romantic than a moonlight cruise among the gas platforms?"

The only problem with Flynn's plan, from a practical point of view, was that he knew nothing about handling a boat. Gabrielle, on the other hand, had been trained to handle high-speed inflatables during her time with RAID.

"We'd better turn off the motor and row," she said. "We're getting close to the complex."

They changed places awkwardly, causing the dingy to rock. She fitted the light plastic oars to their rowlocks and started to row for the outermost platform.

"Just as I thought," Flynn said, "there's only one guard, back up there where the walkway to the store joins the main platform. He'll never see us in the dark."

The platform towered above them, blotting out the moon. To their left and right, rotting wooden pilings from the elevated walkways and other platforms soared out of the water, like titanic reeds. The stench of oil stung Gabrielle's nostrils; it was so heavy, she wondered why it didn't spontaneously combust.

The bow of the inflatable nudged against the piling. Flynn reached out and grabbed a rusted ladder, slippery with seaweed. Gabrielle secured the rope at the bow of the boat and peered up into the darkness. She could just make out the metal mesh and downward-pointing steel spikes of an antipersonnel barrier, halfway up.

"Don't worry," Flynn said, "I have bolt cutters," and started to climb. She heard him working in the darkness above her head, the whispered instruction to duck, and then the splash of something hitting the water near the boat.

"Come on up," hissed Flynn. "It's clear now."

She started to climb. Halfway up she reached the barrier and squeezed through the gap Flynn had made, making sure not to catch the case of the Geiger counter she'd brought on the metal spikes. Then she was right below him, near the top of the ladder, looking across to the floor of the shed.

"Over to the left," he pointed. "There's a hatch for lowering and raising the explosives straight into a boat. If we can reach that, we can climb inside and not worry about being seen from above."

She peered into the darkness. Metal supports for the platform reached under the shed into the darkness. They were very narrow. It was a thirty metre drop to the water, with any number of unyielding struts on the way.

"Can you make it?" she asked.

"No other way," Flynn said, and started to climb.

Gabrielle steadied herself on the ladder until she was sure of her balance and moved her foot. What was it her grandfather had always said, when she was small, about climbing trees?

'Always make sure you have two hands and one foot, or one hand and two feet, supporting you at any one time.'

She let go of the ladder and edged her way out over the water.

'Don't look down,' she told herself. 'Focus on the little details closest to you instead — that rusted bolt, this piece of rotted planking — little things.'

Flynn reached the trap door and pushed it open. She heard a thud, followed by a sharp curse, a distant clang and something hitting the water far below.

"I dropped the fucking bolt cutters," hissed Flynn. "But the hatch is open. Come on over and I'll help you through."

She shuffled over, reached up and felt him pull her into the pitch blackness of the shed. She got her torch and flicked it on.

"Jesus!" Flynn said, looking around. "Whatever you do, don't take out that cigarette lighter of yours!"

Stacked around them in a solid wall, broken only by the door of the shed, were bundles of explosive charges, wrapped in plastic sheeting and labelled with Cyrillic and Roman script. She could make out the words "Demolition Charge Type XIIc" on one of the labels.

"It's just what Komarov told us it was," Flynn said, "an explosives store."

"Perhaps," Gabrielle said. "But what's that?"

A large white object, about the size of a washing machine and wrapped in plastic sheeting, stood in the centre of the shed. Gabrielle moved towards it, pulled out the Geiger counter and switched it on. The distinctive crackle rose to a shrill hiss as she approached.

"What is it?" asked Flynn. "Is it the bomb?"

"I don't know. What does this say?"

An envelope of documents, sealed in plastic, had been attached to the straps that held the protective packaging in place. Flynn reached over, undid the Ziploc seal and eased the papers out. They were all in Russian.

"Shipping instructions," he said.

"But what for?".

"It's an X-ray machine."

Gabrielle swore under her breath. "The source of X-rays is radioactive material. They probably store it out here to keep it away from the personnel back at the main warehouse. Where's it being shipped to?"

"To the Azeroil Oil Company, at some depot in the Black Sea."

She looked around. There was nothing in the shed but the X-ray machine and row after row of explosives.

"It looks as if we've wasted our time," she said. "Photograph the machine and the documentation and let's get out of here."

They made their way back out of the trap door and across the support beams to the ladder, down through the antipersonnel barrier and back to the boat.

"Get the rope," said Gabrielle, sitting back at the oars. "I'll take us far enough off to start the motor without being heard."

She fitted the oars into the rowlocks. All around them, the giant piles of the oil complex loomed like trees in a flooded forest. Support girders arched above like branches and the silvery disc of the moon glittered on the water. The lights of the little fishing village they'd sailed from winked at them.

For a moment, some of them were blocked out by a moving shape, and then reappeared again. It happened a second time.

"Flynn?" she hissed. "There's another boat out there, between us and the land."

"What sort of . . ."

The unmistakeable scream of a ricochet whined just above them, echoing through the darkened forest below the platforms.

Gabrielle dived for the outboard and heaved on the starter cord. The old motor stuttered and died. A bullet zipped into the water close by. A powerful engine roared towards them. Gabrielle yanked the starter cord again and the motor coughed, fired and whirred into life. She pushed it into gear, wrenched the throttle round and turned to face Flynn.

"You look out ahead," she yelled above the clatter of the outboard motor. "I'll steer."

The little boat lurched forward into the black forest of pilings.

The high-powered engine throttling up behind them boomed in their ears.

They were picking up speed.

"Left!" screamed Flynn from the bow. Gabrielle rammed the handle of the motor over and the boat slewed wildly around a massive piling.

"Right!"

She hauled the boat round again, heard the slap of water against another piling and the scream of another ricochet on metal. The booming engine thundered in her ears. The other boat was already under the complex with them! How could it navigate at such speed in the dark?

Her own eyes were only now growing used to the gloom.

A piling loomed in front of her. Before Flynn could call out she had the boat in a tight lock to the left. They were in a stretch of clear water between the walkways and picking up speed.

"Move back!" she shouted at Flynn. "Move your weight back! We've got to get our boat up onto the plane!"

Flynn scrambled to the centre of the boat. Gabrielle twisted the throttle over as far as it could go. The little craft rose up, as if breaking free of some invisible cord, and skimmed across the surface of the sea. Gabrielle felt the wind in her hair and aimed for the next forest of pilings. They had no chance of outrunning whoever was after them. Their only hope was to outmanoeuvre them beneath the complex, shut down their engine and slip away silently in the darkness.

"Slow down, for Christ's sake," yelled Flynn as the complex towered above them. But then they were already in among the steel columns and at full throttle. Gabrielle had the measure of the pilings now. They were in rows. If she could stick between them, in clear water, they would be okay. The boat veered as she brought it round, dropped back for a moment as it lost speed, then shot up onto the plane again, heading in for the shore.

"Where are they?" she called to Flynn.

He twisted round to look. Gabrielle heard a sudden 'smack' and Flynn jerked backwards onto the floor of the boat.

"Are you hit!"

"Shite! Shite! Shite!" shouted Flynn. "The fuckers got my arm!"

"How bad is it?"

"They missed the bone," he snapped. "Just keep driving!"

Another shot screamed off the metalwork. Being in the open lanes between the pilings was giving the boat behind them a clear shot. She hauled the dinghy to the left, into the steel piping.

She glanced back. The other boat was gaining on them.

"Gabrielle! Look out!"

She was thrown forward on top of Flynn as their boat slammed into a piling, leapt up in the blackness and fell backwards, tipping them both into the sea.

22

Chernenko the assassin watched through infrared night-vision goggles as the other boat misjudged the space between the pilings, hit a steel pillar and capsized.

Chernenko had been tailing the occupants of that boat ever since a call had arrived earlier that day to say that an Irishman and a Frenchwoman had been asking questions at Gorshkov's company on Artyom Island and that a list of suppliers had gone missing. It had been a short flight to Baku, a quick briefing by Komarov at Gorshkov's office and a hasty assembly of men and equipment. A call to the local police had identified the two people as having hired a car at the airport and checked into a hotel.

Chernenko had tracked them to a fishing village near Artyom, watched them set sail in a dinghy, and had driven quickly back to the complex to commandeer the security boat. The men with Chernenko were all hand-picked. They knew how to handle a powerful craft at speed in the dark, just as Chernenko knew how to handle a silenced automatic rifle and a pair of night-vision goggles.

Chernenko looked down at the overturned dinghy, wallowing like a dying whale in the dark water, and raised the weapon again.

There was no point in leaving a job unfinished.

Gabrielle's world was nothing but the darkness, the cold and the rising scream of a high-speed propeller. She fought for the surface, burst through and found herself in the tiny space beneath the overturned dinghy. The oily water stung her eyes. A dark shape wriggled in the dim twilight below her. She drew a breath, dived down and pulled it back beneath the hull.

"Jesus!" gasped Flynn. "What the fuck happened?"

"We hit a piling," she stuttered through the cold. "Be quiet! They'll be listening for us."

The propeller softened to a growl as the other boat pulled alongside, searching for them in the water.

Her teeth chattered with the cold. Flynn had his hand to his shoulder. Black trails of blood oozed from his arm into the grey water. The murmur of propeller moved slowly round their upturned boat.

Would they flip it over and look underneath?

The zip of a bullet whizzing through the rubber tubes of their dinghy took her by surprise. It hissed into the water near her head, and was followed by the whoosh of escaping air. Another bullet sliced into their little cavern. Then another . . . and another.

The walls of the dinghy closed in as the tubes lost buoyancy. In a moment, the weight of the engine would pull the ruptured hull to the bottom of the Caspian, and them along with it. To surface outside meant getting shot, to stay where they were meant drowning. Gabrielle could make out the seaweed encrusted bulk of the column they'd just rammed.

"Take a deep breath," she stuttered. "We have to swim underwater and get on the far side of that piling where they can't see us."

Flynn nodded. He was shivering badly. If she didn't get him out of the water soon, he'd go into cold shock.

"We'll dive on 'three'," she said. "One . . . two . . . and three!"

She pushed off from the collapsing hull and dived down, kicking against the water and dragging Flynn with her towards the piling. The boat's engine throbbed in her ears. She reached out for the seaweed encrusting the metal, grabbed it to stop herself shooting upwards to the surface and held on hard to Flynn's jacket with her other hand.

Then she clawed her way round the piling, fighting against the buoyancy of her own lungs and Flynn's body, choking back her overpowering need to breathe, and finally eased her head gently above the water.

Flynn surfaced beside her. She heard his lungs whoop for air. Had the people in the boat heard it? She couldn't see them. Only the low burble of their engine told her they were just a few metres away, on the far side of the piling.

Voices spoke in Russian. Then came the muffled stutter of a silenced automatic weapon and the zip of bullets hitting the water, the metallic smack of an impact on something hollow and the sudden stink of petrol. They were shooting up the dying hull of their dinghy, just to be sure that it sank.

Someone swore and the engine noise rose again to a scream.

"Down!" she hissed, pushing Flynn underwater and drawing a breath as fast as she could before ducking beneath the surface. The engine shrieked as the boat tore around the piling, searching for them. She grabbed at the seaweed to hold her under. Her lungs heaved.

Gabrielle was going to drown. She knew it. Flynn was flailing next to her. She couldn't hold him any longer. He broke free.

She struggled to the surface, bracing her body for the bullets.

But the roar of the boat was fading. It had moved off.

"Shite!" stuttered Flynn. "Maybe it's time we made a move?"

Gabrielle peered through the pilings towards the land. It was no more than fifty metres away.

"Can you make it to shore?"

"I'll try," Flynn said.

"Come on then. I'll hold your head. Just kick with your legs."

It took them an hour to stagger along the shoreline, back to the cove where they'd left their hire car. Gabrielle had ripped the sleeves from her shirt to bandage Flynn's arm, but he was weak and listless from the blood he'd already lost in the water. They'd stumbled a dozen times before the silhouette of the old Volga came into view at the end of a dirt track leading to the shore.

Gabrielle raided the car's primitive first-aid kit, examined Flynn's arm and patched the neat entry and exit wounds near his shoulder. Then she wrapped him in a blanket and drove back to the bright lights of Baku, praying all the while they would not be pulled over by the police and that their attackers were not still watching.

"We . . . we can't go back to the hotel," stuttered Flynn. "Our bags are in the car . . . along with our passports and visas. I vote we go straight to the airport . . . and get the first plane out of Baku to anywhere in Europe."

"And what if you start bleeding?" said Gabrielle. "What then?"

"Then we . . . need a friend," Flynn said.

"Holy shite!" said Gerry Murphy as he opened the door of his apartment an hour later. "What the fuck have you been doing?"

"Research on the oil industry," Flynn said. "It's quite a cutthroat business these days."

"Seriously! Am I going to get deported for this?"

"We just need to get cleaned up and out of here, Mr Murphy," said Gabrielle. "We shouldn't be more than an hour at the most."

"I'll put the kettle on," Gerry said. "The bathroom's at the end of the hall and there's a spare bedroom on the right you can use to dump your things in."

Gabrielle helped Flynn to the bathroom and turned on the shower—warm enough to heat him, but not so hot as to cause what warmth remained deep in his body to flow to his skin and put him into cold shock.

"You're fussing, woman," stammered Flynn, as she tried to take off his shirt. "I'll do it! Leave me alone!"

"We need to get you bandaged and out of here as fast as we can," Gabrielle told him. "So let me help you. I can't have you bleeding all over the plane on the way home."

She pulled his shirt off and threw it into the bath. Pink streaks of blood flowed from the fabric across the white porcelain and into the plug hole. The left side of his vest was stained bright red to the waist. She reached down to strip it from him.

He grabbed her wrist as she lifted the stained garment over his head.

"Leave me alone!" snapped Flynn with sudden venom. "I told you I'd do it!"

"*Mon Dieu!*"

Stretching from Flynn's waist to the base of his neck was a criss-cross pattern of glistening white and purple scars that covered the entire area of his back like melted wax. Gabrielle gazed at them for a moment, trying to imagine what terrible injury had caused them and the pain Flynn must have felt.

He snatched the bloodstained vest, threw it into the bath with the shirt and staggered to the shower. The stench of oil filled the bathroom as hot water hit his skin.

"Get some brandy!" he said. "I'll be out in a minute."

Gabrielle went out into the bedroom and opened the first-aid kit she'd brought from the car. There were still enough bandages and plasters to cover Flynn's wound, with some to spare. She packed their clothes, and made sure their documents were in order. Then she went into the kitchen to see if Gerry had any brandy.

Flynn emerged from the bathroom wrapped in a towel. He had a bundle of red toilet paper clasped to his shoulder.

"It's stopped bleeding," he said. "Now where's that drink?"

"It's not good for you to take alcohol after you've been cold," Gabrielle said. "The rush of blood to your skin could severely reduce your core temperature and put you into shock."

"Just give me the fucking drink!" said Flynn, and slumped on the bed.

Gabrielle gave him the glass and started to treat his wound. It was a clean puncture of the upper left bicep, probably made by a high-velocity bullet.

"You'll need to get this checked out when we get back to The Hague," she said, as she tightened the bandage and pinned it up. "You don't want it to get infected."

Her eyes travelled down his spine to the lattice of scars. Flynn turned to face her.

"My brother Sean used to take me fishing," he said. "Back when we were kids. That's what you're wondering, isn't it, how I got those scars on my back? They're all over my arse as well, but I'd be too polite to show you those."

Gabrielle looked away. Flynn took a deep swig of brandy.

"I was sucked in," he said. "To understand it, you've got to know what a persuasive son-of-a-bitch my brother was. He was the life and soul of any party, the sort of man you'd want as your best friend, the sort of older brother a kid like me would kill for . . . which is what he asked me to do in the end. Our grandfather had been a member of the old IRA, the one that knocked hell out of the Black and Tans in 1916, just like your grandfather knocked hell out of the Nazis in World War II. We grew up on stories of flying columns ambushing army convoys and melting back into the countryside, of how the Brits nearly burned Cork City to the ground and how the mayor died on hunger strike.

"I went to college and studied history and politics. I had all these grand ideas about strategy and psychology. I put scenarios together about how Ireland could have beaten the Brits after 1916 and what might have happened after the Revolution if Michael Collins hadn't been shot—that sort of shite.

"Anyway, one day my brother Sean comes to visit me in my digs up in Cork and he tells me some friends of his are interested in my ideas and want to talk to me about them. So I take the train up to Belfast and that's it—I'm in. So fucking stupid!"

"Why..?" asked Gabrielle.

Flynn held her eyes in his for a moment and then looked back into his glass.

"The thing people don't understand about terrorism, even today, is how young people get brainwashed," he said. "Sean was my hero, like Robin Hood, Michael Collins, Yasser Arafat and even Osama Bin Laden were heroes to the young people who came behind them. They suck the kids in and the training they get once they're in tells them there's only two kinds of people in the world – 'us' and 'them'. That's what I heard all the time – 'if you're not with us, you're against us' – that's how a kid can put a bomb in a pub and blow people he doesn't even know to buggery and not lose a single night's sleep over it. He's doing it to 'them'—people he's been brainwashed to see only as the enemy, not as human beings like himself. He . . ."

But Gabrielle was a thousand kilometres away—back on the platform at Atocha Station, seeing Felipe's face turn towards her, seeing her mother smile and feeling the force of that terrible explosion as it hurled her against the side of the train.

"Do you know what the strongest motivation in the world is?" continued Flynn. "It isn't hunger. It isn't thirst. It isn't even sex. It's the feeling of injustice, the sense of being wronged. That was why I let my brother talk me into joining the IRA all those years ago. I'd heard the stories. I'd been brought up in Cork on the legends of the fighting columns and what the Black and Tans did to our people. I knew what was happening in the North, about the Bloody Sunday massacre. I felt the injustice and I got angry. So I swore the oath, I signed up and all the time it was that burning sense of injustice that drove me, that awful blinding feeling that we were right and they were wrong."

"Is that how you were able to kill those people in England?"

Flynn shook his head.

"Sean and I were on a mission," he said. "We had a van full of Semtex parked in the forecourt of a motorway service area where army coaches used to pull in for petrol and the soldiers could grab a bite to eat. There was just Sean and me in a car on the other side of the car park with the detonator, nobody else. Then a school bus pulls in alongside our van, at the same time the soldiers inside were finishing and about to come out."

Gabrielle stared at him, seeing him suddenly as someone different.

"Sean wanted to blow the lot of them to hell. It was 'us or them' he said. I wanted to save the kids. He gave me a minute to get the kids back on the bus and out of there. Then, when I was trying to round them all up, the bastard panicked and blew the bomb early."

Flynn drained his glass and set it down.

"They shot him stone-dead when he tried to drive away," he said. "My mother never forgave me, to the day she died."

Flynn turned and looked into her eyes.

"So you see, Gabrielle. We're both victims of terrorism, you and me. Now, let's get out of here, while we still can."

23

The train from Paris Centrale pulled into The Hague on time. Gabrielle and Flynn took a taxi to 47 Raamweg, just ahead of the rush-hour traffic and arrived at the headquarters of Europol a few minutes before 17:00. She presented her identity pass and security clearance card, and signed in Flynn as a visitor, with access no further than her own office on the fourth floor.

They'd been on the move for ten days since the Louvre raid. Flynn looked exhausted after their escape from the Caspian. His eyes were sunken and his face was drawn. Gabrielle thought she saw an extra fleck or two of grey in his hair. If he looks like that, she thought, what must I look like?

They'd arrived the previous afternoon in Paris and spent the night with Constance, who'd fussed over them both like a mother hen. Luckily Flynn's wound was clean and the field dressing Gabrielle had applied in Baku had prevented it from getting infected. Constance's doctor had inspected it that morning, applied a few stitches and a new dressing. Then he'd put Flynn on a heavy dose of painkillers and told him to keep the arm rested. Gabrielle thought the chances of that happening were slim to nil.

Her appointment with Parkinson had been arranged for 17:30. She led Flynn up to her office, slipped her laptop into its docking station and logged in.

"I presume the Europol network is password protected?" asked Flynn.

"Indeed it is."

"Because while you're up at your meeting, I thought I might do a bit more background research on our Mr Gorshkov. You'll have databases here that aren't normally accessible from outside. You wouldn't like to share your username and password with me by any chance, would you?"

"That would be highly irregular," she said.

"Even to a member of your own team?"

"COMMETT has been disbanded. I'm supposed to be on sick leave. I'll report what we've discovered to the Deputy Director, present the evidence to support our findings and leave it to him. That's all I can do."

Flynn draped himself on her sofa and gingerly placed his hand over his wounded shoulder.

"When are you ever going to lighten up, mon Capitaine?"

"My username is 'garnault'", she said. "My password is 'COMMETT', with a zero instead of an 'O'."

"Not very original," Flynn said. "But thanks."

She made her way to the lift and from there to the boardroom suite at the top of the building. The receptionist outside Parkinson's office looked up at her but said nothing. Her eyes held the sort of pity for Gabrielle one might give a person about to be executed by firing squad.

"He's expecting you, Capitaine Arnault," she said. "There are also two other members of the Management Board present. Please go right in."

Gabrielle opened the door. Two people faced her from the meeting table in front of Commander Parkinson's desk. She recognised them both. One was Señora Louisa Hernandez, the Spanish delegate to the Management Board who had questioned her with such intensity at the last meeting. The other, an older man with short grey hair, a thin face and steel-framed glasses, was Fritz Heydrich, the representative of the European Council of Ministers for Justice and Home Affairs, to which Europol was ultimately responsible. Both had thick files in front of them.

"Good afternoon, Capitaine Arnault," said Parkinson, a little stiffly, and made the introductions. "Please have a seat. I've read the email you sent me from Paris upon your arrival from the Caspian Sea and would like to talk to you about it. Señora Hernandez and Herr Heydrich would like to do the same. But first of all, I'd like to know what possessed you to travel all the way from Paris to Azerbaijan and what the hell you've been doing when I told you to report here directly to me?"

Gabrielle had anticipated this question, but was still disappointed by it. She felt she'd gone above and beyond the call of duty by taking the investigation to Baku with Flynn and thought that she deserved better than a reprimand.

"I was on sick leave, sir, on my own time."

Parkinson frowned at her. "That does not give you the right to break the law in a foreign country, Capitaine Arnault. Could you explain?"

Gabrielle glanced at Hernandez and Heydrich. They looked back at her, waiting for her answer.

"Before we left Paris, after the assassination of Alexandr Gorshkov in Barcelona, we visited the scene of Jean-Jacques Sabaut's abduction. There were bloodstains there that were subsequently analysed and found to belong to Sabaut. We—"

"But the Préfet de Police in Paris is satisfied that Sabaut's death was suicide," said Heydrich. "According to what Sabaut wrote in his note to this colleague of yours . . . this Doctor Damien Flynn . . he wasn't abducted by anyone."

Gabrielle turned to face him. "Jean-Jacques Sabaut had bookings for a plane to Turkey and his passport was close at hand. His bags had been packed and somebody had hidden them in a high cupboard which Monsieur Sabaut, because of his disabilities, could never have reached. Why does a man with those arrangements in place take his own life?"

"And who exactly witnessed the bags, the passport and the travel arrangements?" asked Heydrich, peering at her over the top of his glasses.

"Doctor Flynn and myself. The young officer at the scene saw them also. The travel arrangements had been made on Monsieur Sabaut's computer. That was still switched on when we got there. That's how we were able to pull out the document history of the so-called suicide note and discover it had been tampered with before it was printed."

"And do you have that computer now?"

"Of course not," said Gabrielle. "The police probably took it away as evidence, after we left."

"I dare say the full file on the case will be on my desk from the Préfet de Police before long," said Parkinson, making a note on the pad in front of him. "In your email to me on your return from Azerbaijan requesting this meeting, you suggest that a certain person connected to the Russian mafia may be ultimately responsible, not only for Jean-Jacques Sabaut's disappearance, but also the assassination of Gorshkov in Barcelona and the theft of paintings from the Louvre. On what evidence do you base this allegation?"

Hernandez and Heydrich stared at her again, anxious for an answer.

"Gorshkov the smuggler had connections with the Russian mafia," Gabrielle said. "He also ran a company that supplied engineering, technology and other services to the Caspian oil industry. Doctor Flynn and I had already cross-referenced various lists of people with Russian mafia connections who might have both the financial resources and the interest in art to have sponsored the raid on the Louvre. A number of names came up that were connected with Caspian oil. Two of those names have interests in companies that Gorshkov already had connections with through his legitimate businesses. One of those operations is about to be supplied by Gorshkov's company with a new X-ray machine. The chairman of that company is known to be a keen collector of art and a particular fan of the Italian Renaissance. That's why we went to Azerbaijan, to gather that information."

Señora Hernandez said nothing. Heydrich opened the file in front of him and took a silver propelling pencil from his pocket.

"My email to you, Commander Parkinson," Gabrielle continued, "simply asks that this man be investigated further using the full resources of Europol. I made no accusations, which might have constituted libel, in that mail nor do I make any slanderous allegations now. I simply suggest that further investigation is warranted."

"Thank you, Capitaine Arnault," Parkinson said, looking up from his notes. "Your point about libel and slander is well taken. In return I would remind you however that, as a member of Europol, you took the same oath taken by every member of the European Commission—to uphold the interests of the European Community. As a serving member of RAID, on secondment to us, you will have also signed confidentiality agreements that are legal and binding. In short, what we discuss here in this room is for your ears only. There is to be no discussion of it outside, with anyone. Is that clear?"

"Yes, sir," she said.

"How long have you known Damien Flynn?" asked Heydrich.

"Nine months."

He ticked a line of type on his file.

"You met him in Dublin when you recruited him to this COMMETT group of yours. Why was he selected?"

"Herr Heydrich, I've already explained Doctor Flynn's recruitment to COMMETT to the members of the Europol Management Board and so has Commander Parkinson. The principal of COMMETT is to use the best experts, whatever their disciplines and backgrounds. Doctor Flynn was recommended to me and to Commander Parkinson by Capitaine Felipe Rodriguez, the man who . . ."

"Was your fiancé?" suggested Heydrich. "That is true, isn't it?"

"Yes. He was my fiancé. And, as I was going to say, was the person who conceived COMMETT."

"Captain Rodriguez was killed in the Madrid bombings, along with your parents?" Heydrich ticked another line of type on his file. "You yourself were injured in the blast."

"Yes."

"So his recommendation was very personal to you? You had a deep emotional involvement in seeing it carried through?"

"I was also instructed to recruit him by Europol ," said Gabrielle. "My personal involvement with Capitaine Rodriguez or my experience in Madrid did not cloud my judgement in any way. Damian Flynn was simply the best person for the job."

"Indeed?" continued Heydrich. "Commander Parkinson, was Flynn security vetted prior to his joining your organisation?"

"Yes, he was," said Parkinson, staring back at him. "His case was fully discussed with the British authorities."

"So they fully concurred?"

"They had some reservations, but not serious ones. In view of Doctor Flynn's unique insights and experience, I instructed Capitaine Arnault to proceed with Capitaine Rodriguez's recommendation and recruit Flynn."

Heydrich was not impressed.

"Please tell us what the British reservations were, Commander."

"There was concern that, as part of his early life in the Irish Republican Army, Doctor Flynn spent time at a terrorist training camp in Libya . . ."

"Where he met other terrorists," said Heydrich. "And could it be that Damian Flynn still maintains those contacts and is himself still part of a terrorist or, at the very least, a criminal network?"

"No," said Gabrielle, feeling the perspiration cold on her face. "It would have shown up on his Europol file and those of the British security forces."

"But they had concerns. We've already established that."

"Only about the past, not about the present," said Parkinson.

"Mmmm," said Heydrich and ticked another line on his file.

"Jean-Jacques Sabaut, the art thief who 'assisted' you during the operation at the Louvre, asked that Flynn be called in to advise," said Señora Hernandez, taking up the questioning. "Did you know that he and Flynn had worked together before, when Sabaut was a dealer in black market art and Flynn was trying to raise money for the IRA by selling stolen paintings?"

"Not until last week," said Gabrielle. "They talked about it openly during the operation. I thought it was common knowledge."

"So your files on Flynn are less than complete?"

Gabrielle nodded. "The version of Flynn's file I was given did not contain that information."

"And you know, of course, that Flynn speaks Russian? He learned it, along with Modern Politics, at university and probably improved it considerably in Libya. That was one of the reasons you recruited him, wasn't it? You needed a Russian speaker to deal with people like Gorshkov?"

"Yes."

"In Barcelona, when Flynn spoke to Gorshkov in your presence, what language did he use?"

"Russian."

"And so you couldn't understand what was said? They could have been discussing the price of cheese for all you knew?"

Gabrielle nodded. She looked towards Parkinson for some kind of support, but his head was bent firmly over his notes.

"And again in Barcelona, just before Gorshkov was assassinated," Senora Hernandez said, "did Flynn use Russian then?"

"Yes."

"There was a police stenographer there also," said Heydrich, looking up from his file, "as well as a lawyer who did, in fact, speak Russian. Was it true that both these people were asked to leave the room so that Gorshkov could speak to Flynn in private?"

"Yes. I was asked to leave too."

Hernandez and Heydrich exchanged glances. Heydrich made another mark on his file. Parkinson looked up from his notes.

"Then both Sabaut and Gorshkov died," said Senora Hernandez. "And the only thing they had in common was that they knew Flynn."

"But you said Jean-Jacques' death was a suicide," said Gabrielle, rallying for a counterattack.

Hernandez and Heydrich ignored her.

"Where is Damien Flynn right now?" asked Heydrich.

"In my office, on the fourth floor."

"Good," Heydrich said, "because I think this Doctor Flynn of yours is far more heavily involved in this case than you realise, and for all the wrong reasons."

"What do you mean?" asked Gabrielle.

Heydrich took off his glasses and laid them on the table.

"To be brutally frank, Miss Arnault, I think Damian Flynn is not so much investigating this case as participating in it."

"That's impossible," she said. "First you question both my judgement and that of my superior officer in recruiting Doctor Flynn, and now you . . ."

"Let's talk about your judgement for a moment," said Señora Hernandez. "And why you've been absent without leave for the last few days. We've already established that you were a victim of the terrorist attacks in Madrid. Your fiancé and both your parents were killed in front of your eyes and you were trapped under a pile of bodies for several minutes before help arrived. Did you receive trauma counselling afterwards?"

"I did. What are you implying?"

"And after this counselling," continued Hernandez, "you took up the project that you and Capitaine Rodriguez, your fiancé, had worked on, the idea of a specialist group to advise Europol on emerging terrorist threats. You were already a dedicated and highly decorated police officer, but this became a real crusade for you, didn't it? You had to succeed, no matter what it cost you personally."

"Commissaire Pichet in Paris was very impressed with your zeal, wasn't he?" added Heydrich. "We have it in his report."

"'Driven' is the word he uses," said Señora Hernandez. "He describes you as an officer who is, and I quote, 'driven to succeed'. Can I ask you, Miss Arnault, in your obsessive desire to see COMMETT survive after its disastrous failure in Paris, did you ever stop to think about the wisdom of rushing off to Azerbaijan on some wild goose chase with a convicted terrorist?"

"We were following a perfectly legitimate lead," Gabrielle said.

Heydrich made a mark in the margin of his file.

"In Paris," he said. "During the operation to recover the *Mona Lisa* and other paintings, you had a minor breakdown in the sewers. Is that true?"

Gabrielle looked to Parkinson.

"I'm sorry, Capitaine Arnault," he said. "Your radio was on for a moment before Flynn suggested you turn it off. Everyone involved in the operation heard it."

"It was a mild attack of claustrophobia," she said, trying to keep her head up and face them. "It didn't interfere in any way with my conduct on the mission."

"And again in Barcelona," Heydrich said, "after Gorshkov was shot. You broke down at police headquarters."

"His head burst open in front of my face, Herr Heydrich! Have you ever had to spit a man's brains out of your mouth?"

"And you're supposed to be on sick leave now?"

"Yes."

"What was your reaction when Commander Parkinson called you in Paris after the Louvre operation and told you that this group you set up with your fiancé and committed your career to was to be disbanded?" asked Heydrich.

"I was disappointed. I felt it was the wrong decision. COMMETT had been the main factor in locating Gorshkov and identifying how the bombs came to Europe in the first place."

"Largely due to information provided by Flynn," said Heydrich. "A man you yourself have already identified as a convicted terrorist, a man who has a file as thick as a telephone directory here in Europol."

She felt a lull in the questioning, as if they were running out of new things to say.

It was time to go on the offensive.

"And what is the European Council's interest in all this?" she asked. "Why are you, a representative of the Council of Ministers for Justice and Home Affairs, here to discuss a purely internal issue in Europol?"

"Because the Council is responsible for Europol and the smuggling of nuclear weapons is a critical international issue, with ramifications way beyond Europe," Heydrich said, without hesitation. "You had your chance to make a breakthrough in Barcelona and you threw it away. You could have followed the trail from Gorshkov all the way back to the source, and instead you let a group armed with nothing more than the casing of an obsolete nuclear shell hold the whole of Europe to ransom. I admire your energy, Miss Arnault, I really do. But your judgement is questionable and, in my opinion, the hiring of known terrorists and criminals to advise Europol is, quite frankly, highly irresponsible."

"You can spend all day insulting me," Gabrielle said. "But the fact remains that Doctor Flynn and I have identified a suspect at the centre of all this and the core of a second nuclear bomb is still out there waiting to be recovered. I've given my commanding officer the suspect's name. All I'm asking for is that he be investigated beyond reasonable doubt. If you have charges to bring against me or Doctor Flynn over the affair in Azerbaijan, then please make them!"

"Capitaine Arnault," Parkinson said. "Europol is taking legal advice on that. I've spoken to a number of people and consulted with those who worked with you in Paris, including Commissaire Pichet. You're an excellent officer, but you've been under a great deal of strain which, I imagine, is the only reason you allowed your judgement to be affected when you went to Azerbaijan. In my opinion, it was this strain that led you to break the law, but break the law you did. The authorities in Azerbaijan are considering bringing charges of trespass and illegal search on foreign soil against you and, by association, against Europol. Until they're answered, I will ask that neither you, nor Doctor Flynn leave the building. I've notified security at all entrances and I will ask you to wait in your office with

184 - JOHN JOYCE

Doctor Flynn until I send for you again."

"But the second bomb?" Gabrielle said.

"You leave that to us, Miss Arnault," said Heydrich. "This case has far wider implications than you can imagine, implications which the Council will be discussing with the Europol management committee. It's no longer your problem."

"And what about COMMETT, Commander?" said Gabrielle, getting to her feet. "What would it take to reinstate it?"

"You have charges to answer, Capitaine Arnault."

"Please tell me," she said.

"COMMETT is dead, Gabrielle," said Parkinson. "The only way to revive it would be for you to hand us that bomb, the *Mona Lisa* and all those other stolen paintings on a plate, along with those responsible. And that doesn't look as if it's going to happen, does it?"

"But Commander . . ."

"This meeting is over, Capitaine. Please wait downstairs in your office."

"Tough meeting, eh?" said Flynn, looking up from Gabrielle's laptop. A stubby memory stick glowed from a data port on its casing, as it copied information. "I just got an urgent call from Constance in Paris. There's something she wants us to look at, something that could be very useful to us."

"It doesn't matter," said Gabrielle. "We're both under house arrest. Neither of us can leave the building. I told you that search of the oil complex in Azerbaijan was illegal. Now the Management Board wants you in jail and me in a mental home."

"Shite!" said Flynn. "Well, we can't let that happen. Not now we're this close."

"We don't have a choice. The Europol building is secured by armed police at all times. They've been told not to let us leave. There are identification scanners. There are . . ."

"Mon Capitaine, as I've told you before, stop thinking like a policeman and start thinking like a terrorist. If you and I are stuck in some Dutch jail, how are we going to reclaim those pictures or get back that bomb? We were right about Gorshkov. We were right about Azeroil and the man behind it. The fact that we got shot at in Azerbaijan proves it. Somebody with a great deal at stake wants us out of the way."

"I smell oil," Gabrielle said. "You heard your journalist friend Gerry Murphy. Oil is big business in the Caspian. America gets sixty-five percent of its entire supply from Saudi Arabia and is looking for an alternative source. The European Union is in the same position. Azeroil is building a trans-Caspian pipeline to connect the various fields in the Caspian and pump it straight across to the Black Sea. The Russian mafia are behind Azeroil. The man behind Azeroil stole the paintings from the Louvre."

Flynn was looking up at the ceiling, examining the light fittings and the smoke detectors. Then he switched off Gabrielle's computer and pulled out the data stick.

"We tried it your way in Barcelona," he said, "and we got COMMETT disbanded. We tried it my way in Baku and we almost got ourselves killed. What I propose is that we pool our resources completely from now as equals and start thinking as a team. How many people work late here in Europol ?"

"I don't know. Quite a few?"

"How many? Ten? Fifty? A hundred?"

"There would be about a hundred people still in the building now."

"Enough to make a good crowd?"

"I suppose so."

"And what is the emergency fire evacuation plan for this building?"

She reached behind the door and took down her coat. Underneath it was a printed floor plan and evacuation drill.

"Great. Do you have a light?"

"A what?"

"A light—matches, that fancy cigarette lighter you carry around with you everywhere, anything!"

She reached into her pocket and pulling out Felipe's lighter.

"Welcome to teamwork," said Damien Flynn.

Five minutes later, the evacuation alarm sounded at the Europol headquarters due to a suspected fire on the ground floor. Smoke from a storage area behind reception activated the sprinkler system around the affected room which, because of its proximity to reception, meant that workers trying to leave the building as quickly as possible, were forced to pull coats and jackets over their heads in order to avoid getting soaked.

Security staff at the reception desk were overwhelmed by the sudden flood of people pouring out of the building, but took the pragmatic view that everyone exiting from Europol had to be a bona fide worker, and confined their efforts to preventing anyone except the Dutch Fire Service from going back inside.

In the ensuing confusion, nobody noticed a tall man with a beard and a woman with a laptop case separate themselves from the crowd of workers gathered at the emergency assembly point on the far side of the road from 47 Raamweg and hail a taxi for the station.

In Brussels, the couple called briefly at Flynn's apartment off the Rue Sainte Catherine to pick up cash and travel documents, before returning to the Gare Centrale for the next train to Paris. Once there they took another taxi to an apartment off the Boulevard Haussmann.

"We can't stay long, Constance," said Flynn. "There are people who may be looking for us. Where's the painting?"

Constance led them into the main room of her apartment. Nicole Sabaut's self-portrait lay on the dining table, exactly where Flynn had left it a few days before.

"I was going to hang it in place of that Dali reproduction in the hall," said Constance. "And then I noticed how heavy it was. Hold it for yourself, and you'll see."

Flynn lifted the portrait from the table. "You're right," he said. "I hadn't notice that before."

"Couldn't that just be the weight of the frame?" asked Gabrielle.

"No. Look at the back. It's much thicker than a normal canvas. See this tiny gap between the frame and what looks like the back of the painting?" continued Constance, taking out a penknife and opening it. "I looked at it and I wondered why I couldn't see the back of the canvas."

Constance inserted the blade of the knife in the gap behind the frame. There was a click and Constance swung the back of the painting open like a window, exposing what lay behind it.

Gabrielle gasped. Flynn laughed.

They were gazing at a portrait of another beautiful young woman. This time the model was sitting on a chair with a scene from a balcony in the background. A thin veil covered her hair, her hands were crossed in her lap and her face had an enigmatic smile. It was Nicole Sabaut's perfect reproduction of the *Mona Lisa*.

"I don't know what you're thinking," said Constance with a mischievous grin. "But I think this gives us the perfect bargaining chip to get those stolen paintings back."

24

Viktor Vorontov enjoyed auctions and he loved Sotheby's. Nowhere else in the world offered him the same exquisite cocktail of refinement, acquisition and the thrill of the hunt. Where else could he flaunt the enormous financial power he now possessed with greater satisfaction than amongst the self-appointed cream of the international bourgeoisie in the hallowed hall of Sotheby's auction room in London, particularly when he knew he could pay ten times the expected price for any item on auction and hardly feel the scratch in his bank account?

He watched as the bidding for the last item reached its peak, and the gavel snapped down on the block to indicate a successful sale.

"Sold," announced the auctioneer, "for two hundred and fifty thousand pounds, to the back of the hall. May I see your paddle, sir?"

All eyes in the room swung in his direction. Vorontov raised the numbered plastic paddle he'd been issued with as a registered bidder at the auction. It irked him that he'd not yet been admitted to the hallowed ranks of those whose face alone guaranteed their accounts at Sotheby's, but that would come in time.

As one of the richest men in Russia his darkly handsome face, with its bright blue eyes, classical Roman nose and wide generous mouth, was already a regular feature on the covers of celebrity magazines but, after his recent exploit in Paris, there might be other reasons for people to be watching him. He'd come prepared. Sitting at either end of the row where he and Giselle his latest mistress sat, were two heavyset men with watchful eyes who had not bid all morning.

It was useful to have them around. The jackals of the paparazzi now thought twice about intruding on his privacy after a number of their expensive cameras had been smashed during the scrum of a photoshoot in Milan, and more than one enterprising photographer had tripped 'accidentally' and broken bones when their subject had deemed their attentions too intrusive in Cannes.

Yes. He, Viktor Vorontov, had finally arrived. He had a plush apartment in Moscow, a *dacha* in the forest west of the city, a house in Holland Park, London, another in Saint Tropez—where another of his mistresses was installed aboard his yacht—and an entire private island in the Black Sea where he could relax and escape the rigours of his billionaire existence.

His wife now lived like a queen, his two sons were treated like princes, and he himself could afford to indulge his passions for beautiful women, expensive toys and his unique collection of Italian Renaissance art.

He dispatched his personal assistant to deal with the payment and shipping details of his latest acquisition. Then he waited for the next item on the catalogue to be placed on the easel next to the auctioneer's polished wooden podium. It was a piece he'd set his heart on acquiring—a breathtakingly intricate drawing by the sixteenth century Italian painter Michelangelo Merisi, known to the world as Caravaggio, and depicting detail of his subsequent masterpiece *The Fortune Teller*.

Vorontov watched. Although he'd never been a soldier, the similarity of strategy and tactics behind the bidding at high-stakes auctions to those of ancient land battles fascinated him. The purpose of the opening bids, like the range-finding fire from artillery, was to reach the confidential minimum selling price agreed between the auction house and the seller in advance. Bidding was slow at first, but in a few minutes the distance to the enemy lines had been gauged, at around half a million pounds sterling.

Then the next phase of the battle began—to determine those who were merely interested to know what troops they'd have to commit before they might have to withdraw and those who wanted to win.

Vorontov wanted to win. He raised his paddle.

"Do I hear six hundred thousand?" asked the auctioneer.

Vorontov nodded.

"Six hundred thousand, at the back of the aisle. Do I hear seven?"

Vorontov thought he would. There were one or two bidders off to the right who seemed serious.

"Seven hundred thousand?" said the auctioneer looking towards a stocky woman with short curly hair near the door. The woman raised her paddle and nodded.

"Seven hundred thousand! Do I hear eight hundred thousand?"

Vorontov raised his paddle.

"I have eight hundred thousand," said the auctioneer. "Do I hear one million?"

Vorontov glanced to his right to see the stocky woman raise her paddle and nod.

Vorontov snapped his paddle into view and nodded twice.

"I have one million pounds," said the auctioneer without the slightest trace of emotion. "Do I hear one million, one hundred thousand?"

Vorontov didn't think he would. The ceiling of one million pounds was a daunting barrier to all but the extremely rich. Passing a million pounds indicated to the room that someone was willing to spend whatever it took.

Vorontov smiled.

"I have one million, one hundred thousand pounds!" said the auctioneer. "Do I have one million two hundred thousand?"

Vorontov was stunned. This was an insult. Who in the room would have the nerve to challenge his bid when it was obvious to all that he had to have that drawing?

He raised his paddle and nodded emphatically.

"I have one million two hundred thousand! Do I hear one million two hundred and fifty thousand?"

The other bidder did not respond.

"One million two hundred thousand? Going once! Going twice! Sold, to the back of the room! Thank you, ladies and gentlemen. Our next lot is number twelve in the catalogue."

This time the auctioneer didn't ask to see his paddle.

Vorontov's mistress squeezed his arm.

"You won *Vitya*! Congratulations!"

"Thank you, *lapochka*, but I'd be very interested to know who was bidding against me."

"She's looking this way, *Vitya*. There, by the door."

The stocky woman with the curly hair had stood up to leave and was indeed staring back at him.

"Excuse me, *lapochka*. There's a small sketch by Caliari I'm interested in. Lot number sixteen. I'll be back in a moment."

He rose to his feet before the bidding for the next item got underway, moved to the edge of the row and, with one of his bodyguards following closely behind him, stalked towards the entrance. The woman stood at the edge of the throng of people in the lobby, as if expecting him. She was dressed in a heavy tweed cape, fastened at the throat with a gold clasp, a grey wool suit over a soft brown roll-neck jumper and handmade leather shoes. She wore no rings and no other jewellery. Her whole appearance suggested good taste and old money.

"Congratulations, Mr Vorontov," she said in heavily accented English. "It's good to see a man so committed to his collection."

Vorontov was intrigued as to how this woman knew his name. He glanced over his shoulder to make sure his bodyguard was close behind him. She would have had to present credentials as a bona fide buyer to be allowed to bid at the auction, just as he had. Therefore it was unlikely that she was a representative of the authorities, on his trail since Paris. But such credentials might be faked.

"You also have an interest in Italian Renaissance art, Miss . . ?"

"Le Clerc," said the woman with a smile.

"Are you bidding on your own behalf, or for somebody else?"

"I was once a close associate of somebody you may be familiar with, Monsieur, a man closely associated with a masterpiece I know you have an interest in. His name was Jean-Jacques Sabaut. Here's my card. Call me if you'd like to do business."

Vorontov examined the card. It simply read "Constance Le Clerc – Art Dealer" above a mobile phone number and an email address. Vorontov never carried his own business cards. He had people to handle that sort of thing.

"Doing what business, exactly, Madame?"

But the woman had already disappeared through the doorway into the street.

Vorontov looked at the card again, turning it in his hand.

On the back, neatly handwritten in black ink, were the words.

"Your *Mona Lisa* is a fake! I have the real thing. Call me."

25

Constance clambered into the black Jaguar at the kerb and slammed the door. She felt more alive than at any time since the first Louvre robbery with Jean-Jacques. She was back on the wrong side of the law, living on her wits, and it felt good.

"Quick," she said, "before he follows me out!"

Flynn pulled off into the early afternoon traffic, raising a volley of angry car horns, and headed south towards Trafalgar Square.

"English drivers!" Constance said. "It's as bad as Paris."

She looked over her shoulder. The thickset man she'd seen with Vorontov appeared on the pavement beneath the flag and awning of Sotheby's, looked up and down New Bond Street and then went back inside the auction rooms.

"Were you followed?" Flynn asked her.

"Please!" snapped Constance. "You can't drive and look in your rear-view mirror at the same time."

"Sorry," Flynn said, "force of habit."

"I can't get used to you without your beard. And the short hair, it makes you look like a banker. I almost got into the wrong car."

"Now that I'm wanted for questioning by Europol, I have to take precautions. How did the auction go? Did you make contact?"

"It went like clockwork," Constance said, beaming at his reflection in the rear-view mirror, "although I was worried that Vorontov wasn't going to top my bid, when the price went over a million. I would've had to sell my beautiful apartment in Paris."

"Did you give him the card?"

"I did, so we can expect a call from him any moment now. Did you book those tables at Fortnum's for me, by the window?"

"Getting through to them on the phone was a pain in the arse, but I did it. You're in the Saint James's Restaurant on the fourth floor."

"And the video link with Gabrielle?"

"Ready to roll. Your laptop's in the back."

Constance took an off-the-shelf mobile phone out of her purse, checked it and laid it on the seat next to her. They'd driven around Trafalgar Square and a mile up Leicester Street before it rang.

"Hello?" said Constance. "Nice of you to call back, Monsieur. You got my message?"

"Yes," Vorontov said. "Is this some kind of joke, Madame?"

"No. It's very serious. You have in your possession something you consider to be a priceless work of art. I have incontrovertible evidence that it's a forgery."

"What evidence?" said Vorontov. "Even if I did have the painting you suggest. How could it possibly be a fake?"

"I'm not only willing to prove that to you, but also to assist you in acquiring the genuine article." Constance said. "I realise we're speaking over an open cellular network, which is why I'm not referring to you or the painting by name and would appreciate the same courtesy in return."

"What do you want?" asked Vorontov.

"I'd like to meet in person. Then I can prove what I'm saying is true. Is that of interest to you?"

"How do I know this is not a hoax, or some elaborate trap?"

"You don't. But then again, neither do I. Shall we say the Saint James's Restaurant of Fortnum and Mason's in Piccadilly at four? It's opposite the Royal Academy. Simply go up to the fourth floor and ask for my table. I'll join you as soon as I'm sure you haven't been followed. Thank you."

She hung up the phone and smiled. This really did feel good.

The Bentley deposited Viktor Vorontov at 181 Piccadilly, beneath the blue and pink façade of Fortnum and Mason's, exactly on the stroke of 4:00 pm. Vorontov liked punctuality. It had helped him in his rise as a manager of the oilfields in the Sea of Azov and he'd insisted on it in his employees ever since. The car slid away to find parking and Vorontov and his bodyguard walked through the heavy wooden and glass doors between the highly decorated windows with their great gold moon faces and across the foyer of the food hall. Tantalising aromas from all over the world seduced him as he climbed to the fourth floor.

"Do you have a reservation, sir?" enquired the frock coated major domo inside the door. "I'm afraid we're very busy today." He glanced to his right. A long queue of people, mostly tourists with guide books and maps, stood waiting.

"I'm here to meet a Miss Le Clerc."

The man consulted a list.

"Which one of you is Mr Vorontov?"

"I am."

"There are two tables reserved by Miss Le Clerc," said the man, "one for you, sir, and one for your associate. Miss Le Clerc was quite specific."

"That is most unusual."

"I understand Miss Le Clerc will be joining you in a moment," said the man. "Perhaps you could take it up with her then? Would you like to see the menu?"

"No, thank you. Not yet."

He settled himself at the specified table by the window with his back to the wall, facing the door. His bodyguard sat towards the back of the room, within sight but out of hearing. Vorontov appreciated precautions like this. You could never be too careful. He glanced at his watch, and then at his hands. The calluses had faded long ago.

Less than twenty years before, he'd been a gifted but highly underrated plant manager in charge of an oil refinery and a score of wells off the Russian coast. His eighteen-hour day had been spent rushing from well to well, sorting out production problems while his director, a lazy man with political connections, had lounged behind his desk back at base and drunk himself into a stupor. There had been hardly enough money to feed his family and his wife had been forced to waste her days in endless queues or to barter foodstuffs at street markets.

That kind of hardship makes a man sharp, which stood Viktor Vorontov in good stead when his boss had taken him to one side early one morning and said, "*Vitya*, I hear things on the grapevine from my friends in high places. Very soon the current regime is going to change. There'll be chaos. But from that chaos will come great opportunities for those who can keep their heads. My friends and I intend to become capitalists. We'll take ownership of this refinery and these wells and we'd like you, *Vitya*, as someone who has demonstrated a great talent for management, to run them for us."

"But how can you and your friends take ownership of something that belongs to the state, Comrade Director?"

"You leave that to us. A new company will be formed called Azeroil, along the capitalist model, and you'll be named as the principal shareholder. That is to protect my friends and me from certain prying eyes. And, for that protection, we'll be willing to pay you five percent of the profits from the company. There'll be great profits, *Vitya*. Oil is power, to capitalists and communists alike. Don't you agree?"

Vorontov had agreed. As manager of the plant and the wells, he was perfectly aware of the enormous money to be made if they were run efficiently, as they would be under his direction. He was also pragmatic enough to know that the only way he could access that profit directly was with the blessing of those in possession of the connections that he himself lacked. If the Communist regime fell and the great state oil refinery and complex of wells in the Sea of Azov became the property of Azeroil, Viktor Vorontov could become rich beyond his wildest dreams.

Vorontov delegated wisely. He thought strategically. He planned methodically and his efforts were rewarded. Then one day without warning, his old boss simply disappeared and another man arrived to see him, along with two heavyset bodyguards who, in previous times, would have been wearing the khaki uniform of the KGB. The man had a thin, skull like face, iron grey hair and eyes as hard and lifeless as ball bearings.

"Viktor Vorontov?" he said. "My name is Igor Kisenko and I represent business interests in Moscow who have recently acquired a controlling interest in your company. Your former boss is suffering from health problems and will no longer be reporting for work. I'm here to represent those interests in discussions regarding the future of Azeroil. Are you willing to remain with the company as managing director?"

Vorontov knew he was now dealing directly with the Russian mafia. There was great danger here, but also great opportunity—if only he could keep his head.

"Of course," he said. "I'm the only person in this organisation who can run it as the current level of efficiency it enjoys and maximise its profits to you."

"I'm glad to hear it. What was your previous arrangement concerning those profits?"

"I got twenty percent," said Vorontov unflinchingly.

"From now on you only get ten," said the man behind the desk.

That had been fifteen years ago and since then Vorontov had taken Azeroil into other profitable markets in shipping, technology, aviation and natural gas. His own sharp eye for business minimised the obstacles in his way and, when those obstacles could not be removed by legal means, a call to his silent partners in Moscow, removed them as if by magic.

It was these silent partners who troubled Viktor Vorontov now. What would they do to him if they knew about Paris?

He looked up, just in time to see the stocky woman he knew as Constance Le Clerc enter the restaurant, give her name to the major domo and march over to greet him. She had a thin black laptop under her arm.

"Good afternoon," she said. "I'm sorry to keep you."

"I'm a busy man, Miss Le Clerc," Vorontov said. "And I've no time for practical jokes."

"Neither do I," said the woman, clearing a space for her laptop amongst the carefully laid out cutlery on her side of the table. "I have a matter of great sensitivity to discuss that could be profitable to both of us. What would you like to order? The Classic Earl Grey is very good here."

"Black tea with lemon," said Vorontov.

"Will you have something to eat? Their Welsh Rarebit is famous."

"No, thank you," Vorontov said. He didn't want to be distracted by food.

"To business then," said the woman. "Two years ago, my very good friend and associate Jean-Jacques Sabaut became the second man to ever steal the *Mona Lisa* from the Louvre in Paris. The robbery was hushed up by the police and the management of the Louvre to avoid embarrassment, just as the much more recent theft has been. Sabaut was permanently blinded in a car accident while leaving the scene of the crime and the painting was immediately recovered."

"That's all very interesting," said Vorontov. "But how can it be of any concern to me?

"Sabaut's wife was a brilliant artist, a genius at forgery and a world expert on the life and works of Da Vinci," said the woman. "She created an exact copy of the *Mona Lisa*, created on aged wood and using only materials that would have been available to Da Vinci during his time."

"I still don't see how this affects me," said Vorontov.

"Sabaut's motive in breaking into the Louvre was not so much to steal *La Giaconda*, as to substitute it with his wife's duplicate and then, when several months had passed, to reveal the truth by returning the original and force the critics who had destroyed his wife's reputation, to accept her genius."

The tea arrived. The woman waited until the waiter was out of earshot before continuing.

"But when he was finally in the restoration area of the Louvre and the painting was his for the taking, Sabaut's nerve failed and he left the museum with the same forgery he'd entered with. When he was knocked down and what appeared to be the *Mona Lisa* was found in his possession, the police assumed he'd been successful in stealing the original from the Louvre and the painting in his case was the real thing. The management of the Louvre was also under enormous pressure to install the painting in the new display paid for by Japanese investors and to open that exhibition the next day. In their haste to keep the whole affair hushed up, the Louvre management put that painting into the new hermetically sealed display they'd prepared, took the one they assumed was Nicole Sabaut's perfect forgery and gave it back to her husband on his release from prison. That painting, which is actually the original *Mona Lisa*, is now in my possession. Therefore I am in a position to offer it to you. Do you want it?"

Vorontov laughed out loud. This was all too ridiculous.

"That's the most preposterous story I've ever heard" he whispered. "Firstly, what on earth makes you think I have anything to do with recent events in Paris? And secondly, even if I did, are you asking me to believe that an institution like the Musée du Louvre would take a forgery in place of the genuine article without first authenticating it?"

The woman looked straight at him across the table. "I'm not asking you to believe it, Monsieur. I'm stating it to you as a fact. The authorities were under pressure to open the new display. Their Japanese sponsors could have withdrawn their funding if they thought something was amiss. The Louvre acted in haste that night and, after all, Nicole Sabaut's duplicate was indistinguishable from the genuine article. Jean-Jacques had even switched the electronic tagging device, which had been hidden under a blob of wax on the wooden panel, to the forgery before he abandoned his plans, but forgot to replace it in his haste to leave the Louvre before the alarms reset. To all intent and purpose, the painting that was with him when he was arrested looked exactly like the real thing."

"And how do you know all this?"

The woman across the table from his seemed to swell with pride.

"My name is Constance Le Clerc and I was Jean-Jacques Sabaut's accomplice on the night he took the *Mona Lisa* from the Louvre. I know who you are, Mr Vorontov. I too have connections in the world of black market art. If you like, feel free to verify who I am and that I'm in a position to know what I know."

Vorontov paused for a moment to think and sip his tea.

"The painting in my possession is the genuine *Giaconda*," said the woman. "Like you, I didn't believe the Louvre could ever be so negligent, so I had it authenticated by an expert whose opinion I trust completely."

"Even if your story was true," Vorontov said. "Who on earth would undertake that authentication for you without either going to the police or taking the painting for themselves?"

The woman opened her laptop and powered it up.

"You and I both know there are a handful of such specialists who will undertake such work for a certain type of collector and remain completely discreet about it, as long as a handsome fee is paid. They can be trusted simply because they have a reputation to maintain amongst their clientele. If that reputation is lost then they either go out of business or, bearing in mind the kind of customer they're usually dealing with, they end up dead."

She tapped the keys of her laptop and carefully turned the screen so that he could see it without exposing what it showed it to the rest of the restaurant.

"I have the original *Mona Lisa* by Da Vinci," she said. "And here it is."

Vorontov leant forward. He was staring at what at least appeared to be Da Vinci's masterpiece, propped up on a chair that had been covered with a white sheet. Daylight shone from the right, illuminating both the painting and the plastic rulers that had been placed at its side and base. To the left of the chair stood a woman in white coveralls, with a surgical mask over her face and a hair cap. It was impossible to make out her features.

"Where's this image coming from?" asked Vorontov.

"Location is not important," the woman said. "What is important is that I have the painting and like you, I have to take reasonable security precautions. I could hardly turn up here in a public restaurant with the original in my handbag now, could I?"

Vorontov nodded.

"Note the size of the piece," said the woman, tapping the screen. "It's exactly seventy-seven centimetres tall by fifty-three wide."

The figure on the screen gently lifted the painting with gloved hands and turned the bottom edge to the camera, which slowly panned along the edge of the bare wooden panel.

"The wood Da Vinci created his painting on has begun to warp, ever so slightly, in spite of the four wooden battens placed across the back of the piece to prevent that happening," said Constance Le Clerc. "That had been the main concern of the Louvre just before Jean-Jacque stole the painting, when they moved the *Mona Lisa* to the restoration area in the first place. It was also one of the prime factors that led them to put what they thought was the original, but which in fact was Sabaut's copy, back as soon as possible in the new hermetically sealed display."

"Can we look at the back of the painting?" asked Vorontov, still peering at the image on the screen. The woman's explanation was clever. It might even explain why the forgery, if it was a forgery, was not detected. She spoke rapidly into the built-in microphone on the laptop in French. The woman on the screen carefully turned the painting and the camera zoomed in again on the back of the panel.

"There are a number of important features," said Le Clerc. "The word *Gioconde* is spelt with an 'e' and not an 'a' and is carved in Italic script along the top of the picture in letters five centimetres high. They are above the name 'Leonard de Vinci', spelt in the French manner with 'de' and not 'da' as in Italian. Also, note the original museum catalogue number 'M.R.31', the red wax seal of the museum, a further blue trimmed certification label with two authentication stamps, the old authentication label, badly faded and torn away, and a leather strap with two attachments to the wood in the top left corner for ease of carrying. There are also four shallow holes in the wood, at the top and bottom of both horizontal edges, where the painting was attached to its original frame by way of metal brackets. Now, does your version of the *Mona Lisa* have these features?"

Vorontov sensed a trap. "I don't have any version of the *Mona Lisa*, Miss Le Clerc. I didn't even know it had been stolen from the Louvre till you came to me with this story."

Constance Le Clerc smiled and shut her laptop.

"Of course," she said, "my apologies, Monsieur. I've wasted your time." She turned to a waiter and raised her hand for the bill.

"If Sabaut did have the original *Mona Lisa* in his possession all this time," said Vorontov softly. "Why did he not sell it before now?"

"Jean-Jacques Sabaut's motive in stealing the *Mona Lisa* in the first place was to immortalise his wife and to confound her critics," said Le Clerc. "He was not a mercenary thief. When Jean-Jacques was handed the painting on his release from prison he was also blind and in no position to know that he had been handed the original by mistake. He kept what he thought was Nicole Sabaut's forgery to keep her memory alive but I have no such scruples. I'll give you seventy-two hours to make up your mind and then I'll make contact with other potential customers. That should give you time to have your version of the painting assessed by an expert. When you've done that, ring me on the number you already have with your decision."

26

Gabrielle Arnault unplugged the webcam from the laptop on the small wooden table. Apart from the chair on which the painting rested, that table was the only other piece of furniture in the room. All mirrors, paintings and reflective surfaces had been removed. The net curtains across the windows of the rented apartment had been closed to prevent even an accidental view of the location being observed by the camera. Gabrielle drew back the curtains, revealing a view of the Seine.

She pulled off her hair cap, surgical mask and coverall, took one of the mirrors and hung it back on its hook above the old marble fireplace. Staring back at her was a young woman she hardly recognised. Her shoulder-length hair had been cut short and bleached dark blonde. Her eyes were framed in clear rimless glasses.

After a life as both a gendarme's daughter and a serving officer in the French police, RAID and Europol, she was having difficulty being on the wrong side of the law.

The cell phone rang. It was Flynn.

"Was he convinced?" she asked.

"Constance thinks so," Flynn said. "The picture quality was excellent and she was able to use the fact that she participated in the first Sabaut robbery to add authenticity. If I was our friend right now, I'd be asking myself some serious questions. We'll return the hire car and get the Eurostar train to Paris. I've arranged dinner tonight so we can meet an old friend of mine. You'll be working with him for a couple of days. Bring a notebook and don't drink any wine. You have a lot of homework to do."

Flynn has assured Gabrielle that the seafood restaurant, in a narrow side street off the Rue Rambuteau, was one of the best kept secrets in Paris. He'd also insisted they arrive there early to talk in private and had booked a secluded table on the first floor, so they could not be observed from the street.

She saw the early evening theatregoers stopping off for a quick meal in the sidewalk terrace outside. Streetlamps blinked into life. The setting sun silhouetted the buildings against the sky.

"If you were Vorontov right now," said Flynn. "You'd be asking yourself questions. You're sure you have the original painting, but not a hundred percent sure. And until you are a hundred percent sure, each time you look at that painting in your collection that tiny percentage of doubt will eat into your enjoyment of possessing it like a worm eats into an apple. And since the whole purpose of stealing it in the first place was to enjoy it, you need to be completely sure that what you've got is the real thing. The question is, how can you be sure?"

He leant back in his chair. With his beard gone, his high cheekbones and hard face made him look ten years younger. But the dark eyebrows and the steely look in his eyes were still there. He could have been a stockbroker or a corporate executive, the predatory type that strikes first and asks questions later.

"Carbon dating," she said. "You could analyse the wood from the panel and the paint from the picture to see if they are as old as they claim to be."

"But carbon dating is destructive," said Flynn. "You'd need to take an piece of the actual wood or a scraping of paint from the original painting, then destroy them during the test. Would you do that to a national treasure like the *Mona Lisa*? Besides, what laboratory in the world could do it for you without exposing you as the thief? No. The best way to find out if you have the original is to have it authenticated by the best expert in their field."

"Ah," said Gabrielle. "But just as with the carbon dating, which top expert in the art world could you ever ask to examine the most famous stolen painting in the world without going to the police?"

"Someone who himself is a crook, and has his reputation to protect," said Flynn. "His name is Guido de Pau and you're going to meet him tonight."

"How can we trust a person like that as part of our team?"

"Because he's an old friend of mine from my days of hawking stolen paintings around Paris, and because I did him a very big favour some years ago, one which he's never forgotten."

"How can we be sure Vorontov will contact him?"

"Two reasons. Firstly, Guido is the one of the greatest authorities on Da Vinci alive today. He's written several books on the subject and even advised on a TV series, although that's not widely known. The second reason is he's a crook, and known to be so by the art underworld. If ever an Italian Renaissance painting goes missing and the thieves need it authenticated, this is the man they turn to. Vorontov, as a collector of black market art, will know this."

"This favour you did for him, what was it?"

"About eight years ago, when Guido had fallen from grace with the Department of Arts and Culture here in Paris because of a drug habit he had at the time, he got into some very hot water with a number of gangsters from Marseilles who wanted him to verify some crude forgeries they'd had knocked up by some unfortunate art student in the hope of conning a museum in Texas. Guido refused, saying that he'd his reputation to think of, so they kidnapped his daughter to put pressure on him. I was just out of prison and working with Guido at the time, so a few friends of mine from Belfast came over and helped us out. This is the daughter you're going to impersonate to Vorontov."

"You certainly have a lot of friends in low places."

"The consultancy business is all about relationships. Ah! Here he is now."

A tall man in a dark suit had entered the restaurant. He looked extremely fit, and the professional way he surveyed the dining area hinted at either a policeman or a criminal. He nodded at Flynn, turned and beckoned in a second man.

Guido de Pau was one of those people whose presence fills a room. He had a large round face, framed by a mane of silvery hair and a narrow beard. He wore a black velvet suit, a purple shirt so dark that it was almost black and a striped silk tie in purple and silver. His bright eyes glittered as he recognised Flynn and a huge meaty hand, the size of a bunch of bananas was thrust forward.

"Damien, mon cher ami! *Ça va?*"

"*Ça va bien*, Guido. Let me introduce my colleague, Madame Gabrielle Arnault."

Gabrielle watched Guido's eyes widen to the size of saucers behind his delicate silver framed glasses and submitted to the customary kiss on both cheeks.

"*Enchanté*, Madame," boomed Guido, his laughter exploding in the small restaurant like a hand grenade. "And in turn, *mes enfants*, can I introduce Sebastian, who is my security for the evening? Sebastian, I'll be doing some delicate private business this evening, so if you could be discreet I'd very much appreciate it. *Merci.*"

Guido squeezed himself into his chair. Sebastian settled himself at a single table near the wall with a perfect view of both the door and the table where Guido was now sitting. Gabrielle could imagine him calculating arcs of fire and escape routes in his head.

"*Et maintenant, mes enfants*," said Guido. "How can I be of service?"

"In a day or so," said Flynn, "a certain person is going to contact you and ask you to authenticate a particular painting. They won't specify which painting it is beyond the fact that it's a major work from the Italian Renaissance and that this authentication must be carried out in complete secrecy. They'll be very insistent on that point. The contract will almost certainly involve you travelling abroad. I want you to regretfully decline to carry out the authentication in person due to ill health, but to recommend that your daughter Antoinette, who is widely known as your protégé, is free to undertake the work on your behalf."

Guido frowned. His voice dropped to a whisper. "I take it this involves the recent incident at the Louvre, the one everyone in our business is whispering about but nobody in authority confirms?"

"It does. But I'm not at liberty to confirm it either."

"And I can take it that, since rumour suggests the 'incident' was carried out by a well resourced criminal gang, there'll be an element of risk to my daughter if she undertakes this work."

"You can."

Guido De Pau shook his big head. "You know I owe you Antoinette's life," he said softly. "But what father could be expected to put his daughter in such a position, particularly after her terrible experience in the past?"

"None," said Flynn turning to Gabrielle. "Your daughter will not leave Paris. My colleague here, who is a trained and experienced police officer, will impersonate Antoinette for the purpose of this job. So I need you to brief her and make sure she knows everything there is to know about Italian Renaissance art."

The cloud lifted from Guido's face. He peered at Gabrielle. Then he grinned and she felt his heavy hand on her shoulder.

"Ah! Now I understand the blonde hair and the glasses. I salute you, Madame. You're as brave as my good friend Damien here. When would you like these lessons to start?"

"Right now," Flynn said. "That call could come at any time."

"To properly appreciate Da Vinci," said Guido as he bent over a steaming bowl of *moules marinières* the chef had prepared specially at his request, "or indeed any artist, you have to know them as a person. What makes a person is what makes their art after all, and Da Vinci was an incredibly complex and inquisitive character, a genius in the sciences as well as the arts."

Gabrielle watched Guido's thick fingers delicately manipulate the hinged shells of a empty mussel he'd just consumed. They were like a pair of tweezers, plucking the plump meats from the rest of his steamed shellfish and popping them in his mouth.

"If we had time," Guido continued, dabbing his lips with his napkin and taking a sip of chilled Muscadet, "I'd recommend that you read and, if possible memorise, sections of Da Vinci's treatise *Traité de la Peinture*, where you'll marvel at the scientific principles he applies to the depiction of anatomy, the drawing of landscapes, the way light and shade falls on a subject and even the way trees branch in different directions. It's as if he could paint nothing without taking it apart, atom by atom, in order to understand it completely. That's what gives his art such depth—everything from his working drawings to his finished masterpieces. You could sit and stare at the *Mona Lisa* for days, taking in the detail and the depth, and still only appreciate the smallest portion of what makes it a masterpiece."

"Time is something we may not have," said Flynn. "What we need is for Madame Arnault to know everything she needs to know in order to appear as expert as yourself about just one painting—the *Mona Lisa* itself."

"Then we need to begin with a background on the times in which it was painted and the life of Leonardo himself," said Guido, taking a lump of French bread and ripping it apart with his thumbs. "You'll need to know who Da Vinci's patron was, the background politics of the day and how the painting came to be commissioned. You'll also need to be familiar with the various theories as to who the subject of the painting actually was, the fact that Leonardo was one of the pioneers of oils paints, over the more traditional tempura method which used egg whites to bind the colour together, and something about the practice of painting on wood instead of canvas, which was common in those days. I also find that, when discussing a painting with a client, it's the little details, the nuggets of odd and interesting information, which impress them most. For example, even though it's small, the *Mona Lisa* is actually the largest painting Leonardo every produced. Did you know that?"

He mopped up the last of the remaining broth from his bowl with his bread and ate it with obvious satisfaction.

"Did you also know that Leonardo was left-handed, as many creative people are?"

"And the history of the painting itself?" asked Gabrielle, feeling herself caught up in Guido's passion for his subject.

Guido washed his fingers in a bowl of lemon scented water, dried his hands on his napkin and drained his wine glass.

"Yes, indeed," he said, beckoning to the waiter to remove the empty plates. "You must know how the painting came to be in the Louvre, how it was stolen in 1911 and how it was found. Then there's all the fascinating stories about how it came to be the icon it is today and how it was protected during the Nazi occupation of Paris during the Second World War. Imagine what would have happened if it had gone the way of so many art treasures across Europe—into the hands of men like Herman Goering, who needed an *entire train* to remove his illegally obtained collection from his castle as the allies moved forward! Some of those paintings are still missing to this day, and a good few examples of the Italian Renaissance period are among them. It's a sad fact that keeps me in business even as we speak. Would you like coffee?"

27

The door of the specially configured Boeing 727 private jet popped open, letting in the heavily scented air of the Black Sea island. Viktor Vorontov undid his seat belt, nodded to the stewardess and stepped out into the lifeless heat of the midday sun. To his left, the sea glittered against the sky beyond the spiky tops of yucca palms and low trees. To his right, soaring up from the base of the island like a scene from a fairy tale, was a beautifully restored medieval castle, its white stone turrets and ramparts dazzling in the sun.

"Have the papers and my luggage brought up to me in the jeep," he snapped. "I have things to attend to." Then he climbed into the back seat of the air conditioned Bentley waiting for him near the wingtip of the jet and told the driver to get him up to the castle as fast as he could.

He was in a hurry. Since his meeting with Constance Le Clerc, the doubt that his most prized possession might not be what it seemed had eaten away at him like a cancer. That night in London, even after a good meal, a show and a very energetic lovemaking session with Giselle, he'd not been able to sleep. Today he'd skipped an important planning meeting in Brussels for the forthcoming energy summit, and had flown directly to the Black Sea as soon as his aircraft could be made ready. In spite of the consequences of missing the meeting, he had to see her.

He had to stand in her presence and be sure.

The Bentley slid beneath a security barrier and wound its way up a short paved road, past the red blooms of oleander, the electric-blue dragonflies and the plump green stems of prickly pear cacti, to the door of the castle. The fortress had originally been built by a Turkish emir during the time of the Crusades to act as an outpost and supply depot for his navy in the Black Sea. It had then been modernised and extended by a far-sighted Russian tsar who saw that the key to domination in the Black Sea and the protection of his empire's southern shores, lay in complete naval supremacy. In those days, ships not propelled by the wind were driven by steam, and steamships needed coal. So the tsar had brought the fortress up to date by installing a coal depot for his fleet of ironclads, just as the Soviets had modernised it to support of their nuclear navy a century later by installing an electronic listening post against any attack by a Cold War aggressor.

The Bentley slid to a stop within the cool shade of the castle keep. Vorontov stepped out, waved aside the offer of a cold drink at the door and marched swiftly through the gleaming marble hallway towards his study.

It had once been the main briefing room of the castle as a Soviet military base. Certain features of its previous existence remained, improved upon and cunningly disguised by the best of contemporary design at Vorontov's personal request. Metal shutters could be dropped over the windows at the touch of a button, hidden microphones could pick up conversations in any of the meeting rooms and living areas and, facing the elegant oak desk that commanded the room, a wooden panel covered what had been an emergency escape route to a bombproof bunker three floors below.

Vorontov shut the study door behind him, ensuring it was locked, and went to the panel. At the press of a button concealed in the scrollwork, the door popped open and Vorontov was running down the narrow spiral staircase. Motion sensor lights flicked on automatically as he went deeper and deeper into the rock of the island until he came to a steel door. He pressed a five digit code into the keypad, watched impatiently as the door hissed open and strode across the carpeted floor.

The bunker had been remodelled and refitted in complete secrecy to serve as a unique viewing room for the most valuable collection of stolen art treasures in the world. Soft lights, designed to enhance the viewer's experience without fading the colours of the collection, shone down from recessed fittings in the wood panelled ceiling. Smooth walls in neutral pastel shades provided the perfect backdrop. A specially designed leather chair on casters could be moved to face any of the score of priceless paintings around the room. There was a fully stocked drinks cabinet and, to complete the experience, a state-of-the-art Bang and Olufsen quadraphonic sound system that could waft classical music throughout the room.

But Vorontov's eyes were fixed on the single small portrait of the woman with the enigmatic smile, hanging alone on the far wall.

He stopped before her and stared, lost in a fog of wonder, worship and agonising doubt.

"Are you real?" he whispered at last. "How can I be sure?"

He stood in front of the painting, wrestling with this question as the calm eyes of the masterpiece looked down on him. When he could take the torment no longer, he returned to his study, flipped open his Smartphone and rang a number in Paris.

"I have a piece of Italian Renaissance art I need appraised immediately," he said when that number answered. "It must be done by a person of the greatest expertise and authority, in the strictest confidence. We've done business before and I'm sure you recognise my voice. Can you help me?"

"Of course I recognise you, Monsieur," said the voice, "and I have the very expert in mind—a recognised authority no less, who has written books on the subject. It will be my pleasure to put you in touch with him."

28

Twenty-four hours later, Vorontov was once more standing at the edge of the runway, shading his eyes against the setting sun. The air was cooler now, and much more bearable, with a light breeze from the sea. In an hour or so, once the sun set and the stars appeared, it would be full of the chirp of cicadas and the flutter of tiny bats. But now, he had to strain against the blinding light of the sun to make out the tiny black silhouette of the returning jet, as it circled to the west, lined up towards the runway and started to descend.

Normally, he didn't greet guests personally, much less drive the Bentley to meet them himself, preferring instead to let them take in his beautiful island, the magnificent castle and the chauffeur-driven luxury car, before being shown into his presence by a liveried servant.

Yet Vorontov had been in a torment of doubt over the painting ever since Sotheby's and the person arriving on his jet from Istanbul had the key to removing his pain. He wondered if he was mad to be taking such chances so close to an Azeroil board meeting, scheduled to be held on the island in two days' time which would include Igor Kisenko himself. Yet De Pau's daughter could still do her work, end his torment and depart in a matter of hours without attracting any attention whatsoever, leaving him with a clear mind to focus on matters of business.

De Pau was above suspicion. His reputation in Paris was second to none and it was in his own interest to be completely discreet where his customers' paintings were concerned. His value to such people had already been proved by the kidnapping case involving his daughter some years ago against services to be rendered.

Why else did he employ a bodyguard for himself and his daughter now? No, Guido De Pau had as much to lose from any indiscretion as he had.

Nevertheless, that had not stopped Vorontov from taking precautions. The crew of the jet were under strict instructions not to reveal their destination to their passengers, whose passports had been thoroughly checked, and all cell phones, pagers, and even the SIM card of Miss De Pau's laptop had been taken into care before the jet had left the ground in Istanbul to prevent her using the internet or email.

The sleek white and blue aircraft glistened with fire from the setting sun as its wheels kissed the runway with a distant screech and puffs of white smoke. Then it turned onto the runway apron, taxied neatly to where the Bentley stood and popped its passenger door. The whine of the engines softened to a whisper and died as steps lowered smoothly onto the tarmac. A slim man in a dark suit peered out through the open doorway. He scanned the steps, the car and the landing field around the plane, glanced down at Vorontov for a moment, then nodded to someone out of sight behind him in the cabin.

Vorontov felt a twinge of unease as the man looked at him. He had the same cold fire in his eyes that the heavy-set men working for Kisenko had, the same look of violence held under control, like dogs on leashes waiting for any excuse to bite.

The man disappeared back into the aircraft, to be replaced by a tall, blonde nurse in a white uniform, who carried a folding wheelchair down the steps and set it up on the tarmac next to the plane.

That fitted with Vorontov's research, but he'd still need to be sure. He fingered the slim plastic cylinder inside his left jacket pocket and flipped off the cap with his thumb.

He saw movement at the door of the plane, and looked up to where the man had reappeared. In his arms was a delicate young woman in a white cotton suit. She had short, dark blonde hair and bright, intelligent eyes that squinted against the sunlight through wire framed glasses. The man carried her gently down the steps and, with the assistance of the nurse, carefully installed her in the chair.

"Madame De Pau?" he said, stepping forward. "I'm Viktor Vorontov."

She smiled shyly up at him and put out her hand.

To Vorontov, who was used to the calculated smiles of models, celebrities and money-hungry mistresses, it was the most natural expression he'd seen in his life. Gallantly, he bent at the waist, took the offered hand and kissed it.

"Welcome to my island."

"You live in a very beautiful place. It's so unlike Paris at this time of year, so warm and welcoming."

"How is your father? He tells me he's unwell."

"I'm afraid so. He sends his sincere apologies for not being able to come in person, but he'll stand over any authentication I make of whatever it is you have to show me. His infection will pass in a few days, if he does what his doctor tells him. I understand the piece you'd like me to examine is here, on this island?"

"It is indeed," Vorontov said. "But before we examine it, can I ask you to introduce your companions?"

"This is my nurse, Lyudmila," Antoinette said, turning to the tall blonde woman. "She travels with me whenever I go abroad. Unfortunately, as you may have heard, I was taken hostage some years ago. As you can see, I lived to tell the tale, but I was hit by a stray bullet during the rescue and now I have no feeling at all below the waist."

"And this is?" asked Vorontov, nodding to the tall dark man.

"This is Damien," said Antoinette De Pau. "He's my bodyguard and accompanies me everywhere at my father's express wish. He was one of the people my father brought in to . . . resolve the situation when I was kidnapped, and has been with me ever since."

The man nodded towards Vorontov. His left hand carried a slim attaché case. He did not offer his right hand for Vorontov to shake.

"I heard one of the kidnappers was killed in that incident," Vorontov said, testing the man.

"All five of them died," said Damien.

That was what Vorontov had been told. He glanced over his shoulder to make sure his own bodyguard was close at hand to protect him. Then, before anyone could react, he whipped his left hand out of his jacket pocket and plunged a needle through the fabric of Antoinette De Pau's white trouser suit, into the muscle of her right thigh.

Damien leapt forward and grabbed Vorontov's wrist. Antoinette De Pau sat looking down at the tiny disc of red blood that blossomed on the white fabric where the needle had entered her skin. Vorontov saw surprise on her face, but no pain.

"I apologise, Madame," Vorontov said, disengaging his arm from Damien's grip. "You must forgive me. When you see the piece you've come here to authenticate, you'll understand why I need to be absolutely certain you are who you say you are."

"Try that again and you're dead," said Damien

"It's alright," said Miss De Pau. "I'm sure Monsieur Vorontov has his reasons. But I hope the bloodstain will wash out. I only bought this outfit in Paris yesterday."

"And I hope that needle was sterile, Monsieur!" said the nurse. "There could be the risk of infection."

"Again, I apologise," repeated Vorontov. "You may dress the wound when we get to the castle. Madame, I'll make it up to you at dinner tonight and of course, I'll replace the garment, if you let me know your size and where you bought it."

The frown on Antoinette De Pau's face softened.

"*Pas de quoi*, Monsieur," she said. "It's nothing. Perhaps we could go and inspect the piece now. I understand time is of the essence."

In less than twenty minutes they'd reached Vorontov's study. Madame De Pau's bodyguard had placed her attaché case on the desk and was standing at a discreet distance near the door next to the nurse, watching them. Antoinette De Pau was already staring at the legally acquired part of Vorontov's collection he chose to display to the world with a look of wonder on her face. It made him happy that, here at last, was someone who could truly appreciate his collection as he did. He couldn't wait to show her what lay in the bunker below them.

"These are magnificent," she said. "Beautiful. You have a Botticelli and . . . that pen and ink drawing? Pisano?"

"It is."

"See how he uses perspective to give the illusion of depth and space. He was one of the first artists to draw that way in the fifteenth century. Until then, all painting looked flat, like cartoons. And this . . ." she gasped. "Is this the sketch by Caravaggio that went for over a million pounds sterling at Sotheby's earlier this week?" Her eyes shone with admiration.

"It is."

"Is this the piece you'd like me to authenticate?"

"No," Vorontov said. "And this is where I must insist on certain conditions before we proceed. I understand your father's concern for your safety at all times but, given the piece I'm about to ask you to inspect and the delicate circumstances that surround its being here, I must ask that you accompany me alone. I'm sure you understand."

"Monsieur," said Damien. "My job is to protect Miss De Pau at all times. Her father would fire me in an instant if he thought I'd left her alone with anyone, even you, sir."

Vorontov saw the look in his eye. The man was not going to budge and he couldn't afford to waste time in argument.

"All right. But you'll observe her working from a distance only. Is that understood?"

"As long as I can see Miss De Pau at all times, we won't have a problem."

"Very well. I must also ask you to show me the contents of your case. Again, I apologise for the imposition. But I'm sure you understand."

Vorontov watched as Damien handed Madame De Pau her case. It contained a powerful magnifying glass, an ultraviolet torch with a viewing shield, pliers and screwdrivers of various sizes, surgical instruments, cotton wool, a half-litre bottle of neat industrial alcohol, a measuring tape, white cotton gloves and a digital voice recorder.

"That's for notes," she said.

"You won't need it," Vorontov said. "Likewise, the sharp instruments must remain here. I'll carry the rest down for you."

He replaced the bulk of the items in the case and closed it.

"Down, Monsieur?" she said.

"What you're about to see must remain our secret," he said solemnly. "If you have even the slightest doubt that you, or your bodyguard, can keep such a secret, please say so now."

She looked up at him. "I am my father's daughter, Monsieur. I follow my father's craft. Damien has risked his life for me in the past. He would do so again. This is not the first job where absolute discretion has been called for and I doubt if it will be the last."

"There will never be another job like this," Vorontov said, "believe me," and stepped over to the panel in the far wall.

Gabrielle heard a click and saw a hidden door swing open, revealing a narrow flight of stairs, spiralling down into the blackness.

"There's no elevator, Madame," he said. "I'm sorry, but Damien will have to carry you."

She turned to Flynn, who raised an eyebrow, bent down and lifted her out of her wheelchair.

"Lead on, Monsieur," she said and Flynn carried her down the winding stone steps, following Vorontov. Lights flickered into life automatically as they descended. Gabrielle felt Flynn weakening, and was about to say something to him out of earshot of Vorontov, when he gestured to the ceiling with his eyes and shook his head. She looked up. Every few metres down the stairwell, the circular glass domes of a CCTV system stared down at her.

Finally, as sweat began to break out on Flynn's face, they reached the bottom and stepped through a security door into a vast and beautifully furnished room, carved from the very stone on which the castle rested and lined with paintings. A single table, bearing a desk lamp, a painting covered in a white sheet and a high-backed chair, stood at the far end. Vorontov gestured to the table and placed Gabrielle's case next to the covered painting. Flynn sat her gently down on the chair and retreated to watch her from the door. Gabrielle looked around the room, recognising many of the paintings from Guido De Pau's forty-eight hour cramming class in black market art.

"Monsieur Vorontov," she said with genuine surprise. "That's the Raphael reported stolen from Florence ten years ago! And there's the painting attributed to Titian which has been missing since the war. Oh . . . and that can't be . . !"

Vorontov had pulled back the sheet.

She was staring at the Mona Lisa by Leonardo Da Vinci.

"Now do you see why I've had to insist on so many security precautions, Madame De Pau?" said Vorontov. "This is what you're here to authenticate. Please examine it and tell me if it's genuine."

Gabrielle pretended to be overwhelmed. It wasn't difficult. Just to be standing in front of such an iconic work of art, to be able to actually touch it, was breathtaking.

"I can," she said, "but it will take me a few moments."

"I can wait," Vorontov said.

She opened her case, removed a pair of cotton gloves and a surgical face mask, put them on and carefully measured the length, breadth and thickness of the wooden panel to the nearest millimetre, while trying to calm herself enough to remember all the important details about the masterpiece Guido had made her memorise.

"It's the right size," she said.

Then she took the magnifying glass, asked Vorontov to adjust the lamp and went to work, minutely examining the painting in a slow sweeping motion from left to right and up and down.

"To make a forgery that will convince an expert analyst, the forger needs to master four things," she said "He needs to find a suitably aged surface which is appropriate to the work, be it canvas or wood.

In this case, Da Vinci used a panel of poplar wood, which is what we appear to have here . . ."

Guido had said that the panel in the original had warped against the battens that ran horizontally across its back. Taking a deep breath and using the gentlest touch possible, she lifted the painting by its sides and stared at the bottom edge. It was warped, although not as much as Guido had suggested the original would be.

"The markings on the rear of the panel look genuine enough," she said, examining the various authentication seals and the letters carved into the wood.

"And the other three things a forger needs to master?" asked Vorontov.

"There are the pigments," Gabrielle said, "which must be authentic to the period in which the painting was created. It was only in 1842 when Windsor and Newton patented the method of sealing paint in resealable tubes. Before then, artists mixed their own pigments by grinding ingredients such as charred ivory, lead and tin oxide and the semi-precious stone ultramarine in a mortar and pestle. Unfortunately, we can only determine the chemical composition of the paint by removing some of it from the panel and having it tested in a laboratory. I take it you'd prefer me not to do this?"

"Only as a last resort," Vorontov said.

"The final two clues are the most difficult for the forger to emulate," Gabrielle said, straightening up from her work for a moment. "The first is the tiny pattern of cracks in the dried paint, what we experts call the *craquelure*. As the oil in the paint evaporates over the years, the paint shrinks and cracks, forming tiny islands. Likewise as the wood or canvas stretches or shrinks with changing humidity, so the cracks form to differing degrees. The only way to simulate realistic *craquelure* in a recent forgery is to find an aged canvas or piece of wood with an old painting already on it, strip that painting away layer by layer to the base coat with its original *craquelure*, and then build up the new painting in very thin layers so that the original patterns of the base coat show through. This is a long and tedious process, because it requires the paint to be baked between each layer."

"Baked?" asked Vorontov.

Gabrielle stared at the tiny cracks over the eyes of the *Mona Lisa*. She and Guido had made up a complete speech that would convince Vorontov that even the genuine painting was a fake, based on the thickness of the cracks in the paint around the eyes. But now, as she peered at these cracks again, there seemed something strange about them, something completely at odds with what she and Guido had agreed she could say. Vorontov was waiting for an answer. Her brain raced.

"Baked?" Vorontov asked again.

"Ah ... the last problem the forger has to overcome is that of making sure the paint on his forgery is perfectly dry," she said, falling back on the speech she'd practiced with Guido while she tried to make sense of what she was seeing. "Oil paint is dry to the touch within a few days of being applied, but it takes years to harden completely, time the forger does not have if he is to sell his piece within his lifetime. The most famous forger in history, whose paintings hung in the Rijksmuseum and deceived Hermann Goering was a man called Han van Meegeren. He invented a way of painting, not with ordinary oils, but with the basic elements of the plastic Bakelite. Once hardened in an oven, his painting was as hard and impervious to alcohol as any authentic master that had aged for hundreds of years."

She peered at the cracks again, trying desperately to equate what Guido had told her about the original with what she was seeing right in front of her eyes.

"What is it?" asked Vorontov.

She felt like a child on a roller coaster, trapped in a headlong flight that couldn't be stopped. There was no other way. She'd rehearsed this speech with Guido a dozen times. But now it had suddenly become reality, and their lives depended on her getting it right.

"It's not obvious even on close examination," she said, lifting the painting gently on the table so that the light shone on it obliquely. "But look at the surface of the painting itself. Not at the image of the woman, or the shape or the colours, but at the *craquelure*."

Vorontov took the magnifying glass and squinted at the portrait.

"Take a very close look at where the eyebrows should be."

"But there are no eyebrows," said Vorontov.

"Exactly. Over the hundreds of years since Leonardo completed it, the pigment in its oil paint had darkened. Pollutants in the air, sulphur dioxide from the industrial revolution in the 1800s for example, darkened the surface of the painting and it lost the incredible luminosity that Leonardo had endowed it with."

"I still don't follow."

"At some stage in the career of the original painting, it was taken aside and an attempt was made to clean it. In those days, before it was first stolen in 1911, the *Mona Lisa* was considered an important painting, but not the unique artwork it is today. The cleaning was careless and some of the incredibly fine lines of Leonardo's misty *sfumato* style were actually removed from the painting, here above the eyes."

"Reducing the impact of the eyebrows?" suggested Vorontov.

"Exactly."

"But the eyebrows are absent in this picture too. How can it be a forgery?"

"Because, to remove enough paint to take away the top layers of the picture, the restorer would inevitably reduce the number and depth of the *craquelure*," she said, quoting her rehearsed speech. "It would be like shaving a block of wood with a knife. Anyone doing so removes the rough surface layers and creates a smooth new surface. Look again closely at the areas where the eyebrows should be and tell me about the lines you see on the surface of the paint."

Vorontov looked. "They're exactly the same depth as anywhere else on the painting," he said.

"Which makes it a fake," said Gabrielle, delivering the conclusion they'd all agreed in Paris. "If we had access to the computer images at the Louvre, which record in perfect detail every crack and blemish on the surface of the original like the scrolls and lines of a unique fingerprint, we would know for sure. But I imagine you are not at liberty to make an enquiry like that?"

"Is there any other way to be certain?"

Gabrielle was confused by what she'd seen. Her head swam as she took out the bottle of neat alcohol from her case, along with a wad of cotton wool. Vorontov's eyes widened. His voice sounded like that of a father whose child was about to undergo surgery.

"You're not going to damage the painting, are you?"

"Of course not, Monsieur, there are smudges of paint on the outer edge of the panel we can test without touching the portrait itself."

She wetted the pad of cotton wool, catching a whiff of the highly volatile liquid in the process, leant forward and gently dabbed the outer edge of the panel. For a moment the cotton wool came away clean . . . and then it started to darken as the paint softened.

The second test confirmed what she dared not believe. The painting in front of her was a forgery. It really was!

The room seemed to move around her. She reached forward and steadied herself on the table. What did this mean? How had Nicole Sabaut's copy come to be here in Vorontov's collection? Was the real *Mona Lisa* back in Paris with Constance?

She looked hard at the painting again, and then at Vorontov. He was staring at the wad of cotton wool. His mouth was open.

"So it's a fake," he said at last.

"I'm sorry," Gabrielle said, with real emotion in her voice. "I know how much trouble you must have gone to get this painting, and how much it must have cost. But the truth is there, right in front of us."

Vorontov looked shaken. "How can you be sure?"

"There are other minor discrepancies," Gabrielle said, blurting out her rehearsed speeches, "in the grain of the wood and the ageing of the seals and labels on the back of the painting. But this is the most telling defect. I'm sorry."

29

Vorontov stared at the portrait. All that money, all that organisation, all that planning . . . all worthless!

"Are you sure?" he said. "Would you like to examine it again?"

The internal phone rang. He tore himself away from the painting to answer it.

"I thought I told you I was not to be disturbed," he snapped.

"You have visitors from the board of directors," said the receptionist. "Igor Sergeyevich, his personal assistant and Anatoly Ivanovich are all here from Novorossiysk and are waiting for you in the boardroom."

Vorontov cursed under his breath. There was nobody in the world he wanted at this moment less than Igor Kisenko. Yet to keep him waiting could be fatal.

"But he wasn't due until tomorrow!"

"I'm afraid he's here now, and he's very anxious to talk to you."

Vorontov slammed the phone back into place. This was the last thing he needed, on top of the terrible news he'd just received from Antoinette De Pau. He turned to her.

"Very well," he said, trying to pull himself together. "I have to meet some important people now. If I could ask you to return with me to the study and wait there for a few minutes, I'll be back as soon as I can. I need to discuss the results of your assessment in more detail. You can leave your equipment here on the table."

Antoinette De Pau nodded and her bodyguard stepped forward to lift her into his arms. Vorontov made sure the door to the bunker was securely locked behind them. Then he led them back up the stairs to his study, and continued through the reception area, up the sweeping marble staircase to the boardroom. Kisenko and the others would want to stay in the castle overnight. That worried Vorontov. It meant that curious eyes might be watching him and the matter of the *Mona Lisa* would have to be postponed.

He paused for a moment outside the polished wooden door of the boardroom, knocked and went inside.

Three pairs of eyes swung like rifle barrels to meet him from around the board table. The first pair was bright blue and belonged to a blonde woman in her mid thirties, wearing a dark business suit and white shirt. Her body was slim and athletic and her face looked as if it had been sculpted from marble. Vorontov knew her name was Irina, that she was personal private secretary to Igor Sergeyevich Kisenko and rumoured to be his mistress. Vorontov also knew, from bitter personal experience, that she was completely ruthless in carrying out Kisenko's orders.

The eyes of the man on Irina's right had the chill of ice behind them. Anatoly Ivanovich Sorokin was tall and impeccably dressed, with the hungry intelligence of a wolf. He smiled welcomingly but Vorontov knew that behind the smile, Sorokin's brain was working like a well-oiled machine to calculate and exploit any weakness his bright eyes might detect. As vice-chairman in charge of strategic affairs for Azeroil, Sorokin was Vorontov's natural successor and his deadliest rival. Vorontov had therefore spent a great deal of time studying his background and searching for weaknesses he could exploit. Sorokin was completely motivated by greed. While his academic parents had been content to live as low-paid professors in the State University of Leningrad, Sorokin himself had developed the philosophy that intelligence was of no use unless it was focussed on the acquisition of power. More than once, Vorontov had narrowly escaped an intricate plot Sorokin had aimed at his chairmanship. In many ways, working with Sorokin was like sleeping with a snake.

The third pair of eyes was as hard and lifeless as steel.

Ever since Igor Kisenko had walked into his office at Azeroil twenty-five years previously and announced that certain "persons in Moscow" now held the controlling interest in his company, Viktor Vorontov had made it his business to know everything there was to know about him.

He knew Kisenko was a major figure in the Solntsevskaya gang of the Russian mafia, based in the Solntsevo suburb of Moscow. He knew that, long ago, Kisenko had aligned himself with the elite of the Soviet Union as a supplier of luxuries such as jeans, Marlboro cigarettes and chewing gum to those who could afford it. This close association with those in legitimate power, combined with Kisenko's criminal connections and his own ruthless intelligence, had quickly propelled him to a position of power in the Moscow underworld. But that power had come at a terrible price, which was paid when his wife and young son were killed in a car bomb meant for him in 1992. Kisenko had never remarried and he preferred to indulge his appetites with female associates who tended to go missing when these affairs broke up.

Vorontov also knew that Kisenko's close association with the state power brokers in Moscow had allowed him to amass a fortune by stripping the assets of Soviet Communism when it collapsed in 1991. Factories, oil refineries and even nuclear power stations fell into Kisenko's hands—along with an arsenal of illegal weapons. He'd also acquired a formidable pool of highly-trained but unemployed operatives from the KGB and Spetsnaz commandos, who had been willing to work for him rather than face starvation, and were used to coerce rival companies into handing over their shares by extortion, kidnappings and assassinations.

As a result, Igor Kisenko was not only a multi-billionaire whose empire included newspapers, railways and shipyards all across Russia—but an enormously powerful man with a private army behind him, a brilliant intelligence and a cold ruthlessness that scared Viktor Vorontov to the core of his being.

But Vorontov had also learned one vital secret about Kisenko—

twelve months before he'd been diagnosed with liver cancer. The waxy skin and the red blotches on his face were sure signs. Igor Kisenko had only a short while to live.

"Viktor," he said. "Why were you not in Brussels yesterday? That planning meeting was a vital part of our preparations for the energy summit, particularly in relation to the Caspian Pipeline project. Why did you come straight here from London?"

His voice sounded soft, but the veins on his forehead stood out angrily against his taut skin. His bony hands gripped the arms of his seat like claws.

Vorontov tried to gather his thoughts as Irina and Sorokin watched him, like children watching a worm die on a sun-baked stone.

"The meeting can be rescheduled," Vorontov said. "I had important things to attend to here in preparation for the board meeting tomorrow."

"That European planning meeting cannot be rescheduled," Kisenko snapped. "The Commissioner and six of his highest officials were there and their diaries are booked up solidly until the middle of next month. You know it's vital to build good relations with the Europeans and to remind them at every turn that they are as dangerously reliant on Saudi Arabian oil as the Americans are."

"I know. I'm sorry."

The faintest hint of a smile curled on Sorokin's lips.

"A pipeline linking the two biggest oilfields in the Caspian with the main artery to the Black Sea and the Mediterranean is as valuable to Europe as it is to the Americans," he smirked. "You need to be fully engaged on this project, Viktor. You must focus! Or is there something else you consider to be more important?"

"Like I said, I had papers to prepare for the board meeting."

"Do you not have assistants?" Kisenko asked. "I'm sure Anatoly could have done that for you, had you asked. He is, after all, your next in line for the Chairmanship."

Vorontov recognised the threat in that soft voice, as clearly as if it had been shouted across the room.

"Anatoly, Irina," Kisenko said. "Would you mind leaving us alone for a moment? I'll join you in the other meeting room later."

Sorokin nodded and got to his feet, followed by Kisenko's assistant. He smiled again at Vorontov as he passed him. "Good luck, Viktor."

The heavy door shut behind them.

Kisenko's mask dropped. "What is this madness in Paris?" he screamed across the room. "What on earth do you mean by entering into such foolishness behind my back? Don't you know what's at stake here?"

"What madness?"

"Don't treat me like a child, Viktor, or you won't leave this room alive. The art theft that money-grabbing fool Gorshkov organised for you!"

"He approached me with a scheme to add a few priceless items to my collection," Vorontov said, knowing now that the only sure way to survive was through at least some version of the truth. "He'd obtained pieces for me before without incident. I had no way of knowing how he was planning to pull it off, or the sheer scale of what he was going to do. I didn't know he was going to bring Paris to a halt or blackmail France with a bomb."

"You're an obsessed fool," spat Kisenko, pulling himself to his feet. "And your obsession with meaningless daubs of paint may cost us hundreds of billions of dollars and the future of Russian supremacy in the Caspian oilfields."

Kisenko stalked over to Vorontov and glared into his eyes.

"I had Gorshkov shot," he spat. "I had his brains splattered all over the wall of the police headquarters of Barcelona before I'd risk him jeopardising what I'm about to do. Why should I even hesitate to do the same to you?"

"I'm sorry," Vorontov stammered, now truly frightened. "I'll do anything to make it right."

Kisenko seemed to regain control. He steadied himself against the board table.

"Viktor, I'm a pragmatist. I deal in realities. Anyone who grew up during the Great Patriotic War in Moscow had to be. In my world, things like love, friendship and charity had to be pushed aside to make room for vengeance, money and power. Do you understand?"

"I do."

"I'm a wealthy man, Viktor, and more powerful than the president of Russia. And yet I have no son, nobody I trust to leave all this wealth and power to, when I die."

He lowered himself into a chair, and his voice softened again.

"When I first met you, years ago by the Sea of Azov, I thought I saw something in you, something I could use. A man in my position, with the enemies I've acquired, cannot afford to take a high profile. But with you as chairman of Azeroil to plan and manage my legitimate interests, with you as a figurehead, I could operate behind the scenes in safety, pulling strings and doing what needed to be done."

The steely eyes measured Vorontov up and down, taking in his expensive suit, his handmade shoes and his expanding waistline.

"You've grown weak, Viktor. The lifestyle of a playboy has softened the calluses you grew on the oilfields and rich food has bloated your belly. You could have had it all, Viktor. You could have been the son I lost in Moscow. But you've pissed it all away."

"What can I do?" Vorontov said.

"You'll restore those paintings to the French, in return for the termination of any further investigations that might lead them back through you to me. You have contacts in the art world, Viktor. You can do it discreetly so that nobody will ever know where the paintings came from."

"But . . ."

"But what? Are those daubs of paint worth more than your life, Viktor? Because that's what's at stake here. I have a project to restore the faith of certain American and European investors in the Caspian Sea project. I've taken enormous risks and incurred incredible expense. And if it all fails because of your stupidity, Anatoly will take your job as chairman of Azeroil, and I will take your life!"

He turned and stormed out of the boardroom, slamming the door behind him with a boom that seemed to echo long after he was gone.

Vorontov stood staring out at the glittering blue sea beyond the windows as he wrestled with the impossible decision he had to make. Then he ran back downstairs to his study. Antoinette De Pau was sitting by the desk in her wheelchair, reading a book on Renaissance art she'd taken from his shelves. Her nurse and bodyguard were by the window, both looking out at the view.

"Sorry I kept you waiting," he said. "My company has an important meeting tomorrow and some of the board members have arrived early."

"That's understandable," said Antoinette, smiling at him. "I wouldn't like to interfere with your business. But can I ask how long you think we might be here? I have other work to do for my father in Paris, now he's sick."

Vorontov tried to calm his mind and think clearly. Now he knew his *Mona Lisa* was a fake, he'd have to deal with Constance Le Clerc to acquire the original. But if he was to deal with her, he'd need an expert on hand to prove that the painting she was trying to sell him was the genuine article. He did not want to be fooled a second time.

"That will depend on the next phone call I make," he said. "In the meantime, there are a number of spare guest rooms on the ground floor, with balconies overlooking the sea. I'll have someone show you to them in a moment and you can rest for a while."

When Antoinette De Pau and her staff had left, Vorontov took out his Smartphone and dialled an English mobile number.

"Good evening," he said, when that number answered. "We spoke the other day at Sotheby's. You asked me to ring you back once I'd had a certain piece appraised."

"Indeed," said the woman he knew as Constance Le Clerc. "It's a forgery, isn't it?"

"Yes."

"Then allow me to offer my condolences. Sometimes it's easier to take bad news from an independent professional than an interested party. Can I ask whose services you used to make the authentication?"

"No," Vorontov said, suddenly feeling protective towards the young woman in the wheelchair who had such a warm smile. "You can, however, honour the promise you made to me in London to supply me with the original."

"There are details we must discuss," said the woman. "My terms are simple. In exchange for the original of the work you desire, I'll require delivery of the other nine pieces you acquired in Paris on your recent shopping expedition."

"That's hardly a fair bargain," Vorontov said.

"In terms of the number of items involved, perhaps not. But if you compare the insured value of eight hundred million on the one piece I hold against the insured value of the nine you possess, not to mention its sheer reputation as an iconic masterpiece of art, then you'll see you're getting more than a fair bargain."

Vorontov thought about this. He had to admit that the woman was right.

"Then there's the simplicity of a direct exchange," she said. "—no currency conversions, no complications with bank accounts and traceable transactions. All we need to agree is a time and location convenient to us both."

"I insist on having my own expert on hand to verify that your item is genuine," Vorontov said. "Given my recent experience, I need to be absolutely sure."

The woman thought for a moment. "Fair enough," she said, "but you must keep the location of the rendezvous secret, even from your expert. The windows of your aircraft are to be kept shuttered as the plane lands and not opened again until it's airborne. The fewer people who know about our business, the better."

"Agreed," Vorontov said, "but what about security? I'll need to bring my bodyguards with me to make sure there's no foul play."

"One man only," said the woman. "The fewer people who know

232 - JOHN JOYCE

about the exchange, the fewer can hijack the paintings from either side. I'll make sure the place I choose can be easily seen from the air, so both of us can satisfy ourselves there's nobody lying in ambush. Both of us will circle the field, check that it's clear, land and make the exchange. Then we'll depart. Is that agreed."

Vorontov thought for a moment.

"Monsieur? Are you still there?"

"All right, I agree," Vorontov said. "I have a business meeting I can't afford to miss tomorrow. The day after would suit me best, anywhere in Europe that has a private airstrip nobody will be watching."

"I'll make arrangements," said the woman, "and check back with you regarding time and place. Can you give me an email address where you can be contacted?"

Vorontov did so.

"One last thing," said Constance Le Clerc. "I'd be grateful if you'd include Nicole Sabaut's forgery of the *Mona Lisa* in your consignment of paintings."

"Why do you want it? It's only a forgery."

"I know, but it has great sentimental value to me. She and I were very close."

"I really would prefer to keep it myself."

"Do you want the real thing or not, Monsieur? The choice is yours."

Vorontov was not used to people standing in his way, but there was too much at stake and he was in a hurry. For a moment he gripped the phone tightly, not knowing what to do.

"Okay," he spat. "Just keep your end of the bargain."

The call ended.

"Who was that on the phone?" asked Sorokin from the door of the study.

Vorontov turned sharply. How much had Sorokin heard?

"A fellow collector from the art world," snapped Vorontov. "And what are you doing spying on me in my own office?"

Sorokin smiled. "Simply checking to see how arrangements are progressing regarding the rescheduling of that European Commission meeting."

"There may be delays," Vorontov said. "You know how it is with the Commission. It's a major logistical exercise to get even half of them into a room at the same time."

"Tomorrow's board meeting is important, Viktor. If you'd been in Brussels yesterday, we'd have had things settled with the Europeans in preparation for the summit. As it is, there are now loose ends that need to be tied up before our major shareholders arrive from Moscow tomorrow. I thought I'd try and resolve them tonight. I trust you have a bed for me somewhere?"

"This island and all it contains is a corporate asset of Azeroil," said Vorontov. "As vice-chairman of the company, you're free to use them as you wish."

"Just as you do, Viktor? I understand you have other guests here now—a man and two women, one of them in a wheelchair. Can I ask who they are?"

"They're personal friends of mine," he said, "people I met in Paris."

"From the art world perhaps, Viktor? Still indulging your passion for paintings? You'll remember what Kisenko said about staying focussed on business?"

"You may be vice-chairman, Anatoly. But I'm still in charge of this company. Please don't forget that."

Sorokin did not flinch. "With respect, Mr Chairman, we both know where the real power lies. Igor Kisenko and his friends in Moscow can take away what they've given you at any time."

"And you intend to be around when they do?"

Sorokin's bright blue eyes fixed Vorontov's. His lips parted in a smile.

"I'm a businessman, Viktor. I seek business opportunities. And the biggest opportunity I see for myself right now is for you to make a mistake."

"Perhaps you'd like to work upstairs in the boardroom?" said Vorontov.

"And the three people I saw leaving this room a few moments ago? Does Kisenko know they're here?"

"Get out," Vorontov said. "My personal interests are no concern of this company."

Sorokin turned to go. "Any day now those personal interests of yours will get you into a lot of trouble, Viktor," he said, and closed the door behind him.

Vorontov cursed himself for his own stupidity. Sorokin was right. As long as profits continued to flow to the shareholders and Azeroil continued to grow, those investors might tolerate his "addiction to art" as Kisenko had called it. But if that addiction were to cause the men from Moscow any embarrassment or loss, those investors would turn against him.

And there was Sorokin, ready and waiting to step into his shoes.

Gabrielle sat in her wheelchair, with Flynn and Lyudmila at her side, and stared out at the palette of colours created by the setting sun over the sea—yellows, oranges, pinks and bright reds. She hadn't dared talk to them inside the building for fear of bugs. She'd noticed cameras in the corridors and various items, that may or may not have been smoke alarms, in their rooms. Out here in the open air, with their backs to the building, they might be safe.

"We have a major problem," she whispered. "The painting downstairs is an actual fake."

"We're away from the microphones now," said Flynn. "You don't have to pretend."

"I'm not pretending. Alcohol softens the paint on it and the *craquelure* is wrong. The *Mona Lisa* downstairs really *is* a forgery."

Flynn stared at her. "But with respect, you're not really an art expert, are you? Is there any way you could be wrong?"

"No. The alcohol test proves it. Even a child could get that right. What Vorontov has downstairs must be Nicole Sabaut's forgery."

Flynn leant forward on the balcony and shook his head.

"Holy shit! What a bloody mess!"

Gabrielle agreed. They were in the hopeless situation of knowing what was about to happen, but powerless to do anything about it. It was like watching a train wreck from a distance. Unless they could contact Constance, their plan to get the original *Mona Lisa* and the other paintings back to the Louvre would blow up in their faces.

"When we worked out that cover story for Constance to tell Vorontov, the one about the Louvre mixing up the two paintings in their rush to get the *Mona Lisa* back into that Japanese display unit in time for its opening, we never thought it could've actually happened!" he said. "The Louvre must have mixed up the paintings for real—"

"Which means the original *Mona Lisa* must be back in Paris with Constance, underneath Nicole's portrait," Lyudmila said.

"We have to call Constance and tell her," Gabrielle said. "Otherwise we'll be swapping the original *Mona Lisa* for Vorontov's fake."

"How can we do that?" Flynn said. "Vorontov's confiscated our cell phones and he's bound to listen in on any landline call you make. We're not even supposed to know Constance, let alone call her up on the phone."

"Let's look at our options. There has to be something."

"What fucking options have we got?" said Flynn. "We're screwed!"

"There are always options. I could tell Vorontov that his painting is real—"

"And you'd look as if you don't know what you're talking about," Flynn said.

"Or we could get him to load the paintings onto his jet to make the exchange with Constance, then hijack the plane and—"

"And all get shot. Have you seen the number of guards around here?"

"Or we could try and get a coded message to Guido and make sure he passes it on to Constance. I could call him and say I've been delayed."

"How would he understand what you really meant, without giving the game away?"

"Or you could come up with a better idea," snapped Gabrielle. "You're supposed to be the expert strategist!"

"I'm thinking . . . All right, our best bet is for us to get a message to Guido somehow."

"But what about the second bomb?" Lyudmila said. "The paintings aren't our only objective."

"You're right," Flynn said. "Nobody's going to die if we don't get the paintings back. The first objective must be to locate the bomb."

"It has to be here on the island," said Gabrielle."They kept it well away from any inhabited area in Baku, out at sea in an explosives store. Here on the island is even better, because they can bring it in and out without being seen. There's a hangar out by the landing strip where they keep the planes. I'd suggest we start there."

"We should wait until after dinner and look for it when it's dark," Lyudmila said.

Flynn nodded. "Okay. Let's do it. Gabrielle, perhaps you could stay and persuade your friend Viktor to let you use a telephone and call Guido. He seems to have taken quite a shine to you."

30

Flynn spent half an hour after dinner sitting quietly on the balcony outside his room with Lyudmila, watching and listening. They saw the moon rise over the sea and heard the chirp of cicadas in the low scrub on the slope below the window. But most of all they watched out for television cameras, guards, dogs or any patrols that could intercept them. They listened for men talking, the slap of footsteps. Finally, when they felt in tune with the darkness and the sounds of the night, they eased themselves over the balcony, down onto the slope and made their way through the low scrub to the path along the shore, where they stopped.

Flynn listened. All he could hear was the soft slap of waves on the rocks below.

"The moonlight's very bright," he whispered. "That could be a problem."

"We'll keep to the edges of the path and to the ditches," Lyudmila said. "We can't go back now."

From the seaward side facing south, they hurried around the soaring walls of the castle to the northward side, where the land flattened out towards the airstrip, and followed the main access road, keeping well within an easy jump to the storm drain.

Twice they had to duck down out of sight as the purr of engines and glare of headlights warned them of approaching vehicles. Flynn felt exposed by the moonlight and vulnerable on the flat ground. He had a fleeting feeling someone was following them. But there were no torches and no noise behind them. It could have been an animal, or just his imagination. He put it to the back of his mind and kept moving forward as quietly as he could.

The airstrip had closed down for the night. Its landing lights were off and the makeshift control tower next to the hangar was darkened. On the tarmac in front of the tower, two private jets stood idle in the moonlight. The whole place appeared deserted, until Flynn saw the red eye of a cigarette burning in the darkness by the control tower ladder and heard the murmur of voices. It sounded like two men, one there to keep the other from dozing off at his post. They didn't seem to be going anywhere in a hurry.

Flynn looked past them to the hangar, signalled to Lyudmila to follow, then ducked down and dodged through the scrub to the far side, where they were shielded from the tower. The main door was on the other side in full view of the guards. It would make a lot of noise if they were to roll it back on its runners. There had to be a fire escape or emergency access of some kind at the back of the hangar. Flynn crept along until he found it, checked all around it for alarm contacts and eased it open, ready to run at the first sign of trouble.

There were none. Flynn and Lyudmila slipped into the hangar, shut the door gently behind them and looked around. The vast space was lit by the moon streaming through the high windows. In the centre of the floor stood a squat cargo plane. Its rear ramp was up, but the passenger access ladder was down and the door above it was open. Flynn and Lyudmila climbed the ladder and, when they were safely inside, Flynn flicked on a torch.

They were standing next to a large white van—an ambulance, with Red Cross markings—secured to the deck of the aircraft by wide canvas straps. The ambulance looked as if it had seen a lot of action, with dents in the metalwork and dust on the windscreen. Flynn wondered why anyone would use an expensive modern cargo plane to transport it. He shuffled around the ambulance to the rear doors and opened them.

There, in the narrow space between the two beds, was a white metal cabinet on wheels with the unmistakable red and white sectioned circle of a radiation warning sign and the sign 'Danger

X-Rays' in Russian. It looked very familiar. The packing material and shipping label lay crumpled on the floor. It was the X-ray machine he and Gabrielle had seen in the explosives store in Azerbaijan.

Flynn and Lyudmila stepped up into the ambulance, pulling the rear doors shut behind them. Flynn sat on one of the beds and looked at the machine.

"It all fits," he whispered. "If you had to smuggle a radioactive device like a tactical nuclear warhead, what better disguise than to put it inside something that's already supposed to be radioactive, something innocent that would command respect."

"Let me have a look at it," said Lyudmila. "Hold the torch over that panel."

She took a Swiss Army knife from her pocket, opened the Pozidriv attachment and began to undo the screws over the inspection plate in the side of the machine. Then she gently removed it and placed it on the bed opposite.

"Give me the torch for a moment," she said and leant forward to look inside. "We have what we came for. Take a look. The bomb is here."

Flynn leant forward, and found himself staring at a mass of wires and metal boxes.

Lyudmila moved closer to him and pointed through the narrow opening. Her hand touched his and, all at once, he felt the same electric thrill he'd experienced when Juliette had brushed against him at the meeting in Brussels.

'Jesus!' he thought. 'Not now, for God's sake.'

"There's the timing device, " she said, pointing with her long fingers. "It's connected to this digital readout on the outside of the machine where anyone can see it. That grey sphere is the plutonium core, surrounded by the shaped explosive charges that would compress the nuclear material to critical mass and create an atomic chain reaction."

"Can you disarm it without anyone being able to detect that you've done it?" asked Flynn.

"I could cut through the wires from the battery to the detonator, then tape over the cuts so they wouldn't be obvious to anyone inspecting the bomb. That would work."

"And no danger of setting it off while you're doing that?"

"There's always a danger, Mr Flynn," she smiled. "But I do know what I'm doing."

"Go ahead and do it then. I'll keep watch."

He left her in the ambulance and climbed out of the plane into the hangar. Trying to start a romance with a woman while she was trying to defuse a nuclear weapon was definitely not a good idea. Besides, he was still troubled by the feeling of being watched. It was nothing he could put his finger on, just some sixth sense of another presence out there in the moonlight.

He waited five minutes then went back inside the plane and into the ambulance. Lyudmila was replacing the inspection cover on the X-ray machine and tightening the screws.

"If anyone tries to detonate the bomb, the timer will still show a countdown, but the electric charge from the trigger will never reach the detonator. So the bomb will not explode. It's safe."

"You're a genius," Flynn said. "Let's get out of here."

Since Vorontov had rammed the needle into Gabrielle's thigh, the anaesthetic Lyudmila had injected into her legs before they'd boarded Vorontov's plane had started to wear off. Feeling was returning, and with it came pain. The needle had gone deep into her flesh and, several times in Vorontov's presence, she'd had to fight back the irresistible urge to reach down and rub the spot where he'd stabbed her. Here on the veranda outside her room, away from the sight of the cameras, she could reach down and run her hand over her thigh.

A soft knock sounded behind her. She manoeuvred her wheelchair back into the room to open the door. Viktor Vorontov stood there, looking down at her.

"I must apologise for not allowing you and your companions to eat with us tonight," he said. "I had important business to discuss with my other guests and didn't want to bore you with the matters of our meeting tomorrow."

"No need to apologise," said Gabrielle. "In my line of work it's vital to be discreet. If, by any chance, somebody was to recognise me, they may wonder what I was doing here and questions might be asked."

"May I come in for a moment?" asked Vorontov. "I'd like your professional opinion."

"Of course, Monsieur," said Gabrielle.

Vorontov sat at the small table near the window.

"I've made a call," he said. "And arranged to exchange a number of paintings I've recently acquired for what I am assured is the original *Mona Lisa*. What I'd like to discuss with you is the proposed price. The person offering me the genuine Giaconda is asking for nine other paintings in return."

"Would these be the nine other paintings that went missing from the Louvre at the same time as the *Mona Lisa*?" asked Gabrielle.

"Correct. I know I can count on your discretion. Do you think that's a fair exchange?"

Gabrielle thought about this.

"Madame De Pau?"

"Sorry. Yes. I think it would be worth even that price. As I understand it, there are several of Da Vinci's slightly lesser-known works amongst those nine paintings, such as *The Virgin on the Rocks* and *Head of a Young Woman*. But that is all they are, a collection of lesser-known works. Nothing can compare with *La Giaconda* in artistic significance."

Vorontov got to his feet.

"Thank you," he said. "I'll talk to you again, in the morning."

"Can you tell me when and where the authentication of the second painting is going to take place? If I'm to be delayed here for several days, then I need to call my father and tell him I'll be late returning. He worries about me when I'm away."

"I've just been informed that he exchange will take place the day after tomorrow at noon," said Vorontov. "The exact location, I'm afraid, must be kept completely secret. But it's at a location in Greece, so I can drop you and your party off at Athens airport and you can get a flight back to Paris from there. Regarding your request to call you father, I can make that call for you myself. Given the incredibly high stakes involved, I'm sure you'll agree that I cannot allow any personal phone calls off the island. That is why I insisted on confiscating all your cell phones when you arrived. I'm truly sorry. But there it is."

He walked to the door and went out.

Gabrielle waited until she was sure Vorontov was well out of earshot then opened the adjoining door to Lyudmila's room to see if she and Flynn had returned. The TV was on but Lyudmila was still nowhere to be seen.

Gabrielle had to tell them something vitally important . . . something that changed everything.

Vorontov had said the exchange was to be made somewhere in Greece.

The arrangement they'd agreed with Constance was for the exchange to take place at a remote and deserted airstrip – in eastern Turkey.

In twenty minutes Flynn and Lyudmila were at the southern side of the castle. Looking up, Flynn saw the light he'd left on in his room and the curtains drawn a third of the way across to distinguish it from all the other rooms in the building.

"Okay," he whispered. "This is where we part company until the morning. I'll check in with Gabrielle before she goes to sleep and tell her what you've done to the bomb. We'll have a talk about where we go from here and what we do about Constance and the paintings tomorrow."

"Understood," said Lyudmila and began to climb towards her room. Flynn followed her for a while, then turned left halfway up the gentle slope and climbed over his own balcony.

He was reaching for the door to his room when he smelt cigar smoke.

"Good evening," said a woman's voice in Russian. "Have you lost your key?"

Turning, he saw a dark figure sitting on the balcony of the room next to his. The figure stood up and moved into the light. She was tall, with close-cropped blonde hair, and was wearing a black silk evening dress that clung to her body like paint.

"Sorry I startled you," Flynn said, in Russian. "I went for a walk by the sea. It seemed much easier to take a short cut back up the slope to the balcony than to trudge all the way through the castle."

The woman stepped to the edge of her balcony and put out her hand.

"We haven't met," she said. "I'm Irina, executive secretary to Igor Kisenko, one of the main shareholders in Azeroil, who own this castle."

Her hand felt strong and warm.

"I'm Damien," he said. "I'm a bodyguard to a guest of Mr Vorontov's."

"It must be an important guest to have a personal bodyguard," said Irina. "Will they be joining us for the meeting tomorrow?"

"No. She's here to meet with Mr Vorontov on a private matter."

Flynn saw the tip of Irina's cigar glow in the dark.

"A private matter?" she said with a mischievous smile. "Would that be business or pleasure?"

"It's not my place to say."

"It's well-known that Viktor is a connoisseur of the arts and has one of the most valuable art collections in the world right here on the island," Irina said. "Would it be anything to do with that?"

"No comment. I'm here to ensure my employer's security is maintained."

"How do you do that?"

"By being close to her at all times and watching for possible threats."

"Do you think I pose a threat?" Irina said playfully, leaning forward so that Flynn could see the deep cleft between her breasts. "You sound very nervous of me. Perhaps you're afraid Viktor doesn't want the presence of your employer on this island to be known to anyone else?"

"That's my employer's business," Flynn said.

"I'm right though, aren't I? You wish them to remain anonymous. Why?"

"You ask a lot of questions."

Irina stubbed out her cigar on the stone parapet of her balcony.

"Let's make a deal, Mister bodyguard," she said. "I'll keep the presence of your employer a secret if you come over here and show me what it's like to really guard a body."

Flynn looked back at Gabrielle's balcony. Her lights were out and the balcony door was shut. It looked as if she'd turned in for the night.

"Just for a few minutes," he said. "We've a long day ahead of us tomorrow." And he climbed over the rails to join Irina, who led him into her bedroom and closed the doors to the sea behind them.

"You speak very good Russian," she said. "But you're not a native speaker. Where are you from?"

"Ireland. I was born in Cork and went to college in Dublin. That's where I learnt Russian, along with modern politics."

"Strange subjects for a bodyguard to learn," Irina said. She looked beautiful in the light. Her tanned skin set off her honey blonde hair and bright blue eyes. Her slim, athletic body rippled under the silk evening gown. "Can I get you a drink?"

"Tonic water, with ice and lemon, if you have it," Flynn said.

"You don't drink alcohol?"

"Not when I'm working."

"Neither do I," said Irina. "I've hated the smell of it, ever since I was a child. Have you been working for your employer long?"

Flynn thought back to the first time he had met Guido De Pau and the incident with Antoinette and the Marseilles art forgers.

"About ten years, on and off," he said.

Irina handed him his drink. Their fingers touched.

"It must be exciting, protecting an important person all over the world. My job is boring. I go to meetings, I take notes, write reports and arrange schedules. One job leads into the next. Sometimes all the meeting rooms and all the faces around them seem the same."

She looked at Flynn over the rim of her glass. Their eyes met.

"Are you bored now?" Flynn asked.

"What if I was?"

"We could do something about that."

She put her drink down on the dressing table and stepped forward. Her eyes closed, her lips touched his and her hand slid over his chest towards his shoulder. He flinched as her fingers pressed the dressing over his wound.

"I'm sorry," she said, pulling back. "Did I hurt you?"

"No," Flynn said. "It's just a scratch."

"Let me look," and before he could stop her, her hands were under his polo shirt, lifting it up over his head.

"That's a nasty wound," she said. "How did you get it?"

"Ah . . . like I said. My job is to protect my client. Sometimes my client needs more protecting than others."

"So it's a bullet wound?" She sounded truly impressed. Flynn had his shirt off already. Gabrielle wouldn't miss him until the morning. His fingers went to the thin straps of Irina's dress and lifted them over her shoulders.

She kissed him again, more passionately this time, and let her dress slide to the floor.

Flynn stared down at her naked body. She was breathtaking. He put his hands around her waist and pulled her to him. Her strong fingers pressed around his neck and drew his lips to hers. For a long moment they kissed as her thigh slid between his legs. Flynn felt himself getting hard. The blood pounded in his ears.

246 - JOHN JOYCE

"Tell me," she said. "Have you ever been to Baku, in Azerbaijan?"

Flynn stiffened as the question hit home.

But before he could break free of her, the strong fingers around his neck found his pressure points. There was a flash of light, the helpless whirl of falling, and then darkness . . .

Irina Chernenko bent over Flynn and pulled his eyelids back. Then she went to her wardrobe, pulled out a slim attaché case and laid it on the bed. Opening the case, she withdrew a syringe, filled it with a colourless liquid from a small glass bottle, tapped the needle to remove air bubbles and injected the contents into a vein in Flynn's right arm. Then she dressed herself in a shirt, sweater and slacks and went out into the corridor. In a few moments she was standing in front of another bedroom door. She knocked, waiting for a response, and went in.

"We have a problem," she said. "Viktor's guests include the two people I thought I'd killed in Azerbaijan, the man and the woman who were snooping around the oil complex at Baku. There's another woman with them, posing as a nurse. She and the man were over at the hangar where the bomb is stored. I think they may have tampered with it."

Igor Kisenko looked up from the papers on his desk.

"Where are they now?"

"The man's unconscious in my room. I've drugged him and he won't wake up for hours. The woman in the wheelchair, the so-called art expert of Viktor's, is asleep in her bedroom. The other woman is in the room beyond."

"And Viktor? What's his involvement in all this?"

"I haven't spoken with him. I thought I'd leave that to you."

"This changes nothing," Kisenko said. "Deal with the man as you see fit and have one of my men help you question the woman who went out to the hangar with him, see what they did to the bomb and make sure it's fixed. I'll tackle Viktor and this 'art expert' of his in the morning."

"Thank you," said Irina. "But I think I can question the woman more effectively by myself."

"I'm sure you can, Irina," Kisenko said. "Just make sure you do it quietly. Tomorrow's meeting is important and I don't want her screams to keep me awake

31

The phone next to Vorontov's bed rang at just after 8:00 am, jerking him out of a fitful and tormented sleep. A dozen impossible questions had buzzed in his brain like flies during the night. What would happen at the board meeting today? Would he still have his position as chairman by the end of business, or would Sorokin replace him? And what about Kisenko's threat regarding his obsession with art? Had Sorokin told him of Antoinette De Pau's presence on the island and, if he had, what would Kisenko's reaction be?

He'd been disturbed at around 4:00 am by footsteps outside his room, followed by the sound of a car leaving the courtyard. Twenty minutes later, he'd been woken by the roar of a jet taking off from the airstrip. Had Sorokin and Kisenko gone home? That had been too much to hope for.

The phone rang again. He lifted the receiver from its cradle.

"Hello?"

"Monsieur Vorontov? It's Antoinette De Pau here. I wonder . . . could I have a word with you?"

"What about?"

"I'm so sorry to bother you, but do you know where Damien and Lyudmila are? His bed hasn't been slept in and Lyudmila is also missing. I know he's a man, like other men, and she's an attractive woman, but this kind of behaviour is not like them. Can you make some enquiries?"

Vorontov thought about her request, as he tried to pull himself awake. The only other person with a balcony room on that side of the castle was Irina and he didn't want to approach her directly.

To make enquiries about the whereabouts of Miss De Pau's staff, particularly to someone so close to Kisenko, was to admit that he'd invited outsiders onto the island during the time of a sensitive board meeting and had no idea where they were.

"I'll see what I can do," he said.

"Thank you," Antoinette De Pau said, and hung up.

Vorontov showered, shaved and put on his best Armani suit. Outside his window, the sun already twinkled on the water. It was going to be a beautiful day. He walked out of his room, down a flight of stairs and onto the corridor below. Antoinette De Pau's room was the second door along, with her nurse's room to the left and her bodyguard's room to the right. Beyond that was Irina's room.

Antoinette opened her door quickly when he knocked, as if she'd been waiting for him. She looked as if she'd had even less sleep than he'd had. Her eyes were sunken and her skin was very pale.

"So," she said, gazing up at him from her wheelchair. "Do you have any news?"

"Perhaps I can help you." Irina stood in the corridor behind him. Two men were helping somebody from her room, somebody who could hardly walk.

Antoinette De Pau wheeled herself to her door and looked up at Irina.

"Have you seen Damien?" she asked.

"Mr Kisenko has asked me to invite you both to a working breakfast," said Irina.

"What about Damien?"

Irina smiled. "Mr Flynn is away delivering a package for me," she said. "I don't think he'll be coming back. As for your so-called nurse, Lyudmila, you might want to stand up now and let her use your wheelchair. She needs it more than you do."

Gabrielle sat at the head of the table in the dining room on the ground floor with her hands tightly bound to the arms of a heavy oak chair. Through the great arching windows, the sun glittered on the ocean, promising a beautiful day. But that was another world, as remote from her as the distant planets. Reality for Gabrielle Arnault was the men and women in this room, and what they might do to her over the next few minutes.

At the other end of the table, sat a sick old man with hard grey eyes. He appeared to be in charge and was flanked by the tall blonde woman, Irina, and a fair-haired man. They were both dressed for business, in dark suits. Coffee, orange juice, cold meat and fruit was laid out in front of them.

Viktor Vorontov sat to Gabrielle's right. His eyes were fixed on the sea, as if he was willing himself out of the room. Lyudmila was on her left, strapped to the wheelchair. Her hands were wrapped in bandages and her face was badly bruised. Her head lolled onto her shoulder and her breathing was ragged. But she was still alive.

"Just to confirm a few facts," said Irina in French. "Your name is Gabrielle Arnault, you are a former officer in the French police force and you and your colleagues are currently working for Europol. Is that correct?"

Gabrielle said nothing. The old man at the end of the table spoke rapidly to Irina in Russian. Vorontov glanced at Gabrielle. She saw fear in his eyes.

"Mr Kisenko apologises that his French is not fluent enough to converse with you directly," said Irina. "However, he insists that unless you truthfully answer his questions, which I will translate, I am to inflict more pain upon the woman who has been masquerading as your nurse. Personally, I don't think she'll survive much more punishment, particularly to those beautiful hands of hers which have already suffered a great deal of damage during the night. So I suggest you are completely honest and open with us. Do you understand?"

Gabrielle nodded. She glanced again at Lyudmila and the bandages around her mangled fingers.

"Very well," said Irina. "Are you, or are you not, working for Europol?"

"No. I am not working for Europol. Not anymore."

Irina translated for the old man. He spoke back to her in Russian.

"Mr Kisenko finds that hard to believe," said Irina. "From my questioning of your colleague Lyudmila, I've already established that all three of you were involved in the recent operation at the Louvre in Paris. Your objective was to save a number of paintings that were subsequently stolen by a gang hired by the late Alexandr Gorshkov and paid for by Viktor. You and Damien, your so-called bodyguard, were also present at the interrogation of Gorshkov in Barcelona. How is it that you're not still working for Europol? Surely this is a Europol operation? How long will it be before this island receives a visit by armed police?"

Gabrielle stared at her, and at the old man at the head of the table.

His eyes were as cold as steel. He nodded to Irina, who got up and stood behind Lyudmila. Then she held out her hand and the fair-haired man passed her a knife from beside his plate.

"Once again," said Irina, "are you working for Europol?"

Irina grabbed a handful of Lyudmila's hair, pulled her head back and placed the point of the knife next to Lyudmila's right eye.

"In case you think this is an idle threat, Capitaine Arnault, I'd just like to mention that the last place I saw you was in Barcelona. You had dark hair at the time, down to your shoulders. The view I had was through the telescopic sight of a sniper's rifle as you walked behind Alexandr Gorshkov, slightly to his left. Tell me, did you wash his blood and brains from your clothes afterwards, or did you just throw them away?"

She moved her thumb along the back of the knife, ready to put greater pressure on the blade.

"This isn't a Europol operation," said Gabrielle. "We're working independently to recover the paintings and the bomb."

Irina translated for the old man. He took a sip of orange juice and spoke to her again.

"Mr Kisenko would like to know why you're doing this. He finds it hard to believe you would take such risks on your own initiative."

Gabrielle looked along the table. She'd been insane to let things go this far. She should have ignored Flynn's advice and dropped the whole thing back in The Hague.

"It was my fault," she said. "I'd been disgraced in Paris when the paintings were taken. The unit I commanded had been disbanded. Everything I'd worked for was about to be thrown away. I did it to prove an idea—the idea that understanding terrorists could help us combat terrorism."

Irina laughed and translated for the old man. He shook his head and asked another question.

"And who came up with that preposterous idea in the first place? Was it you?" said Irina.

"No. It was Capitaine Felipe Rodriguez, my fiancé. He was killed by the bombs at Atocha station in Madrid."

The woman translated back to the old man, who stared at Gabrielle for a moment, with something that almost resembled pity. Then he responded.

"Mr Kisenko says he deeply sympathises with you, Capitaine Arnault, and asks me to tell you that he too lost his family to a bomb. But he still needs to know what communications you've had with the outside world and whether or not his plans are compromised."

"We couldn't reach anyone," Gabrielle said. "Mr Vorontov's men searched us and removed all our cell phones before we even boarded the plane to come here. We have no radio and have not been given access to landlines. We were relying on Mr Vorontov transporting his stolen paintings off the island to a pre-arranged point where we could recover them."

"Where is this 'pre-arranged point'?" asked Irina.

"I'm not sure any more. We'd originally selected an airfield in Turkey. That's where the authorities would have been alerted and Mr Vorontov arrested. But now he's made other arrangements, for somewhere in Greece."

"Very clever, Viktor," said Irina. "Where exactly did you arrange to exchange the paintings?"

Vorontov glanced across the table at Gabrielle.

"On the Greek island of Xanthos," he said. "There's a deserted British landing strip there. I was to meet someone there at noon tomorrow."

"I see," said the woman turning to Gabrielle. "And has this new information been passed to Europol?"

"No," said Gabrielle. "My plan's collapsed now. We can't communicate with anyone outside this island. You can tell Mr Kisenko his operation is safe."

Irina translated.

Kisenko shouted violently at Vorontov, slamming his fist on the table, sending coffee cups dancing in their saucers. Gabrielle witnessed a short, sharp argument in Russian, which Vorontov lost. He slumped in his seat, defeated.

The old man spoke to Gabrielle again. Irina translated.

"Mr Kisenko says you and your colleague Lyudmila are to be held as hostages, in case the authorities threaten his operation because of your actions. I understand Viktor has a secure chamber below his office where he keeps his art treasures. Perhaps he'll give us the combination of the keypad on the door? It seems a fitting place to hold you and your 'nurse' for a while."

"But I told you, Europol have no idea what we're doing."

Irina smiled. "If we don't hear from the authorities, and what you say about acting alone is true, then I'll make your deaths as painless as possible."

"I have a question," Gabrielle said. "What about the bomb?"

Vorontov's eyes widened and stared at her.

"What bomb?" he said.

Irina answered Gabrielle directly. "I followed your two friends out to the aircraft hangar last night," she said. "Then, after Lyudmila was so forthcoming with information in exchange for the continued use of her hands, I had one of our technicians go out and reconnect the detonator. The bomb is once more fully functional. What we intend to do with it is our business."

"And Flynn? Did you kill him?"

"Not yet," Irina said. "Like I told you, he's helping us deliver the bomb."

Three men in dark overalls entered the room. Two lifted the chair in which Gabrielle sat, while the third pushed Lyudmila in the wheelchair.

Between them, they manhandled both her and Lyudmila down a flight of steps, through Vorontov's study and down into his bunker. Then they shut and locked the lower doors and left them in the dark.

Kisenko glared down the table at Vorontov, who held his head like a frightened schoolboy, afraid to look up. After all the years of toil and suffering, after the loss of his family, his plans had been put in danger by Viktor's stupid infatuation with paint and canvas.

Kisenko looked for the words to describe how he felt about this betrayal, took one more look at Vorontov, and found that words failed him.

"Lock him in his office!" he roared to Irina and Sorokin. "I'll deal with him later."

"But the board meeting?" Vorontov said.

"You are no longer chairman of this company," Kisenko said. "You've no place at that table."

Vorontov stared at him.

"Go!" shouted Kisenko. "Before I lose my temper and kill you myself!"

Vorontov walked swiftly to the door. One of Kisenko's men opened it and escorted him outside.

"The board members will be here in thirty minutes," Sorokin said. "Is there anything more you'd like me to do?"

Kisenko stared at him, seeing only ambition in his eyes.

"You have what you want," he said. "You are now chairman of Azeroil. You will take over immediately."

Sorokin could barely conceal his delight. His hands shook as he gathered up his papers and left.

Kisenko turned to Irina. Throughout this whole distasteful business, she had been the only one who could be trusted.

"You've done well," he said. "As soon as we determine it is safe to do so, you'll kill those two women and dispose of the bodies. Is that understood?"

Irina nodded. There was the faintest trace of a smile on her lips.

"And Viktor?"

Kisenko reached down to the table and picked up the knife she'd used to threaten the Russian woman, slowly turning it in his hand.

"You'll bring him before me once this board meeting is settled and the plan is carried out successfully. Then I'll show him the true meaning of suffering."

32

Vorontov walked in front of the armed guard back to his study. Everything he'd worked for had collapsed. All his power and wealth had been stripped from him in an instant. Everything he'd achieved was gone.

And what was this talk of a bomb? That could only mean the inner workings of the atomic shell that Gorshkov had smuggled out of Russia. In his own eagerness to obtain the outer casing for the Paris operation, he'd completely ignored what Gorshkov might do with the bomb itself. What were Kisenko and Chernenko going to do with it? The European energy summit was still weeks away. What other possible target would be of any interest to Kisenko?

Through the tall windows of the main reception area he'd caught a glimpse of sunlight glittering on the polished fuselage of an executive jet landing on the island. The investors from Moscow had arrived—for a meeting he could no longer attend. He had to find out what was going on.

The guard opened the study door, showed Vorontov inside and locked the door behind him.

Viktor stood before the windows for a moment, gazing out at the sea and collecting his thoughts. Then he went to his wall safe, opened it and took out a false passport and his emergency cash reserve of ten million US dollars in untraceable bearer bonds and uncut diamonds. The paintings he'd stolen from the Louvre had already been loaded onto his personal jet the evening before for tomorrow's planned rendezvous with Constance Le Clerc in Greece. He lifted a leather briefcase onto his desk, tipped all the papers it contained into his waste bin and put the bearer bonds, diamonds and passport inside. He was packed and ready to go. All he had to do was to climb down from the balcony onto the slope below the castle and escape.

But, before he left, he had to know what Kisenko was planning to do with the bomb.

He reached into his desk drawer, took a key from beneath a sheaf of papers and fitted it into a concealed lock. A wooden panel popped open in the bottom of the drawer, revealing a set of labelled jack plugs. Taking a pair of stereo headphones from the back of the drawer, he plugged them into the third socket from the right. He could now hear everything that was said in the boardroom.

Kisenko stood back from the sunlit courtyard and greeted the four men from Moscow in the cool dimness of the reception area. Each of them represented a major section of the Moscow mafia and each of them had invested enormous amounts of money in Azeroil and the Caspian oil and gas fields. In return, they'd been rewarded with a convenient way of laundering their illegal wealth from extortion, drugs, weapons and prostitution, as well gaining as a highly profitable investment in an area that was certain to bring colossal returns. Azeroil had been Kisenko's idea. He'd adopted and cared for it as a father would a child. Today, he'd show these men that their faith in him had not been in vain when, with one bold stroke, he'd multiply the value of their investment by a thousand percent.

"Welcome, welcome," he said to each in turn, putting his arms around them and leading them into the boardroom where refreshments were served. Then he took the seat at the head of the table, where Vorontov would normally have sat, and brought the meeting to order.

"Friends," he said, after the wooden doors had been closed and privacy was assured. "I welcome all of you here, on this historic day. For twenty years, we have joined forces and pooled our money like brothers into the Azeroil Oil and Gas Company. We have seen it grow from a badly-run state venture into a commercial giant, rivalling the profits of Gazprom as one of the largest suppliers of energy in Russia."

Heads nodded around the table. Kisenko pressed a button on the audio-visual panel in front of him and blinds slid down across the windows, cutting out the glittering sea.

"Part of that success," he continued, "was due to the efforts of our outgoing chairman, Viktor Vorontov. In many ways, he was the acceptable face of Azeroil—charming, energetic, on good terms with everyone. But today's energy market is not what it was. A new ruthlessness is called for, now that energy reserves are depleted in other oilfields of the world, now that political unrest and war affects fields in the Middle East and South East Asia. Russia is emerging as an energy superpower to rival Saudi Arabia. The Caspian Sea, with its oil and gas reserves off Kazakhstan and Azerbaijan, has enough fuel to rival the output of the Arabian fields, without the political problems associated with Muslim states. Our only challenge is to export that oil successfully from the Caspian, which is a landlocked sea."

One of the men from Moscow spoke.

"And what of the pipeline project?" he said.

"The trans-Caspian pipeline project is temporarily stalled," Kisenko said. "There is a lack of confidence in our technological ability to create and operate an underwater pipeline connecting the Kazakh and Azerbaijani oil and gas fields. Pipeline routes through Iraq and Afghanistan are difficult to obtain. Those problems, combined with the relatively low price of Arabian crude, have deterred our American investors. But times change. To explain these factors to you, and to demonstrate how they can be reversed, I would like to hand you over to Anatoly Ivanovich Sorokin, recently our vice-chairman in charge of strategy, who has today been promoted to the chair of Azeroil. Anatoly, if you please . . ."

From his study, Vorontov listened carefully, imagining the scene in the boardroom and the faces of each man around the table. He pictured Sorokin standing in front of the plasma screen, giving that same presentation he'd rehearsed a dozen times.

"Gentlemen," began Sorokin. "This is a map of the Caspian Sea. Total oil reserves in this region are estimated at over two hundred billion barrels, more than twice that of Western Europe or the United States and putting us in second place only to the Middle East with its seven hundred billion barrels. To the top right of the map off the coast of Kazakhstan, and to the middle left off Azerbaijan, lie eighty percent of the Caspian oil resource. Azeroil not only has investments in each area, but is planning an underwater pipeline to link them across the Caspian Sea. This will deliver the resulting flow of oil directly across country from Baku to the Black Sea port of Novorossiysk, and from there to the rest of the world. "

Vorontov heard him pause for a moment to let those facts and figures sink in with his audience, just as he would have done.

"But we've just been told there are complications with the pipeline," said one of the men from Moscow.

"Indeed," Sorokin replied. "And we've been working with American interests on the Caspian project to overcome them. The Americans have the technology and we have the raw materials. However, underwater work is expensive and dangerous. There are high costs and environmental protests. Investors wonder if it would not be cheaper and environmentally less dangerous to put the pipeline overland, perhaps northwards through Kazakhstan and Russia, or even southwards through Turkmenistan and Iran. But if Azeroil is to control the flow, and reap the reward on our investment, then the oil must come through our own pipeline, linking our two main fields—Kazakhstan to the east and Azerbaijan to the west."

"You mentioned a plan to increase the price of crude oil," said another voice. "What is it?"

Vorontov himself had heard of no such plan. He guessed that Sorokin would have to talk in abstracts now, about energy security and alternative supplies. Sorokin did no such thing.

"The Americans will only invest serious money in the underwater pipeline if the price of oil rises and confidence in Iran falls," he said. "And this afternoon, at precisely three p.m. our time, both those two events will come to pass."

"But how?" someone asked. Vorontov smiled. He could see no way that Sorokin could deliver on this promise.

"Because at that time the oil refinery and shipping terminal of Ras Tanura in the Gulf of Arabia—through which the entire production of Saudi Arabia flows—will be obliterated by a terrorist attack using an atomic weapon," said Sorokin. "That attack will be claimed by Muslim extremists. It will cut off supply from Saudi Arabia completely, precipitating a world shortage that will push the price of oil through the roof and destroy any faith in Iran, or any other Muslim state, as a route for a Caspian pipeline."

Vorontov couldn't believe his ears.

"Surely you don't intend to gamble our entire investment on the actions of terrorists?"

"It's no gamble. Believe me."

"Then tell us. How can you be certain this will happen?"

Vorontov heard Sorokin hesitate. He imagined him turning to Kisenko for guidance and the old man nodding.

"Because we are going to arrange it ourselves," Sorokin said at last. "Irina? Perhaps you'd like to explain the practical details?"

33

The transport plane touched down on the sun-baked runway and taxied to a stop. As the rear doors swung open and the steel loading ramp hit the airstrip apron, a tall Russian in a light-blue Red Cross uniform stepped out into the blistering sun of Saudi Arabia and shaded his eyes against the glare with his hand. A black Mercedes slid to a stop next to the plane and an official in a khaki uniform got out. His eyes were hidden behind mirrored sunglasses.

"You radioed in an emergency," he said to the Russian in English. "You have a man critically injured?"

The Russian's name was Rykov and his English was excellent. He'd learnt it as part of his training with the KGB many years before.

"A worker was flown ashore from a tanker in the Gulf," Rykov said. "He had a bad fall and there may be internal bleeding in his skull. He's been in a coma for the past two hours and shows no hope of recovery. That's why we brought him here—to have a proper hospital make an incision in his skull and relieve the pressure. Without this operation, he'll die."

An old ambulance was backing down the ramp from the aircraft now. Its wheels screeched on the hot earth.

"Just a moment," ordered the official. "I must inspect the vehicle before it goes into the plant."

"Do it quickly," the Rykov said. "The patient doesn't have long to live."

The ambulance driver opened the rear door. There were two men inside; one wearing the white coat of a medical orderly and the other strapped to one of the ambulance beds.

His head was swathed in bandages and his complexion looked very pale against his dark clothes.

A saline drip fed his arm.

The beep . . . beep . . . beep of a heart monitor chirruped urgently beside him.

"What's that?" asked the official, pointing to the large white cabinet standing behind the driver's compartment.

"X-ray machine," said Rykov, coming up behind him. "We needed it to examine his skull for blood clots."

The official scribbled a note on his clipboard.

"Sign here," he said. "And here. Then take a copy for security and one for the medical centre. It's through the main gate and straight down the access road to the end. Don't stop anywhere else in the complex. If you do, the security guards will search you again and there'll be more delays. Do you understand?"

Rykov nodded and took the paperwork.

"Thank you," he said. "We'll be straight out after we deliver the patient."

Then he got into the cab of the ambulance beside the driver. The airstrip gates opened as they passed through into the desert and they drove across a lifeless ocean of yellow sand waves under a deep blue sky. Then the soft lines of the sand were broken by the hard angles of dark pipes and support frames, the skyline became a jungle of oil storage tanks, buildings and derricks, and they were driving down towards the vast petroleum processing terminal of Ras Tanura.

Vorontov listened in wide-eyed disbelief as Irina described to the stockholders from Moscow how she'd obtained the nuclear core of an obsolete Russian artillery shell purchased from Gorshkov and that any security concerns they might have about such an audacious plan had already been addressed. She told them the bomb was, at that very moment, being delivered and would soon be detonated.

The effects on the Ras Tanura complex would be devastating.

Vorontov shook his head like a man trying to wake from a nightmare. It was mass murder on a grand scale. It was an act of war. Thousands would die!

And his company was at the centre of it.

He had to distance himself from it all. The affair at the Louvre had been a harmless practical joke compared to this.

The answer struck him. He could make a deal with the two Europol officers that Kisenko had locked downstairs in his bunker. Leaving the briefcase on the desk, he went to the concealed button on the bookshelf and unlocked the door to the bunker below. He had to talk to the woman he knew as Antoinette De Pau. The automatic lights snapped on as he rushed down the stone steps and into his holy of holies.

The two women sat motionless, blinking under the light. The blonde Russian woman Viktor knew as Lyudmila was bound to a wheelchair, barely conscious. Antoinette De Pau was still tied to the same dining chair she'd occupied at breakfast. Only the chair was now on its side in front of the table where her instruments and the fake Mona Lisa lay, as if she'd toppled it in an attempt to escape.

He reached down, pulled the chair upright and looked directly into her eyes.

"Are you really with the police?" he said. "You must answer me honestly. There's no time for lies."

"Where's Damien?"

"Answer me! Are you with the police? There's something being planned here today that you must know about."

"I am . . . I was . . . with Europol. Yes. What is it?"

"Your bodyguard may be dead by now," he said. "He was knocked unconscious last night and used as a decoy in an ambulance that they're flying to a place called Ras Tanura. It's the main oil terminal in the Gulf of Arabia and they're going to destroy it with the bomb."

"The bomb they got from Gorshkov?"

"Yes. I had nothing to do with this, you understand. I just wanted

Gorshkov to get me the paintings. All I needed was the casing to make the threat to the Louvre look believable. But the people downstairs—Kisenko, Sorokin and Irina—they have the real bomb and they intend to detonate it at three o'clock this afternoon at Ras Tanura. We have to get out of here. We've got to warn the authorities before the weapon goes off."

"Can I trust you, Viktor?"

"I may be a criminal," he said. "But I'm not a mass murderer. You can trust me on that."

"The phone lines? Can you call the mainland from here?"

"All calls go through the switchboard. There's no direct dial."

"Do you still have your cell phone?"

"It's upstairs in my study."

"We must alert the authorities," she said. "And get out of here."

Vorontov ripped at the heavy industrial tape that bound Gabrielle's hands to the chair. Then she was free and standing in front of him.

"Untie my friend," she said. "I need to bring something with us."

She turned to the table, reached under it, pulled out a flat carrying case, opened it and carefully lifted Nicole Sabaut's Mona Lisa into it.

"Why bother with that?" Vorontov asked, as he undid Lyudmila's hands. "It's only a fake."

"It's evidence. I need it." She snapped the lid shut. "Come on, let's go!"

Vorontov looked around the room, at the countless millions of dollars worth of art treasures he'd collected over the years. It broke his heart to leave them behind. Then he hoisted the unconscious woman onto his shoulder and made for the stairs.

He was halfway across the room when the sound of running steps echoed on the stairway. Irina appeared in the doorway, with a silenced automatic pistol in her hand.

"Good afternoon, Viktor," she said. "I hope you're not trying to leave us."

Flynn felt as if somebody had stripped all the skin from the back of his throat. His head throbbed. His lids were stuck tight with mucous and he couldn't move his arms. He tried to swallow, but it was agony. He tried to blink, but it was like his eyelashes were being pulled out by the roots.

He was in some kind of vehicle. The swaying motion made him sick, but he dare not throw up for fear of drowning in his own vomit. The engine's drone sliced through his skull like an electric saw.

The last thing he remembered had been kissing Irina. Then she'd pinched his neck and the floor had opened up and swallowed him. How had she done that? He heard a man's voice now, speaking in Russian, giving orders. He thought he recognised it. Then the lashes of his left eye broke free and he saw the roof of a van and a the back of a big man in a light blue uniform reaching down to lift whatever he was lying on out into the light.

He was aware of a bright blue sky punctured with pipes, the towering frameworks of derricks, the stink of oil and the din of heavy machinery. Then he was in the shade, being wheeled through a pair of swing doors into a cool corridor. A plastic bag of clear fluid danced on a steel rod beside him with a tube falling towards somewhere on his body. He seemed to be in a hospital.

People were talking all around him. He heard the Russian's voice again, braced himself against the inevitable pain of trying to move, and turned his head to see who it was.

It was Rykov, one of the guards from Vorontov's island.

He was standing in a doorway, talking to another man in a white coat, explaining something to him. The man in the white coat nodded and looked down at a clipboard. The doors behind him opened and two more men wheeled a white cabinet into the room. It was the X-ray machine he'd found on the cargo plane before he'd fainted in Irina's room, the one he and Gabrielle had seen in Azerbaijan, the one containing the atomic bomb.

Irina Chernenko took in the rows of priceless artworks, the plush viewing chair, the well-stocked bar and was stunned at the sheer decadence of it all. As someone born into poverty, fighting all her life for survival, the obscene amount of money that had been lavished on this one room, by this one man, sickened her to the core.

"And to think I've killed people, just so you can sit here and stare at your pointless paintings," she said. "You don't deserve to live."

Vorontov stood frozen in front of her, with the Russian woman in his arms. The spy from Europol stood behind him, near a wooden table laid out with instruments and tools. She had a flat carrying case in her hand. Viktor had his hands full, holding the woman. The Europol spy was too far away to be any threat. The hollow point bullets in Irina's gun would make quite a mess on Viktor's beautiful carpet, but with three shots it would all be over. The gun was already cocked and the safety catch was off. He was closest to her. She would take him first.

"Goodbye Viktor," she said, stepping into the room and raising the weapon.

Vorontov dropped the Russian woman to the ground and tried to run at her. Irina squeezed the trigger.

Out of the corner of her eye she caught the flash of movement from the far end of the room and instinctively swung the pistol to cover it, just as the bullet left the barrel. The gun thudded in her fist, a lump of flesh flew from Viktor's shoulder and he slammed back against the wall, knocking himself unconscious.

Then the case the woman had been carrying hit Irina just below her right eye.

Her head jerked back from the impact. She lost her balance and crashed into the work table, falling to the floor in a cascade of tools and bottles. The gun flew from her fist and smashed into the drinks cabinet.

She clawed her way back to her feet as the Europol woman raced for the gun. Irina was angry now and readier than ever to kill.

Viktor was down and the Russian woman was in no shape to fight. So it would be just her and the Europol woman. It would be good to fight someone hand-to-hand for a change . . .

Even as she saw Irina Chernenko launch herself across the room, Gabrielle's focus was on the silenced automatic. Her fingers closed on the long silencer just as Irina charged at her, slamming her up against the wall. Gabrielle raised the gun like a hammer and tried to bring it down on Irina's head.

But she was too fast for her. Irina's arm shot up, catching Gabrielle at the wrist. The weight of the gun, moving downwards with all the force Gabrielle could bring to bear, ripped it from her grasp and went cart wheeling into the middle of the room. Irina's hand swung in a vicious arc at Gabrielle's neck. She blocked that and shot a direct punch at Irina's face. She was fighting on instinct now, pinned up against the wall by Irina and frantically trying to anticipate each blow in the split second before it came.

The Russian's fighting style was unorthodox and deadly, targeted at the vulnerable areas of Gabrielle's eyes and throat. Gabrielle, who had been trained to disable rather than kill, found herself overwhelmed. She blocked a knife hand strike to her eye only just in time. Then brought her elbow up under Irina's chin and felt the satisfying thud of bone on bone.

Irina shook her head, stepped back to give herself distance and kicked at Gabrielle's solar plexus. Gabrielle saw it coming and blocked it with her arm, driving Irina's foot past her into the drinks cabinet. Then she pushed past her and dived for the gun. She gripped the butt and swung it round, just as Irina landed on top of her. The gun went off with a muffled thump and a hollow nosed bullet ripped into the face of an old master on the wall. Gabrielle arched her back, pushing Irina away, and used the space between them to bring her elbow back in a strike to Irina's solar plexus, just as the gun was torn from her grasp and fell to the floor.

Irina heaved as Gabrielle's elbow hit home. Gabrielle rammed her elbow back again, pushed herself away and went for the gun. But then Irina grabbed her legs. Vorontov was out of the fight and Lyudmila was bent over on her knees, tearing at the bandages around her hands with her teeth.

A searing pain lanced up Gabrielle's thigh as Irina rammed a screwdriver into her leg. She screamed in agony, just as her hand touched the plastic bottle of alcohol she'd used to soften the paint on Nicole Sabaut's forgery.

She grabbed it, pointed the neck at Irina's face and squeezed the plastic with every atom of strength she had left.

The cap burst from the bottle, discharging half a litre of neat spirits into Irina's eyes.

For a split second, Irina thought it was water. Then the alcohol blinded her and the stench of spirits filled her nostrils. Suddenly, she was a helpless little girl again. Her father's stinking vodka breath was in her face and his big miner's fingers were clamped around her wrist, forcing her hand into the fire.

She wiped the alcohol away from her eyes with her sleeve, saw the Europol woman digging in the pocket of her trousers and the glint of gold in her fist.

In a flash came the terrible realisation as to what the object was, the awful clicking sound, and Irina's world exploded into searing blue flame and burning flesh. She heard her hair hiss, felt the fire take hold of her clothes and threw herself sideways to roll on the carpet and put out the flames. She tried to breathe, but the fire was in her throat. She threw her arms up over her face and clawed at her hair, feeling it fall away, burned and brittle.

The pain overwhelmed her.

She hauled herself onto her knees and tried to open her eyes.

Where was that Europol woman?

She had to—

The words "Die you bitch!" spat at her in Russian, reached her ears a fraction of a second before the hollow nosed bullet hit her chest, ripped through her heart and punched a hole in her back the size of a dinner plate.

Gabrielle pulled herself to her feet and stared down at the smouldering ruin of what had just been Irina Chernenko. Burning alcohol had set the carpet alight. The stench of cordite, burning hair and singed flesh filled the air. The sound of a fire alarm came to her from far, far away.

She stared across the room. Lyudmila was on her knees, holding Irina's silenced automatic in her shattered hands. Her eyes were shut tight in agony as she lowered the gun.

"I had to kill her," she gasped.

Gabrielle limped over to her and took the weight of the pistol, gently disengaging Lyudmila's broken fingers from the trigger guard. The grinding pain in her thigh had subsided to a deep throb. From the fireplace, Vorontov groaned and pulled himself to his knees, cradling his wound with his hand.

"Can you move your arm?" Gabrielle asked.

She saw his fingers flex. His face contorted in agony.

"Yes. I can."

"We have to get out of here," Gabrielle said. "We've got to warn the authorities about Ras Tanura."

She pulled the sheet that had covered the table out from under Irina's legs, tore a strip from it and bandaged Vorontov's shoulder as best she could. She had to get them both to the plane before they went into shock and their bodies shut down.

"Lyudmila, can you walk?" she asked as she replaced the bandages around her hands. "I can't carry you on my own, and neither can Viktor."

"I'll try."

"Let's go. We have to get to a phone."

Gabrielle unscrewed the silencer from Irina's pistol to make it easier to carry and stuck the gun it into her pocket. Vorontov was in no condition to help Lyudmila, and Gabrielle herself could barely walk. With Lyudmila supported on her arm, she made her way up the stone steps to Vorontov's study. Vorontov staggered to his desk, pulled a cell phone from a drawer and tried it.

"There's no signal," he said.

"Try the landline," said Gabrielle.

"It's no use. All calls have to go through the switchboard."

"You said last night you'd loaded all the paintings into your plane," Gabrielle said. "Is it fuelled and ready to go right now?"

"It is."

"I'm trained to fly small jets. We can call the authorities on its radio as soon as we get airborne."

"How much time have we got?" asked Vorontov, taking a briefcase from the desk.

"Just under two hours, if the bomb is to go off at three," said Gabrielle. "What's in that case?"

"A lot of money," Vorontov said.

Gabrielle went to the door of the study and looked out. Alarms rang and the sound of raised voices reached her from the floor above. Beyond the study door was the reception area and the courtyard outside.

"Quick," she said.

She stepped out into the corridor, with Lyudmila supported on her shoulder, clutching Irina's gun.

The woman behind the reception desk called out in Russian. Gabrielle smiled and limped towards the door with Lyudmila. The woman called out again. Gabrielle didn't stop. She simply pointed the gun at the woman's head. The woman ducked down behind the desk and vanished.

Then they were in the sunshine of the courtyard, staggering

towards the nearest of the parked cars, a Bentley convertible. The keys were still in the ignition. Gabrielle pulled open the passenger door, eased Lyudmila and the case into the back seat and climbed in behind the wheel. Viktor slumped into the passenger seat beside her. Someone shouted. A yellow and black barrier swung down across the courtyard entrance and a man ran out of the kiosk next to it. Gabrielle waved the gun at him, turned and fired a bullet into the front wheel of the Range Rover next to her. The tyre exploded and the car settled onto its front wheel rim. The man ran back into his kiosk and glowered at them over his desk, waiting to see what they would make of the barrier.

Gabrielle turned the ignition key, the Bentley jerked forward and squealed across the courtyard towards the barrier.

"Get down!" she screamed, and ducked behind the wheel. The windscreen shattered and they were racing down the winding road towards the airstrip, the wailing sirens from the castle following them.

Gabrielle heard the smack of a bullet hitting the car, followed by the distant crackle of gunfire. She kept her head down, fighting the wheel as the car bounced across the rough surface.

"How long does it take to get a plane off the ground?" Vorontov asked.

"Less than five minutes, if it's already fuelled. How long does it take to change a wheel on a car?"

"Less than five minutes."

The Bentley burst onto the runway and screeched to a halt.

Gabrielle limped to the jet, opened the door, pulled down the steps and climbed inside. Any space between the seats in the passenger compartment was crammed with the cases of artwork Vorontov had planned to exchange for the Mona Lisa the next day in Greece. She ran to the cockpit and pulled herself into the pilot's seat, flicking switches and checking dials. The fuel pressure gauges and navigation panels lit up. The rising whine of the turbines reached her. She got up and ran back to the door.

Vorontov was helping Lyudmila into the plane. His bandage was soaked in blood.

"Did you get the chocks?" Gabrielle shouted.

"The what?"

"The blocks under the wheels. They have to come out before we can move forward."

Vorontov stared back towards the castle. Sunlight glinted on a moving windscreen. Kisenko's people had fixed the wheel on the Range Rover and were coming after them. Vorontov staggered back down the gangway and went to the portside wheel.

Gabrielle followed him and unblocked the starboard side, before running forward to the nose.

"The other plane," shouted Vorontov. "We have to stop it taking off or they'll come after us. Throw me the gun!"

"No! There's no time."

"You know I'm right. Throw it to me!"

She threw him the pistol and ran back to the steps. Vorontov aimed the gun at the front wheel of the other jet. She heard two shots and then the distant crack of a rifle. Vorontov jerked upright. Then he turned and looked up at her with wide eyes. A red stain blossomed at the centre of his chest.

"Viktor!"

Their eyes met.

"Xanthos!" he screamed above the roar of the engines. "You have to be at Xanthos. Tomorrow at noon! Go!"

He fell on his knees and toppled forwards onto the gun.

The Range Rover hurtled onto the far end of apron. Gabrielle hauled herself up the steps, slammed the door shut and ran past Lyudmila into the cockpit. She strapped herself in, heaved off the brakes and rammed the throttles forward. The jet leapt ahead in a rush, forcing her back in her seat and skidding onto the feeder lane to the main runway.

There was no time for a textbook takeoff. The Range Rover was already fighting to get ahead of the plane and block its path.

Gabrielle rammed the throttles forward to their limit. The airspeed dial crept upwards, painfully slowly, then faster and faster.

The car was level with the rear engines. Its windows rolled down. Someone brandished a gun, taking aim.

Gabrielle Arnault heaved the joystick back as far as it would go and screamed an obscenity.

The aircraft tore itself up off the runway and leapt to freedom in the sky.

Igor Kisenko watched the jet fading into the distance. The plane would have a radio and whoever was on the plane would be using it right now to call the authorities down on him.

The Range Rover skidded to a halt next to him.

"How long to fix the other plane?" he shouted.

One of his guards got out and inspected the burst tyre of the jet.

"Half an hour! Maybe less."

"Make it fifteen minutes, or it's your life."

Sorokin walked over to Vorontov's body and kicked it.

"I think he's still alive!" he said.

"Does anyone have a gun?" shouted Kisenko.

Someone handed him an AK-47.

"Turn the bastard over," Kisenko screamed, slamming his foot into the dying man's ribs. "Viktor. I'm going to start with your feet, your knees, your balls and your guts. Then I'm going to leave you here to . . ."

Vorontov rolled over.

Somebody shouted a warning, but Kisenko was too slow.

The last thing he saw before the hollow point bullet from Irina Chernenko's gun punched its way through his chest was Viktor Vorontov smiling up at him.

"Mayday! Mayday! Mayday! Is anyone there?"

Gabrielle tried to bring her breathing under control as the jet gained altitude. All the gauges looked normal. There was no damage from the takeoff. The GPS showed her location as south-east of Odessa and heading north-west.

A Russian voice came through on her radio headset, asking her to identify herself and her emergency. She asked for a French or English speaker and, when she got one, identified herself as a French policewoman seconded to Europol and that she had a major act of terrorism to report.

After hearing what it was, the voice on the radio connected her immediately to The Hague.

34

Flynn had his left hand out of the strap binding him to the stretcher and was working on the buckle. He had to get to that X-ray machine and do something to stop the bomb inside it going off. Whoever had planted it would have set some kind of time fuse to give them enough time to get clear. But how much time did he have? He wished Lyudmila was there. However much he'd learned about explosives from his training to fight for Ireland, nuclear weapons had not been on the curriculum.

Freeing the strap with just one hand was hard going. There was nothing to press against and the fabric kept pushing against the buckle without going through. He took a deep breath and tried to clear his head. The fact that his left hand was free meant there was more slack in the strap to move his right, so he focussed on that, breathed in and heaved. His right hand came out.

The straps slipped to the floor and Flynn sat up. The room swirled around him and he vomited onto the floor. What the hell had that bitch Irina injected him with back on the island? Two more full syringes of clear liquid lay on a table next to his bed. Jesus! If she'd given him any more of that, he'd be dead. But perhaps that might have been the idea.

He reached down to work on his legs just as an almighty row started outside. Sirens wailed, footsteps clattered in the corridor and engines roared into life somewhere in the distance. Flynn undid the last straps restraining his legs and tried to stand. Another bad idea. The room spun, his legs collapsed under him and he flailed desperately for something to hold onto as he went down.

His hand caught the table by the bed and pulled it over on top of him. Instruments, papers and medicine bottles came crashing to the floor.

An orderly stormed into the room and tried to pull him to his feet.

"Come on!" he shouted. "There's a bomb!"

"I know," said Flynn. "It's right there in front of you in that X-ray machine. Get me a screwdriver. I know how to take the front off it."

"I'll get security."

"No. Just get me a screwdriver."

But the orderly was already out of the door and running down the corridor, shouting.

Flynn pulled himself into a kneeling position in front of the machine. There was no point in running. He'd never get far enough away from an atomic blast to be safe and besides, he couldn't run.

A stupid thought went through his head. Would Siobhan and Aoife miss him?

Then he was scrabbling amongst the instruments on the floor for anything that would undo a Pozidriv screw. He found a thin spatula with a flat end, turned to the machine and applied the instrument to the cross-cut head of the first screw.

It worked. The screw was turning.

Rykov had approached the main security gate in the ambulance. The timer on the bomb was set for one hour, plenty of time for them to get back to the airfield and fly well out of range of the blast when it exploded. He reached into his jacket for the papers he'd been given on the way in.

Suddenly the sirens wailed across the complex. The guard in the security hut was on the phone, speaking rapidly. If it was some kind of general alert, the plant security guards might not specifically be looking for the bomb. Unless they knew exactly what they were looking for, it was unlikely they would find it before it went off.

But if they did know exactly where the bomb was . . . he'd have to fight his way back into the complex and detonate it by hand before it was found and disarmed. Rykov was not afraid of death. He'd faced it so many times before. It was all a question of just how much the people at the plant knew . . .

Then guard looked up from his phone, straight at the ambulance. Their eyes met.

They knew.

"Get out now," Rykov said to the two men with him. "Cover me for a few minutes as I go back inside and then save yourselves."

The passenger door opened and the two men got out.

The guard stepped out to meet them.

Rykov slammed the ambulance into reverse and spun the vehicle round, clipping the front of a car behind and sending workers scattering in all directions. He rammed the vehicle into first gear and accelerated back the way he'd come, towards the medical complex.

Flynn had the first panel off the X-ray machine and was looking at the second panel, with its Cyrillic warnings about radiation dangers. He steadied himself against the cool metal of the machine and started to work on the screws. They were the good old-fashioned type this time, with a simple slot. That made it much easier to undo them. He had four undone and two to go when he heard shouting in the corridor outside followed by a scream, and then silence. The door burst open and Rykov stood staring down at him, his eyes wild with anger.

"Get away from that!" he hissed and lashed out with his foot, catching Flynn in the chest and sending him skidding across the floor.

Flynn pulled himself up into a crouching position. Rykov knelt in front of the bomb. He had a Swiss Army knife in his hand and was selecting the right tool for the screws.

Flynn pulled himself to his feet, staggered forward and tried to kick him. But Rykov saw him coming, turned and caught his foot with both hands, wrenching his ankle round and sending him crashing down to the floor.

"Stay there," he snapped. "Or I'll kill you!"

He went back to the screws.

Flynn's head spun. His ribs were on fire. He caught sight of one of the syringes from the table and snatched it up.

Rykov had the last screw out. He was working on the plate.

Flynn got back to his feet. Rykov had the plate off now. Flynn saw a digital read-out clicking down from 45:36 to 45:35. Beside the read-out was a red button covered by a transparent safety flap.

Rykov hesitated for a moment and lifted the flap.

Flynn yelled at the top of his voice and launched himself at the Russian, falling across him and sending them both skidding across the floor towards the door of the dispensary.

Flynn didn't know which way was up. Rykov was all over him. His hands clamped around Flynn's neck. His fingers probed for pressure points. Flynn brought up the syringe, bit off the cap over the needle and stabbed it into Rykov's neck.

The Russian's eyes went wide as Flynn rammed home the plunger with his thumb. He scrabbled for the syringe, pulled it out and tossed it away, cursing.

He turned back towards the bomb.

Flynn grabbed his waist and pulled Rykov to the floor. The Russian dragged Flynn with him across the linoleum, inch by inch towards the X-ray machine. Flynn's grip was slipping. He skidded in the vomit on the floor. Rykov was getting away from him.

Flynn felt a blow to his head.

The room swam around him.

The blows were getting weaker.

They were almost at the bomb now. He felt Rykov stretch forward as he reached for the red button . . . and collapse.

Flynn was losing consciousness again.

The room was going round and round, exactly like it did when he'd had way too much to drink.

The doors of the dispensary flew open and men in uniforms poured in. Someone was leaning over Rykov to look at the bomb.

He was carrying a tool kit.

Flynn suddenly felt very tired.

He rested his head on the Russian's thigh and everything faded to black . . .

35

XANTHOS ISLAND, GREECE.

Constance Le Clerc stood in the shade of the old transport aircraft's wing and watched as the sun glittered on the polished fuselage of the sleek white executive jet circling the airfield. She'd heard nothing from Viktor Vorontov for over twenty-four hours and, up until five minutes ago, when the distant whine of the jet's engines had reached her, she'd been extremely worried. What if Vorontov had reconsidered swapping all his pictures from the Louvre for Nicole Sabaut's copy? What if Flynn or Gabrielle had discovered she'd changed the venue?

But then the white cross of the jet's fuselage appeared against the deep blue sky and all her fears vanished. She felt alive and excited again, just as she had at the Sotheby's auction with Flynn or back there on the banks of the Seine years before, when Jean-Jacques had emerged from the sewer with the painting in his case. She remembered the sheer exhilaration of knowing they'd done it. They'd vindicated Nicole's name and blackened the eye of all those critics who had driven her to her death.

Then the awful crash had come, the blue flashing lights, the police and the gut-wrenching sight of Jean-Jacques lying in the gutter while a gendarme opened the case . . .

She'd panicked then, and deserted him. It had broken her heart to betray him that night, along with Nicole's memory. But she'd sworn she would make it up to him since, a million times over. And today, she would complete the final movement of Jean-Jacques's ultimate masterpiece—the greatest fraud in art history—by exchanging Nicole's beautiful forgery not only for the *Mona Lisa* itself, but for nine other priceless works of art.

She felt guilty about betraying Gabrielle.

The young Europol officer had been so brave and committed to her mission, so driven to succeed. But she was still young, with her whole career ahead of her. She'd get over it.

The white jet swung on its final approach to the old RAF landing field, touched down and taxied across to the apron in front of Constance. She caught a whiff of jet fuel as its engines slowed from a roar to a whisper. The windows were all shuttered, just as she'd instructed. The jet stopped. The door behind the cockpit popped open and the steps extended down to meet the ground.

Constance reached back through the door of the aircraft behind her, gripped the handle of a slim carrying case and lifted it out.

A man with a brown leather briefcase stepped out of the other plane into the sunshine.

Constance shouted, "Good afternoon, Mr Voron—"

But it wasn't Viktor Vorontov. It was Damien Flynn.

And behind him was Gabrielle Arnault.

They both climbed down onto the tarmac and walked over to Constance's plane. Flynn looked as if he'd been in a fight. One of his eyes was blackened and there were angry cuts on his forehead. Gabrielle was limping. There were bruises and a plaster on her face.

"Good afternoon, Constance," she said. "Why did you change the rendezvous point?"

Constance looked past her, to the door of the private jet, expecting police to pour out at any moment and arrest her.

None came.

"Where's Viktor Vorontov?" she asked.

"He's dead. He was shot by the Russian mafia on the island. There were other deaths also, and a lot of arrests. The Russian police are looking into it now."

"What's going on?"

Constance was frightened.

She didn't want to spend the rest of her life in jail.

"There's a lot of things you haven't told us, aren't there?" Flynn said. "You arranged a whole new deal for yourself with Vorontov."

"But I was just doing what we arranged," said Constance, trying to bluff her way through. "You were to travel to Vorontov's island, persuade him that the real *Mona Lisa* he had was the forgery by Nicole Sabaut that Jean-Jacques had left me. Then I was to offer him Nicole's forgery in exchange for the original and the nine other paintings. That was the deal. There must have been some misunderstanding about the location. That's all!"

"No, Constance," said Gabrielle. "That was my deal—the one we arranged in Paris before I left for the Black Sea. Vorontov was supposed to deliver the paintings to an airfield in Turkey, not here in Greece. Like Flynn says, yours is a whole new deal altogether. There's no mistake, is there? You simply planned to exchange the paintings in another location and then sell them on the black market yourself. You've been playing us for fools ever since Paris, when this whole thing started."

"Now you're being paranoid," Constance said, trying to stand her ground. "You're seeing conspiracies where there are none."

"Then let me suggest a scenario to you," Flynn said. "Let's suppose that Jean-Jacques Sabaut is released from prison after the failed Louvre robbery. He's blind. He's crippled. He's trying to make a living on a disability pension, and he has time on his hands. He starts thinking about Nicole. He starts blaming himself for not going through with his plan to avenge her death on the critics in the art world by leaving the original *Mona Lisa* in the Louvre. But what chance does a blind and crippled man have of breaking back in there a second time? Then it comes to him how much easier it would be to convince a rich and foolish man like Viktor Vorontov to do it for him."

"You're making all this up," Constance said.

"That was Jean-Jacques Sabaut's real masterpiece, wasn't it?" continued Flynn. "He found a way to trick the French into removing the ten most valuable pieces of art from the Louvre themselves, arranged for Vorontov to steal them, and then concocted a brilliant scam to make Vorontov hand over the entire collection to you in exchange for Nicole's forgery, after Gabrielle had convinced Vorontov that the original he thought he had was a fake."

"That's very clever of you," said Jean-Jacques from the door of the plane behind Constance. "I always thought you were a bright lad, even in the days when you were peddling stolen paintings—"

"Which is why you asked for me specifically when you knew I was attached to Gabrielle's COMMETT group," said Flynn. "You needed someone who knew the world of stolen art and wasn't afraid to work outside the law for the second part of your scam to work. You also needed Constance on board to ensure the Louvre's computers were completely under your control. That's why the piece of glass we dropped in the Denon Wing didn't trip the alarms, because Constance was running the whole system. Staging your disappearance, so you couldn't be questioned too closely by the police, was also clever of course. I particularly appreciated the fake suicide note and the bloodspots on the bed to suggest you'd been murdered. That was designed to motivate me into some kind of personal vendetta to avenge your death, I suppose?"

Jean-Jacques shrugged. "I always considered you as a man of honour, Damien. But please go on. Your analysis is fascinating."

Flynn turned to Constance and smiled.

"And having you feed me all those clues to lead us to Viktor Vorontov was extremely subtle," he said. "But then again, you both knew who really had the paintings, because Gorshkov was already using your plan to steal them on his behalf. You're a pair of geniuses. I have to hand it to you. It was a real masterpiece."

Constance tried to think what to do.

She was too old to go to jail. She would die there.

Flynn and Gabrielle were both looking up at Jean-Jacques.

The sun was in their eyes.

Constance reached beneath her jacket, pulled out a loaded revolver and aimed it at Gabrielle's chest.

"Neither of us are going to jail for this," she said. "We've suffered too much as it is."

"I know," said Flynn, hardly acknowledging the gun. "I know how much you both loved Nicole and what her death meant to you. But do you think this is what she would have wanted? Ask yourselves, both of you, did you really steal the *Mona Lisa* the first time for the money, or Nicole's memory? Her reputation is vindicated now. She's recognised as the talent she was and you've pulled off the greatest art theft in history in her name, not once, but twice—along with nine of the most valuable paintings in the world.

"But if you pull that trigger now Constance, you and Jean-Jacques will both go to jail and rot there until you die. If you put the gun away and accept the deal we have for you, you can both go free with enough money to compensate for the pain you've suffered over the years and live in comfort for the rest of your lives."

"Europol knows where we are," Gabrielle said. "And, if we don't put through a call on our radio in five minutes, half the Greek police force will be down around your ears."

"Greek prisons aren't that comfortable compared with those in France," said Flynn. "Listen to our offer, Jean-Jacques, and you'll both be living free anywhere in the world. After all, who would come looking for you now, when everyone but us thinks you're dead?"

"I didn't steal the paintings just for Nicole," said Sabaut. "Not this time. I needed the money. With no paintings, there's no cash. Life isn't very comfortable for a blind beggar, Damien, no matter where you live in the world."

"You were an art dealer once, Jean-Jacques," said Gabrielle. "And there's one final painting you can still sell. You have Nicole's duplicate of the *Mona* Lisa in that case, Constance? Am I right? We'd like to buy it from you, as a souvenir."

"How much are you willing to pay?" asked Constance.

Flynn held up the brown briefcase he had in his hand.

"This belonged to the late Mr Vorontov," he said. "It's his escape fund and neither Europol or anyone else knows anything about it. Gabrielle and I estimate there are over ten million dollars' worth of untraceable bearer bonds and uncut diamonds in here. That would be, if I'm not mistaken, a record price for an original painting by Nicole Sabaut."

"Why are you doing this?" asked Constance, lowering her gun.

"Jean-Jacques was good to me in the old days," Flynn said. "And you've both suffered enough from Nicole's death. Gabrielle and I think it's time someone gave you both a break."

Constance reached down, lifted the carrying case and handed it to Flynn. He handed her the briefcase which she opened, checked and shut again. Then she watched him open the carrying case and gaze down at the familiar face of *La Giaconda*.

"She was a genius," said Constance, holding back the tears. "We both loved her."

"I know," said Flynn. "I know."

Then he closed the case and walked back to the jet, with Gabrielle Arnault limping along by his side.

LATER

Paris

For six days of the week, the Musée du Louvre is filled with visitors from all over the world who come to pay homage to one of the greatest assemblies of art in existence. But every Tuesday, it's closed to the public for renovation and repair.

Close observers of the Louvre on this particular Tuesday in late November would have been intrigued to see a number of black limousines, with police escorts, entering the complex through the underground car park reserved for staff members.

They might also have noticed the unobtrusive but overwhelming number of French security agents positioned around the entrances, exits and galleries.

They might even have wondered why the great glass pyramid in the Cour Napoléon had been cordoned off so that passing tourists could not gaze through it into the concourse below or see the small, but uniquely select body of VIPs who passed there on their way to the newly restored exhibition in Room Six of the Denon Wing.

It was here, at noon, that Gabrielle Arnault stood to attention in her full dress uniform as a member of RAID, on secondment to Europol.

"Capitaine Arnault," said the President of France. "You have done your country, and the world, a great service in restoring the masterpieces we see all around us to their rightful place here in the Louvre. You have shown exceptional courage and initiative in this matter and, at the unanimous recommendation of your own superior officers, those of the collaborating forces and the management board of Europol, it gives me great honour to bestow on you this award. Well done, Capitaine. Well done."

The President took a star-shaped medal on a blue and white ribbon from its proffered cushion, carefully placed it around Gabrielle's neck, stepped back and saluted.

Gabrielle returned the salute as smartly as she could. As applause filled the room, she thought of Felipe and her parents, and how she would have loved them to be here today. Her throat tightened and her eyes filled with tears.

"Thank you, Monsieur le President," she said. "Thank you."

She stepped back, turned smartly and returned to her seat.

Damien Flynn sat next to her, with his left arm around Lyudmila's shoulder.

"Congratulations, *mon Capitaine*," he said. "You deserve it."

There were short speeches by the Préfet de Police, Commissaire Pichet of RAID and the Chairman of Europol. The Chairman laid particular stress on the need for better collaboration between agencies and the use of external advisors in the new world of advanced international techno-terrorism. For Europol's part, he said he was pleased to announce that the management board had unanimously agreed that COMMETT would be significantly reinforced and that Commissaire Arnault would return to The Hague to lead it once her period of leave was over.

The speeches finished. The guests and VIPs enjoyed a glass of wine and an exclusive tour of the Louvre, before returning to their important jobs in high places. Gabrielle received congratulations from the last departing guest and walked over to join Damien Flynn. He stood staring up at the *Mona Lisa*, now secured once more in its hermetically sealed display unit behind two sheets of bullet proof glass and ready to receive the thousands of visitors that would flood into this room tomorrow, when the exhibition reopened.

"I heard you'd given up smoking," he said.

Gabrielle nodded. She thought of her gold lighter, and of Felipe.

That part of her life was behind her now. It was time to move on.

"I never got a chance to thank you," she said. "I hope you'll consider renewing your contract with COMMETT when we resume in a week's time."

Flynn was still staring at the *Mona Lisa*. He smiled.

"Are you sure we took the right one," he said. "I still think there's something not quite right about her eyes."

The End

BIBLIOGRAPHY

Below is a list of books that I found particularly useful in creating *Masterpiece*. For an excellent 'behind the scenes' look at The Louvre Museum in Paris, I would recommend the short film *La Ville Louvre* by Nicholas Philibert which is available on DVD and, of course, a visit in person to this wonderful place yourself.

Bowden, Mark. *Worm: The First Digital World War.* London: Grove Press, 2012.

Kleveman, Lutz. *The New Great Game: Blood and Oil in Central Asia*: London: Atlantic Books, 2003.

Leader, Darian. *Stealing the* Mona Lisa*: What Art Stops Us From Seeing.*New York: Counterpoint, 2002.

Lee III, Rensselaer W. *Smuggling Armageddon: The Nuclear Black Market in the Former Soviet Union and Europe.* New York: St. Martin's Press, 1998.

Richardson, Louise. *What Terrorists Want: Understanding the Terrorist Threat.* London: John Murray, 2006.

Sassoon, Donald. *Mona Lisa: The History of the World's Most Famous Painting.* London: HarperCollins, 2001.

Satter, David. *Darkness at Dawn: The Rise of the Russian Criminal State.* New York: Yale University Press, 2003.

Taylor, Peter. *Talking to Terrorists: Face to Face with the Enemy.* London: Harper Press, 2011.

Varese, Federico. *The Russian Mafia: Private Protection in a New Market Economy.* Oxford University Press, 2000.

Wynne, Frank. *I was Vermeer: The Legend of the Forger who Swindled the Nazis.* London: Bloomsbury Publishing, 2006.

Now read the first exciting chapter of John Joyce's next
COMMETT adventure . . .

MASTERMIND

▬ ▬ ▬ ▬ ▬

DUBLIN

'I AM COMING TO KILL YOU.'

Susan Sheridan stared at the words on the computer screen.

Had it not been for the events of the last twenty-four hours, she might have dismissed the message as a cruel joke by the technical support staff - the sort of prank her fellow students had played on her at college back in the States. She might even have appreciated the way the message had displayed itself straight onto the screen in glaring white capital letters against a blood-red background.

This was no email. This was a direct hack into her computer by someone with detailed knowledge of how to bypass the firewalls of a well-protected system. Someone like herself.

Should she call security?

Her eyes darted around the office and in through the glass wall onto the open-plan area with its deserted islands of empty desks. Rain lashed the windows. Wind howled in one of the worst storms on record. In the daytime, her view would have been out across the modern buildings of the industrial estate to Dublin Bay and the Irish Sea beyond. In the blackness of the night, all she saw were the streetlamps of the Stillorgan dual carriageway swirling like a kaleidoscope of orange and white against the rain swept glass.

The lights in her office went out.

She scrabbled for the phone on her desk, found it and pressed the illuminated shortcut button for the security desk.

"Sean! Who else is in the building?"

She knew Sean. She trusted him.

Sometimes when she worked late, they would chat together

over coffee before she went home. He was an ex-policeman - from Ireland's *Garda Síochána* - strong, kind and dependable, with a wife from Mayo and three kids working in Dublin. He loved to talk about how well they were all doing.

His voice sounded flat and lifeless, like a talking clock.

"Just yourself, Doctor Sheridan. There's nobody else in the building except us."

"Are you sure?"

"The last ones to leave were your research team, Doctor Sheridan. They left at 7.30 after the planning meeting. Is there a problem?"

Sean never called her 'Doctor Sheridan'.

Susan stared out across the empty open-plan office, feeling the panic rise in her throat.

"The lights have gone out in my office," she said in a small, childlike voice that seemed to come from miles away. " Can you come up?"

"It's the storm, Doctor Sheridan. It's getting very bad outside. You should leave now and go home. If you take the lift I can meet you at reception and lock up after you leave."

Again the voice - like a recorded message on an answering machine.

A sudden lash of rain against the window startled her.

"I'll do that. Wait for me."

"I'll be here."

The phone went dead. She felt more alone now than before she'd called him. The cold detachment of Sean's voice and his refusal to come up and escort her down was unlike him. Possible scenarios came to her. Had management found out about the illegal backups of each day's work she made each evening and hid securely against the possibility of a computer virus in the company mainframe . . . or somebody hacking in from outside?

Susan was paranoid about security. She trusted none of her research to any electronic device with a connection to the internet.

She held all her notes on an encrypted tablet with the modem removed and took the personal precaution of downloading each day's work onto two encrypted data sticks which she hid in secret places - one in her office and one at her flat.

Ross had seen her do it. He'd walked in on her just as she was slipping one of the slim plastic flash drives into the hidden box under the lip of office her desk before she went home.

She'd joked about her paranoia regarding data security and sworn him to secrecy.

They'd laughed about it.

Afterwards, she'd thought about finding a different hiding place. The project she was working on had profound implications for the financial success of the company and there was serious interest from a number of security agencies back home in the States.

But she trusted Ross. She left the office memory stick where it was.

They'd been colleagues for the last nine months and lovers for the last six weeks. There has not been many men in Susan's life. At high school she was awkward and unsure of herself - a six-foot tall stick insect of a girl with glasses and an aggressive brilliance that frightened boys away. At college she'd been too intent on making her father proud to have time for socialisation. Then her academic success, and the prestigious A.M.Turing prize for her work on artificial intelligence, made her colleagues so jealous that she left academia behind and accepted a highly-paid research position in industry.

Which was how she'd met Ross.

As a member of the Sheridan clan and the Irish-American community in Boston, Susan was interested in her roots. One of the reasons she accepted the offer to work in Ireland was the chance to do some research on her family history. Ross McCarthy, a fellow Irish-American who worked in the Communications Office, suggested they joined forces. Visits to records offices, hours poring over old papers and family trees had turned into dinner dates.

Dinner dates had turned to something more intimate and suddenly they were lovers.

They shared secrets.

But today, Ross had not showed up for work. And this evening, when she went to retrieve the backup device from beneath her desk and reload it before she went home, it was gone.

She glanced at the open plan area beyond the darkened cell of her office to make sure nobody else was there, snatched her coat and bag and opened the glass door.

The building, which had been purpose built as the company's European headquarters during the boom years of Ireland's 'Celtic Tiger' economy, was constructed as a vast hollow cube. Research areas, offices and meeting rooms lined the inside walls in glass compartments like the cells of a beehive around a vast open space reaching six floors high. At the base of this enormous cavern lay the reception area, staff restaurant and little islands of black leather sofas and chairs between oases of indoor bushes and panels of original art, all tastefully arranged by the parent company in Heuston, Texas to promote the company ethos of 'creativity, collaboration and community'.

Susan hurried between the desks towards the central core of the building and the corridor that would lead her to the lift shaft. Every desk around her was empty. Every monitor was shut down. During the day, this area buzzed with activity and the focussed conversation of professionals going about their business. Now, the only clues that living souls actually worked here were the personal touches on each desk - the holiday postcards, the family photos, the house plant in need of watering, the . . .

The lights in the open plan shut down.

The darkness fell on her like a solid object. She shrieked in terror.

All around her, on desk after desk, the computer monitors flicked into life like the opening eyes of a pack of terrible, malevolent monsters.

And on each screen, in glaring white letters letters against a blood red background were the words . . .

'I AM COMING TO KILL YOU . . . NOW!'

Susan Sheridan screamed. She dropped her bag and coat. She ran headlong towards the light of the central well and the balcony that would lead her to the lift shaft.

She slammed into the edge of a desk and stumbled.

A picture frame fell to the floor and smashed .

She heard the clatter of a phone falling from its cradle.

She was almost there.

Then the lights in the central well went out.

Susan screamed.

In the dreadful darkness, her body hit the rail running around the balcony.

All her senses went into overdrive. She felt the smooth stainless steel of the rail and heard the 'clang' of her impact echo around the central well. The carpet beneath her feet scrunched like dry grass. The blood pumped in her ears. Off to her left glowed the emerald green emergency light above the lift doors.

She heard them hiss open to receive her.

Susan turned and ran to the lift, throwing herself into the dark space within, ready to punch the button for the ground floor and safety.

Instead, her face struck a hanging steel cable and her legs thrashed uselessly in space.

There was a terrible rush of air as she fell . . . the smell of oil and machinery, a whirl of dark glistening shapes and an explosion of light as her body hit the concrete base of the lift shaft six floors below.

To be published by . . .

 **SPINDRIFT PRESS**

www.spindriftpress.com

Also by John Joyce from Spindrift Press . . .

Virtually Maria

Maria Gilkrensky - brilliant, beautiful, rebellious - dies in a car bomb meant for her billionaire husband Theo. Was Theo the real target? Did Jessica Wright, Theo's Chief Executive and former lover, have an interest in seeing Maria dead? And what of Yukiko, the beautiful assassin in the pay of a rival Japanese conglomerate? Was revenge high on her agenda the day Maria died?

Does Maria's spirit live on? What are the mysterious forces that drag Theo back from exile to face murder, kidnap and the incredible possibility that his beloved wife might even now be saved - by harnessing forgoteen forces deep within the Pyramids of Egypt to warp the very fabric of time itself - guided by the new supercomputer that is . . .

Virtually Maria

ISBN 9780955763700

A Matter of Time

Theo Gilkrensky - a billionaire genius obsessed with warping the very fabric of time itself to save his beloved wife Maria from death.

Yukiko Funakoshi - a beautiful female assassin obsessed with revenge against Theo for the death of her parents.

Jerry Gibb - perverted computer games king who lusts after Gilkrensky's 'virtual Maria' for his own sick fantasies.

A Matter of Time

ISBN 9780955763717

Yesterday, Today & Tomorrow

From a bomb blast in an idyllic valley in Ireland . . .
to a pitch battle in the brooding deserts of Peru.

From a massacre in a quiet Japanese fishing village . . .
to mayhem and death in a corporate boardroom in Tokyo.

From the limitless horizons of cyberspace . . .
to the depths of the human hearth . . .

And the breathtaking conclusion to John Joyce's *Virtual Trilogy*

Yesterday, Today & Tomorrow

ISBN 9780955763717

Fire & Ice

At the height of the Cuban Missile Crisis the fate of the world rested not in the hands of Kennedy or Krushchev, but in the minds of two hunted women - 'Fire' and 'Ice'.

A damaged Soviet nuclear submarine receives orders to attack the flagship of the American blockade with an atomic-tipped torpedo. Are the instructions authentic, or are the scientists behind the ultra-secret telepathic experiment that transmitted the command intent on destroying the world?

In America and the USSR the hunt is on for the two surviving telepaths capable of stopping World War III - the two young women code named . . .

Fire & Ice

ISBN 9780955763731

Lightning Source UK Ltd.
Milton Keynes UK
UKOW05f0257041114

240986UK00004B/75/P